C000065370

Klaus Rifbjerg

Klaus Rifbjerg (born 1931) is one of Denmark's most prolific and celebrated authors. In the course of a sixty-year career he has published some 175 works across a panoply of genres, including novels, poetry, short stories, theatre and radio plays, film scripts, travel writing, memoirs, journalism, and children's literature. He has worked as an editor, journalist, critic, translator, restaurateur, and as literary director of the publishing house Gyldendal. He was made a member of the Danish Academy in 1967, and his awards include the Nordic Council Literature Prize (1970). Rifbjerg debuted as a poet in 1956, and his 1960 collection *Konfrontation* is regarded as a foundational text of Danish modernist poetry. *Terminal Innocence* (originally published in 1958 as *Den kroniske uskyld*) was Rifbjerg's debut novel, and is still regarded as one of his most important works. In fresh, rebellious, exuberant language, it gave voice to Rifbjerg's own generation, coming of age in post-war Denmark. It has been translated into eight languages.

Paul Larkin

After winning Ireland's European Journalist of the Year award in 1997 (overall and film category), Paul Larkin made a number of bilingual (English/Irish) docudramas, one of which (*Imeacht na nIarlaí*, starring Stephen Rea) brought him best director (international category) in the 2008 New York Independent Film and Video festival. In 2009, Larkin translated Henrik Ibsen's *A Doll's House* for Dublin theatre company Secondage. In 2011, Larkin translated a selection of Danish painter Asger Jorn's early essays on art and architecture and went on to complete the translations of both Klaus Rifbjerg's *Terminal Innocence* and Henrik Pontoppidan's *A Fortunate Man* in 2014. Larkin is at present translating Martin A Hansen's *The Liar* and is also preparing a book on Asger Jorn's life philosophy. Larkin's debut novel, *Peter Baker's Irish Odyssey*, based in part on life aboard a Danish merchant ship and exploring Danish vis-à-vis English and Irish culture, will be published in spring 2015 by Guildhall Press.

Some other books from Norvik Press

Terminal Innocence

by

Klaus Rifbjerg

Translated from the Danish and with a
Translator's Afterword by Paul Larkin

Norvik Press
2015

Originally published as *Den kroniske uskyld* by Gyldendal in 1958.

This translation and Translator's Afterword © Paul Larkin, 2015.
The translator's moral right to be identified as the translator of the
work has been asserted.

Norvik Press Series B: English Translations of Scandinavian Literature,
no. 64

A catalogue record for this book is available from the British Library.

ISBN: 978-1-909408-13-5

Norvik Press gratefully acknowledges the generous support of
the Danish Agency for Culture towards the publication of this
translation.

Norvik Press
Department of Scandinavian Studies
University College London
Gower Street
London WC1E 6BT
United Kingdom
Website: www.norvikpress.com
E-mail address: norvik.press@ucl.ac.uk

Managing editors: Sarah Death, Helena Forsås-Scott, Janet Garton,
C. Claire Thomson.

Cover photo: Thomas C. Christensen, Rådhuspladsen, Copenhagen,
Denmark.

Cover design and layout: Marita Fraser.

Contents

Terminal Innocence

~

Foreword

Confronting Klaus Rifbjerg

Én, to, tre
uforståelig sammensmelten af to organismer
filihankat
og grunden er lagt til det bedste af alt
at eksistere.
('Undfangelse', *Under vejr med mig selv*, 1956)

One, two, three
a baffling fusion of two organisms
abracadabra
and the ground is laid for the best thing of all
– to exist.
('Conception', *Setting Sail with Myself*, 1956, my translation)

With this playful depiction of the first moment of his existence, the 24-year-old Klaus Rifbjerg burst onto the Danish literary scene of 1956. His debut collection as a poet was entitled *Under vejr med mig selv*, which translates roughly as 'Setting Sail with Myself'. It was startling enough that this sequence of poems described conception, gestation, birth, childhood and youth, but the language employed by Rifbjerg to take the reader on this journey was equally iconoclastic. The 'I' of the second poem in the collection introduces himself as *fosterfisk*, (foetus-fish) – a compound noun at once irreverent, inconsonant, and absolutely right.

For Rifbjerg, and for his contemporary Leif Panduro, the solemnity of post-war Danish literature was ripe for rejuvenation through linguistic experimentation and an engagement with the everyday. Their brand of modernism took its name from Rifbjerg's third poetry collection of 1960, *Konfrontation* (Confrontation). In the decade that followed, this 'confrontation-modernism' enacted the encounter of the individual with a world that was, to paraphrase a famous line from the anthology, blessedly empty, except for *things*. This was a material world of flesh and blood, of technology, and of words that collided to generate new and often joyous perspectives on existence.

Rifbjerg would go on to publish some 175 works in the course of a sixty-year career. Around half of his output has been in novel form, the rest encompassing collections of poetry, short stories, essays, radio plays, film scripts, and many other genres. He has worked as an editor, journalist, critic, restaurateur, and as literary director of the publishing house Gyldendal. He has been awarded the Danish Academy's Grand Prize (1966), the Nordic Council Literature Prize (1970), and the Swedish Academy's Nordic Prize (the 'Little Nobel', 1999), amongst many others, and was made a member of the Danish Academy as early as 1967. Rifbjerg is, quite simply, a colossus of twentieth-century Danish literature, unsurpassed in influence and productivity. And yet it is a rare Dane who would, if asked to identify Rifbjerg's masterpiece, choose anything other than his very first novel: *Den kroniske uskyld*, published 1958.

The Danish *Catcher in the Rye*

Terminal Innocence, as translator Paul Larkin has chosen to render the title – a literal translation would be 'Chronic Innocence' – is narrated by Janus Tolne, a Copenhagen schoolboy whose life is enlivened by the arrival of a new friend, Tore Riemer. Through Janus' eyes, we catch glimpses of life under the German occupation of Denmark (1940-45), but his main preoccupation is his beloved Tore and, by extension, Tore's girlfriend Helle. Locked in a chaste *ménage à trois* with this glamorous couple, Janus navigates his way through the waters of teenage firsts: girls, drinking, graduating from high school. As readers, we live this perplexing and, at times, mortifying process of transformation along with Janus. But we know, too, perhaps before Janus does, that Tore and Helle are caught in some strange stasis, trapped in a web spun by Helle's monstrous mother. As the title of the novel suggests, their innocence seems to be a chronic condition. It is also – as captured by the title of this translation – terminal.

Terminal Innocence can be described as the Danish counterpart to J.D. Salinger's *The Catcher in the Rye* (1951). The two novels share an ambition to give voice to the angst and exuberance of the post-war teenager, as well as their canonical status as literary works whose linguistic and thematic innovations retain enough freshness to speak to successive generations of readers. The author Pia Juul writes movingly of the enduring relevance of Rifbjerg's novel in her foreword to a recent Danish edition:

> When I read the book (at the age of 21) I understood Janus completely. I understood his passionate love for Tore, I understood his odd status as a third wheel to the couple Tore and Helle, I understood him when he went with girlfriends he didn't really like, and I understood the impression he had of his parents as people who didn't grasp what was going on and didn't know what life was really about, as well as his disgust at Helle's mother, who was too intrusive and loomed too large in her daughter's life. Adults can do nothing right. Youth *is* wonderful, and damned.
> (My translation)

Juul's final comment echoes the Danish title of *The Catcher in the Rye*, adopted for Vibeke Cerris' translation of 1953: *Forbandede ungdom* (Damned Youth). Published three years later, *Terminal Innocence* was thus not the first novel to hold up a mirror to the lives and language of its young readers. Rather, Rifbjerg embeds the narrator and his friends in Copenhagen, crafting a profoundly local iteration of that new global species, the teenager. Similarly, Rifbjerg's ebullient prose fuses the eclectic vocabulary of confrontation-modernism with a commitment to capturing the colloquialisms of post-war urban youth, echoing the first-person narration of Salinger's Holden Caulfield. Little wonder that Rifbjerg returned to *The*

Catcher in the Rye almost five decades later, to undertake an acclaimed new Danish translation (*Griberen i rugen*, 2004). Meanwhile, one adaptation of *Terminal Innocence* had almost as much impact in Denmark as the original novel itself: director Edward Fleming's 1985 film adaptation. While popular in cinemas and widely screened in schools, its updating of the action to mid-1980s Denmark was panned by the critics, though this aesthetic strategy was arguably in tune with Rifbjerg's propensity as an author to map the twists and turns of twentieth-century culture.

That it has taken almost six decades to produce a translation into English of Rifbjerg's first novel is, in some senses, surprising: holdings of the Royal Library in Copenhagen include translations into Dutch (1964), Swedish (1965), Italian (1966), French (1969), Polish (1971), Norwegian (1979), Czech (1980), and two German editions (1962, 1971). This delay is less strange, though no less regrettable, when considered in the context of the general dearth of translations into English of modern Danish literature in general and of Rifbjerg's writing in particular. Rifbjerg's novel *Anna (I) Anna* appeared in English in 1982, translated by Alexander Taylor; his sci-fi novel *De hellige aber* was translated as *Witness to the Future* by Steven Murray in 1987; and a handful of Rifbjerg's plays and poems have appeared in English-language anthologies. In the case of *Terminal Innocence*, an important consideration for potential translators and publishers has, no doubt, been the challenge the text presents. As explained by Paul Larkin in the Translator's Afterword in this volume, Rifbjerg's language is not only rooted in the colloquialisms of a specific historical period and the idiolect of an adolescent narrator, but also complicated by its poetic, experimental departures from that linguistic realism.

A sense of place and period

For present-day Danish readers, the novel is a cabinet of mid-century curiosities. The idiolect used by the narrator and his friends is no less 'foreign' than the long-forgotten vocabulary describing the clothes they wear. Even their curse-words seem like relics of a more innocent age; it is not easy to tease out the invented in their language from the outmoded. The translation in this volume attempts to communicate something of this linguistic instability and energy.

Terminal Innocence is of its time in another important sense. It was written barely twelve years after the end of the Second World War, a war which Denmark had spent under the occupation of Nazi Germany. Janus Tolne is roughly the same age as Rifbjerg himself; as in much of this author's work, national history is filtered through his own childhood memories. Denmark was invaded in the early hours of April 9, 1940, as a springboard to the more strategically important target of Norway. Sixteen soldiers died in the two hours before the Danish Government, calculating that resistance was hopeless, capitulated. This pragmatically cooperative approach set the tone for some three years of what the occupying soldiers referred to as *Sahnefront*, the Whipped Cream Front. Government remained in Danish hands, and some concessions were extracted from the occupying forces. From autumn 1942, however, this cooperation began to break down, not least in the face of escalating acts of sabotage by the Danish Resistance, and by summer 1943, a campaign of civil disobedience resulted in an intensification of violent acts of retribution by the occupying forces. These events play out as a subtle backdrop in *Terminal Innocence*, as hints and details that a contemporary Danish audience would immediately grasp. For example, when the suburban schoolboy Janus stays at Tore's apartment in central Copenhagen, he hears gunfire, probably a liquidation of a traitor or Resistance fighter. And then bang! as Janus puts it: the Liberation comes, the Resistance fighters emerge from the shadows, and the city erupts with joy. For Janus and Tore, Copenhagen becomes a playground full of abandoned ammunition and Tommies smoking exotic tobacco, just like in the movies.

Danish writers, artists and filmmakers were caught up in the struggle for liberation, not just as chroniclers of the nation's fate, but also in all-too-concrete ways. Some prominent figures paid with their lives: the poet and priest Kaj Munk was liquidated by the Germans in retaliation for Resistance sabotage. Others, such as the film auteur Carl Th. Dreyer and the novelist Mogens Klitgaard, fled to Sweden to escape a similar fate. An emerging generation of documentary filmmakers, among them Theodor Christensen and Bjarne and Astrid Henning-Jensen, worked with the Resistance to capture footage of sabotage operations and interrogations as well as everyday life under occupation. Being more immediately exportable than literary narrative, their films did much to secure Denmark's reputation in the post-war period through screenings at international film festivals. At home, the literary journal *Heretica* (1948-53) provided a space for poets to react against the realism and modernism which had characterised pre-war Danish literature. Thorkild Bjørnvig, Ole Sarvig and others saw poetry as a means to re-connect humankind with the subjective, the symbolic and the mystical; this was the only way out of the post-war political and cultural crisis. This, in turn, was the literary culture against which Rifbjerg and his young contemporaries reacted, a decade after the end of the war. By 1959, *Heretica* had been succeeded by a new magazine, *Vindrosen* – with Klaus Rifbjerg as one of its editors.

Terminal Innocence is a product not just of its time, but of its city. In this sense, it inaugurates a red thread in Ribjerg's oeuvre: his love affair with the Copenhagen of his childhood, and with the city as it grew and changed through the second half of the twentieth century. The city of bricks and mortar and the imaginative city jostle and collide in poetry such as *Amagerdigte* (Amager Poems, 1965), or *Byens tvelys* (The City's Double Light, 1987). In *Terminal Innocence*, Janus and Tore's night-time perambulations map an urban geography still recognisable to present-day readers. While the trams they catch have been superseded by buses, many landmarks remain. One of the novel's most memorable episodes occurs on the square in front of the Town Hall, a space recognisable to anyone who has visited the Tivoli Gardens just beyond. Towards the southern edge of the square is an elaborate sculpture known as the Dragon Fountain, a detail of which is captured in Thomas C. Christensen's photograph on the cover of this volume. It is into this fountain that Tore falls one afternoon, while trying to impress Helle. Failing to catch a pigeon as a symbol of his love for her, he decides to walk around the outer rim of the basin, much to the consternation of onlookers queuing for buses. Inevitably, he topples into the water and emerges, unfazed, 'like a world champion acknowledging the acclaim of the crowd'. This tableau captures all the joyous impetuousness of teenage love, played out before throngs of city-centre shoppers and commuters. Here, Rifbjerg's genius lies in the ostensibly mundane setting. For his bout of gentle hooliganism, the love-struck teenager chooses a landmark whose symbolism foreshadows his and Helle's impending fate at the claws of another of the narrative's 'dragons'.

It is an older, wiser, less innocent Janus who takes leave of his friend Tore at the end of the novel. And yet, *Terminal Innocence* concludes on an optimistic — or perhaps wistful? — note, as Janus cycles off into the future. Like the just-conceived 'I' of Rifbjerg's first published poem, Janus asserts the unwavering message of this most prolific of Danish authors: that the best thing of all is to *exist*.

C. Claire Thomson
UCL

Chapter 1

My mate Tore was someone you just couldn't help liking. One way or another. One of them lads who can stand up in class and do loads of mad things. Like mimic faces or swing like a baboon, until you've tears in your eyes and you laugh till your balls ache. When the duffhead at the blackboard turns his back and starts writing something, up gets Tore like a mad ape with a banana in his hand conducting a whole symphony, or preening his hair like a rock star and thrusting his hips in and out. Then you just died. Or Tore could entertain us for a whole lesson, mixing his words up, fumbling with things and dropping some daft pencil, eraser or papers, until the teacher was tearing his hair out in desperation, but still couldn't really bawl at him because the kid was the brightest in the class and couldn't help dropping things, and how could he write without a pencil, eraser, or whatever it was he was scrambling round the floor for? Anyway, the duffheads couldn't get near Tore because he was way too sharp for them. In one second he had them round his little finger, if he just smiled his film star smile, and because they knew they needed him. He was just so much better at everything than all the other zombies who just sat there like planks.

And I'm talking zombies. You've never seen such a set of Grade A mutants. Such a bunch of stump-legged mush eaters. Full of half-cock ideas. It's beyond belief what a crowd of little trolls like this can come up with when an adult talks to them or asks them a question. But Tore could always produce something crazy but brilliant that would have us all in stitches. And then watch those little trolls grinning from ear to ear till their faces split. We all laughed that much it was like gunshot howling round the room. Just because what Tore said was so bright and exciting, or maybe because it was like something being suddenly let loose inside of us. It was as if we knew what we were laughing about for the first time and what laughter could do. For a moment, we weren't just little pigs at the trough, all scrambling and gulping at the hog swill. No. We were suddenly something much better and more complete. When Tore threw one of his brilliant bombs it was as if everything fell into its proper place. And I'm telling you, even the teachers had to laugh. It didn't matter how lunatic this kid's behaviour was, there was always something noble and grand about him. As if he was some kind of exotic animal in Copenhagen Zoo. One you don't see in captivity that often. It was like having Superman sitting next to you in class. He was untouchable in some way. He lifted you into a world where delirious happiness zinged through your mind and you became a completely different person for a while. Far away from all those disgusting egg sandwich pongs, schoolboy farts and cigarette dimps.

The classes above and below us were sort of better than us. More aware and mature about everything. Our class was nothing but a gang of mindless sheep corralled into a pen. We came plodding in every day from brick terraced houses and from every possible pathetic area of town, with seriously dedicated labourers for fathers who wore overalls and worked as semi-skilled lathe turners, semi-skimmed milkmen, bicycle repair nuts and obsessive factory clerks with pencils behind their ears. Parents of pupils in the other classes were barristers or doctors and you could smell the difference. We were just a bunch of knuckleheads and dead legs. Me? Well I'm the son of an engineer, of course, so my future is assured. Ha. Ha. Ha. But with the other lads, it was all very much small beer, with weird, shrivelled parents whose only hope was that little Johnny might get that all-important bright white student cap at the end of it all. The cap that signalled you were going to university. That you were joining the ranks of Denmark's intellectual elite. There wasn't even a pretence at academic excellence with our lot. Just trogs at the trough guffing it into them and hoping for the best. The class right above us? Well there was no doubt that they were a different species that belonged up in the lofty heights – the Academy, Parnassus, Rhetoric or whatever it was they prattled on about with their noses in the air. It went without saying that they always had their hair sitting just so, and that their pathetic books had this or that *à la mode* kind of cover, which had been nonchalantly illustrated with their precious pencil flourishes. Damn sophisticated what?! It was as if they were just as clever as the teachers. Because the teachers were forever walking up and down the corridors with them in earnest conversation. Stopping for a moment, looking reflective, showing deference to their opinions. Laughing and nodding in the right places when a horsey guffaw or pearl of wisdom fell from some scholar's lips. And those duffhead teachers who went round with their heads bowed, listening respectfully to those prefects and other snotty clowns? Ah stop. These 'Masters' bent so low sometimes – weighed down by sheer ponderous thought – that their heads drooped below their shoulders and you could see right down their earholes. I mean. Right into the black wax that had obviously been there for years. Truly puke-invoking. Jesus H. And then look at the hair on the heads of those swots. No parting and always effortlessly groomed back from their craniums. Like fake lions. Or the thatch would be massively standing to attention; as if it had been continually pushed up with each strenuous thought, whilst we swamp creatures had to throw water on our heads and part it with a comb to make it behave. We were who we were – mediocre kids, with middling muddling Dads who wore trouser clips as they cycled to work from mediocre Glostrup. We were the lowest of the low, whilst the classes above lorded it with their Flaubert this and Aristotle that. Seeing them swanning round with their ludicrous Latin books. I'm telling you they were crying out for a massive boot up the arse. But the truth was – they WERE actually better than the rest of us. Everything we dreamed about, they could do. Painting, joined-up writing, drama and comedy, reeling off whole poems. Some of them even had girlfriends they had dates with in the afternoon and evening, and they had relaxed conversations with them – the most normal thing in the world for them. Laughing and putting their arms around them and I don't know what else.

I'm serious. Us – we were just the spawn in the swamp. If we weren't slavering idiots and mental retards, we were anally backward coming forwards. There we were all crawling about on a vile average of mediocrity. Some of us couldn't even read a sentence in English, or translate a single line. So you just sat there squirming in your seat feeling like the world's biggest donkey. But never mind English, most of the swamp life in our class couldn't even answer a simple question in their own language. They just sat quivering, squeezing their hands and going red in the head.

It was only force of habit that got them to school every day. Coming in on the S-Train wearing their oversize short trousers and satchels. And then these trogs would start all that wheedling nonsense about how the train was late Sir and Valby Station or Copenhagen Central, or whatever lie they were making up, and pulling out their putrid egg sandwiches with their mothers' pickles so the air was full of them and you couldn't get looking at that Latin text you were supposed to have read the night before. Jesus wept. It was just swamp life. Squelch Squelch Swamp Swamp. And it was beyond unbearable when you started to think about the La De Da scholars on the other side of the corridor. With their posh notebooks. French cuisine and Latin study groups, gorgeous girlfriends and kiss my arse and hope to die and get it over with.

Everything was just claptrap. With dry rot in the chairs and chalk dust everywhere. And the glimpses of girls in the flats across the way who knew precisely what would happen when they stood up or came to their windows. And then the rats scattering from the bins down in the yard when the men came to empty them. There was a permanent mist on all those millions and millions of November days through which the trogs stumbled every morning in their billowing short trousers and fake satchels. But, for all that, there was something that made you glad to see their pathetic faces as they came trudging in – their lunch boxes bulging with those stagnant sandwiches. Younger versions of their dads who'd already gone off to work with their Army and Navy knapsacks and cycle clips. Like dumb sheep blindly following bigger sheep and never would they be anything other than sheep. Bless 'em.

But Tore made everything worthwhile. Because he actually outshone those boring snobs and their Fair Isle sweaters on the other side of the corridor. Because he was a thousand million times better than the whole lot of them put together. Teachers included. Because he was just so Goddamn funny and really did not give one shit who heard him between heaven and hell. Sure, you felt like a pygmy sitting beside him but at the same time so proud to have him there. As if he was a bright galleon in the surrounding swamp. The only thing we could cling on to and boast about. D'ye see lads like Tore? Those very few who can do everything under the sun with effortless ease, without breaking their stride? Everything they do is fresh and new, because it's perfect and right and couldn't be done in any other way. Oh he somehow knew very well what he was and the way of himself. But that was part of the point. That he could just be so out there, yet at the same time remain so modest and charming. He could even ridicule himself, us, the school, the whole kit, caboodle and swamp shebang before anyone realised they'd been had. And the rest of us in class were just sitting there, still working out how to tuck our shirts in. It was actually unbearable sometimes when he got up and we all knew he hadn't read a word of the homework. Because Tore the Man would always come up with some romancing nonsense and your heart sort of melted. Especially when the duffhead up at the desk lapped the whole performance up like the cat that got the cream, then looked beyond chuffed to have been so bamboozled. And when I call them duffheads. I'm telling you those poor teachers were really certified and calcified dumbheads for all their self-importance, ridiculous behaviour and mannerisms. See – that was the thing about Tore. He could make them inconsequential and distant, small and flat as nose pickings.

So you really felt how life had passed them by and how pathetic they were with their fossilized teaching and Stone Age opinions that stank of the must and dank oozing from their common room. You could smell it a mile away and hear their pipe coughs and duffhead wheezing. Tore was so far to the other side of Boy Scout that he was already out of sight, even compared to the champion boxers, football jocks and white-hot tennis players with their cold showers, boxing matches and camping jaunts. Not because Tore couldn't kick a ball. Of course he could. But in a suitably knowing and superior way. There was none of this we'll fight them on the beaches and down in the trenches malarkey and, watching him, you were never really sure whether he belted that ball out of sheer disdain or wicked delight. One thing was sure – the boy Tore could play.

But, to put it bluntly. See all those boarding-school pretensions about young gentlemen, college head boys and *Victor Ludorum*? Tore did not give one shit about all that and, basically, this was OK because they knew he was already out of their league. Never would he have to push his way to the trough like the rest of us. Not that he was any kind of *Führer* of the class. Oh no. Being the official leader was just not his style. But of course he was anyway. Because going to Tore and getting the answer was only natural for all of us. In a way, there was something horrible about a lad like that, who could just not be brought down to earth, no matter what way you went at it. You almost wished that, just once in a while, he would be found to have a flaw. But then you soon remembered that if Tore weren't in class – well, you might as well go right home and let your brain die. So when the swamp really started boiling up on certain summer mornings and the lid was coming off with all the grinning pygmy trolls running to the windows to watch the girls dressing across the way. As if Christmas was coming and goose and rum punch and you were just on a high, standing there gawking out the window with all the other dunces. Well, you started listening to Tore, who one hundred per cent always came out with something that got all them stiff-necked little shits to fall about laughing.

What he said could be so greasy and gross that it ran down the windows in fat globules, but it was always something smart, that we'd never have thought of saying, and it got your funny bone at the same time as you bowed your head in total admiration. The Man.

You couldn't help but fall in love with him. Somehow, not being in love with him was impossible. Though you would never show that or actually make it real. You just needed him there and couldn't do without him. We're talking about infatuation and worship here up to both ears. Because he had that way of filling all those awkward gaps both inside you and in all the world outside. Sure, you felt like a total runt in comparison, but that didn't change the fact that Tore was the one who made you feel more worthy and more adult than you otherwise would have done. One of the initiated. And, of course, one of Tore's magic tricks was that he himself managed to be more effortlessly adult and in control than all us swamp creatures. Even the trogs who didn't turn their heads were watching and waiting for Tore whenever any question of a prickly nature came up. It went without saying that he was the one that would answer it. Because only he had the balls. Take sex right? He just dived straight in if any question was ever asked about sex. Just straight in. And us numpties would just sit there saying sod all. We even knew the answers most of the time, but it was always him who dived in headfirst, and it was sex-mad rabbits this, gelded beasts and eunuchs that. A torrent of big words that left you twisted in your seat but full of respect for Tore the Man. There we were just sitting there. Row after row of tight numbskull heads like beans on a raft, squeezing our thighs and struggling to get our brains, mouths and cheeks in gear because the duffer up there at the desk was staring down at us and might ask us a question. But Tore was as calm as you like, said the right thing and was completely in charge. At the same time, he could afford a little laugh to himself because he knew we were all sitting there like kindergarten kids who'd pissed their pants.

Our day would often begin with all the swamp creatures conglomerating at the windows to watch the harlots across the street as they stood waving their bras as far out of the window as they could possibly reach. And in seconds the trogs were just beside themselves. Spawned to the glass panes and gawping at the mystery of shapes and what it was like down there behind their knicker line till their grunts became audible above the general buzz and quivering coming out of them. Like rutting dogs. And it was as if the teasing bitches over the road were aware of this, even though they never looked directly at us. Because, for ages every day, they would move to and fro near their windows and stand there, or turn around and flaunt this way and that, and them not wearing anything other than a night shift, as if they could sense that a whole pack of grunts was gathered across the way and just on the brink of descending upon them to rip and tear and grab ferociously and drag them into bed and have done with it and then sit on the edge of the bed afterwards, with a torn shirt and tie on the floor and fuck knows where your shoes were and having a cigarette and seeing her stockings and suspenders and roll-ons and roll-offs and lace bras or whatever else those vixens went round with. And at the same time as you were laughing and acting the goat, part of you was mad at them because of that dull ache they gave you in some place when you watched them laughing and gesticulating and jiggling the way they did. But then Tore would appear and spread calm amongst us. You could always trust him to say the thing that was so exactly appropriate that you stood there at the window and felt like crying. Like he knew all about it. Like he'd actually done it. As if he knew every one of those girls over there and knew exactly what you had to do. Even though we knew he hadn't actually done it. He was just our Great Chief. Simple as that. All the other obscenities uttered by everybody else were always petty, farting little grunt expressions, whilst Tore's had wings and would sail across the void and land like garlands around the neck of every girl. He could talk about their tits and say things about them that actually were really funny, or so precise your chest began to heave with the emotion of it all, because you could look forward to all the things he was talking about. I mean. You got the feeling that when you truly were an adult and could do it when you liked. Well, you could mention all them things with your girl. Funny things about different breast shapes, skimpy see-through knickers and French kissing. Then you would both just laugh and jump into bed together having the best of fun for hours and hours like it was normal and a world away from the swamp and the trogs and the grunts. Then you could really feel what it would be like to be a proper adult. Free to do what you wanted and share a life and a whole load of different things with another person. I'm talking being able to do this or that of your own free will and depending how you felt just at that moment. Never mind what it was. At those heightened moments, you just felt totally desperate to get to that point. To be an adult and say what you liked, walk in or out, turn about, whatever occurred to you and without it seeming forced or like a pantomime. I mean. When all that schoolboy crap was finally over, and you would never have to look at row after row of numbskull heads ever again. It would be perfectly natural to put your arm across your girl's shoulders. Pull her in to you. Do and say all them things. The things that made your ears burn right then. Like the names we used and expressions we tried, but they would all be suddenly cool and actually the proper words to use and far more preferable to anything else because the two of you were so close. Tore already had a reserve about him like that, even though he was well able to let rip with the best or worst of us.

And our class remained standing there gawping and tongue-tied, even after the bell went, because there was still loads going on over the road and we weren't worried in the least that the teacher could walk in any second. No. We were different to the class across the corridor from us who already had their books, their poetry collections and notes out on the desk. Just waiting for teacher to appear so they could get going with their bleeding arts and science, scholarship and learning. Fill the room with hot air once again. But the swampies just stayed fixated by the windows, panting at the bints across the way. And when the teacher finally did appear, even some of them couldn't resist joining in the oglefest. As if they weren't grown up and proper adults who had no need to stand staring at the precocious Jezebels on display across the street. As if they didn't get enough from the women they already knew. Because they could do it anytime. But most teachers just strode right in without looking at anyone and were already talking as they came through the door with open page this and did you read that and get a bloody move on because there was an exam syllabus to get through and what did we think it was a bloody holiday camp and you just wanted to walk up and stick a finger right through this kind of specimen to see if they actually were flesh and blood, or whether it was a gramophone record that was sitting up there blaring out instructions. His Master's Voice.

Tore never rushed to his seat. He always had something or other to sort out before he sat down. It might be his little hobby corner where he had his cut-out chalk figures that needed checking. He wouldn't be ready for the rigours of the day unless they were. Or he might have to pass on a message to Anders, his desk sprite, who lived down between the panels of the floorboards. Tore would hold conversations with Anders that lasted for hours. You would see him looking down and talking quietly, as if this were an actual physical human being with opinions of its own that had to be debated. Nobody would interrupt him, because you just never knew with Tore. He could make you feel ridiculous. Like your world and not his was absurd. Nobody tried to tell him what was what.

You could see all the compressed necks of the trogheads, squeezing down into their seats like birds in a tree whenever the shadow of a kestrel passes over them – sheer terror that the teacher would swoop down on them, scoop them up and pick at their knowledge of the lesson we were doing. And none of them knew it really because it was just so mind-numbingly boring that the thought of it was enough to make you sick. The only one who did his homework properly was Georgie, and that was because his mother was a widow and would sit over him and batter him with a ladle if his concentration ever flagged for an instant. She was going to make a lawyer of him, so help her God. And then he would cosset her in her old age and provide a fitting and permanent tribute to her dead husband. Where homework was concerned, all the other trogs just sat there of a morning in their usual S-Train that crept through the morning fog with those sickly overhead lamps turning their blond heads green and the whooshing noise from the self-closing doors. Gazing at mathematical formulas and yawn-tears in their eyes because the whole thing was so pointless and dreary. Some of them even had to cycle in with their dads because he and his mortifying cycle clips were going the same way to work. Some of this particular crowd were already stamped and certified carbon copies. The kind of kid who acted like his father was standing next to him all the time. They spoke as if their words were coming out through their dads' belly buttons and had to be sufficiently soft and podgy. Careful so his paunch wouldn't burst. These kids would drive you beyond rage, they were just so trogheaded and wouldn't do, say, or listen to anything but what was allowed at home, even though they knew the stuff their parents came out with was pure caveman shit. You didn't know whether to cry or just shake your head in pity when they started, in all seriousness, about their bicycle washing on a Sunday and how they wiped and soaped and the old fella there doing his as well, and then off to the forest with their bicycle clips and pannier singing the national anthem 'There is a Lovely Land' as they pedalled along and having a picnic on the wet grass and then going home to pretend to do their Latin lessons for the next day and forgetting to remove their bicycle clips and scout belts before they went to bed. Complete numpties.

You just sat and watched their heads from the back of the class. First picking their noses. Then their ears. Scratching their legs, then diving under the desk to fiddle with their satchels and bringing their lunch box half out and day-dreaming about egg sandwiches with pickle. And then the Ancient up at the desk would clear his throat and start flicking through his book and was obviously getting sick at the thought that any moment he would have to begin conversing with one of the swamp creatures oozing below him and inviting said creature to prove once again how thick he was. Stick or twist, duck or freeze that was the question. So half the class ducked. This was because some psychologist somewhere said you'd be safe from inquisition if you sat bright-eyed to attention and looked as if you were ready and prepared. It was comical to watch the same old routine unfold between teachers and the swampies. First the teacher lets on that he hasn't picked out a particular victim down amongst the morass, and the poor trog is sitting down there knowing full well that he's been eyeballed and lets on that he doesn't give a toss, even though he knows that having to stand up is the most horrific experience known to man. So said trog sits there acting the pretend carefree goat and the duffhead up at the desk gives him a look and you can see he knows exactly what the score is with the swamp boy down there and he's about to dredge him up and give him the big shakedown, but then teacher gets annoyed with himself and the whole predictable farce of it all and moves at random to the trog over there who is just as badly prepared and is sitting there holding his guts in praying that he'll get away with it. Not just because he hasn't a clue, but also because he would rather just be left in peace so he can lean back and doze on.

You see the little twitches in their faces and quivers in their mouths as they sit there half asleep and you want to kill them but at the same time they are your classmates and at least they will never be like those arrogant shitheads on the other side of the corridor. But also because we have Tore and that fact can neither be forgotten nor ignored. Because Tore had no problem talking to the young fogeys across the corridor. They had accepted him as an equal. Not that Tore looked up to them or wanted to be like them or anything. It's just that he can talk to them as if it were the most natural thing in the world to engage with those Latin swots on their level. Then there was the fact that he'd been made joint editor of the school newspaper where the swots spouted off with odes, poems and other bullshit and wrote under pseudonyms, as if everybody didn't know exactly which snothound had done which verse or so-called 'panegyric'.

And do you think Tore was afraid of being hauled up to answer a question or discuss a text? Not at all. They had him up all the time, because he could be both funny and clever. Usually, you were forced to sit there for nearly an hour snuffling at the trough with the rest of them and having to listen to at least snatches of all that guff the trogs would throw up, and at a tempo that would put a snail to shame. Some of the subjects being discussed were actually interesting, or funny, but the brains of most of the dinosaurs up at the desk had been petrified for thousands of years just by the thought of having to get up every morning and head off to the swamp pit and then sit hour after hour looking out across the morass and get sod all from it except trog grunts, snot and lethargy. But every now and again, it was as if there was a rent in the whole thing and you were in a new dimension. Everybody was suddenly grown up and could say loads of things and give replies without being tongue-twisted. You felt that you were something in the universe and not just a leaden lump of bone and gristle. Thinking and speaking was worth the effort. And it was almost always Tore who was the catalyst because he had the balls to say things and go straight to the point. The spark for the explosion.

The whole class could feel how some kind of tingle had entered the room. As if we all bore witness to an important conversation – one you felt could decide the future course of our whole lives. When Tore and the teacher talked to each other, it was as if the teacher stepped out of his duffhead persona and became a different person. Took his mask off. I mean. Obviously we couldn't see him removing his mask but it was as if his face became all relaxed. Like he'd pulled a few cords somewhere and released some muscles that made him more alive. Tore never put a mask on, except when he was doing things like his cartoon characters and the thousand and one sounds he could mimic. But there was never any tension in his face. All those knots and bolts around the jaw you always see with adults because they think they have to carry a certain look, because they think that everybody else around them is

27

thinking that they are thinking that everyone else is thinking if they don't have that particular look then the others will think that everybody else will be thinking and so on and so on till I'm ready to vomit and already dreading becoming an adult and ending up pedalling like mad in your head like that. And the next second, everything is spinning round and you lose your bearings and so just keep staring straight ahead, or fall over so help you God.

Yes. When Tore and the teacher talked to each other, the whole thing was exciting but at the same time also relaxed, because Tore could nice and calmly get duffer to come out with loads of mad things he would normally keep stuffed in a bric-a-brac sack down in his belly, or in his brain, or at the back of his pigeon chest somewhere. And in those moments it was like we were in a Technicolor film. As if multi-coloured curtains unfolded around the walls of the classroom and then pulled back and you found you were in a movie and were a completely different person and could be the Lone Ranger or Tarzan and have special powers and get ready to perform feats that would otherwise be impossible.

Naturally, it was mainly in the classes when we talked about books and literature that things could really be transformed into something powerful and enthralling. Sometimes, things would go so far out that you'd hear little peeps from the swampies and one of the poor trogs would let go of something from deep inside of him and speak about things you never would have thought they had in them, or could have dreamed about in the night. Now this was serious. This was really serious and no messing and you listened to them and lost all thought of trogs and trolls, budgie seed and bicycle clips, and the teacher up there was suddenly sitting wherever he liked with his knee raised on the edge of a desk and all relaxed, so you clean forgot to stare at his mouth which was normally a terrifying furnace that spat verbal thunderbolts one after the other.

And then the whole thing disappeared and the trogs were sitting there again with their numbskull heads and the goon up there braying like an ass that we didn't have time for all that nonsense and pull yourselves together and pay attention and the mask and the jaw clenching like a dog with a bone. And then you just had to try and survive. Sitting there grimly waiting for the bell to ring. You might suddenly pick up the smells coming from the trogs all around you and feel beyond desperate. The smell invading your senses of how it was for them in their beds at night as they lay still and snoring or writhed around and had dreams that wriggled like worms under a rotten log and woke up staring at the ceiling with a light gliding across the room from a car passing by in the street. You would be sat there with the reek of them all around you and study the virgin whiskers on their faces that looked like a screed of dodgy makeup and wonder which of them had advanced to the stage of standing in front of a mirror twice a week and ending up bleeding like a stuck pig trying to scrape that sad bumfluff away. Then you couldn't help thinking how appalling it was that the whole lot of them were getting more pathetic with each passing day and what morons they would be when they grew up and suddenly had to offer their opinions on all sorts of things they didn't have a clue about, but would spout forth regardless because they all had the ingrained delusion that they had to say, think, and do, exactly what their bicycle-clip parents would say, think, and do. Then they were just the most mindless pack of prancing baboons imaginable. You were overwhelmed by the smell of ham bone and pea soup that they all guffed into them every evening in 25 compact and cheerful homes in the suburbs with Dad's gabardine coat and knapsack hanging out there in the hall and the evening paper waiting for him and turn on the wireless love for the news and everything on their disgusting plates gummed and masticated and exhausted platitudes in conversations on this and that and problems and young people today and sex and smut and a thousand petty outrages and agony aunt letters and the little whelps that were supposed to be doing their homework but dodge out of it and keep putting it off and feed the budgie instead and read a comic and listen to Radio Luxembourg and talk for bloody hours on the phone and sneak out to the pictures but keep gumming and masticating on a nagging guilty conscience and then they go to bed and obsess about all those gorgeous bints opposite with salmon-coloured stockings and black knickers that they want to rip off and put on their faces and sniff and bite and tear at and whisper all their dreams into.

So then the bell finally rings in all the corridors and all the zombies begin to blunder out through the door and onto the corridor and then down the stairs to the hall for assembly and morning hymns with all the rest of the school, where we're forced to stand next to the Big Hair boys who somehow or other always managed to look blasé about the whole thing and like they really didn't give a monkey's whether they were there or not, but used the occasion to give each other knowing looks and preen their locks and show off their specially bound hymn books with their own calligraphy on the front, do ye mind. Then we're told to sing this or that on page this or that and there's an eruption of throat clearing and coughs and splutters because everybody thinks it's a great laugh. However, I admit, once in a while, you'd hear a tone that made singing a real pleasure, as long as you could avoid looking at the others around you who were stood smirking or hacked and hawked, or the teachers who were so masked up they couldn't sing because their jaws were locked. But then, you had to put up with the other idiots who roared out every note as if they had they to let the world know that they were proud members of the Copenhagen Scout choir, or whatever it was. Their heads were so boiling hot you got the feeling they were completely naked. Like they'd been discovered with their pants round their ankles. Which just made them roar louder as their heads disappeared deeper and deeper into the hymn book. Trying ferociously to hide themselves in its pages.

Trust Tore to find a way to lift us out of this hellish routine by urging us to try rattling off the hymns and psalms as quick as we could. We soon got what he was up to, because if everyone in our class began to sing at top speed, the tempo picked up right across the hall and the Big Hair boys began pulling faces but trying to let on they weren't bothered by our obvious glee as we stepped on the gas and the organ player going demented and getting cramp in his feet trying to keep up. Our all-time record was 14 seconds for Bjørnson's 'Yes, I choose April'. We were out of the blocks so quickly he didn't even have time to pump the organ and all the duffheads guarding the walls were so slow off the mark they barely had their songbooks open before it was all over. Then we mobbed out of the door before anyone really copped on.

Anyway, the singing master was a dwarf-like muddleheaded numpty who was always scurrying here and there but could never control a class. So he closed his eyes to everything and just tried to teach us the 40 or so religious and patriotic songs the school plagued our lives with each morning. He looked for all the world like a frog perched on a stone by the river as he licked his lips and rolled his eyes whilst watching the luscious Lucies as they pranced across the road, but in fairness, he was one of the few who could take us to magical places because he was a man transformed when sitting at a grand piano, which he played like a virtuoso. The little man could sit there and make that huge thing come alive with stirring chords that made the hearts of all the swamp trogs melt as their heads floated off to a hundred different places. It was as if we had all popped a load of pills and were happy and high because the tones thrummed in our bones and our innards thrilled up and down as the music ebbed and flowed.

Sure, there were a few of them that sat there picking their noses and looking at their toes, or them whose cheeks were flattened against their hands as their hot faces dreamed of bogland, but most of them were up in the musical balloon that floated above all the old maps and plaster busts that just stood and stared mutely at the classroom.

Of course, it goes without saying that a small number of our trogs had to distinguish themselves by becoming overnight music buffs. Straight off unbearable. Complete connoisseurs because they had managed to work out how the gramophone record went on the turntable. Now they did nothing but sit at home every evening listening to Bach, Handel and Palestrina, because somebody mentioned this was the in thing. So Bach it was and nothing but Bach. And they would sit every evening at their pathetic music cabinets turning records over and turning up the volume to drown out the chirping budgie, which would obviously wake up underneath its cage cover and want to join in and thereby ruin the learning by rote enjoyment of Mass in B Minor.

Then they would gather to drink tea and study the 34 LP records they had borrowed from a cultural music library and play all the old favourites and all talk at once, declaring how they so love Gregorian chants and couldn't agree more with the singing master when he averred that there were so many converging reference points between Bach's Brandenburg Concertos and Stravinsky's *Le Sacre du Printemps*. Jesus, would you give me a break. Think of the poor budgie cowering in its covered cage from all the racket.

Tore really liked music as well and never pretended otherwise, but it was none of your old music scores, wonderful key changes old chap, flipping coat tails and highbrow glasses. He was one of those rare people who just knows when something is either right or wrong. No hesitation. No ifs or buts. He could always judge things in a very calm and deliberate way and nothing he decided to do ever went wrong. He was the least false person I have ever known and the complete opposite of a chancer. And if, on one of those very rare occasions when something he said didn't quite come off the way he intended – it happened even to him – you could clearly see that he just wanted to jump out of the window with embarrassment, but more often than not he could save the situation because he would switch on the charm as quickly as the swampies could tear the wrapping from their egg and pickle sandwiches. When Tore had no choice but to be in the company of kids who were really acting the goat, it was plain to see that it made his skin crawl. It was natural for us to worship him. I know I had for quite some time. We had sat beside each other year in year out. Because Tore was the Man and I had to be near him.

Chapter 2

My own name is Janus. I know. I know! My dad is a civil engineer. One of them types that's always running round joining some guild or association, some board, club, or this or that. There's always some do or function he has to rush off to. If it's not this place then it's that place he has to go to, and then of course the members have to have a few beers, but they never get really twisted and it's all very civil. Then he brings the lads back to our place and it goes without saying that they get the munchies and it's *smørrebrød* and snacks on the table and a wee dram, and they all sit there grinning and entertain each other with their technical wit. Not that the banter is overly clever and academic mind. It's not about showing off. Just all folksy and hail fellow engineers and something completely pathetic about it all and them sitting there singing ditties about Nyhavn harbour and ooh ray up she rises and all nearly falling over with arms round each other and the great night they're having and pop open another beer while you're there me old mate.

There was never any question that I would be a grammar stream boy and take the university entrance exam in my final year at school. Because it was just the done thing and what would I do otherwise? It was never going to be a problem. I mean, all I had to do to keep moving up the educational ladder was a bit of calculus and then some dictation and that was it. But the old lady and old man were near crapping themselves for fear I'd flunk my exams for High School. Because then I wouldn't get into this school or that – the very schools that would ensure I came out the other end just like dad with loads of friends and happy days and professional guilds, a well-tuned professional engineer's wit, all daft hats on New Year's Eve and I don't know what else. But that's all fine really, because that's proper order and the way it always was, is and will be Forever and Ever Amen. And yes I was totally bog-eyed and frantic as well with all those tests and marks and ten-minute speed drills and mountains of text and yes I admit I bawled when I couldn't work out the up or down of when a plane flying at such a speed and starting here and ending there did what exactly? Of course I passed the exam but, really, you were still a no-mark little runt.

We budding scholars were nothing more than little swamp-eating gobshites capable of coming out with the purest bullshit about everything and anything. A gang of snotty kids bulging with all kinds of opinions that had been stuffed into us during the hundreds of millions of identical dinners we'd gobbled up in the years gone before. Precious little pricks actually. So idiosyncratic and distinctive that splurging out all that grown-up bullshit we'd gulped up like swamp trogs was never going to be a problem for us. We could bluff our way through any subject till our interlocutors were comatose. And the absolutely worst thing of all was that we thought this was normal – that we were such wonderful child prodigies. Yes we were just so goddamned smart. And the shiny eyes of your folks pressing extra spends into your hands when you came home with a merit mark after you'd just done the most pathetic test ever, where you had to retell a piss-poor tale about a dog that jumps from the world's most irrelevant ship to save the ship's boy and his precious fucking kit bag. Would you stop. Then by God they would talk and shake your hand again and it would be the Law you were destined for, or what about a literary critic, or maybe a glass blower (takes some skill that my boy), or how about a glorified meatball cook with a poncey hat, a connoisseur of arse bandits, or this or that, till your head was so inflated you too started to believe you'd reinvented the wheel. And it didn't stop there. Oh no. Because they could stand starry-eyed for days on end imagining their boy with his rakish student's cap and waving the red and white Danish flag, ah yes the *Dannebrog*, and the ancient Danish beech tree and the superior, but never boastful, Danish spirit of inquiry and learning, the wondrous Academe – the quintessence of our *Folk Geist*, because it raises us to a higher plane, and our ignoble legends are rendered less ignoble and mean if retold in a lusty man of the people's voice and preferably with a jug of beer in your raised hand and surrounded by your fellow guildsmen, the final arbiters and defenders of democracy.

Thus my life as a trusty son and all-round good lad was mapped out for me. One of those stalwart apprentices who never quit when the going got rough. And it wasn't out of badness, or because they were total dorks, but mostly because they were just too tired and couldn't really be bothered trying to stoke up the desire and passion needed to find other opinions than those that just came spouting out of them right that minute. And besides, what was the panic? Everything was in the best and most wonderful order and the world was just right there in front of them, big, bright, cheerful and not a worry did they have of any description.

But then the new school year begins and I start at High School where you're suddenly thrown together with this crowd of weird specimens you've never met before in your life and you're no longer one of the oppos in your street-corner gang, but just a pathetic first year that stands there gobsmacked at the rows and rows of trogs and trolls that get bigger and bigger till their mass of bulging bones and trogheads finally reaches the school hall ceiling. So it's one endless round of ahh mammy's boy spat his dummy bless him, missing daddy is he? Even though all that shit was already mostly going over your head because you were well on your way to mask land with flinching jaw muscles and flickering eyelids. So you stand there gawping at all the other little swampies with their short trousers and summer holiday sun-bleached hair and spanking new satchels, some of them with folders in them, dangling around their backsides, and even the odd pair of long trousers like they were adults and honouring the new institution. And all of them standing there letting on they couldn't give a toss about what was going on around them, but at the same time so wired up trying to work out what new planet they were on, their legs shaking and telling them to bolt for the school gate and back to their familiar street corners and mumsywumsy's soft lap, bosom, whatever. And the tears come even closer to bursting point, because of all them big lads stood there with their huge heads sticking up into the roof space and you just wanted to be anywhere but there, creeping back under your blankets and listening to mammy chatting in the living room as she hummed a tune. Sure we tried to strike up conversations about anything and everything, but we couldn't really look each other in the eye because there we were with our pathetic summer hair and had a load of mates who were everywhere but here and tongue-tied because the only real issue was desperately wanting to run as fast as we could out through that gate and get home right away. But of course none of us did. No. Not at all. We didn't run away because we wanted to be like those big shots as well. The ones that carried that student cap on their privileged heads. So we just stood and mawped and gawped, waiting till some really adult person came along and organised us, so we could begin to feel our way forward.

There was this lad standing next to me. One of them tall, lean lads who always have big angular knees that stick out like building blocks in shorts. He actually looked very friendly, but no one had said a word to him because he didn't have a summer-bleached baby head on him like the rest of us. He was stood there with a sort of half grin on his face. As if he was holding a private conversation with himself that was keeping him amused and disconnected from any panic about running out the school gate as fast as he could. Rocking backwards and forwards on his heels he was, like he was moving in his own time. It looked like he was laughing at us, but not for a minute like he was doing it for badness. He was so deeply tanned he almost looked like a Red Indian who could take scalps with his tomahawk and bring a buffalo down with his slingshot. Like this would be child's play for him.

Now we're out in the schoolyard that has an area with water stands. The kind that spouts water up into your mouth when you press the button. And what does this blade do all of a sudden only step out of our line and go over to the water stands. There he is drinking away just because he feels like it and has a bit of a thirst on him. I mean. He just stood there cool as you like, letting the water spout into his mouth and he drank till he didn't want to drink any more and then just wandered back over to us like this whole pantomime was neither here nor there. And I'm telling you all those little summer holiday kids with their short back and sides and shiny satchels just stood and gawped. As if a Chinaman had popped up out of the ground. All because your man had actually dared to walk over to the water fountain and drink like he didn't give a toss. And the big ones in the higher classes stood and stared as well and then started shouting all kinds of shit about what the fuck them pathetic little toerags thought it was a holiday camp or something where they could start acting the maggot and drinking water when they felt like it when the bell had already rung and wait till tomorrow before school coz they'd get water all right when they were 'dubbed'. But this black-haired lad right? He just saunters back over to us nice and easy. Joins the line again and is like grinning to himself, as if he was deaf to all the commotion, but at the same time knew the score. I moved down to where he was so I got standing right beside him again. He had some seriously tanned athletic thighs that were covered with fine downy golden hairs. I don't know, but it was like your urge to belt out of the gate diminished a bit because you could stand next to this buck and bask in the glory of his having spent the whole summer in the woods with his slingshot and Bowie knife. All on his own and never once was he bored. I continued staring at him until he turned round and noticed me, or let on that he'd just noticed me, when of course he was aware I'd been standing there fishing. I mean. The others either side of us were shooting sidelong glances and shuffling a bit but it was still me that made the move. Stood next to him, as if I was the first that could actually say something to him. As if he had to be claimed from the start. I wanted to say something that might hook him. Stop him from disappearing. Make sure he carried on just rocking backwards and forwards there in his own universe. 'What are you staring at?' says I. Because I'm the biggest, most useless cretin that ever walked this earth. 'What are you staring at?' As if it had been him and not me that had just stood and stared and stared, so bog-eyed that my peepers were ready to spring out of my cranium. I was on the brink of running out of the yard and home to mammy. But he just turns, normal as you please, a grin spreading across his face and goes – 'All right? My name's Tore.'

Ahh, ooh, burh, bah ... me just standing there like the plank I am. And your man stands there grinning and saying – 'All right? My name's Tore.'

I go – 'All right, Tore! My name's Janus.' Jesus wept what am I doing running round with a name like that? Janus, anus, painus, saveus, dickus, brainless, shite. All the same, it felt like I had a hook in him. Like I had hold of him and there was no longer an urgent need to take off home in a blur of legs.

Then he goes – 'State of that teacher over there.'

This was one of the teachers who had come out and started to shout that we all had to go into the gym and line up again. All the other kids in the yard began to catcall and whistle because it was this particular teacher and they knew they could mess. But we all began moving to the gym anyway. I walked beside Tore. We went in and started looking around us at this weird school with all its plaster busts and paintings dotted around the place. Then into the gym where the heat and the bedlam exploded the dream state that had carried us there. I just stuck close to Tore. All the other trogs in our year looked like they'd swallowed a bible that was now stuck in their gullets, especially when they saw all them new teachers who might as well have been aliens from outer space. These teacher specimens were just standing there, breaking into vacant smiles and waving, saying hello to all the older trogs by way of big wide grins, as if they adored them and were looking forward to plaguing and torturing each and every one of them. So we stood for a while like gormless sheep but then quiet descended as the School Principal came in through one of the doors and mounted the steps to a podium. He stood there for a few moments in silence and let the light from the windows fall on him like he was some kind of prophet. And there stood the flag beside the podium and we were all supposed to feel that this was it. Now we were truly on the way to some thing or place. We had taken the first giant step. This was what he stood and said up by that flag, whilst all the big trogs looked down at their songbooks and smirked like they knew what song we were supposed to sing and when the Principal told us the page number they all grinned, and the marionette-like figure at the organ started pumping and tinkling the keys and we all sang along because the Principal told us this was the school's very own anthem – one we all knew and had learned in all the other schools we'd come from. I stared up at Tore. He was standing there singing along with the rest of them. So I began to sing as well because I knew this song and actually really liked it. We sang with them. Sang so we thundered the earth around us. Because here was something we could do to make us damn well belong to this school. All the other first years were looking down into their songbooks but also glancing round now and again to see if any of the teachers were watching them. But the teachers were only listening to the bigger boys in the other classes. So we sang along with even more vehemence because we knew this song and, in some way or other, were acknowledging all that had gone before – a salute to those street corners and avenues from whence we came. 'Oooooooh' and 'eeeeeeeh' said the organ as it closed the song out and then we were told to go up to our classrooms and we gave not a thought to the fact that we would be coming here for the next 7 years, before we escaped and became adults. All we did was mosh through like the rest of them in the scrum for the best seats. There was a background worry for us first years though. We'd been told that we were all going to be dubbed the following day so we better bring old clothes to spare our good ones because it could get a bit rough. It was the teacher himself who came into class and told us this. This dubbing malarkey basically meant that the classes above us were allowed, as per tradition, to 'christen' us first years by pelting us with water bombs, even though there was normally a strict rule about messing with water. They were also allowed to do 'truncheon' and 'fried egg' slaps on us – basically smacks to the neck and back of the head using the bottom part of the hand, so the victim feels like his brain will burst out through his nose.

When we arrived at the classroom, Tore was already down at one of the desks by the window and called over to me to come and sit next to him. It was just brilliant he said that. Just brilliant. I zoomed down to him and sat beside him. Now it was me and Tore and that was sorted from that day forward. We were going to be all right. Tore would make it all right for me. Because he sat there grinning at the whole goddamned pantomime like it was a piece of piss.

Then the teachers. One after the other they came in and stood up there and twisted themselves without trying to show it. This way and that. Some of them were happyclappy like scout leaders, patting our heads and all cheerful till you wanted to puke. And then some of the others were none too happy at having to stand there being stared at by a load of swampies. But there were a couple of them who were just themselves. Relaxed and friendly fellas who made you smile or laugh because they said something interesting or funny and didn't bark words out like parade ground sergeants.

Tore sat and watched every one of them and I sat stealing glances at him, because his expression would tell me whether the teacher up there was all right or not. Just to be sure you hadn't got it wrong.

Then we were told we were free to go home. Back to that island fastness. Our own street corner and mammy's gentle solicitations. Her soft hand and belly. Once out of the gate, I walked alongside Tore. We walked down the red street with its big buildings on either side. Its mass of cars and traffic and jumble of people. On down the street and us kind of looking at the pavement.

'Well, they didn't seem too bad now did they?' Tore says.
'No.'
'Are you heading straight home?' he asked.
'Yep,' says I.

'Right.'

Walking a bit more and gazing downwards a bit more. Me with a good feeling about going to school with Tore from now on. One thing for sure. It wasn't going to be boring. As I walked I got this great urge to do millions of things. We were going to be great and have a laugh. All this because I was now friends with Tore the Man.

'We could walk the same way for a good bit,' I said.

'Yeah, we could go down to the bridge and watch the trains. Do you like trains, Janus?'

'Yeah, trains are brilliant. I could watch trains all day.'

So we sauntered along to the bridge near the station and stared down at the trains arriving and departing, shunting to and fro.

In fact I knew loads about trains, so I start showboating with a stream of patter about this and that machine and they were built in this and that place in Jutland and could pull this and that amount of goods carriages.

'When they raise that signal there, that means they're free to pull out,' says I standing there, as if even the biggest idiot in the world couldn't work that one out. But he just grinned a bit and did his rocking on his feet thing and grinned again till it began to annoy me a bit. Then he just goes – 'yeah?'

As if I didn't know all there was to know about those neverending trains and my father an engineer for Danish Railways who actually controlled the lives of all those commuters down there milling in and out of the trains.

Then he goes – 'Hey ... Janus Trainus. What about this mate? How would you like to just, like, drive off one day with a train. Just head off to Jesus knows where, somewhere out there. I mean out of this country to the back of beyond, or wherever?'

'Er, I suppose ...' says I, because it was a bit hard to imagine, with the war on and Denmark occupied by the Nazis. Train trips for jollies usually meant no further than North Sjælland and a few other spots.

'Yeah, that would be brilliant all right.'

'It would be a great lark. Travelling to all those places, going round having fun and meeting loads of different people.

I mean. I know we can't right now. We're not allowed at the minute but you just get a mad urge to take off when you look at all those trains heading off somewhere. Full steam ahead.'

Then he leaned right over the railing and looked out and away, as if he was already on his way to all those places we'd be steaming through with the train and watching all those people in their summer clothes in the villages and towns, hanging out of windows and waving with white handkerchiefs and smiling in a way we'd never seen before except maybe once in a blue moon. Like everything he saw was one big smile. As if he suddenly longed desperately for a world I knew nothing about, but could now sense was out there somewhere.

'They seemed all right at school,' he said, as he turned towards me once again. 'And our lads. They seemed all right too.'

It was like we could now talk about that school in a real way.

'Yeah, they seemed all right to me as well,' I said. 'Do you think they'll let us play handball, even in the first year?'

'I bet they do.'

'Have you played before?' I asked, exploring whether he was good at handball, like he seemed to be at everything else.

'Naw, we mostly played football at the school I was at. But it's almost the same. Except you use your hands of course.'

'Yep,' says I.

Then we stood for a while longer gazing down at the tracks, like they could reveal a trove of hidden secrets to us if we stared at them long enough.

'Right. Shall we make a move then?' Tore said in the end.

'Yeah, we can move on,' I ventured. I didn't want to lose him just yet. So I left it hanging like that. We pushed our way down from the bridge to street level, which in fact was near my tram stop for home. But I said nothing and we ploughed on, just walking and no words exchanged between us. Then finally he said:

'Janus – that's a funny name.'

'Yeah, it's a mad name,' I replied – more than ready to admit that it was a stupid name. But still, I was peeved that he also thought it was crazy and had said it out loud.

But then he goes – 'No ... I don't think it's a mad name. It's a bit old-fashioned but sounds cool and a bit of fun. Janus, Janus, Janus,' he said, putting his head back and savouring my name in his mouth. Like he'd already swallowed it and was getting the aftertaste from his stomach or heart.

Then he stops, stands there and goes – 'Janus. Janus? ... No, I really think it's a cool name mate. It's like some kind of horse or stone. Janus, Janus. It tastes good.'

He's probably not right in the head. But it felt good – that he was standing there savouring my name. Like a taste of honey.

'What does your dad do?' I asked. Because I was such a little dickhead who couldn't think of anything more grownup to ask about. He goes – 'I don't have a dad.'

I just wanted to die of shame and red-faced embarrassment but Tore just carried on explaining how his mum and dad were divorced and that he did kind of have a dad but it wasn't like a real one, because he lived alone with his mother and his dad was someplace else entirely. He never saw his dad, he said. Now this was a weird one. Like, not having a real father and only seeing him occasionally. Then this about living with just your mother. It was hard to comprehend right that second when you thought about things in your own home with never a cross word or big fight scene or things like that. The folks just there when you needed them. Like when you were sick as a dog and lay in your bed ready to cry. But his mum must have been a good old stick despite everything. I mean. There was Tore with knees like tree trunks sticking out below his short trousers and his head all glowing with sun-kissed warmth as he talked about her.

'You can come up and say hello if you want,' he said all of a sudden. It had completely slipped my notice that we had ended up in a street in the inner city. This was an area we only ever saw when we came into town, because we ourselves lived out in Østerbro. He was already standing on the first step at the entrance to the apartments and all I could do was gawp

43

and look like a first class dick.

'Come on, you nutcase,' says he.

My parents weren't aware we were going to be let off early, so I went in. And anyway, I wasn't going to leave it there, because that stupid grin had started getting on my nerves a bit. Like he knew everything already and didn't even need a dad. Like he was fine with just a mother. Although your mum is the most important obviously.

So we skipped up the steps and then up the stairs to the apartment on the third floor. Riemer was the surname on the door. So Tore Riemer was his full name then.

He had his own yale key. I didn't have my own key. Everybody came home at the time they were supposed to and, on the odd occasions that you didn't, we had help who could let us in anytime. But maybe Tore's mother wasn't always in during the day. So then we get into the hallway of the apartment and I see a load of doors leading into different rooms on both sides. It was dark, so Tore switched the light on and we threw our bags down where we stood.

'Mum!' he called. And a voice shouted back from somewhere inside the place.

'I'm back,' he called. 'I brought Janus back with me.'

As if she already knew who I was and knew that my name was Janus.

'Mum's in here,' says he as he leads me into a room flooded with light coming from a huge window. The kind you see in pictures of artists' studios. All around the walls there were weird paintings and images. The kind that gave me nightmares when I was a young kid. All kinds of lines and edges and disturbing shades of orange and yellow, but some of them were actually pleasing to look at – the ones where you could see what the object was. Or where there were real things like buildings or landscapes. And over in the corner, bathed in light, there was a woman dressed in overalls with a floral pattern. She was fiddling with something on a pedestal. This was Tore's mother.

She was nice looking and much younger than my own mother. There she was smoking a cigarette and her hands covered in clay, which is what she was splurging and splatting with. Presumably for some bust or figure. I stood like a dodo, all squirming and fumbly inside because – was I supposed to shake her hand or wave or what? But she just grinned like Tore grinned. Then he went over and kissed her and she said 'hi Janus' and then it was you're very welcome and how was it at your new school today and sit down and are you boys starving ... so that you just relaxed and knew that everything was going to be fine.

All the same. It was a bit weird seeing Tore kiss his mother on the mouth. That wasn't how we carried on at home. I'd never even seen my dad kiss my mother, except for a peck on the cheek, as if there were nothing more to it than common friendliness. But Tore walked right up to his mum and gave her a smacker on the lips. I mean like he enjoyed doing it.

Fru Riemer just stayed where she was pottering with that figure. There was so much light in the room that everything stood out super clear, and there was a kind of halo shimmering this way and that above her head when she bent over the pedestal scraping some muck away. She was talking all the while - that we should just go out to the kitchen and take what food we wanted and a glass of milk or whatever and wasn't it great that Tore had already found a friend to talk to. But this was mainly for my sake when she knew that Tore didn't need anyone to talk to or hold his hand before he could go anywhere new. He too just stood smiling and watching her. But then without warning he spreads his arms out like aircraft wings and goes – 'brrrraaaaaaaaahhm'. Then we take off down the corridor to the kitchen climbing like two Spitfires just before they perform their nosedives. As he's diving his Spitfire he grabs the handle for his cannons, rams the joystick forward, and swoops down on a Heinkel 111 right below him and lets him have it both barrels so that you see great chunks being stripped off the bomber's wings and the pilot trapped in the cockpit as the plane spins into freefall towards the earth. 'Eeeyoooooooowhm' he cries as he pulls his beast up again and levels her off at that high-pitched whine that rises and falls when the planes fly high over the rooftops of night-time Copenhagen and your heart in your mouth as you lie there listening to them but would die three thousand deaths rather than admit it. Then we sat down at the kitchen table and readied our planes for landing. Nice and easy we came in, smooth descent onto the airstrip with just a few bumps and standing under the control tower in no time with the requisite hand signals to advise mission accomplished.

After that we scoffed a liver pâté and rye sandwich each.

Of course, we'd never really seen a Spitfire, but it was still the ace in the skies bar none. With its pointed nose and gun cannons on each wing. And maybe it was that very Spitfire of your dreams that was droning across the heavens when you lay there at night in a complete sweat and you could hear it whirring and whining way above you and you sort of hoped there would be some kind of 'incident' right then and there but there never was. It was really strange to think of those men sitting up in the air above our heads and flying all the way back to England whilst all we could do is go down to the airfield and stare at boring Junkers and Dornier 215s. And that Donald Duck effort that was supposed to take off from Refshale Island but just kept on revving for ever and ever with its pathetic diesel motor and never seemed to get airborne. It was hard to think that anything in the world would ever be any different, because each day was the same and nobody really knew what was actually happening. I mean, you just knew the Germans were running everything and, even so, you still believed more what they said on Danish radio – that it was somehow more correct than anything that came at us as a distant and surreal voice flitting in and out of all that interference and buzzing on the wireless from England, or that smooth avuncular broadcasting voice from T. T. in Sweden.

So you just didn't think too long or hard about all that. But it was brilliant to swoop down in your Spitfire, or maybe a Hurricane, and blatter the wings and fuselage of a Heinkel 111 so the debris scatters right across the sky and the Kraut turning round in his cockpit to open the window but never managing before the plane goes into a tailspin and disappears in a twister of smoke and flames. This was much easier to imagine, because it was smart and all technical. One machine against another, and much easier than sabotage because that was far more savage – no smart uniforms and gleaming weapons involved, and anyway we were told incessantly on the wireless that sabotage was wrong because it harmed the Danish state.

So there we were. Sitting chewing on dark rye bread and liver paste. The kitchen was nice and comfortable and was really nicely painted. There was a real old-fashioned dresser as well with a row of solid mugs on it.

Then I goes to Tore – 'The biggest bang I've ever heard. I mean. You know, sabotage … was that time they blew up B & W shipyard. Wow that was some blast! I was at home and just getting into bed and I swear I thought the roof was gonna lift off. I'm telling you that was some explosion. There were seven bangs one after the other.' I said this mainly to see what his own thoughts were about all that with the Germans and sabotage.

'You should have been in this house mate when they did air raids on that place, ' said Tore. 'Me and mum just lay down at the windows and watched the planes as they flew in right over our heads. We didn't even go down to the cellar like you're supposed to.'

'I know,' says I.

'There's even gun battles and shooting in the street round this way,' said Tore.

'Yeah, it must be cool to live in the middle of town,' says I.

'Sure is. There's always something happening.'

'What does your mum do? Is she a sculptor or something?'

'Yes. She exhibits her work as well. More when dad was here,' he said.

All this felt awkward – a strange thing to be talking about.

'My father is an architect,' said Tore.

'Oh right,' I said. 'Mine's an engineer.'

Why do we always have to talk and repeat ourselves like little trolls about what our fathers do blah blah. As if this was the most important thing in the world? As if it mattered one bit. But really, it mattered a whole lot. I mean. It was actually a very good thing that Tore's dad was an architect and his mother a sculptor. At least it didn't pull Tore down in the eyes of the world. An architect and an engineer. That was a good mix and now we would be going to school together and cut from the same cloth. It was brilliant that I'd got hold of Tore, because he was just a stand-up kind of fella. You felt so solid and comfortable in his company because you could be dead sure he wouldn't be talking guff every time he opened his gob. Not like most of the other trogs, where your head was wrecked after talking to them for three minutes because you had to stand there letting on that you were amused and interested in their pathetic problems.

Then his mother came out to the kitchen and rinsed her hands under one of the taps. The clay slipped off in long strips. She smiled over at us and asked if we had homework. So we told her we did indeed have homework and how sick and pathetic that was but probably quite right too. And she just laughed even more and said it was just what we needed. That it would do us good to get stuck into something serious and we weren't at Kindergarten any more you know. And this was true. I'd never really bothered my arse at school, but now it was like this both terrifying and exciting prospect. That this was serious and we'd have to get the finger out. In truth, I was a bit stunned that I was going to be learning all these new things with Tore by my side. Discover loads of new things and really take them to heart.

'I'd better get home,' I said at last. 'My mum throws a fit if I'm late. She always thinks I've been shot, or a bomb's dropped on my head, or something.'

'Well, you'd better look smart, Janus, and leave right away,' Fru Riemer said. 'Had you better not ring to tell them you're here?'

'No,' I replied, 'there's no need.'

So I just stand there gazing right at Tore and the last thing I wanted was to go home, because here was so comfortable and easy. I liked where I was.

'Right then. See you tomorrow,' says I to Tore.

'Yeah,' he said, 'we'll probably get a game of handball do you think?'

'Well that PE teacher told us to bring our gymshoes in.'

Tore's mother stood drying her hands and kind of laughing at us, like we were going to be the best double act she'd ever seen.

'Brilliant,' Tore says. He stood up too and began to smile.

'Right then. I'd better go,' I said. As if I hadn't just said that very thing.

'Ta-ta for now,' said Tore's mum. 'Just call in any time you like Janus.'

'Thanks, I will,' says I. The whole thing had been just brilliant, brilliant, brilliant. Just the totally perfect start. I mean. It wasn't like going to one of my mates' houses down the street. Someone you already knew backwards and forwards. This was completely new territory with completely new people, and this Tore fella. Well he gave you the feeling you'd never really had a proper friend before. Like you stood on the threshold of a totally new and fantastic world. Sure I knew he couldn't be my best friend ever just because I'd spent a day with him. But it was as if you got this urge to plunge into the friendship, put your heart and soul into it and enjoy it for all it was worth.

We went out into the hallway and I picked up my satchel, held out my hand and said goodbye to Fru Riemer. Tore followed me out onto the landing and we just gazed at each other for a moment.

'Right. See you then,' I said to Tore. He was standing a few steps above me looking down at me. That was proper order and a kind of a thrill – Tore the Man being up above and me down a few steps and us saying goodbye but, guaranteed, we were going to see each other the very next day. That this was going to be the way it was for many years to come and neverending Amen. Really. It was a bit unbelievable. I mean. Too good to be true and bound to fall apart.

'Right then, see you Janus,' said Tore. 'See you tomorrow.'

I started moving down the stairs saying – 'Yep, see you tomorrow mate,' talking as I went.

And that was how the whole thing started. Like it was a bit mad and surreal from the very beginning. I scooted down the road in the direction of home, managed to get a tram and stood near the driver watching the streets go by. He let me switch the tracks for him at Holmens Kanal and it turned out to be one heck of a trip because there was loads of bother down at Kongens Nytorv – we saw a man being dragged off by the police and there were some German officers shouting and pointing. Next minute the Krauts open up and a huge mob of people begin running down towards Nyhavn, our driver working the handcrank like crazy to get us away from there as fast as possible.

I flew up the inner stairwell at home and burst into the living room all ready to report the news about the Germans, but then thought again. My mum would have conniptions if I started telling her about the riot, and it would be where have you been Janus and why didn't you come straight home Janus. So I just settled for school was brilliant mum and that we had homework for tomorrow and went straight to my room. I'd moved out of my box room and got this proper bedroom after my older brother got married and moved out. Not a word did I say about Tore. I wanted him all to myself for a bit longer ... But he would soon be coming home to visit us. Now that I had my own room, we could sit and yarn away on anything and everything. Tore no doubt had his own room as well, even though I hadn't seen it.

My room was tops. You could see out across the roofs and it had proper shelves because my brother hadn't cleaned the room out when he left. It was a shame he'd taken his two old pistols with him though. He used to have them hanging on his wall but he made sure they weren't left behind. But he did leave one of his stuffed birds behind. And he hadn't taken his air rifle with him. So all in all it was a brilliant bedroom and I was sure Tore would like it too. I really liked springtime in this room because when you opened the window the singing from the blackbirds all around the rooftops came in loud and clear. I mean singing like crazy they were – till their necks were blue with it. Then you got a strong whiff of dad's pipe from down below and it made you feel all grown up and want to smoke yourself. But the old man had already started to drop heavy hints that, if I could wait till I was 21, some serious money would be coming my way.

I pulled out my folder from my bag and began to study the list of books we'd been given. It was some stack of books, but we would be using some of them until the fourth year.

God knows why Tore's mum and dad were no longer married. Maybe they had fought a lot. Screaming and shouting and throwing things at each other, to the point where they couldn't bear it any more? Or what else could it be?

Both Tore and his mum seemed happy enough. But it was impossible to imagine that your parents might not always live together. That was the way life was. You had a mum and a dad. I mean. The earth would just collapse with one Christ Almighty bang if your mum and dad were to part. That divorce malarkey was the most mental thought ever in the world, because look – there's mum running round pouring out the beers and schnapps for dad and all his buddies when he brings them back for a quick one after their guild meeting, and them swapping yarns all pleased and at their ease, and mum standing there with her hands on her hips smiling at the whole thing, like they were all her children and dad most of all. Like Sunday wouldn't be Sunday – when Torben and his wife came to us, and Ernst came too. We all sit eating dinner and the air full of pork roast and Sunday and the clink of plates and knives and forks and the radio on in the background and the hurdey hur of Swedish Radio's weekly lotto and the afternoon news from T. T. wire service. Who knows? Maybe it was still like that for Tore anyway? They'd obviously survived and were still smiling the both of them. And hadn't I felt like staying longer with them? Even stopping over at theirs if they asked me.

It was still real August weather outside, and we had been in the country for the summer, but now we had to get stuck into something totally new and in a new school and things were looking good. Even though of course you felt the heebie jeebies starting something that was strange to you. But it was like you'd struck gold this time because you'd hooked up with this lad Tore and his mother who liked to stand pottering with clay on a pedestal. And it was so bright in that room, and her smile was so winning you just couldn't believe divorce was that bad. And then Tore the Man, who had just stepped out and took his fill of water like it didn't mean squat. And it was just so good that it was 'Janus Trainus' that had got to him first. Really too good to be true. Like a dream that couldn't last.

Chapter 3

Only those who have actually gone through the experience really know what it's like, growing up with a fella like Tore. I grew into Tore, till I was his physical extension. It was always Tore and Janus and Janus and Tore. Every time some stunt or mischief came off, it was Tore and Janus behind it, even though it was mostly just Tore of course. I didn't care what it was we got up to. If Tore was game for it, so was I. Why? Because that was the way things should be.

We soon got going at school and worked out that the other lads we had to share space with were nothing but a bunch of assholes. Though one or two were all right and when we really got stuck into something, we could cajole all the others and, in effect, orchestrate the whole gang and shebang whatever way we pleased. It was always us – down at the end bench near the window directing proceedings. One day we even got one of those gawpy novice teachers to sob like a pure child because we dragged a dead rat up with us from down below and slapped it on his desk, locked the classroom door and hid not only the key but the handle as well so the poor mooncalf could neither stick nor twist. So there's the rat up there just staring at him with its glazed eyes and a rank smell off it and the teacher obviously scared to go near it, not least because it was partially decomposed, but still had its living rat shape. Teacher just standing there paralysed, whilst we incite all the little trogs to start howling by winding them up with low continuous murmurings and chanting till the noise reverberates and becomes a wall of sound that reaches a crescendo and the poor sod's mouth quivering so much he bolts for the door only to find his escape route locked and blocked. So he stands there stock still, staring with all his might towards the blackboard and we just continued with our mantra, till the ones in the front row went quiet and a whisper emerged that the teacher was crying his eyes out like a girl. Soon we all went quiet, because it was pretty weird being in the classroom with a grown man in floods of tears. Not because we felt sorry for him or anything. Just that it was so embarrassing having an adult in our classroom who was stood crying in front of us.

Then Aksel down in the other corner pipes up that the door keys and handle are in the drawer beneath the desk, but this daft teacher just remains standing there as if he hadn't heard a thing. So Aksel pushes on up through the benches, opens the desk and digs out the key and handle then walks over to the greenhorn to offer them up. But Aksel is standing there for ages holding out the handle to the teacher, whilst your man is gasping for air and all the time trying not to let on that he's actually blubbering, as if it would make it less shameful if we couldn't hear his wailing. Finally he takes the keys and handle and goes over to the door and starts futtering at the lock, sticking both things in at the same time, then he drops the keys and one of the other trogs runs out to hand them up to him again, but without warning the teacher goes berserk, grabs hold of the trog's hair and hits him a couple of belts across the ear, as if this trog was totally to blame for everything by dint of him picking the keys up. We were stunned into silence – couldn't even say 'oooohw!', because this was beyond crackers and the young'un starts howling something about telling his dad coz it wasn't fair and he was only trying to help. So teacher lets go of him, finally gets the key in the lock and disappears out the door with a huge snort, which wasn't like anything definite – more like a cross between a sob and a belch. So we sat there and were just totally schtumm because OK we lost the run of it and because your man had gone completely nuts and we had no idea what was coming at us next. You wouldn't believe it but the most pathetic thing in the world happened. Didn't little Cinders go and blab the whole thing to the Principal and the shit hit the fan. There were interrogations and we'll find out who was behind all this and had we ever heard of corporal punishment and we were supposed to be mature but in fact were cretins who had no place in a school like that and we just had to stand there heads bowed and take all that bullshit, as if we hadn't suffered enough having to watch that grown man stand there bawling like a little trog that spat his dummy out of his cot.

Eventually they let us out to the playground and there was no more about it, because everybody knew it was a big song and dance about a minor scrape and the greenhorn teacher was the subject of bleak looks from all sides, as if the school staff went and thought – there goes that numpty who will never get on in this world so help me.

All right, probably we did feel sorry for him but we turned our faces to stone and nobody let it slip.

And yes it was me and Tore that were behind it. What a brilliant stroke – the greenhorn sobbing in front of the class then grabbing hold of that other trog who was completely blameless. Some show or what? Like we'd unleashed an avalanche of things we never dreamed we could make happen. But to be honest it was a real horror story seeing a grown man in the flesh without his mask. I mean. When we were so used to all the other duffheads wearing fixed face masks all the hours of the day. But then. I suppose if we were going to be confronted with an adult totally unmasked like that, Greenhorn wasn't the worst of them. His face hadn't set into that familiar jawbone-clenching grimace. Or hadn't collapsed into ancient petrified aspic. It was just a bubbling mass of grief that looked on the verge of dribbling meltdown, so that only a pair of huge dripping saucers full of snivel would have remained if the meltdown had continued. That and a bare skull.

We had discovered a colossal power within us. Well, it was colossal power he had – Tore the Man. To be able to conjure that whole train of events. Getting a grown adult to disintegrate right in front of us like that. Of course it was a bit bad the whole thing. But only because things got out of hand

and we were left gawping. Saw a human being totally lose it and become diminished – small like us, but more troggy in a way with his scalped bonce and his swimming buggy eyes.

Like you suddenly felt that, underneath it all, there was hardly any difference between us and the adults, when you saw a guy like that become a quivering wreck. Like, when things went wrong and they were out of their depth, they were just as scared as we were.

But me and Tore would never have that problem. We'd show them. All of them. What proper order was. What it meant to be a stand-up guy who just handled whatever came at him. No problem.

I ended up spending all my waking time with him. Both through the day and into the evening. I would just about get an early evening meal bolted into me and then I was out the door on the way to Tore's. His house was now my only destination. Then we could sit there for ages in his room. Chewing the fat about this and that. Everything under the sun. It was just a pisser that we always had to break it up so early because of the Kraut curfew and all the bother that was going on. But sometimes, of a Saturday, I was allowed to stay over at Tore's and then we could lie in our beds and yarn away until cockcrow almost. And I'm telling you there really was major strife out on the street – with live rounds going off and shouts and God knows what was going on. We had no idea whether it was saboteurs, Danish *Freikorps* Nazis or Police Auxiliaries but the hair on the back of your neck stood up and your head froze because it was pitch black outside and the shots were very near. There was one time when Fru Riemer came in to us and it was obvious she was scared, even though she kept on telling us not to worry and everything would be all right. But we definitely heard someone screaming. Bad enough that you felt like screaming yourself, because you didn't know what was going on and it sounded so raw and horrible. It was nothing like how it happened in the movies. In the movies it was brilliant and so cool when there was a shootout and the ones that took a slug fell in that movie kind of way, like going up on their tiptoes, spinning round and going ahh as they fell. But this was totally different because of that screaming – people making that scream noise that was like nothing on earth. I'd never heard it before and I don't think Tore had either. Then a man started shouting down there in the street, as if he was drunk – aaaahwhoooo. Then it came again, that – ratatatatssssss, or a big bang, but totally different to the movies, like more hollow and not so metallic and precise as in the cinema. And suddenly a deathly quiet. Everything just stopped and the next day revealed nothing, even though me and Tore snooped around here and there trying to find some evidence. We didn't even find any bullet casings to add to our collection. But everybody in the area seemed to be an expert on what had happened. An informer had been gunned down. But others said it was a saboteur and others again denied there had been any shooting. Really, it was impossible to be sure about anything, because those people involved in all that in the middle of the night were not like real people. They moved in that midnight world beyond the blackout curtains and vanished as soon as daylight began to show.

Also. Having all those illegal newspapers floating around at my house put your stomach in knots. The old man would lump them home with him and they also got posted through the letterbox. I know we were expected to read all that stuff but you got the screaming ab dabs just seeing them all round the house. I mean. Say if the Krauts came storming into the house and all those newspapers just lying there – that was you caught. You didn't have a prayer. It was the slammer for you mate. But Tore was a lot cockier about all that. Or his mum was anyway. For she was always sending him here and there with a bundle of those papers. Telling him who they had to go to around town. Sure he was nervous, but he still did it. He would walk round openly, his bag full of them papers and that big grin on his head, and I would be shitting myself, no lie, as we walked past a group of Krauts who always hung around a particular café. I was convinced that, any second, they would be running down the street after us and ripping Tore's bag from him. Nothing ever happened. They just sat there every day ogling the waitresses who would strike poses for them with their hair in a kind of a net and all frizzy at the front, grinning coyly and tittering whilst the Krauts popped balloons from their mouths off the whipped cream on their plates. When we got a few steps clear of them we both spat in disgust, but only when we were sure they couldn't see us from the café.

It goes without saying that Tore was over at mine loads of times and mum and dad were just as taken with him as everybody else. I mean. They didn't make it too obvious, but you just knew they were delighted a lad like him should be my best friend and come and stay with me. As if he was bestowing a special privilege upon our home. Or it became a more refined household due to Tore's presence. And he could hold conversations with adults – the kind that adults like to hold when you talk to them. Like you have to be as grown-up as possible – so polite and smiley but with an ironic gleam in your eye. Tore had them spellbound in seconds. Around the dinner table at home, he would have people in stitches when he started his mental stories about all the alien specimens he'd encountered that day. When he started to describe them and give each one of them some lunatic name or other, my dad's face would be all red and nearly bent over into the rice pudding with laughter. Not only that. Tore the Man could even hold a conversation with my big brother Ernst who was already at sixth-form college. Tore could get Ernst to laugh out loud and converse as if they were the same age, even though me and Tore were still only at High School. Sometimes we would take the notion to go off on a dander round the schools, because the Germans took them over as refugee detention centres, and we thought all this confusion was the best of fun. Often, you never knew whether you were supposed to be in school or not.

Then bang. The war was over and we saw them fellas come out of the shadows – the ones we didn't have a clue about, and we saw their armbands and bandoliers of lead and them driving round in lorries, hanging on the sides and sitting on the bonnets with their guns out and shooting into the air and the whole show was brilliant and really was like a movie this time because nothing dangerous really happened any more and everyone, including ourselves, went a bit daft with a sort of crazed happiness.

Dad opened all the tobacco tins he'd been saving during the war, but they were all rotten with mould and mum nearly died laughing. Me and Tore zoomed round all the places where the Krauts used to be. They were still open at that time and you should have seen the weapons and ammo we picked up. We went round to the Tommy soldiers with eggs and film rolls and got cigarettes in return. Then we just stood there inhaling 'Wild Woodbine' and 'Senior Service' like mad things.

I've no idea what happened next. Well. I mean. I actually do know. Because out of the blue Tore is getting ready to leave Copenhagen, because his mother has to go and visit someone or other in Jutland. They just disappear from their apartment and Tore doesn't turn up for school one day. I went round and round like a rudderless boat.

Of course we acted like idiots on that last day before his departure and talked about the world and everything in between. Everything except that other thing. The too real thing. Little trog stuff instead. Going on like that when you really want to do and say important things but just can't do it. So you shrink to nothing inside and puff yourself up outside. Like a clown in a circus.

Tore goes – 'Have you done tomorrow's homework?' As if he didn't already know that I hadn't. As if we hadn't spent the whole day together.

'Nope, and you haven't done your homework either have you?' says I. 'No need. Now you're going to a redneck yokel school.'

'Redneck me arse,' he says. He was going to Ålborg. So I couldn't really call it a yokel school. Anyway it didn't matter squat what school he went to. Be it a hole in the ground. I just couldn't bear the thought that he was leaving me. What was I supposed to do with myself? I couldn't do a thing without him. Because it was him and only him that set everything in motion with his carry-on and cheeky grin.

It was his mum that had met a fella over in Jutland and now

wanted to move over there to be with him. It was the end of the world as far as I was concerned – all that was left was those empty cardboard trogs at school. My mates on my road I hadn't seen since Tore appeared in my life. And Fru Riemer was going to go over there and work at her mess of clay. Playacting and joking with Tore and this new fella obviously. I mean. No doubt they would soon be getting on like a house on fire. I'm not daft and could see it all so clearly. I was so jealous I felt like jumping up and biting into his arm like a bulldog and never letting it go.

'We could go home to mine and drink tea,' I proposed.

'Yeah, that's a good one,' Tore said.

Looked like we were finally going to stop our marathon tour of the streets, because we'd been going round and round up and down for God knows how many hours. So we went home to mine but didn't go into the living room, because Tore had already been in and said his goodbyes, and we weren't going to go through all that again. So we just tiptoed up to my room and threw ourselves down after I'd put the kettle on and pulled out a packet of 'Dover'. I don't know how long I'd kept them hidden. Then we just stared at nothing.

It had become quite cosy my bedroom as time had gone by, because we'd collected a load of different posters and put them up, generally pottering about in it and changing things round. It also smelled of our particular brands of tobacco and not just my brother's any more, as in the old days.

Then Tore goes all bright and looks happy as Larry. Sitting there all of a sudden like he was looking forward to moving.

'Mum's been a bit off her rocker this last while,' he said finally. I knew all this already.

'Like she's crazy about this guy, I've never seen her like this before. I'm talking a bit weird and beside herself,' he said. Then he goes – 'I mean. We have to go over to Ålborg, and I have to join a new school and the whole thing is a bit mad seeing as how we're supposed to be moving up to university grade next year. But I've never seen mum lepping round and carrying on like this. She hasn't done a stroke of work.'

Tore goes on – 'This guy. I've never even met him. And

he's never been at our place. Not while I was awake anyway. She must have met him when she was out at some show, or something. And it's completely mad the whole thing. Us moving from here. But it's nice she feels that way, even though I don't know this fella.'

Then he goes – 'Don't worry Janus, I'll write and let you know how we're getting on.' I just sat there with a daft grin pulling on my cigarette. As if I was delighted by the whole thing. Like, write letters? I ask you. Letters were what you wrote on your summer holidays and only once. Now it was going to be survival by letters. Now I was supposed to survive by devouring Tore's letters. As if these were manna from heaven. When I was so used to having him there right by my side. All I ever needed to do was reach out my arm and there he was with his broad smile and those eyes that seemed to see more than what our boring normal eyes saw.

'And you'll never see Clockhead ever again,' says I. As if this was some lamentable thing.

'No, but you can bet your ass there are loads of them just like Clockhead up in Ålborg,' Tore replied. Clockhead was one of the most demented duffheads of all the teachers we had. One of them total lunatics who goes berserk with rage if you can't say every single word in the set book.

Then Tore goes – 'I'm sure going to miss you Janus Trainus. But we can still see each other in the holidays.'

'Yeah,' says I. 'Yeah,' and nothing but 'yeah'.

Finally I go – 'Do you want a last cigarette?'

So we smoked another cigarette and then he left because he had to go home and pack. We were standing at the communal entrance door down in the street but then I saw dad coming back from somewhere. So we moved further down the street. Neither of us wanted to talk to him right that minute. So we ended up beside the hotdog stand on the corner and some adult trog was waffling on about currency sharks and the haves and have-nots and snot and I don't know what. And we were supposed to take leave of each other here and Tore would walk away and be gone in the morning. The whole thing was pathetic and puke-invoking. When we couldn't stand there any longer, we put out our hands and shook and there was a weird thing because we'd almost never done that before, and we said see you even though we wouldn't and hope you like it mate and would you give me a bucket till I get sick.

I went straight home, chucked myself head first into my bed and thought about girls, girls and girls as much as I could and felt like the biggest loser in history because there was nothing special about me any more. Then I fell asleep. The next morning Tore was gone. But three months after he was back. And never left again.

Chapter 4

One day, he was just sat there. Like he'd never gone away. So it was just a case of marching over to him, saying a big hello, and the old days were back. Or at least, that was my first rush of feeling when I walked into class and saw him there. But when you got closer to him and got beside him it got more awkward. There was something dead now. In the middle of his face. Like you would think someone had ripped open his head and cut something out. There was some sort of gap, but you couldn't put your finger on it, couldn't find it. Something about his face that had never been there before. A hint maybe that he'd been switched off in some way. Or maybe it was down to his eyes, that didn't have the same sparkle as before.

Whatever the answer, the roar of joy rising from your throat at seeing him there again was quickly stifled. You just fought down the elation, because it looked like he wondered who you were a big – whether you'd ever existed. But then things shifted. All of a sudden, he sees that it's good old Janus Trainus standing before him. And then it's all right mate all right and me asking how he got on and him saying it was just great, which he shouldn't have said because I could see three hundred miles off it was bullshit. He shouldn't have said that because it was a dagger in me. And he knew it. He'd just forgotten for a little minute that he was Tore the Man and me Janus. But then there was no more talk because class started and I was so happy that my spine was zinging up and down in my chair, like it was melting with happy juice. Tore had come home, and the show was up and running again. We would show all those big überassholes that it was Tore and Janus now. Back with a vengeance. Yes! Tore again. Tore again. Good old Tore back with us again! And never you worry mate. I'll soon wipe that dust from your eye.

The letters. All those mad letters we wrote to each other. Sure they were brilliant and a good laugh, but nothing was ever said about what was missing – the big gap. Whatever the thing was that had invaded Tore's head was never mentioned. But I'd find that out soon enough. Oh yes. A few of our jaunts and escapades round the streets of this town and I'd have the whole thing dragged out of him and done with. Then we'd recommence our parleys – smoking cigarettes in our rooms, drinking tea and talking talking talking till our insides were talked out and we could look at our innards hanging out there in amazement, or drape them round each other's necks like garlands of celebration.

But this was weird. Suddenly I saw him as a separate individual. Before this, I'd never really been aware of what he actually looked like. Because we were always rubbed up against each other. It was a peculiar feeling, looking at this fella like you would a real person. There he was sitting next to me staring up at the blackboard. I don't even know if he was good-looking. OK. He was good-looking. He gave me the impression he was black. I mean, like everything about him was black, swarthy or dark brown. He had a huge mane of black hair that was pushed back from his forehead and flowed downwards behind his ears. And then maybe it was the shape of his nose that had me thinking from day one he had the cut of a Red Indian. He was a proper Redskin I'm telling you. If you looked anyway close at him. Definitely he was a chieftain. He'd been out raiding but had now returned home. The warrior returned to his tribe, so it would no longer feel itself adrift and rudderless in the wide and treacherous seas. Home to his squaw. The conquering hero and me sat there bowed and humble, just like that squaw. Ready to throw myself into the raging torrent should the Great Chief demand it. Now this Chief had gained even more authority with this new and mysterious look on his face. But three months. Three months of his life that were mostly a blank for me. Squaw was jealous. It was horrible to think that Tore might be possessed by something that made his face look like that. He must have realised I was sitting there probing and prodding him with my eyes, because he turned and gazed at me. My bones thrilled inside me. Because it was Tore sitting there. Tore the Man. Tore the mad bastard.

Then he goes – 'You haven't told me what's happening yet, Janus.'

I ducked slightly behind Erik's broad back so that I could give a report.

'There's loads a things on the boil,' I said. 'You've come back at just the right moment. We're having a party. D'you remember we talked about it ages ago? Coz some of us are doing exams for university list but others aren't? Anyway the duffheads are letting us organise a party. But of course nobody here could organise a fart in a bean factory. But now ... I mean, now with you here Tore. We'll really show them a party. They're letting us use room eighteen. Decorate it the way we want as well. But now we have to ask the duffhead-in-chief how many beers we're allowed.'

To be honest. None of us were great beerheads at that time. Tea was cool and what we lived on. But a party was a party and if we had to get a beer down our throats. Well then. Once we'd had one the next one would be easier.

'Beers?' Tore says. 'We'll have to sort out some vermouth and gin as well man!'

'No chance of that,' says I. 'Not with this asshole of a Principal. He would get full drunk just sniffing a beer cap. So then he thinks we'd be the same. This school Tore. It's got so fucking precious of late. It'd make you vomit.'

I'd only ever been a bit woozy once before in my life. This was at a party my brother had. And even though Tore was well aware that we weren't exactly mad boozers, we still talked about it like two goddamned hell-raisers, so help me. But at least all our talk decided it. We would get a feed of drink in us one way or the other.

This snail-pace class finally finally came to an end. The teacher, who had struggled to keep himself awake for the duration, bumbled and stumbled out the door, yawning so much I thought the top of his head would come off. Afterwards, there was a general hubbub across the class, because nobody felt like going down to the yard. It was Baltic outside and totally absurd that we should have to suffer the degradation of being dragged down to the yard just because some oddball crank or other had discovered it did young people good to get fresh air in their lungs. Pneumonia more like. And as for fresh air. Total joke. You might as well just forget the yard and go down to the coal cellar and eat the stuff raw. But then the teacher on corridor duty comes roaring in and it's get bloody moving you lot and what the hell did we think we were up to. So we cursed under our breath as we filed past him on our way out and he administered precise little smacks across the back of our necks with a perverse little cane he always carried upon his person.

In the yard we ended up standing with the rest of our 'Commitee' over at the bike shed. It goes without saying that Tore became chairman of the group, unopposed. And then there was me, Esben and Kurt. Esben was cool. He could actually get his finger out and make things happen when a man was trying to organise a party. Also, he was an artist. I mean, he could draw. But Kurt? Kurt was a disgusting little creep. A wheedling gobshite. Always insinuating himself into whatever we got up to and toadying around so much like the sneak he was that you wanted to throw up just looking at him. Would you stop. Him sticking to you like shit to a blanket. So bad that you got tired of thinking up new ways to get rid of him and just gave up.

Tore was stood leaning against one of the shed stanchions with his elbow.

'It's ssso brilliant you came back, Tore,' the little sick-bag lisped out. Snake in the grass. Before Tore had come home, Kurt had wormed his way round different lads in the class till he assumed he was going to be the chairman of the party committee, but all that was knocked on the head. Tore was back.

'We'll only be allowed one beer each lads,' says Esben. 'Principal threw the head a bit when we asked him how many we could have.'

'He's gonna tell us after school,' says I.

'Shit what he says down a drain', said Tore. He was still leaning against the stanchion with his elbow. Standing there with all his weight on one leg, the other cocked against the post. Tore the Man totally calm. And that strange look on his face had cleared somewhat now he was full pelt with something. Some stratagem where only he could see the full picture.

'He can go fuck himself. How much money do we have?' Tore asked.

It had to be Kurt that was doing the accounts. It was the only thing he was good at. Just sitting there with his small sausage fingers writing numbers up in neat columns, doing all the reckoning as he moved his ruler across them. Like he could sit there and write – 'Arne owes 2.85'. As if it was the foreword to a calligraphed Bible from the fourteenth century. Now he's prattling on with a stream of bullshit about how much money we had, and this much was for the hot dogs, and the buffet was this much, and so on for ever and ever. Tore just stood there swaying slightly.

Then the bell rang and we dandered over to the stairwell entrance, whilst all the little trogs ran around and in and out between our feet like hundreds of ants. I moved completely into Tore's space as if seeking shelter. We could hear Kurt walking behind us, laughing at something in that very proper way of his that got your goat. Tore was still surrounded by some sort of membrane that I couldn't penetrate. As if he was moving inside a huge film of water. You could still see all of him. Even go near him. But never physically touch him.

'How's your mum, Tore?' I then asked.

Goes without saying that only I Janus Tolne could come out with something like that. I mean. Only a complete dunce could do that. In my head I'd known all along what I should avoid asking him about. But up steps Janus and there you go mate. There it was – my question. Arcing across the air towards Tore's ear, where you could almost see its physical shape as it wriggled inwards like a cold snake. So bad that you wanted to grab its tail and rip it out again. It wasn't like that time on the railway bridge, when I asked him about his dad and he told me he didn't have one because his parents were divorced. OK that was bad enough. But no damage was done. But this time. This time I knew it was bad.

He just carried on up the stairs with his head down. Didn't turn round or even look at me.

Just speaks words – 'Yeah, she's fine.'

Finally he raised his head. But again I saw that look. More like looking at a ball of dust than a face.

The Principal was stood on the landing and called over to me. 'A word please if I might!' It sounded like he was ready to piss his pants with fear coz he had to tell me that we wouldn't be allowed more than one beer each at the party.

Tore hung back on the landing. The Principal fixed his eyes on him and immediately became smarmy as Marmite. Tore just let on that he hadn't even seen him. Maybe he actually hadn't right that minute.

The Principal brushed past me and went straight over to Tore. He had to step round him a little bit before Tore would even acknowledge him. But Principal still looked and sounded like a cross between a choir boy and a toad as he smarmed away about how delighted he was that Tore was back in the fold. An asset to the school blah blah. But then he suddenly remembered what he was supposed to say and out comes his serious face. Once it was fixed in place and jawboned tight, he finally gets spluttered out that it was one beer per pupil and that was it. And he would come to the party himself. If he was invited of course ... ha ha. Sap.

I was stood there looking down in embarrassment and my foot dragging at the floor. Beyond painful when an old stager like that makes a cretin of himself. I mean. A grown man that doesn't understand proper order – the basic code when engaging with a fella of fourteen. All I can say is becoming a grown man has to be the worst affliction in the world. What is it? Do you automatically become a buffoon when you change into an adult? Or maybe that was the way he always was – even as a lad I mean? Take Kurt for example. He was just the same already. A nancy boy. A toady. A lickspittle. They were nearly all like that. Or else they were just little groats in the big swamp who now and again would bubble up with a 'plop-plop' when enough gas had moved for the bilge as a whole to start quivering and free up some slime.

Tore stood tall and erect. As if he was trying to give the impression he was a scout that was just about to be awarded a badge of merit for the record emptying of latrines in the most out-of-the-way and primitive conditions imaginable. Impudence wasn't in it. The old buzzard of a Principal could almost smell that he was being led by the nose. But he just stood there and blattered on incessantly blah, blah, blah bullshit falling from his lips. Like his mouth and head were full of wood shavings. At last we were able to escape and go on up the next flight. The stairs were empty because the Principal had delayed us for so long. We said nothing. I was afraid to open my mouth after that about his mum. We didn't utter a sound. Now there were a few things I really needed to say. Tore was well aware of this. It was as if a vacuum had emerged that had to be filled. But he'd decided there'd be no awkward stuff that day maybe? Or was it me praying there'd be no more awkward moments today? The first day he was back home. At any rate, I mustn't say anything wrong. Something that might freeze the air between us. Nothing awkward today. But I was desperate to rush into that vacuum. Just didn't know how to do it. If I kicked off talking about the coming party, that would be so obvious. I mean. Forcing myself to say something, just anything at all. Tore would pick that up in a flash. So obvious.

Then he turned round to me when we reached the classroom door.

'Now watch us get that fucking booze in,' he said.

I was looking right into his head when he said it, because we had sort of turned right into each other. And I swear that the casing all around him shattered there and then with a report that echoed inside my brain. His eyes were back to those I'd last seen three months ago. They'd been blasted clean. For the first time, I began to look forward to this party so much that I wanted to start running on the spot.

'Yeah, Tore mate. You better fucking believe we'll have booze to beat the band,' says I.

'We can keep it in the backroom that leads onto that small staircase, and then only the committee will have access to it. Then we can keep nipping out to the stash for refills when nobody's looking.'

Me standing there and I lets rip. Roaring almost – 'yes mate and we, we're gonna, we're gonna fucking well ...' I couldn't get the words out because I didn't even know what words. The only thing I knew was that it was all just massively good.

'And we're going to get totally pissed out of our heads,' Tore declared.

And this was utterly true. We were going to get blitzed.

Right after, I began to think about my dad. Getting drunk. That was what it was. I was so engrossed in these thoughts about the old man I didn't even notice the teacher moaning at us because we were so late to class. I mean. Dad got drunk quite a lot but not unconscious paralytic drunk. Just merry and talking nonstop. Like one of those big happy pigs in the cartoons. He just got so happy-faced and you would get the whole spiel about the happy student days and remember to enjoy yourself and you're only young once even though it wasn't all about getting drunk and enjoying yourself you know. But I think really that the people who actually counted for something in his eyes all had the air of a college student about them, regardless of what age they were. That white cap you got after you'd passed your exams to get to college – that cap had to be got, or at least the prospect of achieving it. If you didn't, you weren't up to much. Not so much because you would become so much cleverer. Just the idea of that cap and the guild, association or fellowship it brought with it. The sense of belonging that sent the old man into fits of delight as he fell into a reverie about the buildings and halls, the gravitas of his dear old Alma Mater.

Then I couldn't avoid the stark realisation that I was made from exactly the same mould. I think it was possibly the first time it struck me that it would possibly be a nightmare to end up as an exact replica of all the other specimens who went round acting the goat with each other – for whom life revolved around having a few beers and a stiff one at the monthly get-together, a couple of slices of *smørrebrød* and page 48 of the guild songbook, and synchronised raps of the table and the clink of glasses and come all ye boys as the flushed mood took such a hold that tears had to be fought back when recalling the thousand million other times they had been just as goddamn all colleagues together in the same place, with the same people and those same goddamned fucking red and white heart of the nation Danish slices of rye bread with Danish toppings. Ah Jesus mediocrity or what? Would you stop. No. This party with Tore in charge would be something else altogether. Why? Because it would be our twenty-one gun salute to his homecoming. We'd become blood brothers again. Drink beer and booze together. A foster-brother pact consummated in beer, gin and vermouth, through which we would rediscover the core of each other again. It was going to be so pure and cleansing the whole thing. A totally different form of intoxication than those old ones with their reunions, where they just sat and got all maudlin staring into their cups. No comparison. Ours was going to be a right roaring ancient Viking *Berserkerfest*, where they drank themselves so twisted they ran full pelt head-first into trees and walls and so what, coz they just kept running man, coz they were indestructible. Because we were young braves – warriors. And I knew that Tore was still the Man and could do anything. Tell you what. He could jump from a window that was hundreds of feet up and him on one almighty bender, land on his head and easy as you like walk back into that goddamned building again and zoom up to that fifth floor no bother to him. Me? I'd never been full drunk before so hadn't a clue what I could really handle. Headfirst into it.

Kurt it was who disturbed my deep thoughts. The little snake in the grass. He was sitting there bowed before a piece of paper writing diligently, even though it was nothing more than how much we were in credit and how much crepe paper and decorations we'd need. I threw it over to Tore. The worm was almost wrapped around himself at his desk from sheer subservience as Tore ran his eye over the accounts. In a flash, Tore ran his pencil right across the page in a mighty crisscross that all but obliterated its contents. The snake was up his own hole – gone. He looked for all the world as if he'd swallowed his desk. All that fine computation and calligraphic flourishing gone in a puff of smoke. The fawning Nancy boy's whole world blown to kingdom come.

'We're gonna get drunk, right?' said Tore.

Little snake just sat there as if he was swallowing his own retch. Not daring to say anything, even though Tore had ruined his accounting masterpiece. Jeez – it was so good that Tore was back.

'You're going to get rat-arsed, Kurt,' Tore said. 'Aren't you mate?'

'Er yeah, course Tore,' he quivered.

'Right. So what's this about crepe paper and decorations then?'

Er berh bah boh ... Kurt sitting there like a cross between Laurel and Hardy. Of course we wouldn't be having streamers and bunting, even though I'd gone along with this as well, before Tore's return. Like hell were we gonna have decorations and streamers. Now the Great Chief was amongst us once again. Now we were heading towards something massive, absolutely massive.

Little snake had got some of his rattle back by the time we were standing in room eighteen getting the place ready for our 'feast'. I was still mad on this idea of a mental Viking night. That way we could put drawings of the teachers up on the wall with them in Viking gear. With no extra effort, Clockhead could be made to look an even bigger noggin than he was already. And the Albino Rabbit, who was another fine specimen of the whey-faced dummies at this school – we could transform him into a prancing elf.

There was a spark and urgency in the air as we moved around the room getting things ready. Tore was standing on a chair putting one of our drawings up on the wall. At the same time he was directing the rest of us who were on the floor painting onto large sheets of industrial paper. We sang. This was a fantastic song we'd made up about the Principal. Tore had written most of it. And we sang and sang. Sang our hearts out for a half hour or more. Our version of Oh Come Oh Come Emmanuel.

'O the Principal is a duffhead and a clown ... and ransomed captive Israel.

His farts they sound like thunder here ... in clouds of methane gas and tears.

He's gross He's gross. The Principal is gross ... shall poison thee O Israel!!!'

We burst our lungs for these last lines so the walls resounded and the whole school echoed with the din. Kurt roared on into the next verse:

'Oh hide thy cock thou big Jesseee ... and stop acting like a faggot and a queen.'

Then I chimed in –

'From the depths of hell your breath did come ... and now you want to bite us on the bum!'

The whole thing blew up to a right orgy. I don't think weasel Kurt had ever said that word in his life before. I mean. That word 'cock'. He had definitely never roared out stuff like this to the tune of – 'Oh Come Oh Come Emmanuel'. But snake-features was right in it with us now. Tore meanwhile was still up there conducting and directing the song – 'And if you take your trousers down in school ... the Principal will stick a ...' but he got no further because who'd walked right in amongst us at just that point only the star of the song. We'd neither seen nor heard him as he skulked into the room, as he always did. And now here he was. Stood there fumbling and awkward and not a clue what he should say. He coughed slightly, cleared his throat, and finally managed to mumble something about it not being appropriate to murder such a lovely psalm by roaring and shouting, especially not when preparing a school celebration. Then he stands there a bit longer and eventually gets out – 'After all, we are talking here boys about one of *wehld litteracha's moohst praceless gehms*.' After he'd slithered out the door, we collapsed on the floor with laughter. We laughed that much we couldn't get up again and spent the next hour walking round putting 'ah' at the end of literature and an 'a' in the middle of 'priceless'. In the end we had to stop because we were nearly ready to puke with laughing. Kurt was still shocked that he'd come out publicly with such profanities, and probably because we now knew he wasn't such a goody two-shoes. But at the same time he was as proud as a Henry Hotspur. Like a kid who'd just learned to ride his first bike.

Tore said very little as we walked home from school on Friday evening after decorating the room. Rain was drenching the streets, and it was strange to look back at our school and see it enveloped in darkness. The cars seethed in a different way as their tyres squished along over the wet asphalt, but maybe it was all those reflections of the neon lights and the whole thing dizzying your head. School was a daytime place. But we were the chosen few who could go there of an evening and turn school rooms upside down. Brilliant feeling. If only Tore would say something soon though. Now we were alone. If only he would open his mouth and tell me what it was. This strange thing going on inside him. But maybe it was something I would never understand. Maybe something had happened between him and somebody else over in Ålborg and it was nothing to do with his mother. Then all my worries from the other day about mentioning his mum had been pointless and it was no big deal and yes – maybe that was the problem. Maybe there was some other kind of Janus over in Ålborg and he felt awkward. So why could he not just say it, so I would know? Just let it out. It didn't matter anyway. I didn't give a damn. Why should I care if he had found another mate over there? A mate who'd become a best friend. A better friend than me. OK. Maybe it wouldn't be all that nice if he came out and said it there and then. No. We'll wait till after the party. If only he leaves it until after the party. Then that would be the party done and dusted. Our party. Then we could go back to being mates like in the old days, when there was nothing wrong with us two.

Right that moment in my head. This blurry image came to me. A figure or something. Some person maybe, or a dress, a skirt, just something random almost; but it scared me so much I nearly jumped into his skin as he walked beside me. I reached my hand up to his mouth and shouted –'Wait just a second.' He stared at me as if I was this mad loon and I actually was of course, because what the hell was I doing carrying on like that?

'What? ... what?' he said. 'What's wrong with you?'

'Nothing,' says I. I was almost completely breathless and fighting the urge to pant like a dog.

He just stared right ahead of him and we ploughed on. I mean. We didn't plough on. We sloshed on through all that rain falling in sheets over Town Hall Square. I stared up at the electronic clock above the corner building as we cut across. I was going to have to take a tram if I wanted to avoid walking home.

'Right. I have to run over to catch number 14, Tore.'

'OK then,' he said.

'Right then. See ya.' But I hesitated, swaying there in front of him. Then I goes – 'I'm looking forward to that party, mate.'

'Yeah, me too,' he said. 'See you then Janus. Safe home mate.'

By now I'd jumped up into the tram. 'Yeah, same to you. See you Tore.' The whole thing was as if it was me heading off to Ålborg. What was it, this comedy we were playing? There I was hanging off the back platform waving a salute to Tore, as if I was never going to see him again. As if that was it between him and me forever. When really it was just a normal Friday and he'd only come back to me a couple of days before. And there you are standing like a sap with your heart in your throat and on the verge of blubbering. Would you stop.

'See you!' I yelled into the rain. 'And safe home yourself!'

And then you went home and went to bed, got up the next day and went to school, saying to yourself it wasn't that long now. Just so many days and hours until the party and saying to yourself not to think about it and then the time would go quicker. It was a brilliant feeling just talking to yourself about it and just keeping it running in the background.

Big Chief Tore had planned and arranged everything. He

got Esben to buy the beers and the gin. These were kept in the garage at Esben's house. So then it was a question of smuggling them into the school. There was nothing we could do about the official entertainment that had been lined up for us. Goes without saying this was going to be horrendous – with our French teacher scraping on a violin and another teacher declaiming some poem or other. Of course the real reason they were going to be there was to keep an eye on us. But we'd roped them into our trick. I mean. Tore had roped them in as usual. Round his little finger.

That Saturday, at around three o'clock, Esben arrived with the hooch. Getting it into the school was easy. We just put the bottles of gin under our jackets and waltzed up to room 18. Just as bold and breezy, we marched up the back staircase with more of the contraband and neither cat, mouse nor teacher saw a thing. Down with us again for the beer and at first we just stood there looking at the four crates, because officially we were only allowed one. But there was nothing for it, other than handballing them up to the room and seeing if we got away with it. If anyone asked, we'd just say that of course this crate was the only one. Then we began hauling them up. It worked like a dream. No one said as much as boo. But then when we were halfway up with the third crate, who should come traipsing down the stairs only the Principal himself, looking like he knew he had an appointment but just couldn't remember where. We just hauled away. But of course, with courteous nods and a bit of a curtsy and all big smiles, and he said something lunatic and irrelevant that made us bite our tongues before we threw up with laughter. Then he disappeared. With that, all the crates were safely stowed under the old stairs in the back room behind the classroom. Next thing was to just pop open the beers. It was the usual sensation in your throat. As if the first beer has to be forced down your gullet like a ramrod. But we said cheers lads and clinked our bottles. Kurt got tears in his eyes at the first gulp. Jesus he deserves a clip round the head the Nancy boy. Tore just stood the beer down by the side of his foot as only he could. As if he was a bricklayer or something. I mean. There was the beer stood to attention. The whole scene so calm and professional. By four o'clock we'd necked two beers each. I could already feel it. By now we were rowdy and roaring and wired up about the whole thing because it was our party and we had sorted it and there were 200 beers out the back just waiting for us and gin and vermouth as well. It was like we'd won the football pools or something and a giant leap to being mature and an adult, because we had all that hooch and it was up to us what we did with it, even though it was banned.

Then came a few hours of weird interlude that we had to get over before things began properly. A strange lull in which your happiness made you uneasily giddy. We went round and round doing the same unnecessary things two hundred times, just to have something to futter with – so you didn't let yourself think too much about how you felt inside. We went off and ate a meal in some place that was a bit of a dive but felt self-conscious and weird because we never went to restaurants. Kurt just sat there the whole time staring down into his wallet to see if he definitely could afford 3.50 for liver and onions. I mean. A clip round the ear for that boy. Maddening the way he didn't understand proper order and the way to behave when you were out with your mates.

We went back to school a quarter of an hour before the show kicked off. By now everyone else would be on their way in. There they all were in their merrygoround of trams and bells and just as wired to the moon as we were. And there the school was. Just standing there. Like it could have exploded into smithereens at any moment. Like it was now filled with so many new things that it had to go *whamkewhooonnnng* in one huge bang. As long as them beers hadn't gone and blabbed the whole thing by clinking too loudly. In the back of your mind, the stroke we'd pulled was so barefaced that some disaster had to happen.

But the main doors swung open like normal when we went through and all the plaster statues and busts stood there staring out into the gloom just as always. Jeez you nearly felt bad for them lads. I mean. Never being able to close those peeled-back eyes that always stared straight out into space.

We went up to number 18 and lit the candles at the tables and the others began to arrive. The trogs looked like they'd woken on Christmas morning and were coming in to see the presents under the tree. They had big shiny elf eyes and blue clothes that looked too tight because they were growing and their voices were breaking. 'Hoyee!' would erupt from their gobs every now and again in the middle of a sentence. So then we ringmasters went round glad-handing and making grand hand gestures and showing people to their places. Then the teachers who were going to entertain and watch over us came in and shook our hands so you felt like the greatest idiot. The Principal walked in last, just like at morning assembly, so you were waiting for him any minute to ask us to open our psalmbooks and start singing 'The Lord is my Shepherd' at no. 77 in the new book and 218 in the old one. But he just stood there and mumbled something about what a great job we'd done decorating the whole room. Not a clue did he have that we had a whole bootleg booze factory out on the back stairs. Just ten yards away from him on the other side of the back wall. There was so much booze he'd never have seen that amount before in his whole life. Now the party itself began and we dealt the *smørrebrød* round on paper plates. Then we got that one single beer we'd been officially permitted. Woh! How the mood went up after that beer, man. We sang the official song that had been written about all the different teachers and each of us 'head boys' took a fair slug of gin or vermouth every time we nipped out to the back room for something or other. When things really got going, up gets Tore and delivers a speech addressed to the Principal, to thank them for allowing the party and also for taking the time and effort to attend the festivities that evening and to look after us so splendidly. All the swampheads mooed, bawled and laughed. But we laughed even more because we knew we'd hoodwinked the Principal. And would you give over now because doesn't the Principal get up again and splurge out a whole spiel about how life was starting for real now, because some of us would now be going into the university stream and others the technical stream. You were left in no doubt that the others were lesser mortals. But now there was a great big world waiting for us out there, he said, and other such platitudes as he droned on way past the pain of cringe. But for all that. It did make you think as you were sat there listening about getting a bit older and how brilliant it would be to be really grown-up because now we were starting to have some kind of importance in life. We'd even been given permission to smoke this evening and sat there puffing one fag after another right up into the faces of the teachers and Principal.

The entertainment was to proceed on a raised platform that had been set up at the back of the room. It had a curtain behind it, which made it almost like a little stage. The door leading to the back staircase was behind this stage, exactly the place where all the beers were. A break was called so we could all go down to the yard and get some air. Most of the boys needed to pee as well. But while they were using the toilets in the schoolyard they all knew they could just creep back up again via the back staircase. So they just blundered right into the beer stash. One after the other they appeared and disappeared, skulking up and down the backstairs, getting themselves a beer, maybe two beers and a gin, and there was a tittering and sniggering and a scraping and coughing out of them, so I thought the Principal, the caretaker and teachers would come bursting in on us at any moment. But Tore had ensured there was always a few swampies in the classroom to distract our visitors. But when the trogheads were sent back down to the yard again, so that they could go up to room 18 the proper way, the noise out of them as they made their way downwards was worse than an air raid because their heads were turned with the hooch. There they were running round the yard like some mad football match.

Getting the beers down your throat was no longer a problem. I gulped one beer down after the other. Kurt was already well on the way to being stocious. He sat there weirdly with his arm in the air, as if he was hanging onto the bottle. It looked like one side of his mouth was beginning to lurch a bit as well. I went over and told him that he'd have to get a grip of himself and stop acting the goat. So he goes – what the fuck was it to do with me, so I told him to fuck right off outtathere this minute. In truth, he looked relieved at having an excuse to avoid drinking the rest of the beer. Then I stood there and drank that beer and it came to me that I was well on the way to being like dad when he was two sheets. I heard Tore's raised voice inside the classroom and I threw out the rest of the trogheads from the backroom 'bar' so they could join the entertainment by going through the yard and up the proper stairs again. It was pandemonium in the classroom as I walked in myself. What with all the booze-induced shouting and general clamour. All the swampheads sitting there were at boiling point and the teachers were all screwed up because they were going on stage any minute. Tore had gone up onto the stage and was stood there with his cheeky smile, waiting for quiet to descend. There he stood. Like he knew that it was him who was the director in this comedy and all was proceeding exactly as he had envisaged. Suddenly, my hands began to shake a bit and went all clammy, because all this was starting to remind me of the rat escapade and how things spiralled out of control. What if the whole thing began to boil over all around us? But then Tore the Man looked right down at me from the stage, like we were tying a line between us, a telephone line, along which a whole load of strength came from him to me. It was like getting a blood transfusion, and I immediately didn't give one hot damn about anything. Yes, sure, I was also getting a bit hot and dizzy from all the hooch I'd poured into me. I was on the verge of being properly drunk. Esben looked like he'd shit his pants. He had obviously never been way out in such deep waters before.

Tore introduced the French teacher who slinked up to the stage with his violin under his arm. He would like, he declared, to play something from Bach and I noticed straight away that Kurt tried to adopt his Bach demeanour. I was very close to roaring at him but could really feel how drunk I was so I reined myself in. Your man fiddled away up there like a mad thing till the whole school was shrieking with it. Then he played stuff from Mozart and Brahms. But the real laugh was the great finale when he tried to step on the gas and go superfast. Man.

He looked like a canary on crutches and nobody had ever seen or heard such a brutal thing. Then there was such grinning and laughing in that room that the candles were bent sideways and the poor creature up there thought he was Stravinsky himself, and his little legs went even faster, till in the end you felt sorry for the cat that had donated its guts for the string only to be abused like that. At last he came to a halt and stood there mumbling something and accepting all the whistles, shouts and claps that came up to him, wave after wave. This gave me a chance to slip out of the classroom. I was sat right at the back and so the door was very handy. I bundled down the dark staircase and got down to the yard. You could see some of what was going on up in number 18 and even faintly hear Tore's voice coming through the open window, as he thanked Hr Andersen for such a virtuoso performance. There was a light rain and I stood there belching and burping from all that beer. It was the happiest rain shower that ever had fallen on that schoolyard. I was standing right in the middle of the yard and was as black as the dark itself and just let the rain fall onto my hair and listened to the sounds coming from the classroom and from the cars driving by somewhere on the other side of the school wall. I was so pleased and happy, because it was a brilliant party that was going on up there at number 18, and because Tore had come home and had done things the right way. The Tore way. I walked over to the cycle shed and hit one of the support columns of the shed a right slap. Because I needed to let something out. Tore had finished talking and Hr Neesdal had begun his reading. Snatches of words came from the window and bursts of laughter every now and again. I went over to a wall and leaned my hand there while I pissed and really enjoyed it. Then I crawled up the back stairs to the treasure trove. On the other side of the door, they thundered on with themselves, just as I managed to kick two thousand beer bottles and felt the world was going to collapse around me. But nothing happened. It was pitch black back there in the back room and I was staggering weirdly round in it. But I got hold of the gin bottle and took a brave heave at it. Fire tearing round my guts it was. But it gave some kick I'll tell you. Tore would soon be sitting in my bedroom again. Telling me a rake of new things about what happened to him since. And we'd open the window and lie on our backs and look across the rooftops and watch the rain running down the roof gutters and then gurgling down the pipes like a flood. We also needed to start getting hold of some girls. It was about time we got started with all that. Saying that. It would be weird if there should suddenly be a third person and not just him and me. But anyway. We'd still be doing all the things together that we'd been doing before, because the girls we got would be really sound and would actually want to do the same things we wanted to do. Otherwise those girls just couldn't be with us. Simple as. No reason to start getting jumpy though. As long as Tore stayed, everything would be just fine. As long as he didn't head off to Ålborg once again and then come back with those strange vacant dust-filled eyes. And there would be no problem with finding the right kind of girls. Well, no problems for Tore anyway. I took another swig of paintstripper before pushing the bottle away from me. Course there would be a girl for Tore. Yeah, but it was a bit off that there should only be a girl for Tore and none for me. I mean. If Tore was going out with a girl, what about me? What about me eh? So Tore gets a girl because definitely there was a girl out there for him and so … but now I knew I had to get back down the staircase and then up into number 18. Otherwise there was going to be bother. But there was something about this girl waiting out there and Tore that was getting at me. I couldn't work it out though.

It was like walking into an iron curtain when I walked out into the schoolyard, the rain was that heavy. I went up to the classroom again and slipped inside. All the swampies stared at me because I was soaked. But then Hr Neesdal threw some shape with his book and they all swivelled round to look at him instead, grins in their heads. Tore had kept his eyes on me, but somehow seemed not to be looking at me really. Just like that day in our own classroom. There was something freaky about him. As if he had suddenly seen an evil spirit and was now blind to all else around him. It cut into me like a knife.

What was going on with this lad? What had happened to our brilliant party? I went dizzy and my guts heaved. If only that asshole would soon give it up says I looking at Neesdal, who was doing his best not to lose his false teeth as he read from his book.

Finally, finally. It was over. And then the French teacher managed to blag a couple of the trogs up onto the stage to sing a duet, while he accompanied them on the violin. Then some others went up to tell a few stories. The whole thing rolled along in a kind of fog, with me sat there muttering in my head and trying to keep down the rising nausea. It was almost eleven before the Principal switched on the main lights and declared his thanks for the evening and all the boys began to go home. Some of them came over to me and asked if there were any more beers left and I told them we were going to send the empties back to the store and get money back on them and the unused bottles. With that they trudged off. The *virtuoso* Andersen went off with his violin, and the Principal came over to say goodnight and could we tidy up please before we went home ourselves, and I said yes of course and just wanted him the fuck out of there because I wanted to get a grip of Tore.

He was standing over by the backstage curtain waiting for me. We stood in opposite corners of the room. I was stood by the door and there was a sea of tables and chairs between us. The light from the white globes above us was harsh and palls of cigarette smoke still hung in the air. It was just all glare and morass. The waves of white paper tablecloths, white paper plates and white song sheets made things worse. The whole thing began to run away from me. If only he would throw a rope overboard and haul me ashore. Pull in Charlie Chaplin and Laurel and Hardy, Tore. 'Laurel and fucking Hardy,' I roared right across the tables. 'And bringing up fucking father,' I barked after that. 'And Maggie, lovely Nora and Goddamn lazy Ethelbert, Donald Duck and Uncle Tom Cobley and all. Tore! Tore, you bloody ancient old fart! Shall we go down to the yard, get our cocks out and piss crossways? Shall we?'

Then I smashed across the tables and chairs to where he

was. He grabbed me into him and kept a good hold on me. All the time staring right into my mug.

'You're blind drunk man,' he said at last.

'You're fucking right I'm blind drunk and so what? Am I not allowed to be as drunk as I can possibly be? It's not up to you. Is it? It's not you who decides everything.'

I was on the point of roaring. I mean a real drunken man's mad roar, because the whole thing was beyond me, and because he was standing there not letting go of me and staring right into my face.

'Move your hands,' says I. 'Fucking let go of me.'

'Yeah, yeah,' he said. 'Sit down in there.'

I reeled into the back staircase area. Kurt stuck his head through the open door. I screamed at him to fuck off. He mumbled something or other about being supposed to tidy up, but then disappeared again.

'Give me that bottle,' I said to Tore.

He thrust a beer over to me but I wanted the gin bottle. I wanted the gin bottle, because he was damn well not going to decide what I should and shouldn't drink. So I got the gin bottle and gulped a shot into me. Tore took it afterwards and drank three slugs.

Then we sat and stared out into the half-dark with everything wriggling and jumping in my head, and the whole world around me heaving and sucking. There was a furry beast down in my guts that was fighting all the time to get up to my throat.

'What did you come back for anyway if you're gonna be like that all the time?' My words were almost under my breath. 'Why didn't you just stay where you were? What the fuck is wrong with you? That mad look on your face the whole fucking time. Like a clown? Eh!? Why have you gone like that?'

I knew I was saying all the wrong things as usual but I was that far gone I had to say something. He just sat there with his empty face in the air.

'Jesus Christ, say something man will you. Any fucking thing,' I roared. 'Can't you speak any more, Tore?'

'Yes I can still speak, Janus.'

I lurched over to the bottles and got hold of the vermouth. It was like getting a mouthful of glugging canal water down your throat. I was sure I was going to throw up. Like, what was going on here? This mental, unsettling scene on these back stairs with their smell of old sacks? Why did they never use the lights? Or did they keep them off on purpose?

'Have you forgotten that we have to get our cocks out and piss across each other,' I mumbled to him.

'My mother is sick,' said Tore.

He wasn't allowed to say something like that. Not when I'm talking about cocks and piss. He just couldn't say that.

'What did you say?' I asked. I mean. I knew exactly what he'd said, because he was so clear and precise, as if the words were made of flashing neon tubes coming out of his mouth.

'You see, that Poul fella ...' There it was. More neon tubes emerging from his mouth and I sensed something dreadful – a thing that any moment would be written large in the air between us and deep inside of me. So deep as to be unbearable. Poul? So that was our man. And of course. Turns out he's a psycho. Now here it comes. What I knew all along. That it was this guy Poul who'd ruined everything. Then Tore began to speak normally.

'We went over to Ålborg and moved in with this fella Poul, and mum arranged things so she could do her work there. And that was OK by me, but it was a bit strange seeing mum with this man, when you were used to having her to yourself, just me and her, you know ...'

Then Tore went quiet and I tried to focus my eyes on him like a camera but it was hard. The words began to run out of him again.

'See that Poul fella, there was some kind of twist in him all the time, and then all of a sudden, when we hadn't been there that long, mum comes to me and tells me they're going to have a baby. Her and Poul. I just stand there, not really sure what to say there and then, because it's this Poul fella, and because they'd not been married that long. And when she saw me just standing there, not saying anything, her head went kind of funny and she just walked away from me. I felt like I would die on the spot.'

He levelled his gaze right at me. Fru Riemer with the sun-kissed hair and clay on her fingers had turned her back on Tore. But I couldn't really imagine it as a fact right in front of me. The whole thing was just too far-fetched. I said nothing. I just sat there rocking backwards and forwards, the booze rearing up on me. In my innards.

'I was so scared,' Tore says. 'Because Poul disappeared and was away for weeks. Just gone. And I thought he was dead or something – and I wish he had been.' His voice dipped down between all the bottles in a strange, dull implosion. He stopped for a long time and his head was just dust. He came to resemble Pierrot himself. But with his red lips drained of colour.

'I can't say the next bit,' he said. Now he was rocking backwards and forwards on the staircase, till I thought he'd fallen. His whole body was washed out in the sickly light, and the rain still falling. Eternal gobs of rain. Then I thought he let out a scream but it was his mouth going mad - '... and in the evenings I could hear her crying in there but we couldn't talk. Then he came back home and came into my room and says what did I think I was playing at treating my own mother like that, especially after he'd agreed to let her bring her fucking little snotbrat with her, but then mum came in and there was something wrong with her like she'd been drinking and she gave Poul a shove and he fell backwards. Then he starts shouting and roaring and what the fuck did she think and hits mum in the face. Mum fell over towards me and I couldn't understand a thing. Could not understand a thing ... but he disappeared again and mum was shaking in every part of her body but didn't say a word. Just kept staring right ahead of her and was as white as ice. And then she went to bed and I went down to mine and then things went quiet. But I could hear her yammering and then she let out a huge scream and I ran into her room, but I was almost too shit scared because the whole thing was a nightmare. Because her baby had come far too early ...'

Tore sat without moving, holding on to the banister rail

like it was the only thing keeping him alive. Then I threw up because a word was cannoning round my skull the whole time. Because that word was choking me. Because someone somewhere was echoing 'miscarriage!' on that staircase, even though there was nobody else there. Just me and Tore. Because the word miscarriage was scrawled across my stomach and on the walls and in the vomit on the floor. I tumbled down the staircase and stood in the yard. Staggering and leaning my head against the whole goddamn building that was toppling over me more and more till I threw up again. Then the Big White Mask emerged from the school door and I followed it till we came out of the school gates. There was sick on my jacket and it reeked of bile. I couldn't speak to that mask. I walked right up to it and kept telling myself that it was Tore in there behind it. Then I took his hand and we walked down the street like that.

Chapter 5

Gradually. We became great mates again me and Tore. Just like before. After many days just sitting either in my bedroom or over at his and talking talking till our ears rang. Fru Riemer was there at Tore's but she had changed somehow and her way of speaking was different from before. It was like someone had stuck a tea cosy over her head. So that she had to talk through a wall of padding before the words got to you. She worked flat out at her sculpting but you felt that what she really wanted to do was throw all that clay up on the stand and just batter at it, squeezing and pummelling like you would a mound of dough. She pulled herself together, working non-stop and taking great pains with everything, as she stared and stared. As if she could see that baby in front of her. The child that wasn't there and had never quite been there. Me and Tore never spoke about her.

Things weren't like that in my home. There, everything just carried on in its usual cock-eyed way. My folks were all chuffed because we were doing university entrance exams and would be proper students before you knew it. The old man had even told a smutty story in front of me and mum one day. It was funny all right, but still weird and horrible hearing your own father coming out with that sort of stuff. You curled your toes and screwed your backside into your chair as his tongue ran away with itself. Afterwards, he shot a knowing glance over at me, as if to say that I was an adult now and had been ushered into the real world and all its complexities. Mum said something or other, because there was a weird feeling in the room and the laugh I came out with just hung there and hovered like a little damp cloud over the carpet. Dad just blurted on and, as soon as I could, I sneaked off to my own room and sat staring out of the window and thinking of the time I threw up. Man, all that vomit. And you couldn't help but think about the big difference between something like that and the other things you now realised were going on all about you.

The days passed by with little difference between them. We went to school every day and slouched home again and made attempts at reading the set books but never really did because we didn't need to. I mean. I was already studying far more than I actually let on to Tore, because I had to pedal a lot harder just to keep up with him. As for him, he didn't do a thing at home except read a whole load of books, which I then also got stuck into. These were not exactly a barrel of laughs, but I tried my best because he was doing it.

But we talked about girls non-stop. It was brilliant to imagine having a girl on your arm. Like she belonged to you or something. Just going up and down the road with a girl on your arm. It had to be a brilliant feeling. But really we didn't talk as much about that, we talked a lot more about what it would be like to go to bed with a girl. When you were thinking on your own, it was like your powers of imagination couldn't stretch the whole way like that. Even beyond the wonder of how it would be to just be walking up and down Strøget in the middle of town with a girl on your arm. Goes without saying that we'd been to dances and there were loads of girls but it was like they were a million miles away from us and we daren't approach them because they already had their noses turned up at us.

At the start of 2G year, we were told a school ball was coming up where our whole class was to act as escorts for girls in a 2G class from another school. If we were honest, we hadn't a clue what role we were supposed to play in this whole carry-on. Weirder still. A lot of these swampies from deadendsville and their potato row houses actually knew far more about how we were supposed to 'escort' these girls. The truth was that they'd learned all this from their church youth clubs and Sunday Schools, or whatever it was they called them, and handled girls in a much more natural way than me or Tore. Me and him were like two balloons, all blown up and bursting with weird notions of what girls were actually about. All them lads just zoomed right over to the girls and off they danced with a spin-turn this and *chassé* that and I don't know what else. As if they'd been born to it. Even that little runt Kurt was out on the floor quick as you like, still with his bicycle clips on mind, but snapping up a girl and dancing off with her. But of course he'd received strict instructions at home about what to do.

The invitation had actually been passed through the respective Principals at the two schools and this made the 'occasion' a bit too official for our liking. But me and Tore decided to go anyway and we looked forward to it. I mean. It was always a good laugh to go to a party. Now I knew him inside out once again, it was brilliant that we were going to a party together.

The dance was being held in the sports hall at the girls' school and me and Tore went together. I'd been out and bought a new set of clothes and felt weird. As if everything was too big for me. Tore was wearing a short tweed jacket and grey trousers, and to me he looked fantastic. He was wearing a tie. It made his head even blacker and more Red Indian looking.

When we got there, everyone was in the midst of taking their coats off. We just pushed our way through without looking left or right, because we reckoned this made a more dramatic entrance. But of course we didn't miss anything. It was a bit strange walking into a girls' school. The smells were totally different to ours. I noticed that Tore's breathing was more intense as we went through the door and I could see his nostrils flaring slightly as we stood and groomed ourselves in front of the full length mirror that had obviously been pulled out of the changing room next to the gym. The girls were all talking too loudly, laughing and generally making an awful racket. Made you not even want to look at them. Tore leans into me and goes – 'Hey Janus, it's mad when you think we could actually have kids with one of these girls if we both wanted to, isn't it?'

I grinned back at him. I was a bit thrown to be honest. I mean. I liked the idea but didn't really believe I'd be able to do it.

'Yeah, we could soon sort that one out, mate,' says I to him.

By now we were in the sports hall, which had been all spruced up and decorated, but all the same was still a school sports hall. It was cold in there. We stood chatting with Esben for a while and Tore started this whole comedy where he played out some scene from a Gary Cooper film – the hero is a dead shot with a rifle and is lying in a trench picking off Germans one by one like a turkey shoot. Tore aims his rifle and has the way Gary Cooper shoots his gun in the film off to a tee. Then he's brilliant at showing the Krauts and the way they fall when they get hit. Anyway, we start a whole commotion, grinning and laughing because we sensed through the back of our necks that we'd attracted the attention of some girls.

A girl prefect from the school's debating society went to a podium and bid us all welcome and hoped we were all going to enjoy ourselves, thanks to the two Principals, the teachers the cleaners and all that nonsense you're always forced to listen to at these things.

'Her arse is shaped like my old aunt's inkwell,' Tore whispers to me.

'Yeah, looks like she could shit straight down the neck of a beer bottle,' says I.

'Do you know what, she actually can,' Tore replies, 'How did you know that?'

He leans himself and his big fizzog right into me and goes – 'She won the female chicken-shit championship in the Back of Beyond.'

But there was no more of that because there was major movement all around us and it was dance time now and some appalling school band or other began playing 'Olga Polka'. Me and Tore made a quick retreat to the wall rails of the gym and watched the dancing from there. We glued ourselves to those rail-bars because there were girls looking around who'd still not been asked to dance. There they stood looking all forlorn and disgusted, casting the odd glance over to the boys' side of the floor. We were flattened against the bars because we hadn't a clue what to do. In the end, we went down to the little bar that had been set up in the corner at the other end of the hall and got a beer each. I bet there's never been a beer in the whole of history drunk so slowly. We talked and talked about everything under the sun without thinking what we were saying or listening to each other. Just standing there staring at Aksel and Kurt and all the other trogs tearing off across the dance floor with one girl after the other. It was an impossible dream to actually have a girl on your arm and be walking round town with her. And then the smell in the air because it was a girls' gym where they would all usually be jumping around, legs and arms going up and down. The whole situation made us so jumpy that we just talked away spouting on and on to each other till we nearly got lockjaw, but at the same time our beady eyes were never still for a moment in our beady heads. Constantly sweeping the dance floor so as not to miss a single glimpse of leg, breast or eye – anything that might show awareness of our presence. Some of the girls shot glances over at Tore but he was blind to them. In the end, we went over to talk to some lads who'd come with the band. Standing there giving our opinions about jazz and all that, as if we gave a flying shit whether Bing Crosby or Louis Armstrong was the best crooner in the world, when all the time this weird tingling fragrance was hovering all about us. A feeling that wouldn't go away and couldn't be ignored.

A number of female teachers from the girls' school had been stationed in the hall to ensure that nothing immoral should be perpetrated upon their little angels. If only those dumb old bags realised that we had no idea what we were supposed to do with ourselves. I mean. Even the thought that, at some point, you would be forced to actually go out and dance with one of those girls – just because it was expected, so that you didn't feel like a total numptyhead for the rest of your life. If they knew all that, those teachers wouldn't have had that stewed prune look on their faces.

So we just stood there in an awkward pose, blowing into

our empty beer bottles. The next minute it was like somebody threw a light switch at the other end of the hall. Or at least, me and Tore both looked up at the same time. And right away, with a brilliant feeling that bloomed like a tropical flower down in my gut, I knew she was the one. It might have been a hundred thousand years before anything happened, but I knew straight away that Tore's girl had just walked into the hall. I glanced up at him, but for a change he wasn't paying any heed to me. His eyes had latched onto her, and now she was dragging them round wherever she moved. Like they were attached with pins. She was dancing with a fella we didn't know and you saw right away that this was the kind of girl who only chose particular dance partners. She was tall and very slim. She looked like she could lean right back on your arm and laugh out loud as she danced with you, like in the movies. This she would do totally naturally. Like she'd forgotten all the losers around her and was going to laugh if she wanted to. Right that minute though she had a serious look on her as she concentrated on her foxtrot steps. But this was Tore's girl I'm telling you and I wasn't one bit jealous. Not one bit. Because it just went without saying that it was no use trying to compete with him where all that was concerned. I mean. He was going to win and that was that. I fished a cigarette up out of my pocket and lit it in a new way I had learned – using just one hand. Then one of the fellas with the band asked if we wanted a beer. They'd brought some extra supplies with them inside the instrument cases. Me and Tore had still not looked at each other but we said yes simultaneously. Our empty bottles were replaced in a flash. These second ones got necked a lot quicker, because the whole occasion was now charged with meaning.

Tore turned his whole focus onto us. He bent the whole of his will to our entertainment. But at the same time he projected his wider aura out from the back of his head and across the dance floor like a long extending searchlight. His inner self was already fully engaged in the act of encircling that luminous girl out on the floor, and I knew from the start she wouldn't be able to resist that radiating pull for very long. We just stood for quite a while, acting the goat with the other lads, tapping our feet and swaying our bodies, but then doesn't a totally dopey female cousin of mine, who was at a junior class in this school, come over to me and request my arm for a dance? I could feel the way the others were going whoh! Phew! All quiet sighs of relief and smirks of *Schadenfreude* that it wasn't them that got caught. She dragged me out onto the floor anyway and before I knew it we were flat out with something I realised to my horror was the tango. I hobbled and jiggled around like a live eel getting stuffed in aspic. Just grimly concentrating on not losing complete control of all my bodily functions. Then I saw that Tore was making his way down the wall-rails in the direction of the exit. And then I saw that the luminous girl was also on her way out of the hall. But then the cousin has a grip of me again and pulls me off with her in a couple of mental kangaroo jumps. Kurt dances past me with his superior Clark Gable grin on him, so that I nearly grabbed him to throw him headfirst down the nearest toilet bowl. He looked for all the world like a wind-up-doll that had been set to keep going till half ten exactly, at which point he would frogmarch himself to bed. Jesus Christ man.

In the meantime, the band had switched to a waltz. My cousin spun me round and round and my one leg went totally lame in my efforts to keep myself upright and moving at the same time. And all the while, I was keeping an eye on the exit doors at the end of the gym. As if in panic that Tore had snuck off with the girl. Three times I tramped right over my cousin Nelly's patent leather shoes, but she said nothing. Anyway, she should be thanking me really given that she was the one who'd dragged me out here in the first place.

Then an interval was announced and the drummer gave an extra whack to the big cymbal. I followed Nelly out to the wall rails and gave a bow and she says thanks for the dance, a smile on her face. Then I went back to the lads at the band and I asked would they play 'Pennies From Heaven', when they started up again. I was standing with my back to the dance floor wondering how Tore was getting on out there. He'd looked like he was just waiting for that girl to turn up.

Suddenly it occurred to me that all things actually follow some kind of predestined pattern, because it was so obvious what would happen next. Or maybe you weren't completely sure, but you kind of suspected something beforehand about the way things would go. Nothing ever came as a total surprise.

Then the band struck up again with 'Pennies From Heaven' in a really slow tempo and I could see my own self as I turned to face the dance floor. I looked a complete shambles but utterly superior. Like I was looking out over some speakeasy in Jersey City, rather than a dreadful sports hall in a girls' school in the middle of Copenhagen. And that was just perfect because right then in comes Tore steaming straight at me with the girl, who had proper breasts under her dress. Breasts that didn't carry a milligram of doubt about them. A little fit of terror attacked my hands when I saw them walking slap bang towards me and part of me wanted to run for it, but my face was fine, so I stood where I was. I mean, I knew it wouldn't change anything anyway, even if I did do a runner. I stared straight at Tore, and he looked right back at me. We were exploring whether there was a problem here, because a lot was going on all of a sudden. But what Tore didn't see was my hands going all clammy right that second. I mean. It was idiot stuff from me. What was the first thing Tore thought of when he got a girl like that? Only to drag her over to meet me. A wave of clarinet tones came bouncing all over my bonce right where I stood. It was 'Pennies From Heaven' tumbling round my head and falling at the feet of this girl Tore had eased in front of me. So close to her now, I could clearly see that she had freckles, but it was the radiance of her hair that had illuminated the hall. Incredibly well groomed, this hair. I mean. What was I supposed to say to all that hair and then the girl beneath it? But Tore had already said that my name was Janus Tolne, and this was Helle Junkersen. Helle Junkersen. The very name Junkersen made me see past her and, instead, I saw Count Bismarck in his *Junker* days, proud on his charger as his horse leaps right over an enemy trench. Dimwit stuff to be thinking of I know, but the image hit me from an old picture book that has always stuck in my mind. And she was the image of a real *Junker's* daughter. The way she looked. I squeezed her hand and she smiled. Then we just stood there for a while and did nothing.

'Do you want a glass of vermouth?' Tore asked her.

She shook her head and said no thanks and let out a little laugh, because he had said it a bit like a film star offering the best champagne in the house. And I would have loved to see the outcome if she had said yes. Because Tore didn't have a red cent on him. Not for vermouth anyway. Not if we were going to get the tram home.

The band started playing 'Alexander's Ragtime Band' and foxtrot was one of the few I could do and I gets this mental idea that I wanted to dance with this Helle Junkersen. So I ask her if she wants to dance. She passed her bag over to Tore, as if this was the most natural thing in the world. That he would just stand there and mind her bag while me and her danced. She was mighty easy to get around the floor with, because she instinctively knew how to adjust herself to the mad steps I would throw in every now and again.

I looked straight into the freckles she had on her nose. Then I asked her what class she was in and she told me she was in 2G and I really felt for the first time the huge difference between boys and girls. It was a massive shock to be dancing with this girl all around the floor. I mean. Holding her around the waist. That she was moving and her legs gliding in and out in sequence with my own. That she was so alarmingly different to me. And then I looked up into her eyes and nearly bolted out the door, because I could see she hadn't a clue what was going on in me. I bowed to her after the dance and said thanks, and then we walked side by side towards Tore, who was stood there with a big grin on his head. You could see just by looking at him that he was delighted I had danced with her. It meant I had more of a part in the whole thing, and it was reassurance that I wouldn't go getting jealous.

'Are you two doing maths for one of your specials?' This Helle Junkersen asked, as she laughed with her whole body.

Straight together we let out a scornful laugh. 'You must be joking ... you mad thing,' says we, two voices in one. 'Modern languages we are.'

'I'm Classics,' she said, looking at us with anticipation. We just gawped.

'Jesus Christ,' said Tore, looking at her with open admiration.

'Like, loads of Latin an' all that?' says I. My look of disbelief all too obvious. She nodded. So we were just trogs in comparison to Helle Junkersen.

'I'd like to study the history of art at University,' she said. 'I think ancient history is just fascinating.'

'Yeah, I do too,' said Tore. 'The only thing is that we have such a wooden-top teaching us lot that Janus has to tie his jaw up to stop yawning all the time in that lesson.' He shoved me with his arm and Helle laughed again.

'I've been to Italy two summers on the trot with my mother,' she said. I could see from Tore's face that it had never occurred to him she might have parents, a mother, or anything like that. He flinched for a second.

'It was fantastic going to Rome, after reading so much about its history before we went,' Helle says. She's completely serious now. Me and Tore couldn't say much in reply because we'd never gone further than across the channel to Malmø and a short holiday in Norway. In my mind's eye, there she was walking round in Rome with her bright dresses and getting ogled by millions of black-haired swarthy Italians. But I could also see that Tore thought it was brilliant she had been to Rome. She was even more fantastic now, because she had walked around down there and seen all those things that felt mentally remote and unreal to most other people. He looked so happy Tore the Man. There she was. This girl so pretty. Casting a bright glory over Tore, the like of which I'd never seen since the time before he left for Ålborg. I took a deep breath and held it. I'm not sure whether it was the oxygen in all that air I gulped that made things go a bit dizzy, or whether it was the mad elation in all of us – just at that very moment when the three of us went silent and we were kind of set apart from all the commotion around us. Forming a bond that would tell a new story. Starting from a new and empty chapter that waited for our lives to fill it.

One of the female teachers gave some sharp claps as a signal to the band to stop playing. It was nearly eleven and time to think about getting home. The last waltz would now be played, she declared but the hall lights would remain on. I saw Kurt the metronome making his move and clocking his puppet head tight into his dance partner's cheek. Tick tock. As if a new gear started up in him when the tones of the last waltz struck up. Tore had pulled away with Helle. I just stood where I was in front of the band. Letting this goodnight waltz drift past my ears in waves. Tore was talking to Helle as they danced. Asking her about Rome no doubt. I'm sure it was already in the back of his mind, wondering when he'd get the chance to go to Rome with her.

I was still working out what I was supposed to think and feel about all this. She was a competitor. No doubt. But not really. Because she wasn't going to break what me and Tore had. That we were great mates. I trusted Tore. And a girl he had to have at some point. And she was the one. I already knew that. We'd get on all right. Really all right. Because she just had that right way of laughing. So now we had to set off as Three Musketeers instead of two, and that was maybe more natural. I mean. It was mental that this huge thing had happened and it hadn't caused an explosion or some other mad sensation. The thing we had dreamed and fantasised about, right up to two hours ago, had now come true for Tore, and it was like it was true for Janus too. Coz now I could carry on and see how you were supposed to handle it. Everything was now right up close and I could scrutinise Tore and Helle through a magnifying glass whilst still being their most intimate friend. A willing go-between amongst all their innermost secrets. This role was me down to a T, because I had no duties other than offering my views on life every now and again like the worldly-wise bachelor I seemed cut out to be.

The music came to an end and the whole world began draining down the exit and the cloakroom. We held back nonchalantly however. We didn't have to make the last S-train like most of the other poor creatures. Tore was holding Helle's hand. Even a day ago, he would never have dreamed of doing that. I shot a look over at him and managed to catch his eye. He smiled back. I kind of rocked backwards and forwards and from side to side as we finally descended the staircase for outside. At the bottom, Helle went into the ladies' cloakroom. Tore came over to me.

'Well, what do you reckon mate?' he asked.

'She's great,' I said. 'Really pretty and really nice.'

He pulls a face and goes – 'Nice? Fucking nice? She's a goddess.'

I looked up at his face. He was looking directly towards the door she would come from. He goes – 'We're walking her home right?' Then he turned his head to look at me.

I was just about to say something along the lines of I'd probably best head off home on my tod, but ate my words when I saw his face. That he did not want. He didn't want to be left alone with Helle. So I was going to play a role in all that as well.

'Yeah, all right Tore. Sound,' says I. 'In fact if her house isn't too far away we've even enough money for a taxi!'

She came out of the girls' cloakroom and walked straight at us. She had combed her hair with the effect that it was even more radiant than before. But maybe there was also some kind of new lustre in her eyes. In a way I couldn't work out if she reminded me of something I was sure I already knew. But damned if I could work out what it was.

Tore helped her put on her coat, and we walked through the door and out of the school. We walked for a good while without saying anything to each other. I mean. Walking either side of her. So I could feel the vibrations going on through my side. If we were going to do a link, it was best if she linked both of us. Then it would have been more like all friends and Musketeers together and less formal. Like we already knew her. But we didn't offer the arm or touch her.

'Shall we get a taxi?' Tore asked. He skenned down at Helle. She looks up at him, shakes her head and says very quickly:

'Ah no. Walking's more fun.'

'Least it's not raining. Lovely evening,' says I. She turned to me and smiled once more.

'Yes, Janus. I love this kind of weather as well,' she said. She threw her head back slightly and inhaled the night air. On down the road. We went from one pool of lamplight to the next as we passed each streetlight. Tiny drops of it clung to our hair. The fall of light from the lamps was more like an artist's drawing.

There was something very intimate about us as we walked down the street. We spoke in dampened, confidential tones about the weather. Sure, the subject was a bit meaningless but in talking about the weather you could say an awful lot about yourself. I loved the way she appreciated this kind of weather, because it was just this sort of weather that suited our town best. Tore and me as well. I mean. It was real - this is our late evening *justwalkinghomeafteraparty* weather. With a just a few cars gliding on by and not another soul on the streets. Just us three together. Tore and me and *wouldyoueverbelieveit* a girl whose name was Helle Junkersen, who had no objection in the slightest against walking home with us. Even looked like she was enjoying it. Of course, it had always been just a matter of time. Because when the girl of girls finally appeared, she would of course feel totally at ease with Tore – and with me.

His big Geronimo head hopped up and down every time he took a step. We stopped at a crossroads and let a car pass. Just as we went to move down the street again, Helle lifted both her arms and stuck them through ours. She gave a little pull at us, so that we moved into her. It was like getting home to mum after you'd hurt yourself as a little kid. We both went stiff in the face to hide how totally shocked we actually were. Yes, Tore had held her hand before, back there in the sports hall, but that had been in a kind of disguised way. Because it was the leading hands from the dance routine that had gone on a bit longer than normal. But here we were, just walking down the street with a girl under the evening sky, as if it was the most natural thing in the world.

Helle laughed suddenly.

'You two are a right pair I must say,' says she as she looked up at Tore.

'All compliments gratefully received madam,' he said, bowing slightly. 'Janus is in fact quite funny sometimes. But with big gaps between the sometimes.'

I grinned like a simpleton without saying anything.

'It's just that when you're talking ... well there's no real sense in what you're both saying,' said Helle. 'You just say individual words, or maybe a clump of words, and you understand the whole meaning. To me, it's almost like a secret code.'

'Ah yes. Again very true,' said Tore. 'But you have to speak baby talk to Janus, otherwise he doesn't understand. God knows I've tried to instil some manners and breeding into him, but in truth he's a right little delinquent.' Tore said this last bit in a brilliant stuffy old-maid voice.

'Less of the little delinquent Tore,' says I, looking dead ahead.

Then I turned to Helle. 'See. We've known each other so long it's like it changes your language. We save on loads of words when we're talking together because a lot of it is already understood. Doesn't need to be said.'

She nodded. And I started to think how strange it was that she hadn't spoken much to the other girls from her class. As if she was slightly cut off from all of them. I mean. It was obvious she didn't speak 'mate talk' to anyone at her school.

Maybe girls were always a bit more cut off, even when they were with their friends. Maybe they just didn't have the same kind of friendship as me and Tore. They could be friends all right, but I don't think they grew into each other's flesh and bones the way me and Tore had. But now here she was slap in the middle of us and holding both of us tight. And maybe she'd get to find out what it meant to really belong to someone else.

Tore goes – 'All right, let's sing something.'

We laughed out loud at him. And he began to sing what is actually a great song, even though it's about ancient Denmark – 'Denmark's Song is a Fair Young Girl.' And he sang so that the words bounced off the buildings and houses. Then he abruptly switches over to a quick waltz and rips Helle away from me. Dancing off with her away down the footpath. I stood back under one of the street lamps. The place where the crook of Helle's arm had rested against me still throbbing slightly. They whirlygigged round and almost crashed right into a man who was out taking a leisurely stroll. Tore let go of the girl and bowed deeply to the unsuspecting victim who just walked on shaking his head.

'That man has no feeling for *Art* and *Artistes*,' Tore shouted over to me as he pointed at the disappearing figure. The man sunk his head a few centimetres more into his collar and picked up his pace. Tore tried to get hold of Helle to start the dance again but she held him back and called me to join them. So I went over.

We were going in the direction of moneybags land out in Frederiksberg. And by this stage we were in Frederiksberg Allé. The streets were devoid of people and the trees looked glossy and weird in the street lighting. We were walking at a fair lick now.

'I have to be in before midnight,' says Helle.

We both turned and looked at her.

'Where do you live?' I asked. 'It's no trouble getting a taxi, honestly.'

She shook her head. 'No, it's fine. We're nearly there,' she replied.

It wasn't exactly a shock that she had to be home before twelve, but still and all – it was a bit early. It being a Saturday and just after a school party.

I had ended up walking on my own again and was concentrating on not stepping on the lines in the flagstones. But when I stood on them anyway, I just told myself it didn't mean bad luck or anything like that. I x-rayed their power but watched my step anyway because I'd decided that the punishment for treading on the stripes was that I would only live till I was thirty. Then I realised that I was completely alone going down this avenue. Fear tugged at my guts when I saw that the other two weren't by my side. So they'd sneaked off on me had they? My upper body was pitched forward in the air and my feet planted right on the edge of a line as I hit the brakes. I stumbled a bit and then stood stock still. It wasn't a quick turn I made. Just swivelling slowly on my heel and there they stood back at a corner. They laugh when they see me stumbling. Standing there like a dolting duffhead.

'Jeez little Janus, were you sleep-walking?' Tore calls over to me. 'We were just about to leave you in the lurch but we couldn't in the end.'

Then we clearly heard the distant sound of the Town Hall clock striking midnight in those familiar swaying tones. Not all its strikes reached us, but we knew what hour was being struck.

'I better get home,' said Helle.

She gave a hint of being uneasy and some kind of change came over her. I mean. She wasn't going to fall about laughing in our arms any more. The radiance was gone.

We turned down one of the side streets off Frederiksberg Allé. We were all completely schtum. It was all going to be over with this Helle girl very shortly and talking became a bit awkward. Because we didn't know when we might see each other again. Also because she'd stiffened up. You suddenly realised this was actually a girl we'd only known for a couple of hours and didn't know diddly squat about really. I skenned over at Tore, because it was his girl. I wanted to see if he felt the same as me. But his face told me nothing. His nose was still cutting its way through the damp air, as steady and certain as a ship's bowsprit. I'd started sweating a bit under my coat. Helle stopped outside a large villa that lay back off the street a bit. It was one of those real Frederiksberg fortresses with towers, climbing vines and heavy gate work. The place was in complete darkness.

We stood around a few moments and scraped at the ground with our feet, whilst Helle fussed at her handbag. Tore all the time looking at her. For the first time ever, I felt he would have seen me anywhere else on the planet rather than where I was standing right that second.

Helle retreated slightly and stood right by the garden gate. A patch of light fell on her face, so that her nose cut a long shadow across her cheek. Tore's face though was hidden in shadow. I turned on my heel and looked at Helle.

In the end I goes – 'Blimey that was an atrocious band you lot scraped together for the party. Which lunatic asylum did you get them from?'

'They're from Christianshavn Grammar School,' said Helle. 'We were out there once to one of their dances.'

I waited then. In the gap. Waiting for Tore to say something meaningful, but he just stood there like a black splat and said nothing. It was him that was supposed to talk now. I didn't feel like it any more. I'd actually started to believe that we were on the way to being quite adult, because it had gone so well with Helle. I mean. The whole thing had just been so natural. But now it was like everything had turned into a minefield. I'd taken in how fragrant she was. But it was as if that scent betrayed something deeper that was beyond my ken. Probably, you needed a long time to get used to it, because it was a strange bouquet of things that weren't just part of her but of all that she came from and that was part of her as well. But now she was almost as far away from me and Tore as the time when we never knew her at all. Now she looked a bit like a little doll that was all alone and cut off from the rest of the world. She looked so weak. But at the same time dangerous. Because that scent of otherness was all about her like a killer animal. She was on pins. Nervous.

Helle was just about to say something when a light went on inside the villa. Tore gave a start and his face was completely lit up. The house light looked as though it was shining out through an alien body. One of them where all the insides, the intestines, veins and blood vessels are completely transparent. Beating away. It was like someone had cut a framed hole in a stomach. A big square-shaped hole. And the only reason all the innards didn't fall out of that square of light was because a film of glass had been fitted across the hole. There was something far too revealing and abnormal about what we saw. Right in the middle of the window was a woman. Staring directly at us. She could have been standing in that black squared belly the whole time for all we knew. Staring at us without us knowing it. Now there she was. A black silhouette.

Unknown to us. But terrifying in her nearness, with that glaring light coming from behind her, revealing chairs, tables, shelves and lamps. The woman stood rock still and made no sign of wanting to talk to us. She just stood there looking out at us with her hands resting on the inside window sill.

Helle gasped and I went stiff with shock. Tore put out his hand to Helle, as if the whole point had always been just to see her home and leave right away. And she put hers out and shook his. Then she said a quick farewell and thanks for a lovely evening. She looked right at me and uttered my name when she said goodbye. Then she bolted down the garden path and up the three steps to the front door. She had the key in the lock before she stood still again.

The shape of the woman in the window removed itself and we saw the light in the hall go on. The door opened and a cut of light fell out onto the steps. Then Helle disappeared inside, but in the instant she went through the door I saw Helle's face. She had turned round to look for where we were. As if she wanted nothing more than to run back to us. Then she was gone. Maybe it was just the light on her face that made her look that way. But to me it looked like she'd suddenly grown old and not suited to me and Tore at all. I really wished I'd never see her again.

I turned to Tore who was still standing there looking at the house. I mean. He was just standing there like he'd already forgotten the woman in that big window and only remembered that he had danced in the street with that girl Helle. He hadn't noticed me freezing up at that moment when I stared deep deep into that yellow square of guts out of which the woman stared back at us. But then Tore wouldn't be shook the way wimpy me would be. Not now. When he was on the verge of it with this girl. Nothing horrible would get through to him. No chance.

'Right come on mate,' says I. 'Giveover standing there gawping like a mad Romeo will ya?' I said it that way so he wouldn't pick up my own heebiejeebies. But then he goes –

'Jeez, there must be some bother with that mother of hers for her to race off like that.'

We were back down at Frederiksberg Allé by now and it was like returning from an expedition in some frozen wasteland in the Arctic Circle. It was brighter as well, because the moon had risen. Down by St. Thomas Plads I stopped a taxi.

For a moment, when me and Tore got in, I saw his face in clear light again and there was some flinch of unease there that made me think what happened back there at Helle's house had maybe affected him more than I first thought. He must have picked up something. Must have. Tore usually noticed things a hundred times quicker than me.

Chapter 6

Sure, this new situation was a bit weird. I mean. It was strange having to go round like a third wheel on a tandem, even though it was Tore and Helle's bike. But I learned loads of things. I learned, for example, how long it can take for two people to say goodbye to each other. You sit in another room and wait and wait, and you can't hear a single sound from the others. Before this, I'd kind of believed that all kissing involved some kind of slupping and slucking sounds. But now I knew different. Kissing is completely silent and can last for hours. I waited and waited for Tore to come out, but there was nothing happening except total quiet, and every now and again a slight noise that could have been mumbling or clothes being ruffled. I just stared out at the sky and saw nothing, only darkness, and felt, more than saw, that the garden lay out there on the other side of those window panes, and that there in another room were two people kissing each other. And one of them was my best friend.

Finally finally I would hear them standing up, and then it was a case of getting my face arranged so it didn't look like I'd been waiting for ages and was also sufficiently adult to deal with the situation in a nonchalant way.

Tore would always come out first through the double doors of the sitting room. His big head and face screwed up into a grin that was innocent enough but still a bit uneasy. Trying to read me for a sign that I was pissed off because their snogfest had lasted so long. Helle always came out second. He would pull her out from the darkness by her white hand. Now there they both stood all pale under the crown of light hanging from the ceiling that I had turned on just beforehand. My heart bulged for them. Like they were my own children. I had sat guarding them as they said their goodbyes and were so vulnerable to the outside world. I knew what needed to be done if anyone appeared to disturb them. A whole comedy of how are you and lovely evening and, ahem, oh there's Helle and Tore now. They'd had their precious time alone together and now we had to get moving if we were going to make that last tram.

'Jesus what took yez so long,' says I, grinning at Helle.

'Ah you're just jealous Janus,' she said and regretted it immediately.

I looked up at Tore, who was stood pulling on his windcheater. I wasn't devastated. I mean. It wasn't like I went to pieces inside or anything. I just looked up at Tore and understood that he now had a girlfriend and that they'd been kissing each other goodbye for over forty minutes.

I put on my cotton-coat, because it was easier to run for the tram with it on me rather than over my arm. Anyway, my mum was forever telling me you cut a much better dash if you had a coat on when you were out in the street. Helle had gone over to Tore again and stood there eating his face bit by bit. I turned slightly away from them. Then she tore herself away from him and in two bounds was over at me, takes my arm and turns me about. She leans over me and ends up kissing me in a weird place between my chin and cheek, because she'd almost stumbled. I deserved something too because I was such a star. It was all a bit too much, but then it suddenly felt like we were all actors in a movie and that made things go easier.

'Right, that's enough. You two can't drag it out any longer,' Tore called.

Me and Tore burst out of the front door of Helle's house and bombed it to her garden gate. We turned just the once and waved to her. Then we legged it down the quiet street and reached Vesterbrogade just as the number 6 tram left the stop. It was the last tram of course. We said nothing to each other but set off walking into town.

It was great to have Tore all to myself as we made

our way out of that oh so quiet residential Frederiksberg neighbourhood. I tried to convince myself that him going out with Helle wouldn't affect me really. In fact, I managed to persuade myself that our friendship had actually been strengthened, because now we had to start thinking about it. Strengthened also because we had grown in number. We were now Three Musketeers, with the new addition being feminine into the bargain. A young, pure and feminine thing like Helle. I whistled slightly at the thought of it. Pure love. The purest, the youngest and freshest love possible had happened to us. Had happened to Tore. It was brilliant walking round in the night with my summer coat unbuttoned. Tore hadn't zipped up his windcheater either. He turned his head in my direction and started talking, whilst I looked straight ahead.

'I asked Helle today if she would go to bed with me but she said she didn't want to,' Tore says. Just straight out like that.

I reacted by just staring straight ahead of me. I mean. It wasn't such an astounding thought that Tore would want to go to bed with Helle. But at the same time the words that had just come out of his mouth were amazing. I still hadn't quite grasped the full meaning of what he had said. But I understood that he had exposed a lot of deep things to me by uttering that one sentence. Helle go to bed with. Helle not go to bed with. Helle wouldn't go to bed with Tore. I suppose it wasn't that surprising given that we were barely adults and the thing we mostly aspired to was getting to walk with a girl on your arm up and down Strøget. But that said, it was unbelievable that she wouldn't go to bed with Tore. The way they were with each other, it seemed natural she would want to go to bed with him. 'Engage in sexual intercourse with him,' it suddenly said in my head, as if someone had shot a canon off.

'That's unbelievable,' says I.

He grinned widely, but there was a bit of rage there as well. 'Yeah. You would think she would do it. Even if was just to get back at her mum,' he said.

Sarcasm didn't really suit him right at that moment. It didn't feel right. Because if Tore or his girl were going to do

111

something – anything. Well, it had to be totally pure and pristine. It had to be solely because it was the two of them and nobody else in the whole world that had been chosen for just that thing. But Tore starting to *talk* to Helle about these kind of things was perfectly acceptable. He had to go gently and make sure she wasn't offended or frightened. He was just being very careful to prepare in the right way for the massive events ahead. Those sacred moments mustn't come as a shock or huge surprise. They had to build slowly to huge life-changing discoveries.

'I just don't get that she said no straight out like that,' Tore said. 'It was as if the very thought of it was so off her scale that it was a bad joke. She went a million miles from me after I said it.'

By this stage we'd walked a good bit towards town. Tore seemed distracted. As if the whole thing had left him shocked. When I edged closer to him as we walked, I picked up a scent I found familiar but had never truly taken in except in my dreams. A scent that takes your breath away.

'Ah, you know the way it is, mate. With girls and all ...' says I, bleating into the night air.

We walked past a side street where there were loads of pubs in full swing. To cover my awkwardness, I asked Tore should we go for a beer. Not that drinking in pubs or going to restaurants had become normal for us. We never had the money and pots of tea lasted a lot longer when we were having our marathon chats. But the tension in the conversation we'd just had cried out for some kind of distraction.

We turned into the street and went past one pub after the other with their brightly lit windows and signs. One place reeked of smoke and piss and we weren't sure which to choose. In the end, we tumbled into the only pub we kind of vaguely knew. It was called *The Lord Trevelyan*. The kind of pub that was supposed to be the haunt of people who might have held a pen in their hands at some point in their lives. As usual in these situations, we were a bit wary. The more so because we didn't have much money. And what little we had wasn't supposed to go on bottles of beer.

I had my hands in my coat pockets and shoved the door in with my elbow. At that same moment, some fella was on his way out and got the door right smack in his forehead. Now I was scared, but this just made me look more devil-may-care than I had intended. The man staggered back and stood looking at us with bleary eyes.

'Fucking idiot,' he said, as he leaned forward and grabbed me by the shoulders of my coat. Then he launched himself out of the pub doorway using my shoulders as a springboard. But instead of letting go, he kept his grip on me as he blundered forwards and tore my coat. Then he fell down the three steps leading into the pub and stayed on the ground cursing and swearing. Tore's head had turned white as a sheet. He shoved me quickly into bar itself as the door swung shut behind us. My whole body was shaking. And the bedlam inside hit us straight in the face. I was worried that the door behind us would swing open again and there would be the dipso coming after me. But nothing happened.

There was table service but no tables were free. A barman edged his way past us and swept us towards the side wall with his weighty gut. 'You young gentlemen can sit at that big table over there if yez are going to order something!' We took our coats off and sat down on a hard sofa by a square table that had a bench on the other side containing a selection of choice pub specimens. All knocking beer back. The waiter's gut appeared again and we ordered a beer each. Tore leaned towards me as if to speak but he just grinned and I said something about having a proper night out on the town. This late hour on a Saturday evening meant the racket in the place was a killer. Our bottles of beer arrived and we poured them into the glasses. I had come to sit next to an older woman who seemed on the brink of collapsing over me the whole time. Not a violent collapse. But I could just feel the way she constantly edged into me. So that I was forced to discreetly nudge her back from where she came. In the end she sat still and turned her face towards me. She slobbered with her lips a bit. As if she had to get them going before she could say something. A drip of spit drizzled down her chin.

'Letssh have a beerh together Mr Ssshtudent,' she says right into my face.

'Well I would love to but the problem is I've no money,' says I, smart as you like.

'Errrgh,' she goes. Squawking and spitting all over my mouth. 'Itssh jusssht he has no bleedin munneh! Heeeh!' She wailed, looking round at all the others. 'Heeesh! Shsstony broke he ish!'

Finally her stream of words ebbed out and she toppled herself over one of the men at the other side of our bench.

Helle wouldn't go to bed with Tore. It wasn't exactly pleasant thinking of Helle while we sat in here. It wasn't exactly pleasant thinking of the old hag next to me with no clothes on. Me sitting there getting furious with Helle, because she'd said no to Tore. What the fuck was she playing at? She just had to do as she was bid and no messing about. She should be grateful. I mean. Tore was asking her to do something for fuck's sake. I would personally stand guard outside their door as the event took place with a huge gleaming sword in my hand.

Me and Tore clinked our glasses and leaned our heads back as we drank. The cold beer tasted good. Through the bottom of the glass, I could see the people out dancing beyond our table. All milling around out there in the middle of the pub. Their backsides were huge and deformed in the play of the glass. I put the glass down and looked more closely at some of the women and a few girls who were dancing. I don't think many of them would've refused if you'd asked them.

We talked into each other's faces about that. About Saturdays, and about the others sat at our table. Sitting there talking past each other, because it was hard to say anything that meant much in this place. A fella at the table called out for more beers – for de schtudentss ass well! We smiled over at this man and said thanks and joined the round of new pilsners when they landed. Then Tore rose from the table and edged his way towards the jacks. I stretched my legs out under the table and came to kick the old bag next to me. There was no reaction whatsoever. She just sat there saying 'pusssh pull, pusssh pull, pusssh pull' all to herself. In a flash, I became aware of my complete independence and anonymity in this place. I could do just as I pleased, and the immense power of this surged through me like a thunderbolt. I would show them! I got up and steered myself towards the young woman who looked most presentable in this dive, bowed ceremonially, if a bit skewed, in front of her. She looked up at me with a bit of a lunatic smile and stubbed her cigarette out. Then she hooked herself tight to my arm and we blundered out onto the dance floor. Helle wouldn't go to bed with Tore but what was that to me? Didn't stop me losing my virginity if I felt like it. Anyway, before when I danced with girls I'd never asked myself whether they were virgins or not. This time I was sure she wasn't. The girl was right into me. As if she was paid for how closely she could lodge her breasts into my chest. The line between innocence and not being innocent any more had always been a distant idea, a massively distant idea in my thoughts. Now it was dancing right in front of me. But Jesus Christ. This wasn't Helle. It wasn't some big debate. It was just the thing I was dragging round with me here and now, then a few formalities that needed addressing and that was it. Job done.

'You're a good dancer, young man,' the girl said, looking up at me. We'd moved about two feet across the floor in the last five minutes. I was only a bit drunk from the two beers we'd had. The girl I was dancing with was not exactly electric but everything considered, I could probably work myself up to some kind of amorous state without much bother. Me. Janus Tolne. And his virginity. That should be sorted out sooner rather than later. I mean. Why waste any more time fretting over it when life threw the chance right into your hands? I looked over to our table to see if there was room for my girl and saw that Tore was talking to a man. Some dipso or other had sat down at our table. We danced on. I looked right down at her hair. It was actually nicely done up. All curled upwards bouncy and without a parting. I cleared my throat and asked her what her name was.

'You can call me Inger,' she said, as she looked up at my

face with a blue gaze. 'You can call me Inger.' Phew. Sounded a bit dodgy to me. All the same, I couldn't help feeling a kind of tenderness for her. Everyone played some kind of game. Time to be an adult in an adult world. Time to step up and live that world - the wonderfulness of it. I had absolutely no fear of this girl and her: 'You can call me Inger' carry-on.

'I can handle this no fucking problem,' says I to myself. Then I looked over at Tore at the table. He looked weirdly green in the face. The stranger he'd been talking to was leaning right over him. Tore jerked his head away as if trying to avoid this fella's bad breath and then he half turned and looked at us as we danced. I got the feeling I'd better get over to him. I moved my hand from Inger's waist and we both went to Tore and this other man. Tore looked up at us. He didn't smile and his greeting was terse as he went to stand up for the girl; then this stranger put his hand on Tore's knee and shoved him back onto the bench. I stared at this fella and then it hit me. I knew who it was. It was that Poul. His mum's ex. My mind started to spin but, in the same instant, Inger starts lisping about what kind of gents were these making her stand there staring at them and not even bothering to stand up for her or anything. I was just about to tell her to shut her trap but Tore stands up and asks whether we should leave. I nods and Tore takes a step away from the table. But Poul throws himself over Tore and wraps both his arms around him. Tore's eyes go stiff as this Poul fella's arms slip down around his hips. My girl starts tittering.

'Can't you get her to do it for me?' the man gasps, 'You can have a word. I know you can!' He continued hanging on to Tore with his arms, and Tore almost dragged him from his chair as he took another step back to free himself. People at the other tables began to swing round and crane their necks. Suddenly Poul lost his balance and as he fell towards the floor he threw his hands out and caught Tore in the crotch and he doubled up at the blow. The man hit the floor like a sack of spuds and Tore knelt over him. Then he lifted his clasped arms above his head and brought them down over Poul. I was stunned for a second. Then this Inger starts shouting something and I jump across to Tore to tell him to stop. I roared in his ear to stop but his big Red Indian hands just kept on laying into the man beneath him. Someone must have heaved me away because I found myself skittling across the floor and could feel someone dragging me by my tie. Next I see that Tore had stood up and had pulled Poul up as well. They stood facing each other as Inger drew back from them. A waiter rushed towards them just as Poul raised his right hand and smashed it right into Tore's face, which went rigid from the blow and the stifled cry that followed. Tore didn't see the fist coming. Or at least, his face met it full on. I only noticed my own blood trickling from my nose after the sound of the hefty smack had died away and the whole pub descended into mad commotion. The blood was seeping between my teeth and running down my chin. The hand that had a grip on my tie pulled me upwards and kept on pulling till it was more like a noose. I managed to stand, and then staggered over to the thing that just minutes before had been Tore. The punch had rammed his upper lip, which was all smashed and shredded. His face was shut tight in the glimpse I caught just before I kicked out at this Poul with all my might. I missed completely and then felt myself being pulled backwards by an arm round my throat. Something was dripping down my shirt. The girl Inger held onto one of my arms as I was vaulted through the door via my other arm that had been twisted up my back. A bit down the street, I turned and waited for Tore. Then he came out. He wasn't thrown out like me. He'd just been shown the door.

I rushed over to him. Reached up and put an arm around his shoulder. Then I starts mumbling in his ear: What kind of a shit evening was that? What was all that about? And all that with Helle? What had she said exactly? I couldn't remember any more. I didn't give a damn about that any more. But it was the thing that had led us into this shit evening. It actually was. Wasn't it? I stood there muttering all this into Tore's head. My arm round his shoulder all the while. Really … what was all that shit about purity and sacred discoveries? The crucial passage into that great moment. When here we were. Dribbling blood and gore down our mouths and onto our shirts and looking like total trogheads. Just kids who couldn't hold their drink.

Tore straightened up and pushed the back of his hand against his upper lip. The angle of light from the street lamp made it almost look like he was grinning at me. Then Inger walked up to us.

She came straight up to me and put her hand on my elbow.

'You never told me your name in there ...' she said. She was deadly serious. Looking straight at me.

'Janus. My name's Janus Tolne,' I sniffed back at her. It was clear that she took it for granted I would have such a mad name. After the weirdness of all that had just happened.

Inger goes – 'Better get cleaned up.' Then this right floozey dragged us off. As if we were two camels that had lost their bearings after a storm in the desert. The one sleeve of my cotton coat was in tatters and hanging off me. It was also filthy because they'd thrown our coats into the gutter after ejecting us. Inger had picked them up. She was all eager now she had a task to organise. She tottered off in her high heels and Tore followed like some huge gliding lighthouse.

But what had happened to that fella Poul? When did he get thrown out? I hadn't a clue but I hoped that they'd battered him first. Smashed up against a wall and given him a right doing.

'It's like when you eat an orange,' said Tore as he turned his face to me. 'It's the same feeling. With all them strips and shreds in between your teeth. A real blood orange.' He grinned but then grimaced when his wounds cracked open.

I laugh and go – 'Yeah, we used to call them bloodsuckers when we were kids.' A sense of pride emerged amongst all the weirdness. A bloodsucker wound had once been a badge of honour. Now it was just horrible though. I mean. Getting a smack from a low-life like Poul was not funny.

Inger goes – 'What's your friend's name?' She was walking beside us now and holding my hand. She was at least 25.

'My name's Tore. Tore the Main Man,' says Tore, laughing again from some corner of his mouth.

'Jesus. You two are a right pair aren't yez,' the girl said. 'I bet you're not even allowed out this late.'

That got me thinking about all those gallons of tea me and Tore had sunk during our endless conversations. Now here we were walking around in Vesterbro with smashed-in faces and a girl who straight-faced said – 'You can call me Inger!' Brazen.

A few people passed us by every now and again. But they didn't pay much attention to us. I suppose round here they were used to seeing this kind of pageant being played out on their streets. We turned a couple of corners, and I started to get the feeling we were on Søndre Boulevard - or some such mad area under the dark curved wall that guarded the railway tracks. Then the girl stopped and pulled us through an outside door that led directly onto a staircase. My head thumped as we ascended the stairs. The girl in front, then Tore, and me bringing up the rear. 'A rag-tag army fleeing the battleground,' says I to myself. 'Bloodied and cowed and commandeered by a girl.'

We might just as well have gone home to our own beds.

On the third floor this young woman stopped. I suppose it had taken us a while to get up there because as she stood fumbling with the key the light on the staircase went 'plop' and darkness descended. We stood like statues whilst she worked at the door lock with her key. But she finally got the door open, stuck her hand inside and put on the light in her apartment.

It was one of those strange bedsits where you walk right into the flat itself. No entrance hall, lobby, corridor or anything. It felt disturbingly intimate just to crash into someone's bedroom, kitchen, sitting room and toilet ike that. Inger went over to the window, put her bag down, turned round and looked at us. We were still stood at the door. Like lost sheep. Just staring blankly.

'Well, don't just stand there. Come in.' There was a hint of abruptness in her voice.

We edged our way past the door and entered. Tore pulled himself together and began swinging his arms in some attempt at playing a man of the world.

'Sorry we've got you caught up in all this bother,' he said. He stopped like a plane that suddenly stalls and it looked like he was going to faint. It was grotesque to see him illuminated by that bare light. With his hair all down over his forehead and a smashed upper lip. I walked over to him and took his arm. But Inger stepped between us and shoved me away. She pulled Tore over to a curtain in one of the corners of the room where there was a sink. She pulled off his windcheater and jumper and sized him up for a moment. Then she pulled a chair from her table and sat him down. She doused a cloth at the sink and began very carefully to wipe the blood from his nose and mouth.

It had to be because he was in worse shape than me that she looked after him first, says I to myself.

I walked over to the window and stared down at a long street that was totally quiet and abandoned.

Wonder what he was at that Poul fella? Everything had happened so fast. One, two, three, and now here we were in Søndre Boulevard or somewhere near there in the bedsit of a young woman we didn't know from Adam. Standing there feeling sorry for myself. I turned round to the others when Tore mentioned my name.

'This is like being some big potentate,' he said. I gave a laugh in answer. 'With a manicurist to hand,' says I.

He got up when she was finished with him and then she told me to come over and sit in his place. Behind my back, I could sense that Tore had gone over to her bed, and she turned her head and said he should lie down for a while. He mumbled something like a protest but lay down anyway.

So that was the upshot of the day. Tore asked Helle if she would go to bed with him. She had said no. And now he was lying on a strange girl's bed with a smashed upper lip. Was this Tore the Man of legend?

I felt Inger's breasts against me as she leaned into me and tenderly washed my head and face. The clean-up was no big job. Though I shivered a little bit. But then I got the notion that I should put my hands on her hips. She wriggled away a bit in the first instance but let my hands stay there after that.

Over on the bed Tore had started to snore. Little wheezes were coming out of his big inflamed nose.

Inger turned and hung the cloth on a hook at the side of a mirror by the sink. Then she turned and looked at me without smiling or anything. I flinched on the chair.

'Looks like he's out for the count,' she said. I glanced over to the bed, where Tore lay sleeping. Very pale. Then I felt pure terror when she moved right into me and, with a friendly look in her eyes, proceeded to unbutton my trousers. A sacred moment with Tore snoring on a bed, whilst 'You can call me Inger' stood there undoing my flies. I actually didn't move a muscle as she began fishing around inside my underpants. But then it struck me that it was a bit too crass and troglike really. Me just sitting there without taking any active part in the proceedings. I had no desire to kiss her but instead took hold of her breasts. I obviously grabbed her too hard because she gasped a bit, but then she threw herself over me and we did a sort of soft roll onto the floor with her still holding on fast inside my trousers.

'Any second now Tore wakes up,' I thought to myself but didn't get to think it through because I got a throbbing in my head and inside my pants and the whole scene rushed at my eyes. And Inger seemed to understand this because she began heaving her dress up and her knickers down and she whispering all this stuff in my ear and the whole thing ended up as one crazy mess and rolling round and me not able to work out what was up or down.

This was all skewed and somehow split from the day before. Midnight was long gone and we were close to dawn and all that about Helle not wanting to go to bed with Tore, and that Poul who wanted to get back with Tore's mum again. That was all yesterday. Now we'd just get up, walk down the street together, and try to get back to the old way. No. We couldn't do that now. Because Janus Tolne had gone and put his signature on the papers that made him a different person to Tore. And the sequence was all cockeyed.

It was almost unbearable to think how skewed it was. Because, of course, it was Tore that was supposed to be first, and in a different way. Tore the Man was the one elected to do it first and give it his seal of approval. Then I would come afterwards and enter the noble arena that had been prepared for me.

He hadn't stirred during all that carry-on and noise we must have made. Inger lay there laughing at me. Not unfriendly but still she was actually lying there laughing at me, whilst I was doing my best to get my shirt back in my trousers in that awkward position I was in.

'Good job Mr Student. Nothing for it but to lie on the floor in your own room when the night turns out like this,' she said, giggling. I would have preferred it if she had pulled her dress down, but it was still lying there like a long curled-up sausage above her breasts.

I managed to get myself up on my knees and came to put my hand in a pool of wet on the floor. I pulled my hand back rapidly. Then I got up.

Daylight was rising outside. Tore looked macabre and strange the way he lay on the bed. He slept in complete silence. Inger had got up too and was standing at the sink with a toothbrush and glass. Clinking and banging clatter clatter noises and then groaning from the pipe.

'We better get home,' says I out loud. She'd begun to brush her teeth but told me through brush and toothpaste foam that we could stay if we wanted. 'I can just lie back down on the floor again now I'm used to it!'

In truth. Inger wasn't being coarse or mean when she said this. It seemed she was just used to talking in that way. A bit brash and the whole thing had to come out as sharp punctuations between her teeth. Damned if she could be told what was what by anyone!

I bent over Tore and shook him very gently. He gave a weak grunt. Then he opened his eyes and saw my face. The next second he was wide awake. As if he'd just been lying there spying on us with half-closed eyes.

'Right, we better get home,' he said. His voice carried neither praise nor reproach. No sense of a hidden awareness in his tone. He heaved himself up from the bed and was just a big block of a Red Indian, groggy with firewater sleep.

His arms flapped like wings as he pulled on his windcheater.

When his coat was on him, he strode over to Inger and put out his hand. Then he thanked her for bringing us back to her place and getting us cleaned up.

Mad stuff seeing him standing there with the girl. As I watched them, the nagging feeling I'd done wrong came back to me.

I didn't want to wear my cotton-coat, because it was so tattered and anyway it was bright day by now. I wrapped it over my arm instead as I waited for Tore to say his farewells. She followed him over to the door and ushered him outside. As he eased through the door she looked up at me with a big smile on her face. There was now a bond of sorts between us. She took hold of my jacket and pulled me towards her a bit. Then she leaned right into me and whispered: 'Bye bye kiddo.'

We emerged onto the small landing directly outside her door and she closed the door right after us. I'd cleared the last hurdle, I felt. I'd done it all now.

We tramped down the staircase and came out onto the street that was all pale morning. A blackbird on a rowan tree was belting out notes so clear and sharp you wanted to hold your ears. I bet we looked like shipwrecks. Anyone coming across us would laugh and say: 'Ha Ha! Ha! Those two bucks have been out on a right gallivant.' In a way, I was shocked that what had happened up there hadn't changed me more. No doubt I was now one of the Damned. But actually I didn't feel much different. Thought it was supposed to be like some butterfly in summer emerging from its pupa. What I felt was more like the way I was right that minute. With a wet sticky patch in my underpants. So I bowed my head slightly as I walked along by Tore's side. We'd no money for a taxi after we'd drunk those beers in that insane pub. Nothing for it but to start walking again.

'I'll walk with you to your house first,' I told Tore in protective tones. We let out a laugh at each other. The bridge with all the trains underneath was right ahead of us. Great clouds of steam plumed upwards from the early morning express train. The smoke was almost blindingly white in the grey morning. Tore shot a quick glance down to the train. The locomotive was an S machine. One of them with the small wheels that run at thousands of revs when the train starts to move with the wheels not engaged yet.

Our old urge to jump the train and take off overwhelmed us again, and we stood there hanging over the railings for a minute. The departure signal went up and the engine began to hiss because of the pressure build-up in the machine's boiler. Then the train driver engaged the throttle and the train bulged its way forward under the bridge, gliding further along the curve of tracks and disappearing out of sight.

My shoulders hunched involuntarily. I was cold because I'd no coat on.

'Things would've been better if we'd got that last number six tram last night,' Tore said. 'We'd have got more sleep. That's for sure.'

'That fella Poul said he's come back to get hold of mum again,' he continued. 'He was going on like a mad thing. Begging me to see if I could sort it out. As if he thought it would help things if he got me on his side. He was pissed as well. I just don't get it with him and my mum. Maybe she found out she was pregnant and then married him for my sake. Or I don't know what.'

Some office workers were going into Tivoli funfair park as we walked by.

Tore goes – 'I mean. Course it was crazy to go and hit him but I got my reward for it.' He laughed and put his hand up to his fat lip.

'Just imagine if we could go into Tivoli in the early morning. I could kill a fresh roll or two,' he said.

He swung his arms around like a pure mad gymnast and heaved the cool air through his nose.

'Let's find a baker's shop that's open, Janus.'

We ferreted about for quite some time and finally found a baker's shop at the other side of the Town Hall. I had a massive need to wash my hands.

The woman in the shop nearly had conniptions when she saw the state of us.

Tore goes - 'Can I have eight million rolls, love.'

124

'Yer can giveover with your million rolls as well,' she said.

'Sorry. We'd like a few rolls please,' says I.

Then Tore goes – 'Madam, I can't believe you're turning down a chance to make a mint. Selling us all those rolls.'

The woman tutted with a snap of the head and brought a paper bag. 'How many?' she asked with a snarl.

'Six,' said Tore gravely.

The woman smacked the rolls into the bag. One after the other. Then she scrunched and strangled the top of it.

We strutted out the door.

'She didn't put butter in,' I informed Tore. About face for Tore. Back in to the bakery again. The woman was positively spitting by the time I got back in.

'You young fellas can get yourselves to a dairy shop if yez want butter,' she roared and we fled out the door into the street, giggling like mad. A cotton coat and a bag of rolls flapping round us.

We got butter in a milk and dairy shop and sat on the bench outside the Glyptotek eating our rolls. Officially no longer a virgin, I sat there whilst Tore lurched forwards, his pocket knife full of butter, and an innocent, busted upper lip flapping down over his teeth. Why wasn't I worried more about me and my own concerns for fuck's sake? No. Tore was in a worse place than me. Never would they be allowed to destroy him, those bastards. Tore and Helle. That was the touchstone of everything. I mean. Was the honour of the king and queen going to be dragged through the mud? No chance.

Some pathetic street sparrows were jumping round our feet for crumbs. I flicked out at them with my feet just for the hell of it.

'If they hadn't stopped us, we could've battered that Poul fella. No doubt about it,' said Tore with a crooked smile.

In my mind, I could see his face at that second when it was down there hanging between the tables. Just waiting to get kicked in. And I knew he would've been dead meat from that point on. Never would he beat up another person again. The truth was we weren't up to that kind of malarkey.

'Might have been a bit chicken of us. Two against one like,' says I, but knowing very well it was bullshit.

'I hate him, because he stinks,' said Tore. 'I couldn't stand it any longer. The reek off him. Right in my face like that. And then when he grabbed hold of me. Jesus man – like getting covered in shit.'

I chewed on my bread roll. The truth we had led sheltered lives. Wrapped in soft cotton wool. Never getting our hands dirty. As if we wore surgical gloves. To guard against contact with all the shit life threw up. It occurred to me I hadn't got round to washing my hands before eating the bread. The bread rolls weren't exactly appetising any more. Inger hadn't washed her hands either prior to us leaving. But she'd brushed her teeth. Jeez a bath would be heaven right that second. My skin crawled with swampy feelings. I rubbed my hands vigorously together and stood up.

Tore sat chewing in a very studied way that sought to avoid engagement with his crushed upper lip. All his thought and will was bent to this task. I dangled on the precipice of leaning down and telling him about me and Inger. It was unbelievable that he hadn't twigged the whole thing. But as usual he was the Great Champion who, untroubled and effortlessly, evaded all that was base and impure. He had reposed sound and serene in the realm of sleep. Proudly bearing his battle wounds as only a king can, whilst I had grubbed around in the murk of his moat. I had this mad urge to bellow and roar here in this square named after Dante and his infernal comedy, but instead I bowed before my Chieftain with folded arms and my cotton coat dangling between my knees. He had completed his dawn repast and sat calm as a stone statue gazing out into the morning. He didn't have far to go, but I had a tram to catch. Tore got up and held out his hand. My need to roar died away. We shook hands and the peacock in Tivoli gardens opened its throat to crow at just that moment. As if thirty pieces of fat corn had been strewn at its feet and it was about to croak in strangled pleasure. We stood like Brutus and Marcus Antonius on the steps of the Senate in Rome and began suddenly laughing at each other where we stood.

There was only one other person in the otherwise deserted

tram – a morning-sharp cleaning woman who showed no interest in me, even though I must have looked like a walking disgrace.

The milkman was just leaving the entrance to our stairs as I walked in. Now tiredness came like a wall rushing at me. I dragged myself up the stairs. Feeling like it was a thousand years since I'd walked down them to go to Helle's place. At our apartment, I finally managed to work my key into the door and ease it open. In one movement, I took a step into the hall and shut the door behind me. I barely made a sound. But when I turned to go down the corridor, there was dad standing right in front of me.

My father standing right in front of me. And I had the weird feeling that I lived the whole of his life right that second. This was the culmination of his life. His youngest son had come stealing home after daybreak on a Sunday morning. He had gone through exactly the same ritual with his two eldest sons and now here came the youngest. It had all gone as he'd hoped and he couldn't ask for more. A knowing smile lit up his face and he was on the verge of shaking my hand. Congratulations on my passage into the realm of manhood. It struck me that he'd already picked up my scent as I'd walked down our street. Nosing his way to an awareness that I'd been with a woman and in a pub. Now he stood there in his pyjamas to present me with the victor's crown. A laurel wreath.

I tried to edge past him with a guilt-ridden nod of the head but he stood in front of me to block my way.

'Bit late coming home, eh?' he said. I couldn't bring myself to look into his face because I knew it wore a conspiratorial smile. His all-lads-in-it-together familiarity sent shivers down my back.

'Yeah,' I said tersely.

'Your mother was starting to get worried but I told her that young bucko …'

I pushed past him with nothing but black in my head. But just as I went through the door to the sitting room his hand brushed my shoulder with a light pat of approval.

'Night.'

'Good night, Janus,' he said through the door as it closed behind me.

I ran through the living room and out into the other passage that led down to my room. I could hear a blackbird singing from the top of one of the gable walls opposite. I pulled my jacket off and slung it into a corner. Rubbed at my shoulders as if someone had spat on them. When I'd managed to flay all my freaky clothes off and was in my pyjamas, I sneaked out onto the corridor and down to the loo.

I was now an adult. So if I wanted to sit on the jacks at half six on a Sunday morning and me wanting to throw up. Well, there was nothing stopping me any more, because all of adulthood's privileges were now mine. Bit of a lad our Janus, eh? Chip off the old block.

I washed my hands and face and tiptoed back to my bed. You really needed to be like Tore the Man to handle this kind of thing properly. Tore hadn't washed himself like a mad thing before going to bed. Not a chance. He wouldn't have felt the need I bet. And there actually wasn't any need for him. Bet you he lay there sleeping now. All big and blocky, and a refined sort of snore passing through his imposing but now slightly crooked nose.

Chapter 7

In the time just after Tore and Helle started going out together, I didn't see that much of them. All I knew for sure was that they met after school and walked round the streets for an hour before she went home. That was as far as it was allowed to go. They hardly ever went out in the evening, because me and Tore had our reading and homework to do. We usually did this together, but whenever we stopped in the middle of our crucifying Latin, Tore would start to talk about her; how they discussed everything under the sun. I just sat and nodded and confirmed to myself yet again that she really was perfect for him.

One evening, Tore blew into my room like a whirlwind. His eyes a bit wild in his head. He'd actually been out at Helle's place on an official visit. His mum had come into his room a few days before and told him a lady had been on the phone. It was none other than Fru Junkersen, Helle's mother. She had, she said, nothing against Helle socialising with young men. Nothing in the least. But she would really like to see the young men in question, be able to speak to them. Nothing more.

Tore was in fits laughing. So the upshot was he'd been invited out there for dinner. When he rang the doorbell, a young girl opened the door wearing a white cap and apron. She took his coat from him and then he was left standing there in the hall like he was waiting for an audience with the Queen of Sheba. There was no sign of Helle.

In the end, Tore knocked on a door and went in. There sat both Helle and her mother. The mother was around forty years of age and they had conversed politely about politics and literature, whilst Helle just looked uncomfortable the whole time. He was sent off home at ten o'clock. 'Helle has to be all bright-eyed and bushy-tailed first thing tomorrow,' Fru Junkersen told Tore.

Tore was lying on my bed rattling on breakneck about this fantastically posh inaugural dinner.

'Madame herself was appalling,' he said. 'The whole time, you got the feeling she was inspecting the stains on your trousers or other defects.' He stroked his nose in thought. 'Though she's good-looking for a mum. She puts you in mind of a lion, I think. She's the type that scares you a bit as well,' he said, smiling at me.

That made me think of the effect she had when she stood in front of that window. I knew exactly what he meant.

'But Janus, I'm telling you. Helle is just wonderful,' Tore said. 'I've been invited to dinner at theirs again. This is for Helle's birthday, and she proposed that you should come along too this time, you young rascal you.'

He said all this in a glow of besottedness. I flinched a bit, but at the same time was delighted that I too was being invited into the magic circle. At last, I was going to see what lay at the heart of the beast.

Me and Tore went out there on the birthday itself. The avenue on which the villa stood bore a completely different character to that night after the school dance. There was nothing mysterious about it any more. Just a row of ancient gardens with flowers and some houses that looked like something out of a sepia photograph from the 1860s. The whole road felt dead and empty. As if it knew it was neither here nor there. We were hours getting past the garden gate because we played a game of polite boys. Bowing and scraping to each other and insisting the other went first old chap. I mean. We had to get used to this polite society malarkey. It was Helle who opened the front door this time. Tore just stood there for a second but then stepped forward and gave her a kiss. Just a glancing brush of lips. We wished her a very happy birthday and I produced a book I'd bought for her. It had cost a fortune, but she looked very pleased with it. I wanted to be popular.

Me and Tore had a quick sken at each other as we entered the hall. He straightened his tie with exaggerated gestures.

Never in my life had I seen such a giant room. Had to work hard to convince myself I wasn't actually in the banqueting hall of Rosenborg Castle as I waited for an audience with the Great Queen. Though the vast room seemed empty apart from ourselves. But then a slight rustling sound emanated from the other end of the room and a woman rose up from a sofa. Behind her was a shelf with beautifully bound volumes that seemed never to have been touched.

Fru Junkersen remained standing where she was and suffered us to approach. We lurched over the thick pile carpet and I became all prickly heat. Right in front of her, we stopped and undulated for a minute. Then she extended her hand to Tore, who took it and bowed as he offered his congratulations for her daughter's special day. Then the lady turned towards me with a smile that seemed to chill her eyes somewhat.

'May I introduce my friend Janus Tolne,' Tore said. I bowed my head and mumbled some numbskull nonsense about being grateful for the invitation. Her hand was as dry as tinder and felt like it was weighing my own in hers.

Then we were invited to sit and Helle offered us cigarettes from an enormous silver case that was very like one we had at our place. Dad had got it as an anniversary gift from all his guild buddies. Only thing being there was not even a hint of an inscription on this one that Helle was offering round. Its surface was clear and shiny and when right that second I thought of Dad's case I was filled with the smells of the dining room in our home. But now we began conversing. Helle looked mighty pretty. She had put up her hair in a particular way. Like a crown on her head. So you saw far more of her neck and ears, which still carried some kind of tinge of baby glow. Extremely pleasing. The way herself and the Red Indian suited each other. Made me sit back in my chair a bit. Just wallowing for a moment in the whole idea of this perfect couple.

Fru Junkersen was startling to look at. The yellow hair pushed up and back gave such a powerful Queen of the Jungle impression that I was on tenterhooks waiting for her to let out a roar. Her low-cut grey dress made her neck, which did not show one wrinkle, rise into the air like an obelisk that held this arrogant head aloft and thrown back slightly. Her replies came staccato out of her with barely a twitch from her face as she spoke, but in a voice tone that stung your eardrums. If her figure was no longer youthful, you wouldn't know it from looking at her. Her breasts stuck out proudly to each side, but with no more exaggeration than was becoming for her species. She was the Big Cat.

Tore hadn't described all this properly. He had merely given me an impression of an unbearable upper-class snob, but this was something far far worse.

In the meantime, the maid had set a cocktail down beside us and when I first sipped at it I enjoyed a little moment of feeling I was a true adult. I started to tell Helle about something going on at our school and leaned over towards where she sat. I felt an intimacy between us but was this was soon dispelled when I noticed that her attention had swung over to Tore who was chatting to her mother with a fanatical display of charm. It was as if his hostility to this woman had ignited all his most irresistible attributes. His hand movements were a perfect accompaniment to what he was saying and his enthusiasm made waves in the air that rolled into this woman's space. She goaded his performance into new life with her responses that continually unleashed yet another inspired tale from Tore the Man.

In the end, me and Helle just watched the drama being played out in front of us. Helle gazed upon Tore with pride and enchantment. I couldn't tear my eyes away from Fru Junkersen's face. Her motionless demeanour and air of superiority banished any thought I'd entertained of being truly grown-up.

The maid appeared through the double doors to announce that dinner was served. She then pushed the doors right back into the walls. You didn't feel the absence of a father figure in this house. You actually felt there wouldn't be room for him. A thought entered my mind that Fru Junkersen had eaten him. Like the female spider. After he had impregnated her. Now it was Tore that was caught in her web.

I was placed beside Fru Junkersen at the table. Tore got permission to have Helle on account of her birthday. The food was fantastic. A lot of work had been put into its presentation. We were served with white wine for the first course, and then were each given a carafe of red wine to accompany our main course. On top of the cocktail, it had quite an effect. I started getting flimmer-flammer feelings and slurring lips. Found myself talking at the top of my voice about all manner of pathetic things, whilst Fru Junkersen just sat there with the hint of a smile threatening to fall out the corner of her lips. I got this fantastic urge to get hold of it and stuff it back in her trap. I talked so much that it came as a shock when I suddenly shut up. I felt all disgusted and guilty with myself. I mean. It would be Tore carrying the can if things went wrong. Then Fru Junkersen rang a bell that was placed under the table. The noise went right through me. She did it in a particular, discreet kind of way. Like her movement almost didn't happen. So the secret chain down to the domestics was barely noticeable, but it was still like the alarm bells at a fire station. The maid came in again and we rose from the table and went back into the other room, where God strike me dead there was another maid serving coffee. I still had just about enough sense to decline the offer of cognac.

So there we sat again, and the anxiety worked its way inside and amplified my intoxication. Helle's mother gave a little yawn. But all in her eyes without opening her mouth. Then she sized us up and released the pressure by saying that we could go to the cinema if we wished. Helle's face lit up like a lamp and she raced off to get the newspaper. We could just make the nine o'clock performance. We didn't bother ringing to reserve tickets because the very thought of all that fresh air outside. Of the streets. And talking and laughing about it all, lifted the atmosphere in the room up to the heavens. We said a very courteous and careful goodbye and thanks for a lovely dinner.

'Helle must be straight home after the cinema,' she said, looking directly at Tore. He flinched infinitesimally. Then the woman half turned her back to him and began gathering up the newspapers.

We got our coats on. I put my own on, but the maid helped Tore. He had a cigar clamped in his mouth and looked every the bit the dude when he straightened up and pulled his coat about him. He was right back to his old self again and I took a step backwards so as to make way for the two of them as they moved to the door. He put his arm about Helle's waist as they went down the steps from the front door, but removed it as they went past the big front window. Smoke clouds from his cigar sailed upwards in large pulses and wafted around my head as I walked behind them. And I took these as signs from a signal fire showing favourable portents. Fru Junkersen was not standing at the window.

My earlier drink-induced high coursed through me again when we hit the cold air. We had melded together. Nobody could pull us apart or make us feel down. Even as we walked our force was expanding like crazy.

'Hey, can we not take the car?' I asked Helle. I had seen that the house also had its own garage.

'Ha! You don't even have a driving licence, you big pansy,' she said, and Tore laughed.

'Believe me. My driving's so good, I don't need a licence,' I replied, and meant every word of it. With Fru Junkersen as the radiator mascot and Helle and Tore in the back seat, I would tear off down the coast road with a blaring horn and flashing lights. That might even get the old bitch's hair to fall down so she'd go from lion to sheep. Her eyes wouldn't change though. She was like a figure from the Apocalypse. A hybrid creature. Part lion. Part snake. With a lowering mandible and pulled back head that seemed poised to strike.

But Helle was big now too. Grown into an adult together with Tore right there where they walked in front of me arm in arm. Now I had a great feeling that she was part of us. Now I could play the court fool. Act the goat and play up with low and high jinks before my Lord and Lady. I would have turned somersaults in front of them just to please them. Bark and growl like a mad dog and rip out my teeth. Juggle them this way and that, moving forwards and back in the dark of the evening if they so wished it. Perform a backward double jack-knife over their heads, landing on the tip of my tongue at the very edge of the pavement, as I simultaneously declaimed nonsense verse just to see them giggling.

After the picture, which made us laugh so much we were in cramps, I bade farewell to the two of them. My head was pounding. It was better to get it over with straight away. So at least they wouldn't have to worry about having to dismiss me before they walked off on their own.

They turned left and disappeared down Vesterbrogade, whilst I remained standing in front of a shop display, then looking at cars without really seeing them. When I finally turned in the direction of town, who do I see but Kurt across the road from me. I quickened my pace like a paranoid squirrel to get away from him, but it was too late. He had already seen me. Damn.

'All right Janus,' he called. A demented grin flowing down his chin.

'All right mate,' I said, already exhausted.

'We may as well walk together ...' he ventured expectantly.

I made no reply. Just let him start walking next to me. He'd obviously been wandering aimlessly about because he was going in the opposite direction when I saw him and now he was meandering back with me. Kurt had this unique ability to jump out at you from nowhere at any possible moment and then follow you home to get a cup of tea. We trudged on as he started telling me about some new thing he'd got for his bike – a cyclometer. Hadn't he worked out exactly how many kilometres it was from his basement cycle shed at home to the cycle shed at school? And he knew with mathematical certainty how long the trip took going against the wind, then wind-assisted, then in fog, sleet, frost and ice. So help me God. He stole quick glances at me every now and again. Then he just walked on without saying anything for a while. By this time, we'd passed a few stops where I could have got a tram but I was in that trance-like state where you keep saying to yourself you'll get one at the next stop until you find you're almost home.

Kurt wiped his mouth gingerly with the back of his hand. A sure sign that he felt awkward or was getting red-faced over something. Then he goes – 'Tore and Helle. They're going out together, aren't they?'

'Yeah they are,' says I. So he was going to stick his snout into this now.

'Must be great going out with a girl like that,' he said, without looking at me. There was something sick about the way he said it that made me frantic. There was nothing perfect, whole and rounded, in this world. Everything belonged to everyone and could be pawed at, as and when it suited. The body. The mind. Words.

'Aye, she's a lovely girl,' I said. Once Kurt got in. You couldn't get rid of him. He latched himself on. Shit to a blanket. And it didn't matter how big a hint you gave for him to disappear, he just never got it. Or maybe he did get it, but prided himself on ignoring you and hanging in there. Would you stop. In a bit he was going to say that Helle had gorgeous tits and I would tear him limb from limb.

At last, I got a seemingly perfect excuse to jump on my tram because I could see one was going to pull up just as I reached the stop. I stepped up the pace a good bit. Kurt came stomping after me.

'Right. See ya Kurt,' I called as I began to run. He was on the verge of starting a jog beside me. But like an idiot I hit Spitfire speed to get away from him and landed at the stop way before the tram. My brain fried at the thought that he would get to me before I jumped up onto the tram. I walked out into the road as I felt him get up beside me.

'Bet you're trying to get into her knickers as well, eh Janus!?' I heard him say as I jumped up onto the back step.

I turned just in time to see his grinning mug. All red now behind his raised hand. Then the tram took off and I felt such a spluttering rage I couldn't utter a single word back at him. 'Just shut it. Just shut the fuck up Kurt,' I heard my brain say to my head. 'Shut your trap you pathetic swamphead. You dirty dirty little scut.'

As I walked up the stairs to our apartment, a massive thirst came over me. There was nobody in the kitchen, and probably nobody at home, so I let the water run until it was cold as could be. The water tasted good and I stood drinking and thinking until I started to long for my own room and loving being at home and taking a drop of water whenever the fuck I wanted to. We were always walking goddammit. We spent the whole of our lives walking. We walked home from school. We walked when we wanted to talk to each other or were just going somewhere together. It was like we spent the half of our lives footslogging up and down those streets. When we'd sat for long enough in one mate's room, we trudged across town so we could sit in another mate's room.

When I got to my own room, I just stood there for a second inside the door looking at everything. It was a good room. In spite of everything, that lived-in feeling remained there. Still. Quiet. In the air, there were still remnants of my brothers' time. The pipe and fag smoke had bestowed a family aura upon the place that appealed to me. There was a sense of vintage about it all. I mean. When you considered all the cigarette brands that had been fired up here in past times. Flag, Red North State, Lucky Strike and Tory, and then hand-rolled tobacco with Virginia essence. Not to speak of the more sophisticated ones that we now smoked. God knows whether those rascals had even brought girls up here? I'd never picked up that dangerous scent in my room. If Mum had noticed it, the whole room would have been scrubbed and fumigated in a flash. There were some books on my table. I sat down and began to browse through them without taking in a single jot of what was written in them.

Tore and Helle would be back out at hers in Frederiksberg by now. It was a totally weird feeling to be in love with two people at one and the same time. On top of that. One was a girl and one was a boy. The words sounded ridiculous in my head – 'to be in love with them'. Was it not just a case of 'loving' them? Thinking about all this so clearly right that minute made my bones shake and my mind go to jelly. 'Janus Tolne is delighted to announce his forthcoming engagement to Hr. Tore Riemer and Frøken Helle Junkersen.'

I sat there sucking on an empty pipe. From the start, it had been me and Tore the Man. And then Helle. For us to survive, I simply had no choice but to include Helle. Because losing Tore was unthinkable. So it was the two of them. Had to be. And now we were tighter because we had this demon that stalked all three of us – Fru Junkersen, the lioness with the jaw of a rattlesnake. And she had to be fought tooth and nail if our thing was going to succeed at all. Thinking of the sheer power she had made me put the pipe down and start rubbing my hands together very slowly. Kurt was just a snake. A low-life snake but. Fru Junkersen, on the other hand. She was both a snake and a lion with a head raised so high it would be difficult to stamp on it until it was totally crushed. It was my duty to protect them. And definitely this would not be easy. I thought of Helle's eyes widening in fear. And then Tore who was so open and amenable that all his seemingly enormous strength would collapse if he fell victim to a sneak attack, a venomous bite from the fangs of that monster who had beheld him with her hateful stare. Oh yes. I'd seen that hate revealed in all its power when Helle's mother had constantly fed Tore full of leading words that evening. Till he was sat there all full, warm and enthused. Wide open to her as he slipped obliviously into her clutches.

When I lifted my hands from my writing table, the impression of my palms remained there. I was just about to get up to wash my hands when I heard a low whistling from down below. It could only be Tore.

There he was. Standing in the inner courtyard. He came over to me when I opened the back door and we crept upstairs to mine via the kitchen stairs. He was whispering things the whole way up. Humming a tune now and then also. It was only when we got to my room that I saw his glowing face properly. That big, black head had a rapturous glow. As if the huge rush of it all had only really gripped him this night.

'Janus Trainus,' he said as he launched himself onto my bed. 'I'm so completely off my fucking head in love with that girl. She's the most wonderful thing you could ever imagine.

She's just ... I mean. We walked out to hers and I'm telling you mate. We stopped at every fucking street light and kissed like mad things. I've never known the like of it.' He rolled off the bed and down onto the floor. 'You should have seen us man. People staring at us as if we were from the loony bin. And at this time of year!' His voice had reached such a pitch I had to shush him.

'I'll have to make sure she gets out to us more. Sees my mum. So they can get used to each other.' He gave me a look full of radiance, because he knew his mum and Helle would get on really well. He was so certain of his mother. And I was also certain that Fru Riemer would rather die than let Tore know she might be jealous of Helle. Not a chance would she.

Tore just blissed on about all that was wonderful in life. Her. Him. They. But then he goes - 'Strange thing though, Janus. That Fru Junkersen was stood there lurking near that big window. She's nearly always there when we get back to Helle's.'

The idea of this couldn't dampen his joy. He'd got up from the floor and was putting on his coat on. The room was too cramped for him. He had to burst out. So that he could move properly. Swing his arms again.

'See ya, Janus me old mate,' he said. 'And thanks for coming with me to the dance that time.' I followed him to the door of my room and let him out. Then he disappeared down the back staircase. I stayed where I was. Standing there listening to his footsteps. When he had got a good bit down, I heard him stop. From far below came his voice. 'She is just gorgeous. Just fantastic ... Night Janus.'

'Yeah, night mate,' I whispered.

I managed to heave the door back into place without too much noise. My pipe was still there on the table. I got my head in gear, went over to it and began filling it. By now it was one o'clock in the morning and the whole house was quiet. I hadn't even heard the others coming home. The smoke from my pipe drifted slowly upwards and settled under the ceiling, whilst I sat at the table not in the least bothered about going to bed.

Tore's laughter was still clinging to the walls and all around in the room. But gradually, I couldn't help seeing those laughing mouths turning into sneering leering masks.

Why was I a Janus? A real Janus that saw things with a second sight in which everything was skewed and cockeyed? And a second nose that could sniff out all those insane odours that existed in the world? All those different disgusting vapours rising up out of the earth, regardless of where I went?

No doubt it was really only the mad heebie-jeebies that sent ripples of gooseflesh all over me whenever Fru Junkersen came into my mind. But the kind of paranoia she unleashed felt genuine to me. Definitely. She had set her Evil Eye upon Tore. She was a hagwitch. And until she was burned at the stake we would have no peace.

Truth was that you could go round in this world trying to keep a steady gaze or a keep your ear tuned to uplifting things that made life bearable. But be damn certain that in the next second your visions might be swamped by shit, and discordant tones will split your ears asunder.

Chapter 8

In truth, Helle had come as a shock to my whole existence as well. Things feminine were always something you considered from a distance, except your own mother of course. Girls were always deemed to be either slags, bitches or proper ladies, and when you mentioned them and thought about them as girls, there was always something untouchable and out of reach about them.

When Helle became a sudden reality, the explosion was so huge it was difficult afterwards to waft the gunsmoke away. To get your eyes in focus enough to see her clear and true. I don't think the sexual element started for Tore until a long time after he first met her. Loads of other factors about her had to be in place before pure lust. In fact, thinking about it. Sheer get-your-knickers-off lust seemed to be lamed for quite a while after her bombshell appearance. It did kick in though eventually.

But just trying to make out the contours of her person was difficult, because I was forced to accept her without any of the usual opening manoeuvres.

Bit by bit, she emerged through the mist. The aura which had shone around her that night in the sports hall had remained there with more or less the same shimmering intensity. She was a dazzling nymph, because her femininity sent light beams radiating through her skin and bewitched the eyes of anyone who gazed upon her. I was completely bowled over by her. If I had any sexual feelings towards her, they were rarely allowed to burst through in any conscious way. Only in exceptional moments, when she looked at me without seeing me at all, and me feeling her gaze piercing my breast, did those undeniable tightening pangs I felt in my stomach tell their own tale. But that kind of thing only happened in tiny slivers of time when some kind of mental exhaustion buried my conscious knowledge that Tore existed and Helle was his girl.

Other than that. I knew more than anything in this world that Helle was Tore's girl. Right from the moment that Tore met Helle in that pathetic sports hall, I knew that bells were going off all over the place and, ever since then, I had fought to work her out and win her favour, because this was vital if my existence was going to have any kind of legitimacy.

She was a strange girl, because gorgeous girls are nearly always strange and very different. All that tittering awkwardness that scared me with girls was just not present in her. It never had been, I think. It was as if that had been refined away in a previous life.

When she smiled, the aura about her glowed more brightly. But the thing that became even more astounding was the gleam of fear. And I'm talking pure fear. That sometimes shone from her eyes. There was something Fairy Tale about it. Some kind of feeling that a witch had once pronounced a curse upon her that she would, at a predestined age, be turned into a frog, and the old hag was suddenly there in front of her to see the prediction fulfilled. It made Helle weird and mysterious, but at the same time gave me a feeling of being her fellow foster child.

I'm sure Tore had seen this terror himself, and his face would have reacted to it. But it was like he would always emerge from those dark waters again, purged and towering with his proud Red Indian face jutting forward as he bestrode the shoreline. Taking in the clear light rays of the new life that was ahead of him. But me. I was like one of those metals upon which the acid of life's progress etched itself as a set of indelible images. And it was the most base and grotesque experiences that stood out in greatest relief. No doubt Helle had it that way as well.

On the other hand, Helle's fineness of being had the effect of making my own behaviour and speech more refined. She had a particular way of smoothing our rough edges. So that, imperceptibly, we were transformed in her presence. More poised. So our sentences didn't always come flapping out of our mouths like gangling half-starved birds looking for a branch on which to settle. We felt a sense of duty towards her. But at the same time, she bestowed rights and favours upon us that seemed colossal after spending so many years as solitary male animals. It was mainly Tore who got the benefit of all this of course, but I could feel the greatly expanded space to move that she gave me. And the paralysis that usually fell upon me when confronted with the opposite sex fell away.

We formed our own solar system with Helle and Tore as the sun and me as the circling satellite. That's how we were viewed by the rest of the world. And that image was more accurate than anyone could imagine because they really were Sun Gods and my own glow nothing more than a pathetic moon, whose very existence hung upon the continued pulse from their glowing star. The spellbinding force of Helle was magnified, because in truth we didn't know who or what she really was. Sometimes I would go round thinking – Jesus, maybe she's not of this world at all, and simply vanishes into the cosmos as soon as she crosses the threshold of her front door and we could no longer see her. I mean. She had no girl friends. And she'd only vaguely told Tore about her father who was apparently dead or lived abroad. Or maybe it was just Fru Junkersen being so versed in smoke and mirrors and hag spells that she materialised this wonderful being out of thin air so as to tempt us into her lair.

But then, the everyday knockabout Helle we encountered so often turned any doubts about her earthly veracity into some kind of old wives' tale.

All three of us would often meet up on a Sunday and head off on a forest trip. Maybe it was those Sundays just in themselves – long, happy Sundays where everything seemed to go off just right. It was hard to distinguish these trips from each other. But it was like there was always a bit of rain around and a tang in the air. The mornings were always easy as you like and the tram ride carrying an uneventful but wonderful satisfaction with it. All our thoughts on the hours of good companionship ahead of us. On the face of it, the actual journeys were completely meaningless but for us had an almost religious mystique because this was a rendezvous day outside of the run-of-the-mill week. Confirmation we needed each other, even on Sunday, when the rest of the world was in bed breathing zzzs up to the bedroom ceiling or gawping over their lunch. All those rainy November-to-February Sundays when we would meet on the misty platform and wait for the S-train, nudging each other and yapping about the week we just had and about ourselves. The two of them arm in arm and me a step away with my hands behind my back and a slight stoop of my head if I said something funny.

Then the train would arrive and we'd get on board. It was always half empty with just a few bodies carrying potplants all wrapped up in tissue paper. They on their way to Sunday lunch somewhere. We would usually head over into a corner of the train where we could sit opposite each other. The two of them together. Me facing.

Helle was always a little pallid on these mornings. A bit sleep-haunted after the late Saturday spent with Tore. Kissing each other for hours on end. Sunday was the day when she was free of her mother, and now she sat there for a while composing herself with closed eyes as the train thumped its way through the tunnel at Nørreport. The grey ambience beyond the carriage as the train emerged from the tunnel at Østervold would lend a fey colouring to her countenance, and on one occasion I found myself stubbing out my cigarette in the ashtray in case the smoke should upset this delicate being sitting opposite me. By her side sat Tore all big and imposing on his throne and exuding heat beneath his massive scarf that could go round his throat twenty-six times. He always wore his windcheater on our Sunday forest trips and often got soaked through because he refused to wear a raincoat.

We spoke slowly on these train journeys. Just enjoying each other's chat about one thousand trivial things that sometimes made us laugh so much that that dappling of potted plants in the carriage swayed in our gusts and half-awake couples gave a start in their seats. Big clumps of rain came in from Øresund Sound as we got off at Klampenborg station and went down to the platform exit. Then across to the red gateway into the deer forest.

The certainty of the day that was ahead of us. The recurring element. Made these forest trips even more fruitful, because it was like we grew as people as we walked and talked. We always had something to say about the horse-drawn carriages once we were in the deer park itself. Often talking about hiring one for a ride, but we never did. Getting up in a vehicle and lording it like that would have required some really special occasion like passing your student exams or something. And doing that would have also broken our Sunday ritual.

Even the mad arrangement that I had to go all the way to the main railway station to meet them, instead of just getting on at Østerport, formed one of the ceremonies that we performed on Sundays. There would be a kink in the day if we didn't follow the pattern that at some time or other we had mysteriously agreed on as the proper course of events.

We ploughed on through the befogged and dripping beech trees without saying an awful lot to each other. I lay like a destroyer in and around the heart of the convoy. One minute up forward and the next prancing in their wake. We never met anyone we knew on these sodden excursions. We had the world to ourselves. Helle's face was completely at peace, once we had walked for a while, and she would instinctively lean into Tore, who walked by her side linking her elbow and forearm with his own arm. We plashed right through the middle of big puddles without giving it a thought. Because the quiet and sense of fellowship invigorated us, like batteries slowly being recharged.

The route we took invariably led us along the edge of the bare plain, so we couldn't see its full extent, but just followed the road up to the castle. Once at the castle, we stopped and stood there for a while, staring out into the mist. There was a big clump of old snow. I fashioned a snowball in my bare hands and stuck it onto the nipple of one of the reclining sphinxes. We had a laugh about freezing brassieres but then the sloppy snow fell down, and we turned to walk over to one of the main roads – Fortunvejen.

Only now and then did I feel the urge to complain about having to play the gooseberry. But that soon passed because it felt like I was in a church. A place where you have to control any mad outbursts like that. Your thoughts kept on higher things.

At the Fortune coffee house, we shared tea and cakes. The waiter would always come with the tea and cakes in one hand and a particular way of swinging his arm as he served us. This was an obligatory feature of our Sunday tours as well. We steamed like racehorses once we came into the warm and our faces began to glow as we drank our tea. No matter what we got, it was never enough.

Dark settled in again as we completed the rest of the tour. We took the main roadway to Lyngby, a bit more skittish and the onset of a whirring in our legs. Now we sought to stifle thoughts of our impending separation and the Monday morning studies awaiting us. Soon we would all be moving on that shadow side, which had already enveloped Helle. The house in Frederiksberg loomed large with its withered ivy, turrets and spires and a big black window.

We would normally get to Lyngby around 5 o'clock and stood there smoking until the S-train could be heard out on the coastal rail track. When we took our seats, a heavy warmth entered our legs and dragged them to the floor. We sat dull and lethargic, staring out at the myriad shifting lights speeding past the window. Our Sunday walk was already no more than a dream residing somewhere in the body. We turned to face what was ahead of us.

They got off at Hellerup to change to the Frederiksberg train, whilst I stayed on to Østerport. I leaned back in my seat and looked up at them as they got up. Tore taking Helle gently by the arm as she rose. He took his cap from the net overhead and pressed it down over his hair. Then they stood there for a few moments saying goodbye before going out to the corridor as the train entered the station, the noise from the tracks becoming more penetrating in the covered platforms.

Before they disappeared into the other train, they turned and waved to me, but they were never turned to pillars of salt. Just went on and were eaten up in the throng. Uneasy but with a huge sense of being replete in my heart, I could settle back and move on. These Sundays were meant to be alive in precisely this way. Full of deep assurance but ending with a pricking unease at something not having been quite fulfilled, something that cried out for us to try again. Try the same ritual, and still with that hope in our hearts of a miracle that would transform the world. Make it look and feel different.

It's true that Helle was still some sort of stranger in our midst. But on days like this she seemed to act as a stronger coupling between Tore and me. On the occasions when I was bold enough to take her arm, it was like touching Tore at the same time, in an intimate way that otherwise could never have happened. When I got home after our walks, I would sit in a state of distraction and eat Sunday dinner with the old folks, my brothers and sisters-in-law, not taking in much of what was being said. When they asked me whether we'd enjoyed ourselves, I couldn't say either yes or no. Just sat there mumbling into my bumfluff beard and my eldest brother remarking that I could be a right miserable bastard sometimes.

As soon as I was done, I slipped down to my room and sat perusing my books without reading any of them properly. Then I would stagger into bed and sleep like a beast, dreaming about white window ledges flowing with green plants and no flowers, but tropical and steamy as a jungle.

I seldom saw Helle of a weekday. Tore biked it every day to meet her at school and see her home, but otherwise she was curfewed during the week. The door closed behind her and she disappeared like mist into that huge house.

But very occasionally all three of us managed to meet up in town. Say if she had to run an errand, which gave her liberty to be abroad in the afternoon. So we would head for Strøget. And parade around as Tore gave free rein to our secret dream. He strutted off with Helle on his arm, whilst the court jester ran amok. Dancing and prancing by their side, up and down

147

the gutter, in and out between the citizenry, all the time trying to keep step with the Royal Couple ploughing their way through the crowds that parted before the Great Chief's nose.

Helle took to the street atmosphere like a butterfly to summer. She was more beautiful than most of the girls around her and walked with a natural confidence that broke something inside me. She rarely wore anything on her head and whenever they got a few metres in front of me in the jostling crowd, I would see her beacon of golden hair, as if one of God's own sunbeams fell directly upon her crown.

When we had marched up Strøget right from the Town Hall to Kongens Nytorv, back we would go. Wending our way along exactly the same route in reverse. Except on the opposite side of the street.

I had my bike waiting near the Town Hall. And when we got back there we'd start our leave-taking. We could be ages doing this. I'd be standing with my foot on the pedal for the thousandth time and then someone would get some idea to do something and the others had to tear that or this person to shreds, or there was a book in a shop window that we just had to see and so it went until at the very end Helle had to leap onto a tram and the last we'd see of her was that golden head above a green dress disappearing down line six.

We stood there dazed for a bit, me and Tore, staring out into space. Then Tore turned to face reality again and shoved at me and I jumped up on my bike and sped off with my satchel out front on the handlebars.

Sometimes we'd manage to get to a dance together. There was always some kind of school dance going on in gym halls round about, where brutal dance bands sawed away and all the trogs and swamplife thrashed around the room with their more or less presentable *ladies*. I always got stuck with right uggbags that hadn't got beyond the embarrassed tittering phase – the total opposite of Helle and Tore, who only danced with each other. Like a soap bubble gracefully floating over a pot of bubbling stew. I got two dances with Helle.

I held her as if at any second she was going to vanish. Right there in the middle of the dance floor. And then where would us two be left? I was also terrified because it felt like the palm of my hand would simply pass through her elf maiden waist. But then her body scent overwhelmed me. Jesus. I switched my leading dance hand so she wouldn't feel the heat running through me. Tore was stood talking to my dance partner, but every now and again looked away with a distracted air, his gaze scanning the dancing crowd until it found us and a reassured smile lit up his towering head. Me and Helle got roped into one of those appalling family dances where you were made to dance with all kinds of woeful *bella donnas*, and she was gone from my side. Tore strode across the floor and joined the line on the men's side. Then the band struck up Laurel and Hardy, and we all started shambling around like a herd of wildebeest. The music stopped abruptly and even though Tore stood at least four *donnas* away from Helle, he brazened his way over to her and gave the subtlest of shoves to the young hopeful who was just about to bow to Helle. I swear she never even saw the little tyke in front of her. Just settled in with Tore like a bird alighting on a familiar branch and easing itself into its favourite position. I tramped round with this total virgin in a ridiculously lilac confirmation dress, sending despairing looks over to Tore who had his head cocked slightly to one side. The perfect angle, I knew, for him to take in the scent from Helle's hair. He signalled back his sympathy for me.

In the time just after Tore had met Helle he went into himself a little bit. Not that he went cold or distant on me or anything like that. More that the pace of his exponential advancement at school was moderated. Sure he was still the undisputed leader of the pack, but now as the most adult and mature head amongst us. Now we looked to him and leaned up against him, basking in his Olympian radiance. He was now the man who not so much assumed the role of leader but quite simply flowed into that position borne by the collective will of the rest.

Helle had done this. She it was who had led him to that point without any conscious effort on her part. But her magic aura, as powerfully bright as her mother's was ferociously dark, had finessed Tore and made his own magnificence even more startling.

It was seldom I had Helle all to myself. After all I only really saw her when she was with Tore. But one evening, one of those golden Saturday evenings, they were both supposed to be coming over to me because I had got hold of some red wine and then bought more on top of that. At half eight, the doorbell rang and sure enough it was Helle. But without Tore. It was obvious that I was looking for his big Red Indian head but it wasn't there and she laughed at me, because I looked like a total idiot. I finally managed to pull myself together and hauled her inside.

'Er, where's Tore then?' I asked like a first-class dope.

'He's on the way,' she said. 'But he's a bit delayed.'

'Ah right,' says I, so intelligently.

As she eased out of her coat, she said: 'He was balancing on the edge of Dragon Fountain at the Town Hall as we were going across the square to get the tram to here and didn't he take a nosedive into the water.' She burst out laughing whilst I stood there. I mean. I just stood there gormless and open-mouthed but beginning to see the scene unfold in my head.

'Janus, you should have seen it. I mean the state of him.' At which point she bent over with laughter and I saw a part of her bare back beyond her hairline.

'He was in water up to his neck. Lying there like a dying fish. The big lunatic.'

We both set off laughing and my mum came out into the hall and asked what had happened.

Between suppressed bursts of laughter Helle managed to blurt out a 'Hello Mrs Tolne' and stammer out an explanation for the hilarity.

'Oh dear dear. Oh that's terrible,' my mother said. This was her time-honoured response to things like this, perfected over many years of marriage to my father.

'And now he's off home to dry out and get changed,' said Helle. As we went down below to me, she explained how it happened. They were walking across Town Hall square and Tore spots a lonesome pigeon flying overhead. He decides he's going to capture it and present it to her as a symbol of his undying love. When capture of the bird proves impossible, he becomes determined to demonstrate his passion in some other way. It was then that he jumped up on the edge of the fountain, much to the consternation of the people in the queue for the bus to Amager. With both hands sticking out like a tightrope walker and singing at the top of his voice, he began to walk around the edge of the basin, but just as he was negotiating one of the large sea monsters that grip the edge and spout water inwards, he stumbled and ditched like a gunned-down Stuka dive-bomber headfirst into the fountain. All the people in the square were stunned and unsure how to react. The whole escapade had looked really dangerous and the chances of broken bones were high. But then the Red Indian emerges with his hands aloft. Like a world champion acknowledging the acclaim of the crowd. He was sopping wet and clambered unaided over the edge of the fountain and down next to Helle. She was furious. The shock of it had made her furious, and she had sent him home to change his clothes. His misery knew no bounds when he saw her reaction. But he took off straight away, his shoes squelching and his soaking trousers flapping after him. Helle got the tram out to Janus on her own, so that he wouldn't be sitting there by himself wondering what to do with all that red wine. As something of a punishment for Tore also. But now she was laughing about it till her body shook.

I had brought one of the good chairs from the living room into my room and showed Helle to her seat, whilst I sat on my desk chair. Then, when we had done with joking and laughing and fell to ordinary chat, we finally noticed that we were alone together for the first time in our lives.

She was wearing a light grey skirt and a red jumper with buttons at the back.

Helle took the hiatus with ease but obviously noticed that I sat there all awkward and squirming inside.

'A cigarette would be nice, Janus?' she said.

I sprang up and began to rummage and fumble all over the room and of course completely forgot that I'd bought a packet and set them on the table so my guests could smoke.

She'd already taken one from the packet and I fumbled some more in getting it lit.

I took a cigarette myself and the break in conversation intensified as I lit my own.

'How's your mum?' I asked in the stunning way that only I can.

A little shadow flickered between us and hovered there for a second before disappearing, and Helle replied smoothly that her mother was fine thank you.

We smoked a bit more in silence. I went across and turned on my little wireless, even though I knew Tore would hate it being on when he came. He hated radios playing when we were supposed to be talking.

To confirm my ability to be a first-class idiot, I ploughed on down the same route.

'I think your mum really likes Tore,' says I. Helle looked straight at me.

'Do you think so?' she said. Her face was completely open, but just as quickly as those hopeful words had flown from her mouth, her face turned to stone.

It was a weirdly stilted and old-fashioned conversation for us to have as well. But the genie was now well and truly out of the bottle and hung there. Shaking the air. Like trouble looking for just the right spot to hit home.

All words were useless anyway, because deep inside we both knew very well that where Fru Junkersen was concerned liking or not liking didn't come into it. Fru Junkersen was not blessed with likes and dislikes. She just conquered and that was it. And what she couldn't conquer she despised.

The aftershock of delight in Helle's eyes at the thought of Tore's drenching in the Town Hall fountain was gone. Instead, you just saw this angst pulsing behind her pupils somewhere like a vague, threatening glow. The golden aura from her hair became tarnished and, for a moment, the colour in her face disappeared altogether. I felt that my legs had been knocked from under me and I was free falling in the dark void of an awareness, on both our parts, of a malignant force in our universe that we neither could hold in check nor even properly understand. This gave us once again a sense of being a cursed fellowship. Our gaze met briefly across that space, but I looked away and began like a mad mental thing to mess with glasses and the bottle of Chianti I'd been given. I'd already taken out the cork to let the wine breathe but stood there now trying to put it back and then taking it out. In out in out for an eternity, whilst the smoke from my cigarette streamed into my face and tears formed in the corner of my eyes.

The atmosphere in the room was at breaking point. But release came when Tore rang the doorbell soon after and he bowled into my room gesticulating wildly and wearing a blue suit, which he hated and never ever wore.

'I've just come from a confirmation ceremony,' he roared with joy. 'The occasion was held at the dragon fountain in Town Hall Square, but I dropped my precious amber cigarette holder, a traditional gift at these celebrations as you both know, so I had to damn well dive in for it. I found it, much to the relief of the local populace who carried me all the way out here in a golden sedan chair as a token of their gratitude!' He strode across the room and embraced Helle. Then he sat down on her lap and roared aloud: 'Red wine, Janus. Red wine my man. Buckets of it!'

Chapter 9

Following my first, ahem, real sexual experience (yeah, yeah, stuff it where the sun don't shine!), things started to move at a quicker pace, you might say. I occasionally managed to get relief here and there, but mainly with slagheaps you wouldn't normally be seen dead with. But I was still spending most of my time with Tore and Helle. Sometimes, it felt to me like the whole thing was a bit too precious. Sometimes I felt like screaming – 'For fuck sake! Enough of this goddamn tea drinking and talk talk. Time to get down to it. I mean. Jesus guys, get cracking!' But the whole thing was gnawing at me anyway if I'm honest, because I had nobody I could walk up and down Strøget with.

We would often sit together over at Tore's on a Saturday afternoon, having a laugh, listening to the radio and letting everything just go in one ear and out the other. It was a brilliant way of putting your existence on hold, but at the same time living in a way that had life whooshing past your ears. We could totally disappear into the upper realms of sheer delight by talking about one little thing and then building it up so that it took on the dimensions of a fantastic hot air balloon of nuttiness. When one of us said something that got the other two laughing, someone else would quickly come with a top-up, and so we would go on egging each other on to kingdom come. 'Weekend Miscellany' on the wireless droned and clapped in the background with soloists from Iceland and doleful men who were forced to tell of their doleful experiences on woeful trips to weird places like Venezuela.

Fru Riemer's tea trays would appear from nowhere and we'd

be at them like a shot. Ravenous and greedy as thieves. These tea tray rituals were our form of orgy. Momentarily easing our unconsummated hunger for something else entirely. These were our oblivious days in our own little *Shangri-La*.

We always sat in the same spot – around a broad-brimmed hanging lamp in a corner of her artist's studio, bathed by a corona of light, which clearly marked the line in the room where brightness gave way to murk and where Fru Riemer's figures stood like frozen sleepwalkers. The wireless was placed on a shelf beneath the big window and was so far away from us that when it was switched on, none of us could be bothered to go over and turn it off again. We would often wake up to the world around us at such a late hour that the wireless was just buzzing and humming to itself. The presenter and musicians having packed their bags and gone home long ago. Just like small children who can abruptly fall asleep in mid-bawl, we could conk out slap bang in the middle of the most animated of conversations. It was not uncommon for me to wake again and see Tore and Helle sitting on the sofa opposite me holding hands, with Fru Riemer having gone to bed aeons ago. Then that massive irritation would come over me once again. They'd petted and pawed at each other for so long now that something would have to break pretty soon, or the whole thing would descend into little more than the romantic potboiler stuff you get in those women's magazines.

I got up and went over to the big window. I felt in the small of my back that the two of them barely registered me. You couldn't see the street down there through the window. Just feel a vague hum whenever a car went by. It was a lunatic sensation to be standing there in Fru Riemer's studio feeling lonely. I mean. I'd been living there for a thousand years and knew the odour of dry clay and all those colours. As if I'd made them myself. I'd known Tore for a thousand million years as well. Right from when we'd been in first year together. So it was lunatic. Standing here feeling lonely. And on top of that, I'd done far more than him. I mean. I'd done it. The whole way. I half turned towards them and went to shout something at them, but saw that they were snogging. Best to get home, I said to myself. A light went on in one of the windows across the way. So I hung there for a bit to see if anything exciting came into view. But it was just a doddery old gent, walking round in his braces and picking up newspapers. So here I was. Suspended here. Some place in mid-air between an old codger going round tidying newspapers and those two sat there kissing on the sofa. So maybe feeling lonely was not so strange after all. On the other hand. Nobody had claims on my time. I was king of my own castle. But what good was that?

The light across the way went off. I'd forgotten to keep my eye on what the old fella did next. I bet he's lying over there now staring up into the black void, unable to sleep. Poor granddad.

'Right, time to make tracks, oh castle king,' says I to myself. 'Home-time.'

I turned quickly enough to see a hand disappearing from a place that I sometimes managed to reach when I got hold of a girl. Tore rolled backwards off the sofa and looked up at me. This huge specimen of overgrown youth.

'Right mate,' I said. But I just stood there lurking. A skewed smile on my face. He knew by looking at me that I wasn't exactly shouting halleluiahs at the way things were. But he refused to acknowledge it. He had too many other things on his plate.

'Sit down, trog features,' said Tore.

'Nah mate. I'm gonna get home. Right now.'

'Why are you going home now?'

Ha! Ha! Ha! 'Why head home now?' Because there's fuck all entertainment for me here. Is there?!

I sat down on the corner of the sofa near Helle.

She looked up at me. 'Do you know what you're gonna do tomorrow?'

I stared down at her. 'Haven't a clue.'

'Well, I'll tell you what you're going to do,' says she after a pause. 'You're going on a country tour with your aunty Helle.'

'My sister-in-law Helle. Please,' I admonished.

I goes to myself – 'So I'm going for a spin out in the country with you two and the poisoned Sphinx? Well fuck me. Fuck me stiff. Or is it just us three maybe? So is something finally going to happen? Is tomorrow the day? Am I going to play chaperone and sole witness to the crucial deed?'

'My mother asked if we'd all like to go to our house in the country. She'll drive us out there herself.'

'Well that takes the biscuit,' I said. 'Count me in.'

'So good of you to grace us with your presence,' said Tore. He was still stretched out on the sofa.

'But you'd need to be rising at cock crow, Meister Janus.'

'Yes indeed. Hardly *plaisant*,' I lisped. Not too far from us, the Town Hall clock clanged out the hour. Strange that they'd not said anything about this before. Maybe they thought I wouldn't be keen and had to be jumped with it at the last minute. So I was going to be sat up front next to Fru Junkersen, tearing up the coast road in that grey BMW.

Cool or what! At last there was some action again. A thrill went through me and I could literally feel my almost dead batteries getting a kick.

'We were supposed to be up there this weekend, but mum was invited out somewhere. That's why we haven't said anything until we knew for definite,' said Helle.

OK. Maybe not a perfect situation with dragon-features being there but still – maybe something could finally go off.

Tore sat there filling his pipe.

'I'll see you home,' he said. As if there was otherwise some goddamn doubt about this.

I lifted my coat off the chair and moved towards the hall. The two of them came after me.

'I'll bring my swimming trunks,' says I, trying to stop my teeth from chattering at the very thought.

This was the month of May.

'My hero!' Tore pants behind me.

This was more like it. The three of us on a great jolly up country. And stuff that old hag anyway. As long as she can manage to drive us up there without crashing into some telephone pole.

'All for one, and one for all,' I roared, as I jumped down the indoor stairwell, nearly breaking my neck because the light went out with a PLOP.

'SSSHHHHH!' said Helle.

'Darling, je vous aime beaucoup,' Tore crooned somewhere in the pitch black.

'Be quiet on the stairs, you two,' the young Vestal Virgin protested.

I stood at the bottom and with a *chevaleresque* flourish opened the door onto the street for my Lord and Lady. 'Your carriage awaits,' I cried, bowing deeply.

They launched out onto the street arm in arm as a taxi rolled by. Tore went right out to the edge of the pavement and pretended he was opening the door to a coach and horses, grovelling and scraping, he held his hand out to Helle, who with her left hand lifted her voluminous skirts and stepped into the carriage. A nod from Tore and I sprang forward to take up the reins. Then a practised appraisal of my four trusty steeds snorting and straining to get the coach away. '*En avant*!' Tore bellowed, and then us firing down the empty street as the world and his wife wriggled and turned over in bed cursing them bleedin hooligans and all their bloody commotion again.

We stood totally jiggered at a street corner, panting like wild horses. Helle looked simply gorgeous in that breathless state. I looked and looked. Milady. She was Milady personified. All right. A sweet, innocent version of Milady de Winter. Because she can't be a spy for Cardinal Richelieu like in the Musketeers. No chance. Tore a Danish Mohican Indian and Helle his Danish Milady. And me? I'm a Danish d'Artagnan. A commoner but with my feather hat cocked and musket primed. Ready to split any Rochefort or Richelieu that comes within a hundred paces of my Lady and Liege. Come out from the shadows ye cowardly poltroons and I'll blast your skulls for yez. For this is my bailiwick and none shall pass without my say-so!

'What's the actual time of departure tomorrow then?' I asked Helle.

'We're heading off at eight thirty from my place,' she said. 'Mum wants you and Tore there at quarter past eight, so we can get away right on the half hour.'

'Off to bed with you then, Hit Man,' said Tore sternly.

'Yes boss,' I replied.

I patted the breast of my jacket just below my upper arm with a conspiratorial look. As if wishing to ensure that my revolver was securely stowed.

'Got enough ammo?' my boss asked.

'Full clip, boss,' I replied.

'Ah, you two are off your rockers,' said Helle, who at first was not quite sure what was going on.

'Keep your trap shut, woman,' Tore says to her.

'Want me to fix her, boss?'

Tore gives a brief nod, and I swoop on Helle and pin her arms behind her back. I hold both her hands together with just one hand and put my other arm round her neck. Tore goes up to her and pretends to slap her across the face with the flat of his hand. Three, four times. Meanwhile I kept a firm grip on her. People going past began to stare. Then Helle dug her heel right into my shin and I jumped as high as a kite.

'Ow! That's not in the script, you witch,' I cried with no little venom. Tore just jumped about like an ape, laughing his head off.

Then we stole away into the night. We were talked out for that evening. Thoughts of what was to come that very next morning had unleashed a massive energy ball. Now those two had to sort the rest out. In truth, I felt not a pang of jealousy right that minute. I was heading home to my bed and as soon as I woke in the morning something new was going to break out. I mean. Right from when I got up. The next day promised a million possibilities. There was Tore and Helle together in a large forest. There was Fru Junkersen behind her steering wheel in the grey BMW and me sitting next to her up front. All of us up there in a new place I'd never set eyes on before, but still felt I knew in a way because Helle had spoken so often about it.

We stopped at Frascati's Corner where the tram terminus is and mumbled our farewells. The last tram was about to depart. The two lovers were in each other's arms again. 'A two-headed animal,' was the first thing that came into my mind. 'Him and her nosing through this soft May evening. On the way to cascades of virtuous kisses up against billboards and street lamps, and serenaded by the quiet song of dreamy cars sissing by on the asphalt.'

'Friends, Romans, Countrymen, I bid you good night. Number fourteen leaves pretty soon,' says I, as I set off walking.

'See you tomorrow, Janus,' Helle called. Tore had already started swinging her round and steering her in the direction of Frederiksberg.

'Night, gangster,' he said. Truly, his hugeness was amazing to behold.

I cut across the square that struck me as being sedate and a bit provincial, with its red lantern signalling the departure of the last tram of the day. The hands on the clock seemed almost petrified. Like someone just about to dive into a lake but sticking a toe in first to check the temperature. It stood on the brink of half-past twelve.

My fatherly feelings towards the other two had evaporated. The sense of loneliness I felt was more real to me. I was on my Jack again now and just going home on the usual fucking number fourteen tram to Østerbro. But tomorrow my man! Tomorrow things would take off again.

Bell cords were pulled by a million and one tram conductors and soon all the trams were in motion. Like you would think they were fairground Dodgem cars going to smash into each other at each road junction but nothing happened.

I'd just pulled out my wallet and was stood there near the back of the tram rooting after change for a single ticket when I saw a couple scampering after the tram. Like their life depended on it. I kept an eye on them, like you do, to see if they would make it. Not turning to stare at them. Just glancing back over my shoulder. They ran like charging bulls, with their heads lowered, especially the man. But just as they were about to leap onto the back platform, your man raised his face. So close to me now that I could almost have eaten it as he jumped. It was that fella Poul.

He recognised me straight away, but just turned his back

to me and heaved the woman aboard. My heart beat like bats out of hell beneath my jacket. As if it was me that had run for the tram and not him. What was this cretin doing on the number fourteen? He was standing right next to me and even though I avoided looking at him, I still got a far better idea of him than the last time, which had been more like a heap of mad shapes being flung into the air. He was quite stocky, and tall as well. His hair was very blond and exaggerated the red in his face, especially after he had busted his gut running for the tram. Jeez. You had to admit he was quite handsome. His girl was a bit of a mixed bag. But she was tall as well and had a good chassis on her. But Fru Riemer? I mean. How the fuck did she end up marrying this balloon and taking off to Ålborg with him? Was it just a case of him being really really good at doing it? I'd never connected Tore's mum with anything like that. And that thing with some being able to do it better than others. What was all that about? I mean. Chrissakes. There couldn't be that many ways of going at it? But yes. For the right people. There were all kinds of possibilities. Helle and Tore could do amazing things together. They had to get it done properly and without any further hanging around. I just knew they were meant for it.

I turned to stare right at this Poul fella who was pushing his bird further into the tram. He could get more of what he got before, that dickhead – a smack in the nose.

'All for one and one for all!' I cried to myself. Then I remembered how that night ended, after we had met Poul. No denying a bomb went off that night. Whoa. Things moved. Something big happened all right. My guts tightened and a fire went through me like molten lava spilling out over the crater from pure excitement. I had totally forgotten about tomorrow. No denying that loads of things were on the cards for tomorrow as well. And I'd forgotten to ponder all this because that Poul fella had jumped on the number fourteen.

In a few hours I'd be pulling my bike out and off with me to La-De-Da Land in Frederiksberg. Then I'll park the bike at the kerbside, walk through the gate and right up to the house. I ring the bell. If Tore has already arrived, he'll open the door.

If he's not there yet, either Helle or the maid will. No. That girl will probably have a day off because *Madam* is going to the countryside. So Helle opens the door. Fru Junkersen wouldn't dream of doing so. But I still have to go in to her to say hello. She, of course, is busy organising something or other. I let her have my film star smile when I greet her. Thank you so much for letting me come as well. But I'll say something smarter than that. She says hello Janus and turns back to her packing or whatever, whilst Tore stands back a bit. Them two rubbing up against each other. In the most discreet way possible of course.

The movie running in my mind was interrupted because I noticed this Poul guy looking at me via the reflection in the window. I sensed no danger from him here in the tram. He was also completely sober. But it was not a nice feeling. I knew so much about him. It was if I'd been following him and he'd found me out. Him and Tore's mum had been naked in bed together and he'd smacked Tore in the face. And here he was now. Standing there in the number fourteen tram with a jacket and tie and some slag on his arm that I didn't know from Adam. I felt a great urge to give him the finger and then run like fuck. But I was too old for that kind of stuff.

I kept an eye on him, right till they got off at Little Triangle. He marched off across the road with the doll. As the tram set off again, he turned and stared back in my direction. His eyes shot at me like two chameleon tongues snaking out and sticking to the window just in front of my face.

The tram rattled onwards and I turned to look out across Sortedam lake, which was as black as its name. That Poul. He was a like a vampire appearing in the night. By rights he should have just vanished into the black air across the lake instead of walking down Classensgade like any other normal human being. He should have had huge dark wings. Up into the air with his white hair and red face. Way out over the lake and begone with him forever that fucking ratbag.

But it was a good feeling to get off at my stop and walk the last bit home. It was always unbelievably quiet and peaceful in my street at that hour of night. That slight hum you could hear must come from all those hundreds of breathing mouths and noses snoring away behind those walls. I longed for my bed. I was going to dive under that duvet, pull it up over my head and sleep. But no more than a second will have passed, then it would be light and I'll be up and making tracks.

The hum in the street was brought home to me when I opened the hall door. Dad's zed drones were barely dampened, even after travelling through several closed doors. 'You get the best relaxing sleep of all after a few beers for a nightcap,' he would often say. Tonight it sounded like he'd swallowed the beer bottle as well.

The window in my room hadn't been open all day and the sun had shone in right through the afternoon; so the place carried an air of heat and dust and the scent of all those weird objects I'd thrown together during my time there. But it was a lovely welcome back. For once it felt like a real homecoming.

I was down under the covers in seconds and pushed out my legs and toes. So that I could touch as much of my bed as possible in one mighty stretch. Night, Call me Inger! Night, Helle! Night, Tore! Night, Poul, you fucking vampire you!

It proved to be a really restless night, where one minute I was running after trams and then trying to kiss that woman who was with Poul in the tram. In my last dream, Fru Junkersen was waiting for me down in the street, blowing her horn. I jumps out of bed and throws on my clothes in a panic so as not to keep her waiting. I tried to call down to her that I was nearly ready and not to leave without me but the words wouldn't come out.

I finally managed to wake up out of my dreamstate. It was bright in my room and it was twenty past four. Everything was clear and concentrated in my head, and I wanted to cry, because I knew I would never get back to sleep. A second later I was asleep again.

My alarm clock goes off like a grenade sending piercing hammer blows into my brain, and I dive over it as if trying to save a whole company of soldiers from death by sacrificing my own life. My head felt as heavy as a medicine ball. So I staggered out to the bathroom and stuck my skull under the shower. It was ten past seven. The time I would normally be getting ready for school. But the tap was singing its Sunday chorus, and with the rush of water my elation came right back. Hahah! The night was survived and just lay there now, shrivelled to a tiny pea pod under the mattress. Now things were going to happen. I checked myself in the mirror and smiled at the beginnings of a suntan, as I knew it suited me. Janus Tolne looked a bit more grown up with a tan. I made sure my underwear and shirt were clean and fresh. I chose my tie judiciously and knotted it with extreme care in a Be-Bop knot – the wide manly knot. Then I brushed and combed my hair with enthusiasm and precision.

None of the old ones were up yet. I had the whole ship to myself. There was no need to go out for fresh bread, but the morning paper was jammed in the letter box, as fat and gorgeous as only the Sunday paper can be. Dad's snoring had become reduced to an amiable morning wheeze that paused for a moment when I pulled the newspaper out of the letterbox. I lifted up the paper and sniffed at it.

With obsessive precision, I dug a hole in my bowl of oats and filled it with sugar. I poured in the milk from the litre bottle without shaking it first, so that all the cream landed good and fat onto the oats. Then I scattered more sugar on top. With the newspaper on my left and my spoon in my right hand, I ate my fill.

It was fourteen minutes past eight when I swung into Helle's road on my bike. I had set my watch by the Town Hall clock. The road and all its expensive villas looked weird in this different light. I'd never been there at this time of day before. The garage port was open and the grey BMW had been brought out. The folding roof was down, and the long low vehicle with its buffalo leather interior and trimmings was truly wondrous to behold. The boot at the back was open as well and half full with all sorts of bags and luggage. Helle emerged from the house as I was leaning the bike up against the kerb. She had her arms full of badminton rackets and balls and God knows what else. She was showing off her legs like I'd never seen them before and her hair was bound up in a short headscarf. I quickly got my brain in gear to avoid falling into a trance and said loads of hellos and lovely mornings and here let me help you and so on.

Tore's big billy-goat bike was already parked in the road and I could hear him somewhere inside talking to Fru Junkersen. They came out of the front door together. Tore just a few steps behind Madam herself who gave you stars like a boxing glove in your face when you looked at her. She must have got up at three in the morning to look like that. She was surrounded by a kind of electrically charged mist, which I nearly knew the name of but couldn't quite put my finger on that second. Tore seemed oblivious to it and spoke to her in his usual way – showing interest, engagement, but with all his real attention on Helle. Both of them said hello and I looked a total gawp when I bowed my head slightly to Fru Junkersen. She looked straight at me and said something quick that lamed me like a snake bite. There were still a few small things to be put in the car. I hauled some boxes out with bed linen in them. Did I actually smell or just imagine a scent of secrets arising from the bedclothes? But I dismissed these thoughts as I could feel my imagination starting to run wild. Fru Junkersen was stood leaning against the car door when I emerged from beneath the lid of the boot. I couldn't help staring at her breasts. She was unbelievable. She had to be getting on for forty-five.

The maid came out onto the front steps and asked if Madam needed anything else. But no, there was nothing else. As if by silent agreement, Helle and Tore sat together in the back seat, whilst I glided into the smooth seat up front with the great and terrible Sphinx.

I revelled in Fru Junkersen's expert movements as she started the car. It responded to the ignition with an instantaneous roar and revved up like a mad thing as Madam's high-heeled shoe shoved down at the accelerator. Helle had, at some point or other, mentioned that this BMW had a specially built racer motor, and it seemed she was right. It pulsed through my body and I just had to fire a quick glance back to Tore. Ah would you stop! It was delicious to just go with the flow and let yourself be totally swept up in this upper-class lifestyle. Fru Junkersen depressed the clutch and put the car in reverse. Then we rolled out down the road and were soon bombing down Falkonerallé en route to the coast road.

The conversation was all put on and blasé don't you know. Even though, in truth, what I really wanted to do was stand up in that goddamn car and shout and yeehah yahoo because the whole thing was so totally pure dead brilliant. The sun gleamed on the leather, whose smell was now even more intoxicating, mingled as it was with the scent of these two women. So powerful that it lashed your senses. In third gear, the car's acceleration roar transformed to a low solid hum, which was its superior way of letting the world know it was still only playing, even though we were now doing about ninety on the coast road. Fru Junkersen never stopped overtaking. Waiting behind other cars? Not for her. No No.

I noticed that she kept a careful eye on Tore and Helle via the rear-view mirror, and the summer day paled a touch. It was also maybe a bit chilly. Us whistling along in an open car in the month of May. I flinched and shuddered slightly in my tweed jacket. Madam Sphinx continued to keep one of her eyes on the rearview mirror at the same time as she overtook other cars in the most lunatic way. I turned around and started talking to the pair in the back. Just like all our other days together, this was a day for them as well and I had to play my part to make sure that happened. Helle's head scarf flapped in the wind and she narrowed her eyes slightly against the constant blast and the bright reflection from the water by the coast. Tore straightened up in his seat and with his hand lifting an imaginary top hat, acknowledged the bowing and curtseying of the commoners we passed along the way. The Emperor and Empress on tour through their empire with a Sphinx as private chauffeur and Janus Tolne as escort.

'Do you want to put this on, young man?' Fru Junkersen asked me as she pulled a leather motoring helmet from the glove compartment. There was a hint of scorn in her eyes, or maybe that was just my fancy. I accepted the dead smart helmet with my best smile, put it on my head and fastened the strap under my chin. What a shame nobody had a camera to record this special moment.

The car simply devoured petrol and the road, spewing both after it in long streamers. Fru Junkersen's hands in her white gloves were resting supremely at the top of the steering wheel. I bent forward slightly towards the windscreen and watched the road throwing itself under the car at blinding speed.

The car's wild animal roar came back a few times as we drove through Helsingør and had to drop down to second. But north of the town we started bombing once again. In between two small villages, Fru Junkersen turned right and drove along an unmarked track, which led through some trees down to the seashore. Then, when we had passed through the thickest part of a clump of spruce trees, the landscape opened up again and a house came into view. A house that stood in stark contrast to the Sleeping Beauty castle in royal Frederiksberg. This summer house was in Spanish hacienda style with an elegant sun terrace looking out to sea. The terrace also featured an enclosed patio area with floor tiles, which could just be glimpsed through some window frames that were devoid of glass. Fru Junkersen parked the car outside the garage, which was completely covered in clematis. The air was heady and full of salt tang. You only got its full effect once all movement had stopped and the emerging quiet gave you the chance to sense things other than mad speed, buffalo leather and white gloves on a padded yellow steering wheel. With a measured elegance, I removed my white motoring helmet.

The gravel path gave an auspicious crunch as we walked up to the house. Fru Junkersen walked ahead carrying her keys. We followed at an appropriate distance. Tore and Helle walked apart from each other.

'Wow. This is a gorgeous place,' said Tore. He did a half turn and nodded at the sea. 'Are you going in, Janus?'

'Brrrrrhh!' says I. 'Looks a bit nippy, doesn't it mate?'

Helle goes – 'No. No. No. There's no way in hell you are going in that water. Are you mad? It can't be any more than eight degrees or something.' She shivered as she spoke.

This was a challenge. I stared across at Tore. 'No harm in dipping our toes in,' I replied.

Fru Junkersen had opened the house door and the strong smell of a long closed summer house streamed out to us. A smell redolent of embalmed sunshine. Helle wafted past and proceeded to pull up the window blinds in a wonderful room that looked out onto the sun terrace and the sea. She shoved the French doors back and the wind from the sea blew in across the floor and sunshine flooded the room. By way of the kitchen, you got to an enclosed courtyard that was being warmed close to summer temperatures by the sun overhead.

We emptied the car and brought everything into the house. The others went before me with all their paraphernalia. This gave me a chance when I was left on my own to bend right down and put my nose against the rilled leather of the front seat.

Hunger pangs were already attacking me as I went back to the house. But it was only half ten, so there was a while to go before lunch. Helle had taken off her headscarf and her hair was all fuzzed upwards. Tore was rooting through a stack of gramophone records.

'Is there anything else you want me to do, mum?' Helle asked. Her mother was out in the kitchen.

'No, you can all go for a walk or something. But be back for twelve to help me prepare lunch,' she called.

'Playtime at school,' I thought to myself.

'Well. Shall we?' Tore asked.

I looked at him with a question mark face.

'Shall we dip our toes in it?'

Being honest. My bones rattled at the very thought of it. Like ice going down my back. But there was no way out. I could feel my skin blanching under my shirt.

'No. Come on lads. Stop acting daft,' said Helle.

'Think we're pansies or something?' says I, and Tore burst out laughing. Then he shot off for his swimming trunks.

'Where can we get changed?' he asked.

'No. You're not allowed to go in,' said Helle. 'You're just not and I mean it.'

'Ah now… Now it's you that's being daft, Helle,' says I. She looked almost angrily at me.

'The two of you are just being total idiots!' she cried.

'They can decide for themselves if they want to swim or not.' The hooded hydra was stood at the door ready to bite. Her smile was no smile at all.

Helle turned sharply to face her. Then she turned to Tore. I stood nearly frozen to the spot but Tore gave Helle his best Clark Gable look.

'Let's do it!' he beamed.

I fished out my own swimming trunks and the towel from my bag. Then I followed Tore and Helle. We were to get changed upstairs.

Up above there was one big bedroom and three smaller rooms. They all seemed very well equipped, with solid beds and mattresses. Me and Tore got changed and Helle went downstairs to wait for us. We could see the sea from the window. It looked summer blue on top, winter blue beneath.

The Red Indian's body was just as brown as his face but I looked like a sick asparagus by comparison. The beach wimp. Sand kicked in his face.

We plodded down the stairs and into the sitting room where Helle was bent over a suitcase, fussing at various things. She didn't turn when we entered.

'Aren't you coming with us, Helle?' Tore asked.

She gave no answer.

'The Queen does not wish to observe her Musketeers making a watery spectacle of themselves. *Enfin, d'Artagnan mon ami*, we must go alone,' he said.

We marched out of the room, letting on we were a flock of ducks waddling in the forest.

It was bone-shakingly cold outside and I wrapped my towel around my shoulders to try and stem the onset of pneumonia. Then we went mental and bombed it down to the sea.

A jetty went out to where the water was deep enough to bathe. So we had no choice but to go out to it. I turned around for one last forlorn look at the warm, living world before launching myself into the arctic sea. I swear. I caught a glimpse of a female figure in the big bedroom on the first floor. Helle was nowhere to be seen. Then I just went with the inevitable and turned to go after Tore, who was already whoohooing and splashing about in the pack ice.

The water smacked my forehead like a baseball bat driving a block of ice into my skull and in fractions of a second a paralysing frostbite spread through the rest of my body. Toe cramp. Heart cramp. Jaw cramp. 'This must be the way it is - death,' said my brain. My windpipe refused to function, once I'd got my head above water. Only after the second try, when I came up for air again, did I manage to get some air in me. I flapped and splashed like an electrocuted frog and finally managed to get to the jetty where Tore stood shaking like a hunting dog.

We said nothing to each other. We couldn't. Just smiling like village idiots through chattering teeth and then tearing down the jetty and along the beach, which was far too stony for a barefoot race. Just as well our feet were numb. We were running that fast it felt like I'd left my body a few steps behind me and I was nothing but heaving breath, then a warmth that gradually bloomed and returned my lamed body to its physical shape. Tore was ahead of me, but now he turned and we raced back for the towels that were back at the start of the jetty.

'Fucking hell, man. Madness. Total fucking madness,' I muttered. I was still quivering like a cocktail shaker full of ice. 'That is just the coldest ever. No argument.'

'We're going in again after lunch. All right mate?' said Tore with a massive grin.

I made do with waving my numb forefinger from side to side in front of his face to show my thoughts on that idea.

The water and cold had scoured all trace of perfume from my nose. I think both of us had actually forgotten where we were and why we were there. It was just the two of us. Like back at the start. In the good old days. Sharing a happening, an experience, that was ours and ours alone. We'd been in the water together for the first time that summer. And even if we'd never done anything like that before, it was still somehow right for the way we did things – our own way. Our towels chafed and scourged across our backs, till we looked like two boiled crabs.

The water glugged below us at the jetty. All withdrawn and self-aware. Like it knew it had ambushed us. But its surface calm gave nothing away. It was just there. Deceptive blue and ice-cold.

Then we sloshed our way back to the house. I felt a rising apprehension. As if I'd done something that wasn't allowed. Tore bounced along all sprightly. Relaxed after his dip.

Helle appeared in the doorway when we got to the sun terrace. She shaded her eyes with her hand to get a good look at us. And couldn't stop a bit of a smile from lighting her face. Maybe it was because I came back looking like a ghost. But I'm sure she was more interested in Tore. 'You two are actually nutters,' she said.

'Compliment accepted,' Tore said as he went straight over to her and kissed her on her mouth.

'It's you two that are the bloody nutcases,' I mouthed to myself as I pushed on into the sitting room and then up the stairs for my clothes.

Food smells gradually began to circulate in the house and by this time my morning oats were reduced to the bare minimum. Food smells were totally good. Tore came into the room.

He pulled off his swimming trunks and as my gaze passed across him, I couldn't help thinking: 'Untouched by human hand.' But that had to be bullshit.

'I'm fucking starving man,' he said.

'Yeah, we might need to be,' I answered. 'I mean. Can she actually cook do you think?'

'I don't know whether she's ever had to. But surely she could manage to fry an egg?' said Tore.

The smells drifting up to us were more than just fried eggs.

We descended the stairs like two grandees. The staircase was just suited to the scene as well, because it delivered us right into the middle of the sitting room. Our hair lay smooth against our heads after our bathing escapade. Tore's hair was almost dark blue. My tie knot was perfect.

But the sitting room was deserted.

Helle's voice came from the kitchen – 'We're eating out here, you two.'

We filed out to the kitchen, where the closed door leading to the patio had been thrown open. Fru Junkersen was sitting at table out there. We were both a bit awkward. Seeing her sitting there like that. Our walking speed dropped the nearer we got to the table. How were we going to cope with this woman? I had a hopeless feeling that we would never find the answer.

'Do please be seated,' she said.

We hovered and scraped with chairs a bit but in the end were properly assigned so that Tore ended up sitting opposite Helle and me opposite Madam. There was a delicious spread on the table. Every pot of herring and sardines, every jar of sausages big and small that you could imagine. And for the hot plate, you could sense the cooked mushrooms and boiled eggs before you saw them. My mouth watered like mad. In front of each napkin stood a bottle of pilsner. The suspicion that had crossed my mind two seconds earlier almost left me: that Fru Junkersen had forgotten to sort the poisonous mushrooms from the edible ones when preparing the hot dish. We shovelled the food into us like men possessed.

Not that many million words were spoken during that meal. And before we knew it, the whole thing was over and we sat there stupefied by wind and sea, lunch and pilsner.

'Janus can do the dishes,' said Tore.

I nearly reacted with my usual tetchiness, honed to perfection in my own home, but I gritted my teeth and suffered it because of where I was. I shot a glance over at Fru Junkersen.

'I'll wash up, mum,' said Helle.

Tore smiled at her.

'No, that's fine. If you will dry, young man, I'll wash the dishes myself,' Fru Junkersen said, looking straight at me. Her bracelet clinked, as she took the cigarette from her mouth.

The smell of perfume was not as overpowering out here on the patio.

My whole clock just showed an idiot grin and at the same time I felt my gut wrench.

'Right then. That's that sorted.'

Helle got up. We offered our thanks for the food and began to clear the table.

Fru Junkersen remained in her seat and watched us. 'She's too gorged with kill to bite right now,' I thought to myself. Helle and Tore were laughing about something in the kitchen. A flock of seagulls strafed the inner courtyard and both Fru Junkersen and I looked up at them. When we looked down again, we were looking right at each other. We did that for a moment or two. 'Who has the right to what here?' we asked without saying a word. 'Who has the right to whom?'

I lifted the empty beer bottles and went into the kitchen. Helle was stood at the draining board rinsing plates, whilst Tore hung at the wall.

I turns to Tore in exaggerated outrage – 'You always get the lucky breaks.'

'Janus mate. If you really understood the character-building aspect of housework you wouldn't be complaining!' he retorted with his big mad head. 'And don't forget I've my own obligations to attend to,' he continued, looking over at Helle.

'God. You think you're the cat with the cream don't you?' she said.

'Me? I am the Emperor of the world,' he said.

Fru Junkersen appeared at the doorway and filled the room with her presence.

'Well, that's us all finished here,' Tore said with a big smile.

Helle looked searchingly at her mother. Her mother turned away.

'Off you both go then for a walk,' she said as she looked out the window. Helle's glance held me for a second and I saw exhaustion in her eyes.

'Come on Helle!' Tore cried, pulling her away. 'Leave the skivvying to the slaves.'

They could be heard rummaging for things in the sitting

room and then Helle said something that made Tore laugh out loud. I grabbed a tea towel that was hanging on a hook. It was impossible not to feel like a rookie lion tamer alone in the cage for the first time with that year's circus sensation – Roll Up Roll Up! For the fabled snake-fanged lioness never before seen in Scandinavia!

Fru Junkersen lost some of her *grandezza* as she stood there with a cigarette lolling from her mouth. A constant stream of smoke flowing into her eyes whilst she was bent over the sink. The soapy water disarmed her for a moment.

Without looking at me, she suddenly asked: 'How old are you, boy?'

She lobbed the question across the draining board like a grenade. How long did I have before the blast? The fuse in the question hissed in the quiet of the kitchen.

'How old are you, boy?' the woman said. But it was the 'boy' that carried the dynamite. It was as if her hands were already upon me.

'Old enough to stick one on your beak Mrs,' I wanted to shout. I clinked and clanked with some plates.

'You're still green anyway,' she said.

I tried to think of something to say that might soften her hammer-blow description of me. Something I could handle.

'But I know you're not as green and wet behind the ears as he is.'

She took the cigarette out of her mouth and chucked it through the open window. Her hair shone in the sunlight but in a different way to Helle's.

'We're both in 2G,' I said, like a cretin.

She turned for the first time and looked straight at me. She looked nothing but vulgar. That gave me breathing space. I picked up the plates but then remembered they belonged in the kitchen. But the ashtrays now. They had to go back to the sitting room. I lifted them and began to walk towards the door. Maybe Tore and Helle were still there.

'I'll just take these in,' I said.

The room was empty. The spacious and elegant room with the sun spilling across the floor. Totally quiet. I ploughed on with the two ashtrays in front of me, like a drunken altar boy holding the burning censer in church.

'Put them on the coffee table.' Her voice directing me like remote control radio-waves. I caught a glimpse of her back there drying her hands with the tea towel. When I got to the coffee table she was right behind me.

A block of ice exploded inside me when I felt her hands running up the inside of my thighs.

'I can't stand looking at his big innocent face,' she snarled at me, shoving my knees apart from behind as she spoke, so that I toppled over on to the leather sofa in front of the coffee table.

'She is at least forty-three,' I said to myself. 'She is at least forty-three. At least forty-three.' The pungency of her perfume thrust deep down into my throat and struck my chest so hard I felt something give and let out a sigh. A strong smell of buffalo leather invaded my nostrils. I reached out for her and she lowered herself forward, but at the very point when I thought I was going to drown, she brushed me aside like a pathetic insect.

Not once did I think of Tore in those moments. Or if I did think about him, I wasn't aware of it.

I saw her back disappearing into the kitchen. The serpentine demeanour still with her. She rolled on her hips a touch, and her movements were redolent of a reptile gliding through the grass after a well-executed ambush. The warm, throbbing numbness lodged inside me wouldn't go away. Now I was going to rush out to her in the kitchen, grab hold of all her posh clothes, rip them off and then thrash that bitch inside out, up and down, and then tell her exactly what she was – nothing but a stuck-up old hag with a wrinkled head on her, who would be better off crawling into the nearest trash can and pulling the lid down over her.

Rattling and tinkling sounds came from the kitchen and I realised how weird it was to be lying on that sofa. Floating the way I was. The heat began to leave me like unnatural tidal water draining rapidly from my body.

My thoughts about Tore, that had not materialised up to

that point, now began to take shape. Here was the proof of something I'd felt all along: traps had been laid for him and I'd already run into some of them grinning from ear to ear. What was it she'd said just before? That she hated his big innocent face. It had to be Tore she meant.

I managed to get up, but felt like my undercarriage was shot. As if someone had been tugging forever at my crotch. 'But I'm only human,' I thought, rather theatrically. That was going to be some epitaph – the noble knight with the gleaming sword to defend his Lord fell to his death, because his nerve failed him as he stepped out onto the rotten floor. What the fuck was I going to say to the old witch?

What was I going to say to Tore?

Any time soon, he and Helle would be back with red rosy cheeks after their walk, chatting and laughing and then there's me sitting here like a guilty schoolboy caught with his pants down. They'll breeze in like swaddled cherubs, smelling of milk and honey, lanolin soap and pure love, and there'll be me sitting on the sofa – not like a shining nobleman ready for battle, but a blowfly, reeking of filth and baseness. And then from the kitchen she will emerge like a hideous, brown spider with slaver spilling from the thick thread around the sides of her mouth. The spider and blowfly should have fucked each other and then the world would have gone under. But those two kids won't notice anything. Just prattle on, and I'll sit there and say nothing, nothing, nothing. Because the venom from her perfume, the venom from the car, the venom from her breasts and those mushrooms will already have paralysed me. Utterly and completely. I'll just smile back at them and not do a damned thing because I actually lost something a long time ago they've never even thought about. Because they couldn't see that my armour was not made of a crusading knight's burnished steel, but was just insect shell, an empty husk with nothing but filth and maggot spawn in it. She came in from the kitchen and I brought my hands down from my face.

'Would you like a cup of coffee, young man?' she said.

I looked up at her as if I'd been expecting a bollocking but was offered sweets instead. She stood in the doorway with a coffee cup in one hand and a cigarette in the other.

'In the books they always smoke a cigarette at the edge of the bed after they've done the business,' I said to myself. But we hadn't done any business whatsoever. And anyway, I hardly ever drank coffee.

'Yes thanks, that would be great.' The politeness that had been drummed into me rising to the occasion.

She turned around and came in again moments later with a cup of coffee from the kitchen. She placed the cup on the coffee table.

'Madam taking her coffee,' I thought. 'The spider with its embalmed fly cadaver.'

Fru Junkersen looked very prim and poised there with her legs together and her back erect in the chair. She had folded up all that risqué and vulgar side of her like an umbrella and left it in the kitchen, but the chill remained in her eyes like permafrost.

'Here comes the chat about the weather,' I said to myself.

'Cigarette?' she asked.

I leaned forward and took one of the cigarettes from the little case on the table. They must have been there right through the winter. They were yellow and dried out.

'No young man, take one of mine,' she said and shook out a cigarette from her own packet. I put back the old cigarette and took hers. Quiet reigned in the room and outside the sea could be heard having its usual conversation.

The cigarette smoke hovered under the ceiling and drifted towards the window where a soft draught from a crevice sent it back in small plumes.

'Haven't you got the right to something now, Janus,' I thought. 'After the way she behaved just then, you can make demands. Say what you want.' But it was like I wasn't really convinced by the conversation going on in my head. Though I desperately wanted to say something.

'I've known Tore since I was in first year,' I said. She turned her head fully towards me with a look that seemed to expect more.

'We've been mates ever since. For years.' She smiled out of the corners of her mouth.

'He's my best friend really,' I said. It wasn't hard to see the connection with the issue that was staring at both of us, but it still felt like sheer blather.

'What subject would you like to do at college, Janus?' she asked. It sounded like she was pulling a packet of cigarettes from a vending machine.

Her words floated over to me like an iceberg, and I hooked myself fast on it. At least that would keep my head above water for a little longer.

'I think I'd like to do linguistics.' She set her cup firmly away from her on the table. 'Now that, young man, is an excellent idea,' she said. 'And then will you teach afterwards?'

'Yea...hhs,' I said. Sounding like I suddenly had swamp muck in my throat. First the weather and now this!

'Of course, Helle is a classics scholar,' I said. 'So I suppose ...'

Helle's name made the shards of ice in Fru Junkersen's eyes glint like daggers.

'Yes, she's mentioned Latin a few times, but I'm really not sure how serious she is. She's still so young of course.'

'Aye, she's young and you are an old mare,' I said to myself. Why couldn't I start using her first name now we were intimate? Why was I still letting her boss me about all the time? It had to be because she was a lady. A woman.

'Your father, of course, is an engineer, so I would've thought that the polytechnic was more your line?' she said.

I went under again. Flailing.

'Don't you understand that Tore and Helle, that they ... I mean. Don't you see Fru Junkersen that it's. I mean they have ... The thing they ...' The water began to go over my head. 'Tore and Helle can't. You've no damn right to ruin it ... to ruin it all.'

'Yes, Janus. I think the polytechnic side of things can offer a great career these days,' she continued, looking straight into my face.

'Yes but,' I said. 'Yes. But listen to me.'

'Ah little Janus, you're in love with Helle too, aren't you? In your own little greenhorn way.'

Everything in front of me went red then black.

'Ha, you thought you hit home there, didn't you Madam,' I roared. 'Thought you got me right bang where it hurts. But you're wrong, lady. You could not be more wrong!' It was like screaming into the mouth of a storm. She and that fella Poul and Kurt too. They couldn't be fought against.

They would always be there no matter what.

I slumped back into the sofa but reared up again like a rabbit that was waiting for the snake to strike. Yes she had struck home, but in a perverse way. It was both true and not true. Impossible to disprove. The wound sat in a place where I couldn't lick it. And the heart of the matter was not me but my proud Red Indian chief. And what could I do? What could I say to him?

'But if you become a teacher Janus, you'll never be able to afford anything. Most of them can barely support their wives.' She lit a new cigarette as she spoke.

I wanted to get up and flee from the house.

'What is it. This game you're playing?' I asked, knowing already that it sounded pathetic.

'As a student at the polytechnic,' she began. But then she just sat and stared at me. A waft of her perfume hit across to me. I fought for breath. 'Any second. She's going to come slithering over to me and mount me again and then I'm lost forever,' I said to myself. And I so much wanted her to do it. Because I just so fucking wanted to do it. The black water rose over me. Round me and in and out of me again and I knew that feeling as if it had happened a thousand times before.

Fru Junkersen just sat quietly.

'I am not in love with Helle,' I said. 'I really like her. Both her. And Tore … I mean.' What did I really want to say about Tore? That it was him I loved? But I couldn't do that. That was completely impossible. That word 'love' was pathetic. Fucking useless.

Yes it was him. But also about the right to just be yourself with all that meant and understanding each other and having great fun together and being mates and sticking up for each other and also that he was whole and pure of heart. Not cowed or smashed that made me go berserk in my head and most of all made me want to get the fuck out of there. That was what I 'loved'. Again I got the urge to hit back.

'It's pretty obvious, Madam, that you love yourself more than anything.'

'You mongrel,' she fired back.

She was sat there straight up and down as her cigarette oozed smoke.

'Little pup,' she said. 'Go and piss on something your own tiny size. Because I'm out of your reach, boy.'

We sank back in our seats and some kind of lethargy filled the room. I was wrecked inside. There was fuck all more I could do or say. I had collapsed. No. The Sphinx hadn't beaten me. But it was a complete collapse anyway. Because everything was lost there in that room. Because I was a coward. Because she was such a tramp. Because I had fallen fallen fallen fallen and couldn't stay on my feet with my back straight but always had to glide and sink down into the black water and the mud and shit at the bottom. My shoulders were as tense as bomber wings with a full load and my jaw flinched. Then the whole thing just fell away and I felt like slime running down a wall and there was not a thing I could do to stop it.

Far away, like a cry for help from a drowning man, I heard Tore shouting. The cry came as a quiver in the air and disappeared immediately. The voice was borne aloft by the sunshine coming through the window and died away above our heads. Neither of us reacted. A short time later came a new sound. A harmony. Like birdsong. Quite soft at first then closer with more strength. Mixed now with feet on gravel. They were nearly home from their walk.

The chloroform silence in the room remained, but I began to fight my way to consciousness. The effort moved in my throat. Like when you try to scream in your sleep but can't utter a sound. I flapped my arms a bit, like a sick bird, but still couldn't stand up.

'That's them now,' I gasped.

Fru Junkersen got up and stroked her hand down across

her skirt. As if that was enough to wipe the whole situation clean. She calmly bent over the coffee table, picked up the cups and took them out to the kitchen.

And me? With a huge effort, I managed to stand up on my legs. That self-esteem which, despite everything, still remained inside me after 'you can call me Inger' and those other exploits, was strangled in these moments. It was like being on Death Row. Waiting for the Padre and Hangman.

The voices outside were now clearly recognisable. I could hear every word they said. One last ripple of air in the room and then a violent crunching of gravel. The porch door opens and Helle steps in with Tore right behind her. They appeared like divine revelations from another world.

'Well. Did you get those dishes washed up?' A hint of guilty conscience in her voice.

'We're done and dusted,' I said. 'Ages ago.'

'Jesus, cheer up Janus. Less of the misery guts,' said Tore. I looked up at his face, like a dog that had just been whipped.

'We went for a brilliant walk, mate,' he said, as he looked scrutinisingly at me. 'Almost right out to the lighthouse.'

'They've even had time to drink coffee, the layabouts,' said Helle, pointing to the mark of a cup on the table. 'Where's mum?'

'She must be out in the kitchen,' I said.

Helle looked at me uneasily. So I got switched on.

'I'd say she's taking a break, coz we've been sat in here talking nonstop,' says I, with an attempt at a smile.

'Do you have any cigarettes, Janus?' Tore asked.

I offered my own pack to him and offered one to Helle as well. 'No thanks,' she said.

'Think Janus has a Painus somewhere,' said Tore. 'Looks like he went a bit mad on that coffee.'

Fru Junkersen came in from the kitchen. Her whole head was radiance itself and Helle breathed a little sigh of relief.

'Enjoy the walk?' she asked. 'Did you take Tore right down to the end of the beach?'

'Yes, mum. We went right out to near the lighthouse,' said Helle.

'How can she do that so bare-faced?' I thought.

The three of them moved around one another like planets whose poles were completely balanced, whilst I felt like an ill-fated moon that had been knocked out of its true path. The two of them entirely unsuspecting and the third utterly confident in her feminine wiles. The two of them innocence personified and she the epitome of evil, who perhaps can live alongside such chasteness for a time, but who eventually must either devour it or herself be crushed by it. And me? I was just the dregs.

The afternoon began to fade and the rest of the day disappeared into some kind of sea fog where not even the lanterns, never mind the shape of the ships could be distinguished. But vampires were abroad. Very close to the bloodbeat of the house.

Yes, it was far too early for St Elmo's Fire, glow-worms and sulphurous flames in the night sky. But I swear. I sat there as we drove home and watched them all, with the portents falling around me and the nauseating smell of buffalo leather lodged in my nose and throat.

Chapter 10

We had finally arrived at the beginning of the end. And things looked set fair for a successful outcome. We had begun the revision period for our final school exams. In truth, it was totally mad to think we wouldn't be going to school any more after the 24th of June. But then, maybe that wasn't quite true either because we would be going to university. Although it actually was different. I mean. We wouldn't be forced to sit at an insane desk for six hours day in day out. We'd come and go as we pleased. Study when and where we liked. That was what students did. Finally finally we would be proper grown-ups. Our dream fulfilled.

We felt mighty important when we bowled into Østre Anlæg park with a stack of books under our arms and sat down to read them. Folk gazed upon us with an affectionate air. As if they could already picture the scene – us as merry students, pondering life and cavorting beneath the verdant canopy. Just as with every other pre-exam revision period we'd been through, there was a real buzz in meeting our study subjects once again, but in a much more intense way. I mean. I was reading in a really concentrated way now. Because I had no choice. Because I had to get that pathetic qualification. But also because it was exciting. There were more revs in the engine than normal. And we ransacked each other's brains, enjoying the dare of seeing how far we could push each other before falling off the plank. My sense of terror was unbearable when I realised it was going to be simply impossible to get some of the subjects read through properly because I was so far behind. I looked over despairingly at Tore as I gripped a bundle of around 100 pages of Latin texts I couldn't remember ever having seen before, not even in my dreams. So I shoved the book down to the bottom of the pile quick as I could. It was a waste of time even looking at it really, because we still had to do history revision and my mind was almost as blank on that as well. But at least the history texts were in Danish.

The sun warmed our necks as we sat on the bench revising *Faust*. We were both good at German. Me and Tore immersed in the text and embraced by the sun. Our heads still stuck in our books, a scraping sound suddenly emerged in front of us and, in my wild imaginings, it was *Faust's* demonic black poodle that had jumped out of this dog-eared book and now stood pawing at the ground by our park bench. I looked up from my book. It was Kurt. All ready to start barking.

'Howdy pardners,' he says with disgusting cheerfulness. Like we were characters in an American cartoon series suddenly landed on Danish soil. Tore looked up and his face resembled a sour lemon.

'Gettin any work done lads?' Kurt asked.

'Yeah loads,' says I.

'Your mum told me you were both over here Janus, so I thought I'd take a stroll over. Is there any chance I can borrow your Latin notes?' This last sentence spoken with all the politeness and evil that only Kurt could pull off.

'Ah, would you give over,' says I. 'Ask Tore, not me.' Kurt knew rightly that my Latin notes would be about as much use as a first year's.

Tore was way ahead of me. He'd already heaved his notes out from the bottom of his pile and handed them to Kurt. 'I'll need them back by the day after tomorrow,' he said.

'Perfect!' said Kurt. 'I'll get them back to you on time. Scout's honour. It's just that I thought Janus might have some good notes too. I mean. You two always revising together like you do. Thought Janus might be able to spare me his.' He stood there talking at some point beyond Tore.

'How's things otherwise?' he then asked. The sun was shining right into his face and he stood there squinting. The devil appears in many guises. Dog and snake.

'Good mate. Brilliant,' says I.

Kurt standing there. A grin spreading slowly across his face like a bad thought. With his politest of Copenhagen suburb accents he then goes:

'And how's Helle getting on these days?'

I mean. In theory, a question like that bears no malice. But this was Kurt. What the fuck did it have to do with him? The little runt.

'Yes, she's up to her neck as well of course,' said Tore.

Kurt's grin spreads and he goes – 'Yeah. Shame she's doing Classics. Otherwise you could have all revised together.'

When Kurt said anything. Anything at all. It always sounded more like he'd just kicked a dog and was delighted with himself.

'Yeah. That would have been handy,' said Tore without smiling.

We sit there for a moment. Silent. With our legs crossed and books turned face downwards on our laps. Kurt would soon become a free adult too, and he already knew exactly what he was going to do with that freedom. The whole university and career plan had already been agreed with his father. And he was even more smug because it was himself who had decided what he wanted to do. And Kurt was self-satisfied for other reasons. He was going to 'cut loose a bit' in the summer holidays he told us. Before he went 'back to the grindstone' in September. No point 'hanging about' once the summer fun was over, he said. It was a lot harder trying to imagine Kurt 'cut loose' than see his nose at the grindstone in September. The latter was his natural state. If Kurt had any kind of problems or complexes, he did a good job of hiding them. But my guess was that his idea of 'cutting loose' was no different to the way he would be in any situation – ultra-polite, snide and relentless, with a mountain of pomade in his hair.

'I'm not even thinking about doing any of the German,' he said. This wasn't meant as sarcasm or a cutting remark. He was just scratching around for something to say. A space filler.

'Aye. I've thrown my Latin primer away as well,' says I.

'Ha, ha,' Kurt said. 'Ha, ha.' Him meaning by this that I'd mentally thrown my Latin book away a long time ago like the little hooligan I was. I fished some cigarettes out and without saying anything offered one first to Tore and then to Kurt.

'No thanks, I don't smoke,' said Kurt. The height of politeness.

'Oh yeah ... that's right,' says I, trying to make this sound like he was nothing but a pansy. It didn't bite.

'Who's going to do the student speech?' said Kurt, looking right at Tore. Tore was back reading and had forgotten Kurt.

I gave Kurt the dirtiest look I could to shut his trap and this time it succeeded. There was of course no question that it would be Tore and none other than Tore who did the class's student speech on leaving day, but it couldn't be decided in that way. 'It's not been decided yet,' I told him.

But Kurt pushes on. Makes his move. 'Oh! Forgot to say I saw Helle yesterday.' Looking to see if this would get a reaction from us. 'She was in her mother's car.'

'Imagine that. There was us thinking she was at home doing her revision without a minute to spare,' I said. Tore looked up from his book and smiled.

'I hope you waved to her?' Tore asked.

'Yes I did actually!' Kurt said with real excitement in his voice. 'And she waved back.' Jeez. The way he talked about it. Like a little boy who unexpectedly gets an extra piece of cake. 'And her mother has certainly kept her looks,' he said.

I turned my book over and started to read again. But Kurt was like one of those pathetic dogs which, even when you give them a brutal kick to the head, always come back to you, wagging their tails and barking excitedly.

'God knows how many parties and dances there'll be,' Kurt said. This utter numbskull. He was going to look so ridiculous with a student cap on his daft head.

'Well there's about eight or nine we just won't be able to refuse,' said Tore. In truth, thoughts of all those parties united us for a second.

I chucked my cigarette onto the ground and trod it out.

'Right. We better get on here.' Kurt didn't budge a centimetre.

'Who's going to be your partner for all those dances, Janus?'

he asked. 'We all know who Tore's bringing.' His fake coyness was sheer old school vaudeville.

So I looks at him all innocent – 'Will you be my partner Kurt?'

'Fuck off. Do you think I'm H6 or something?' he said trying to act like he was an expert.

'No Kurt. I don't think you are anything whatsoever,' I said, not even trying to hide the contempt that was oozing out of me. 'Tell you what. I know you're a complete swot who knows all our subjects off by heart, but I'm nowhere near that. So I wouldn't mind the chance to learn even a small bit of this stuff.' He attempted a laugh and looked down at me with narrowed eyes.

'There's a while to go before we have to face the examiners,' he said.

Tore ducked his head up from his book.

'There is, but I'll tell you one thing Kurt old chap. Doctor Janus here really enjoys reading *Faust* and would now like to avail himself of the peace and quiet prevailing in this park so that he can peruse said manuscript at his diligent best. Besides we'll see each other beforehand in the classroom.' Tore's voice was pure stage farce.

Kurt looked down and pulled up his plus-fours. For all the world, it was like he was putting on his bicycle clips. He might just as well go home and polish his bike if he had read up on all his subjects. I didn't have the time to think of anything else but *Faust* and the rest I had to learn. But Kurt's presence here was pounding so much else into my skull. Stuff that didn't bear thinking about right that minute.

I tried to get back to my reading but just kept going over the same three words again and again. Like my eyes were glued to the page. I took a deep breath and tried to push Kurt out of my mind, but he was like a bluebottle always buzzing back to the same spot. So instead of trying to read on, I raised my eyes and looked out across this tranquil park, where old-age pensioners dragged themselves around for a while and then collapsed onto the benches. Rocking themselves into a good position. Even if they hadn't walked that much. Summer had come early. Saying that, summer always seemed to arrive as soon as we started revising for exams. The tension from exam nerves felt good. Madly productive in your mind and body. Now there was no doubt something was happening. A feeling of something clean, pure and uncomplicated. Something reduced to its sheer essence that no doubt affected your feelings but didn't feel lethal. Just challenging and exciting. I mean. We weren't going to totally fail. No chance. So it was just our parents that paid close heed to, or were upset by, poor grades. And we'd make sure they heard about any good results we got.

It seemed we'd successfully boxed Kurt into a corner. He was stood there. Pawing at the ground like a bashful school kid.

'There was some fella sitting in the backseat with Helle.' So he had kept this ace up his sleeve and was slapping it down now. His final gambit.

I was already half out of my seat and snarling, but Tore's foot curled round the base of my shinbone for a second and held me back. It happened so quickly that Kurt saw nothing.

'My God. Was there?' said Tore, highly animated. 'Wonder who that was? You don't think Helle would go and two-time me? And behind my back as well?' He sounded like a shocked nun. 'That's very hard to believe. I mean, she's such a lovely, sweet girl.'

Gradually, Kurt twigged the ironic tone in Tore's voice and he tried a grin. 'No. Not that,' he said idiotically. 'But I just ...' the rest ebbed away in a mumble.

'Like I've already said, Kurt,' Tore continued. 'Both Doctor Janus here and my good self get such a buzz from Margrethe in *Faust* that we really would love a bit of peace to get to know her even better.'

This jumped-up poodle Kurt would never be transformed into an even half-decent Mephisto. He would always be nothing more than a dog.

He turned tail and slunk away. The utter scrote.

'Phew,' said Tore. He then picked up his book and began reading again.

But I'd been knocked completely off my stride. Foreign bacteria had once more burrowed their way into the open wound I always carried round with me. And these bacteria soon found their way to my brain, from which they unleashed a million thought processes to distract me.

For one thing, I couldn't stop thinking about the confusion that seemed to reign over my life. A mess that got bigger and bigger with each day that passed. Whilst the world everybody else inhabited seemed to become more and more streamlined, mine just became steadily more chaotic. Tore and Helle were going out with each other. Talked to each other. Enjoyed each other's company. Fussed over and petted each other and so it went and so it went and nothing ever more than that.

But what was it to me? I mean. Why did more things than that have to happen anyway? Ever since that day when Tore told me Helle wouldn't go to bed with him, I'd been obsessed by it. It was the thing that would bind them ever closer together. It would be the magic ritual that would make them stronger. Powerful enough to ward off Fru Junkersen's ensnarements. Overall, it would wed them together in a united front against the world's lurking malice. Their virtuous union being a source of great strength. Both for them and for me.

Never had I breathed a word about my little wrangle with Helle's mother to Tore. It was very hard not to let him in on something that was so major and so troubling. Normally, I would tell him everything. Not a word this time though. I'd scratched my head trying to work out a way of telling him so that he could be on his guard, but something scared me. I don't know whether it was embarrassment or anxiety. Or just that the whole thing was so shocking it would make him do something reckless. It would be just like him. He wouldn't stand for anything like that. But I couldn't bring myself to act. It would remain one of my innermost secrets. Sitting there in my gut like fermenting yeast, sending its rancid venom into my bloodstream.

Ever since that whole affair in the summer house, I'd made

sure I never ended up on my own with Fru Junkersen. She for her part had never in any way indicated that anything untoward had happened between us. She was back treating me the way she always had. It was 'young man' this, or 'Janus' that. Tore's old friend and schoolmate. Someone she had to put up with. And as with every other time, up at the dungeon in Frederiksberg, I would sit with Helle and Tore at the dinner table and listen to her ever-so-intelligent conversation, as she slowly inveigled Tore into her witch's web. I would catch Helle looking at Tore with real apprehension in her eyes as he listened to her mother. As if she saw him slipping slowly towards the edge of some pit so dark and deep that looking into it would be unbearable. We did the same things we'd always done together. The life we shared had a particular rhythm that was full of rituals. Like magical staging posts in our daily lives. But all the same, we sensed some kind of shift within our firmament. As if all three of us were heading towards a destination that was not yet clear to us. A point in the future that refused to reveal what lay in store. For good or ill.

Fru Junkersen's *attaque* had unleashed something ferocious in me. As if the sheer vulgarity of her had infected me with a similar strain of corruption. Now it was lodged there like some great dread I had to frantically work out of my system. So I dug out an office girl four years older than me whom I worked at in secret. I treated her like the worst kind of bitch. And this can be the only reason she wanted anything to do with me. When we were together I mocked her in the most horrible of ways. Told her how pathetic she was, how boring, how totally ordinary, how ugly, how unattractive, that she reeked of body odour and needed to wash far more often. Our so-called love for each other was actually a perpetual war zone. An obstacle course which left both of us shattered, but to which we always returned with the same ferocious hunger and disgust. She had her own small flat and I holed up there as if it were some kind of latter-day opium den. Occasionally I would take her out to the pictures, but mainly I just went up to her room and ripped into her. Flayed her apart.

Whilst lying in her bed, I would see Tore and Helle in my mind's eye as they took a stroll hand in hand along some broad boulevard. Talking together. Sharing good, interesting and funny things. I couldn't say many words to Ellen without calling her a fucking idiot and a scrubber. And she laps all this up. As if all her life she had been called 'little petal' or 'sweet pea' and now needed to hear the total opposite. My good mood left me the minute I was with Ellen. Only rarely would a sliver of gallows humour cut through the surrounding gloom. Like the times I would be looking in the mirror in her toilet and couldn't help saying to myself: 'Hi there Poul! How are you today, you sad sack?'

With Ellen, I thought I knew better. That I was feeding a superiority complex. But every single time I went home after seeing her, I was left feeling dumb and small-minded. The darkness I entered at the bottom of the stairs from her flat was real enough. I got waves of nausea every time I left her. Both over myself and the trauma of being with her. And then because I wasn't getting enough sleep. When we'd spent the evening together, I would very often fall asleep on her bed. But I always dreamed like a lunatic and woke with a jump. She would stare at me in terror and ask me what the matter was. My folks noticed the state of me but said nothing. That must have been dad holding my mum back. But then, there hadn't been any of his reaffirming winks or nods in the last while.

Whenever I got to Ellen's place, I would race up the stairs as if trying to lose someone that was on my heels. She'd barely have the door into her little apartment opened and I was on top of her. Throwing her around the room, fucking and blinding, snarling like a rabid dog that didn't know whether to bite or sit. I loved her like a relay runner that just takes off like a headless chicken so that he can hand over some totally meaningless baton and then fall over seconds later. Tank empty and utterly fucked.

She would try to calm me down by telling me about things going on at her work. Or she would ask about my studies or Tore. But I had no time for all that. No time because I was either ripping into her or having a nightmare in her bed or flying out the door and down into darkness. Though it has to be said that, in the occasional breaks from all this mayhem, she did succeed in teasing a lot of stuff out of me.

Tore she already knew, because he was with me on the night I met her. As usual where my girls were concerned, I'd picked Ellen up in a bar. Me and Tore had wandered into this place and were sat there scraping the money together for the one pilsner we could afford between us. We were still nowhere near professional barflies. So there we sat, unobtrusively in a corner, following the events going on around us.

There weren't that many in the bar. We'd just come from a university scholars' association meeting, so it was about ten o'clock in the evening. But just across from us there was this couple. They were sitting with their heads low, nearly touching. The way couples sit in a bar when they are either canoodling or having a row. The girl was of the thin, black-haired variety. It looked like they were in fact having a row. Just beyond Tore's conversation, I could hear your man was giving her stick about something. In the end, he stood up, grabbed his cotton-coat with an angry flourish and stormed out. She just stayed sitting there staring straight ahead of her. Suddenly, this fella comes back and throws a fiver on the table. As if he was saying – now I owe you fuck all. Bitch. She still carried on looking dead ahead of her. The guy hesitates for a minute. As if he was hoping she might call him back. But then he spins on his heels and disappears. Me and Tore followed the whole drama under hooded eyes.

The girl sat there, fiddling with the fiver as we carried on talking. She was actually quite pretty. Finally, I went over to her and bowed my head slightly as an invitation to dance. As I stood there bowing, it struck me that the music they were playing in the restaurant section would be impossible to dance to. Another problem was that there was no dance floor. I could feel my face going a red hot colour. On the spur of the moment, as it was, I didn't have time to tell Tore what I had in mind and I could hear someone roaring with laughter behind my back. The girl then looked up at me with big eyes and smiled. Making me even more furious. Trying to get back to what looked more like a normal posture, I mumbled some kind of apology. I think much of my rage at her started from this very point.

The end to it all was that Tore said she should come over to our table, and that is what she did. Gradually, we made our pecuniary situation known to her, which resulted in her paying for another round of pilsners.

Then it was home-time. Tore going one way and Ellen, as she told us her name was, going in my direction. It was a cold evening in November, and I allowed her to take my arm, still half-choked with rage. She put up with it. Just as she put up with all the other things that followed on from it. Even though my rage increased time after time.

She was massively frustrating, because her lack of sexual guile reminded you more of gullibility than anything else and her vulgarity was of the kind seen in those tacky, garish adverts for anti-BO products and bad breath.

She was as many light years from Tore and Helle as she was from Fru Junkersen. But she stuck it out with me. She opened my veins and bled me, so I could still return to the core of my world without getting sick. Tore and Helle and our forest promenades were the Saturday and Sunday of life. What I otherwise did were my run-of-the-mill duties or cesspit stuff under the cover of darkness. Stuff that was my business. And mine alone.

The four of us only ever met once. Me and Ellen had just completed one of our rare expeditions to the cinema and were walking down *Strøget*. Helle and Tore were walking straight at us and I caught them too late to nip down a side street, or drag Ellen into a shop doorway, or some getaway. Like a condemned man, I walked straight towards them with Ellen latched onto my arm. Not a clue did she have. I felt like some kind of mass murderer or a churl from a lower caste. But Tore and Helle just came on, like two brightly illuminated ships, calmly and confidently nosing the water aside as they made way, whilst I felt like a U-boat that had inadvertently broken surface with no time to submerge again.

Then Helle spotted us. She was obviously stunned for a

second but then let out a quick call: 'Hi, Janus!' Tore looked up straight away. His face bore a slightly droll expression as he looked at us. 'Well hello there kiddies,' he said.

'Hello there back,' says I, as I steered Ellen in front of me a little bit. Helle began to take her off her glove. I was just about to say there was no need for any kind of formality, but my Ellen had already taken hers off. She was just about to introduce herself when Tore broke in and explained to Helle who this girl was and then told Ellen who Helle was. For a moment I was lamed and dumbstruck. We stood there for a while without saying much, but I did manage to communicate that we'd been in to watch a film. I noticed that Ellen couldn't take her eyes off Helle. It really was a case of a sparrow in the dust being dazzled by a regal bird that wings its way past swooping whooshing to the ground.

We parted soon after. I nudged Tore with my elbow as we passed and he nudged back. Not one word did I speak to Ellen as we went home. Up in her room, I was the worst I'd ever been with her and she cried till I wanted to get out to the toilet and throw up. Why the fuck didn't she just throw me out? I didn't understood any of it, but carried on torturing and abusing her till the blood boiled in my brain.

Once I was back in my own home, I was seized by restlessness. I couldn't concentrate on anything. Never got a book or lesson read. At our family meal get-togethers of a Sunday, they would all say I was turning into a right oddball. Only when I was with Tore and Helle did I truly relax. Or rather, when we were alone together without Fru Junkersen.

Even though nothing menacing had happened any time after our *tête-à-tête* in the Spring, my hands still went clammy every time I set eyes on the hagwitch. I mean. How was I to know whether she might not out, of the blue, throw some kind of bomb amongst us that would blow us all to bits? But nothing like that ever happened. For reasons I didn't understand, she backed away. And there was Tore sitting opposite her with a face as open as a target disc.

I had never viewed Tore as being naive. No. He was not naive, but after meeting Helle he seemed enthralled beyond sense or reason. So it was natural, I suppose, that he would also be oblivious to Fru Junkersen's machinations. Tore the Man, who otherwise immediately saw through anything sham. I just didn't get it. He accepted Fru Junkersen, because she was Helle's mother. Not because he was that keen on her. But there was no denying she could fascinate him as well. He just couldn't help being interested in her in an insidiously dangerous way. She was placing him under her spell with words.

In all areas but this, Tore was still superior. His calmness and maturity, and not least the wit he always demonstrated, made people deferential to him, almost servile. Everybody loved him, and most would even enjoy being mocked by him. It was always better than him just ignoring you.

But still. I couldn't pass on my suspicions and greater awareness about Fru Junkersen to him. Every time I worked myself up to it, I was stopped dead in my tracks. It was almost as if he didn't want to know.

I was left carrying a strange feeling of perpetrating a deception. As if I'd been trying to spin him a yarn that held no truth. In the end, I just gave up trying. I didn't want to raise an issue between us that might put a twist in our friendship. As time moved on, I began trying to convince myself that my view of Fru Junkersen was probably more to do with my own peculiar take on things.

In the main, I suppose you could call the year that had just passed a fairly normal year. In truth, nothing sensational had happened. I just felt a bit shook up. But now this revision period for the exams had come as a great relief. I burrowed myself down into the reading and information ran through me like a purgation.

When I looked up from my *Faust*, I realised I had been sitting there staring at the same sentence for quite some time. Yes. Kurt had triggered that whole distraction. Tore was sitting next to me on the bench, still concentrated on his reading. The sun had crept round into the start of a decline and it had begun to feel a bit chilly sitting there in the park.

'Do you want to go to mine for a cup of tea?' I asked.

'Mmmmm?' asked Tore.

I sat there observing him and saw that he was actually just reading *Faust* for the enjoyment of it. Not translating or making notes. I looked down again at my own copy. The German text in front of me looked more like an obstacle course. I did my best to concentrate again, but failed miserably.

Tore stopped reading. He put his finger firmly at the place he had reached.

'Won't it be weird, Janus? To be finished,' he said. For the thousandth time, we were going to talk about this.

'Wonderful,' I said, as my shoulders sank.

'Do you know what? I'm going to go up and down every possible street with that goddam student cap on. Doff it and put it on again every time I meet anyone,' he continued. 'I'm gonna wear it like this ... pushed back, resting on my neck. And I won't forget to put the storm strap under my chin, when we do the fun fair and big dipper thing. That storm strap is so cool. I've always thought it was one of the coolest things about those caps – that they have a strap you can put under your chin. Remember those pictures from the Nazi occupation Janus? Where you see all those students on the demonstration against Scavenius or whoever it was. I'm telling you man. All of them had their storm strap around their chin.'

'Yeah I know mate. It'll be unbearable when we get the caps before the exams but have to leave them lying there in a bag till the big day.'

An S-train went past and let out a whistle. Weird discordant sound.

'I'm getting a new suit,' I told Tore.

Tore looks over at me. 'Do you mean a tux?'

I admitted it and felt like an idiot because I was also embarrassed. Truth was I was really looking forward to that tuxedo.

'Yeah I know. Bit over the top, isn't it?' says I. 'But really it's my dad that wants me to get it,' I said. For some pathetic reason, I started thinking about Ellen. She wouldn't get much joy out of me becoming a student. Sure I could go over to hers in my tux. And feel like a complete jerk.

'We should go on one of our forest tours to Dyrehaven. If we can get ourselves organised,' said Tore.

I nodded. That was a brilliant idea. We'd never been out to the deer park together in the summer.

'We could go out there and treat ourselves to a slap-up lunch,' I said. This was all good. Fun and exciting things to look forward to. There couldn't be that much of a crowd of a weekday.

'We should take our swimming togs as well,' said Tore. 'That would be the first time this year.' A smile appeared on his face. 'Do you remember that time we went out to the country with Helle?'

My thought processes hit an emergency stop and before I knew it I was on a helter-skelter ride full of blinding images of women.

'Yeah. It was fantastic,' says I.

'It's actually a bit strange we've never been invited up there since. I mean. It's a gorgeous place. And what a house, man,' Tore said, as he laid his book to one side on the bench.

'Yeah, I guess,' says I.

'But it was like you didn't really enjoy it or what?' he looked inquisitively at me.

'No. I had a great time, honest,' I said nervously. Jesus. Was he going to start dragging the truth out of me now?

'Didn't you end up doing the dishes. Standing at the sink there with Helle's mother?' he asked, between a tease and a dig. 'Did that knock you out of your stride, mate?'

'Right, here goes. Fuck it,' I said to myself. 'I'm going to blab the whole thing.' The words were on the tip of my tongue but at that very same moment, I saw that he might not even believe what I was telling him. He would actually laugh at me. Joke that it was my devious mind making me delirious.

'OK, I admit it. I was out of my depth with Lady Junkersen,' I said.

After that, I knew I would never tell him. It was no use. It had all been left for too long. It would sound unbelievable. And anyway. What did it really have to do with Tore? Him and Helle would still be the same. They had each other. So who cares about Fru Junkersen?

Another thing hit me then. The only person so far who'd been affected by the whole escapade was yours truly. My attempts to predict the future were certainly no more than my wild fantasies. I mean. Who was I to pronounce good or bad on other people's lives? Did I have some kind of crystal ball that revealed their destinies? All my outlandish ideas seemed to me to have reached even further shores of crazy. And lookit. The person who was being driven demented by all this was me. And of course it shook me up. But Tore wasn't me. And Helle wasn't me either. So no doubt wrong of me to put them in my shoes. But still. Tore was the rock of hope upon which my troubled head rested. He was still the Man.

'Are we not going to my place for that tea?' I asked.

We packed our books together and made our slightly dazed way to the exit gates. A scraggy water bird gliding by in the pond reminded me of Ellen to an alarming degree.

I goes to Tore – 'I'm still going out with that girl. Remember the one we met that evening?'

'Yeah well. I can understand that, mate,' Tore replied. 'You're not slow in getting that end of things sorted.'

He didn't say this in a malicious way. Nor was he peeved or being vulgar for the sake of it. But there was something patronising there. As if he was saying he was above all that grubby shit.

I flinched. I don't think Tore even noticed the tone his words carried. And anyway. Maybe it was more the thrumming membrane in my ear that picked it up wrong.

'I tell ya, she's a nice girl,' he said. 'Why d'you keep her hidden away? You'd think she's this big secret in your life.'

'Nah,' says I. 'She's no secret.'

By now it was around four in the afternoon. People and cars were thundering by. They looked like they expected a prize or something if they got back five minutes early to their swamp pits. We trudged on to where our bikes were parked and unlocked them. Then we mounted up and manoeuvred our way into the cycling throng. Our pedal tempo was way below theirs.

Tore waited for me while I put my bike down in the basement. Then we went up the stairs to our apartment. Mum was stood in the hall when we walked in.

'Helloo helloo boys,' she said as she put her hat on. 'Kurt was here, Janus. He was asking for you.'

'He came over to the park, mum,' I said.

'Ah good. So he got those notes he was talking about, did he?' she asked.

'Oh yes. He got what he needed.'

'We were the height of friendship with him,' said Tore.

'Why are you two always so down on that young man?' mother asked.

I gave her a pleading look.

'He's such a polite and pleasant young man,' she continued.

'Ah mum, giveover,' I said. Begging now.

'But Mrs Tolne. Honestly. Me and Janus are always polite and pleasant with him,' said Tore, flashing his most charming smile.

'Ah. You two. Pair of rascals,' mum smiled back at him.

I stood there, tapping one foot impatiently.

'Right come on,' says I to Tore.

'Yes. You two have a lot of work to do,' mum said to Tore.

'I know. Not long now,' he said.

I turned round and stood facing away from them. Mum lets out a big sigh and goes – 'Well. We're hoping and praying ...'

Tore moved to help her. Gathering up her shopping bag from the floor. And then opening the door to the staircase for her. He gave her a 'your servant Ma'am' hand salute as she passed him.

'Ah Tore, you're always such a gentleman,' my mother said.

I felt the hidden reproach run down my back like cold water.

'Is Tore staying for dinner, Janus?' she then asked.

'Jesus. Would she not just be gone down those stairs,' I said to myself. With a loud and clear voice I said:

'Yes, mother. Tore is staying for dinner.'

'Very good. That's fine,' a bit hysterical now. 'I'll have to get something extra then. I'll see if I can think of something so we can ...' The rest of the words died away as she descended the stairs.

Tore smacked the door to and turned round to me with a grin. Then we went down to my room.

I slung the books onto my desk.

'Right. I'll make tea,' I said.

'Ah great,' said Tore as he launched himself onto my bed. 'By the way, have you heard I'm getting engaged?' he continued, as if giving me a casual reminder that he took sugar in his tea.

'Who to?' I asked. Shocked to my core.

'To Helle, of course, you daft fucker!'

'Are you really getting engaged like?' The idea of Helle and Tore as an engaged couple seemed brutally ridiculous. They couldn't be any more engaged than they already were.

'She's throwing a party just after the exams – on the 22nd. And we've kind of decided to announce to the world that we're engaged.' He looked out of the window. A bit askance. 'It's not me that wants it. But Helle thinks it's the sensible thing to do.'

'Sensible?' I asked. 'Yeah well. If you think so, mate,' I said, with no enthusiasm. Common sense maybe. But it wasn't really the Tore I knew. The very idea of getting engaged.

But then maybe sensible was OK. If only because it would stop Fru Junkersen in her tracks.

Then Tore goes – 'Helle thinks her mother would be much happier if we became officially engaged. To me. It's one of the most horrible ideas I've ever heard. But I felt suddenly so old and tired with it all. Like I couldn't be bothered either way.' He lay there with his hands under his head. Then he goes – 'And then full steam ahead Janus to our Student Ball. White caps and coloured lamps. Sniggering and snogging in the bushes. The only thing missing will be the old drinks on the back stairs trick!' He chuckled to himself. 'Pushing it a bit. Would be good though.'

I smiled back at him, my hand on the door handle on the way to the kitchen.

'Wonder if she'll go to bed with him now,' I thought to myself.

'And do I get to do some kind of best mate's engagement speech,' I asked in all innocence.

'Depends on how drunk you are,' the voice from the bed said. 'If you're suitably shitfaced, you'll be given leave to kiss the female half of this marriage arrangement. On the cheek!' he said.

I bowed theatrically and went to make the tea.

Making my way along the corridor, I reflected on this pathetic situation. My best mate Tore Riemer who'd always poured scorn and invective on the idea of engagements, rings, parties – he too was now going to put himself through that whole charade. God only knows what Fru Riemer said about it. She probably just smiled in her quiet way.

In the kitchen, I cut some French stick for us both.

Of course, this meant I could now take Ellen to Helle's party. What an engagement bash that could turn out to be. A really top table double engagement party amongst the cream of society and in the best surroundings. Jesus. Imagine the way they'd stare if I came bowling in with that drossbag hanging on my arm. And the outrage will boil up in all those little trogheads, at the same time as they're snot green with envy. Because the things I get up to with this Ellen will be clear as daylight to them. They were still. Years down the line. Hanging out of the classroom windows at school. Slavering at the girls getting dressed over the way. And two guesses what they did when they got home. That is, if they even bothered to wait that long, or just scooted down to the shithouse instead to work off their predicament. I nearly felt superior to them. But the thought of me and Ellen – the way were with each other, hardly filled me with pride. I didn't have a clue how Tore dealt with that thing. Maybe he just moved all those thoughts and needs to some higher level.

I lifted the kettle off the gas and poured the water into the teapot to scald it. In a way, I was a bit shocked it was Fru Junkersen who had proposed that Helle and Tore should get engaged. Surely she would much rather see the whole affair quietly peter out, rather than making some big show of it – an idea I knew she hated. But maybe it was Helle herself that had come up with it, as a manoeuvre to grab the snake by its tail before it got a chance to strike.

'From dust you came,' I said, as I dropped the tea leaves into the pot. 'To dust shall you return.' The final words of this ritual anointed the water. Falling like one long sigh into the pot and sending tea fragrance into the air in the kitchen. I carried the tray with the bread and cups in one hand and the pot in the other. Then I shoved open the kitchen door with my foot and went back to Tore.

He was sitting on the bed reading when I entered my room. I put the cups and teapot down on my desk without saying a word. Tore looks up at me and says:

'You think it's all totally pathetic don't you?'

'Erhm,' says I.

'Go on say it,' he continued. 'You think it's a fucking pathetic idea.'

'Well yeah. I mean. It's not exactly what I expected, but sure ... I can see ...'

'See what?' Tore asked.

'Well. That it makes sense,' I said.

'And how exactly does it make sense?'

'I mean. You two are kind of stronger. Shoulder to shoulder against the world. Against ...'

'Against what?' He persisted.

'Tore. You know exactly what I mean,' I said.

'What? So they won't object so much if we go to bed together?'

I shrugged my shoulders and put my hands up.

'Maybe they wouldn't even mind if we had a baby?' He edged himself down the bed a bit. Closer to me.

'They would let it go because we're engaged? With rings and the whole heap?'

It was like being grilled by the cops. I said nothing. Anyway it was more himself he was grilling.

'I mean for fuck sake. It's loony talk when we've not even had sex! I've never been to bed with Helle. But you know that anyway. You've known that all along.'

'Maybe when the rings are on and all that Tore ... then she

might. I mean. She might ...'

'Horse shit!' He cut my words off like a knife.

I'd never seen Tore so wound up since that day when he told me about Poul and his mother. That bloodless white expression in his face was back.

'Do you know what? I just don't get any of it,' he said. 'She says she daren't do it. That she's scared of her mother. But I don't believe Helle's that scared. Helle's game for anything.'

I spoke now. Softly. 'She'll probably be happy to do it once you're engaged. Don't you think?'

'I just don't understand any of it,' was all he said. He looked beat out.

'I don't understand any of it either,' I said. Me? Maybe I'd expected something different. Suitably mental. Maybe an elves and sprites type wedding in the forest. The wedding party in flowing robes and fine long gloves. Wreaths of mist. A fairy hill lined with glowing torches. Bridesmaids bedecked in white. The scene hallowed by heavenly music.

Then Tore goes – 'I mean. You sort your end out mate. You make sure your needs are satisfied.' He spoke in almost accusatory tones. Like when a piece of clothing is being torn and ripped.

'Phrrrrrh ... I suppose,' I said, blowing my lips out.

He seemed to steel himself for something. A silence stole into the room. A silence I'd never met before in my own place. Like it could hear my heart banging.

'Janus, can't you see the whole thing is a fucking nightmare?' He looked at me. Pleadingly.

It was on the tip of my tongue to say – 'Well actually there's loads of lads out there who'll have to wait a lot longer than you,' but I ate my words. I felt suddenly that our roles had been reversed. Tore was me and I was Tore. But what I really saw was that Tore had become more like Janus. I got scared then.

'Just wait, things will start happening,' I said. 'No doubt about it.' I didn't want to hear his voice any more. Didn't want to see him crumple as I looked on. He had to stay the way he'd always been. The last time we'd talked about this, he'd been completely different. It was easier then because it was nothing urgent. Just talk. I was sure that Tore would get all those boxes ticked double quick. Nobody was even close to him. Now he was just sitting there and becoming a stranger to me. I hated hated hated his lack of certainty.

'You still want tea. Yes?' I asked. He nodded. I put a cup over on the little table by my bed. Noticed it shaking slightly in my hand. We sat there cradling our tea. Like two Tibetan monks with their prayer wheels.

It was desperate really. The urgent need we felt to pronounce a death sentence on the last surviving innocence in the world. Helle had become nothing more than a slab of meat and could we for God's sake get her fucked as soon as possible. It was now or never.

'But it's not the be all and end all.' I hadn't a clue how to say this properly. 'I mean. It's not the end of the world if you don't do it.' This was me trying to sound like I meant it. It sounded so fake. I wasn't used to giving him advice.

'I don't even think I could do it anyway,' he said. His voice was as dead as a grave. I flinched in my seat.

'I couldn't get her to do it, Janus,' he said and then looked at me. 'Because I don't think I can do anything with that girl.'

My old need to just take off like a shot welled up inside me with huge force.

There was something dirty and horrible talking about all this with Tore in that way. We normally discussed this kind of stuff with an air of cool superiority. But here we were now in a cold sweat beside each other and deadly serious. In the last while at least, I'd stopped revealing really intimate things to Tore. Things that I wasn't sure about myself. But I'd never been in any doubt about his supremacy. Never. It was just that I didn't want to bother him. Anything that might put cracks in that dream-like bubble in which we moved, I kept away from him. Now here he was spewing out a load of things to which I didn't have any answers.

'That is utter rubbish,' I said. 'Total rubbish.'

'Janus. We went so fucking close,' he said. 'But she resisted and pleaded with me and went on and on about her mother.

Till in the end even I couldn't any more.' He sat there and crunched himself up on the bed.

'That was no way to talk about Helle,' I thought to myself. 'Never would I have allowed anyone to talk like that.'

'Ah come on, you're making a bit too much of it, mate,' I said. That goddamned perfect innocence. Goddamned perfect innocence.

If the whole building had collapsed right that minute I would have welcomed it. But a different *deus ex machina* appeared. I heard footsteps in the corridor and, as they came nearer, I realised it was dad. I grabbed my teacup.

A second later my bedroom door was flung open and my old man bursts in. Already talking and words belting out of his face:

'Your mother told me Tore was here, so I thought I'd come down and say hello,' he said. He headed straight over to Tore, got hold of his hand and shook it with all his heart. 'How's Tore then,' he said. 'Are you getting anything drummed into that head of Janus's?'

Everyday life had returned.

I was never so glad to see dad. One of the great days in his life was about to take place. Very soon, his youngest would become a student. His most important mission was accomplished. Because now all three of his sons would be university graduates. Nothing could have made my dad happier.

'I hope you're staying for dinner with us?' he asked Tore.

'Mum's already invited him, dad,' I said. There was none of the usual exasperation in my voice.

'Thought as much,' he said. 'How's the revision going? Have you two covered nearly everything?'

'We're revising German at the minute,' I said. Tore sitting there in turmoil.

'Ooooh Janey,' said the old man. 'That German. I could never grasp a bloody word of it. The only German I know is "Pilsner bitte!" But I tell you boys, you can get a long way with just that. But I've never liked the sound of that language.'

'We're reading *Faust*,' said Tore.

'Lord above,' dad says. Then he bursts out with – 'Habe nun ach ...'

He was as far from *Faust* as we were gripped by it. We had laid our plans for the deflowering of our very own Gretchen. Trying to make excuses would not help her any more. It was just a question of how best we could assist her in yielding to the dreaded deed. True. The fact that our *Faust* was under some spell of impotence created another difficulty. But surrounded by snakes and diabolical dogs as we were, our scheming would still win through, I reckoned.

Dad launched into some tortuous and complicated story about a group of foreign engineers who'd visited his office. So I busied myself with collecting the cups and taking them down to the kitchen. As I moved away from the room, I could still clearly hear the old man's voice. Every now and again, he laughed so loudly that my stuffed bird was probably blown onto the floor. But I didn't try to make out what he was saying. Let it all flow over me.

Tore was still sitting on the bed. Smiling politely. Like a young boy that's been dragged along to see Father Christmas, but is at that age where he doesn't really believe in fairy stories any more. Just smiles anyway so as not to disappoint his mother.

Chapter 11

When we finally got started, all else was forgotten. The wonderful sprint to the finish line devoured us completely. We went from one examination board to the next and everything happened so quickly it was over almost before it began. Tore took it all brilliantly in his stride and I handled it well enough. After being up in front of the examination panels in the morning, we usually had the afternoon to ourselves and went to the pictures or some park or other. Talking non-stop and winding ourselves down. The sunshine that warmed us suffused our skin and went deep into our bodies. The feeling of getting things done and over with for good and all. Of gradually nearing the goal that for so many years had been the cradle of our dreams was blissful. We were there now and nobody could deny us that plain fact. All thoughts of past and future disappeared the moment we pulled out the first of our exam slips with our subjects on them. Only these days remained in your consciousness as a time that was dazzlingly alive and exciting. A bright crown that was slowly but surely being placed upon our heads. We didn't even pretend to be blasé about it all, because of the sheer joy we felt at approaching the finish line.

The last subject was English. For me and Tore it was plain sailing. No dangerous rocks here for us.

We stood with the rest of the class in an empty classroom waiting to be called up to the panel. The atmosphere put you in mind of Christmas Eve. All the pathetic trogheads we'd gone to school with for so many years were stood there, pissing their pants in delight that the whole mad circus would be over in just a couple of hours. I was one of the first that would be called up and Tore one of the last. Even though, by this point, most of those present couldn't have cared less about the result of the exam, a lot of them were still reading their course books so ferociously they made the room glow. The tension had to be released one way or another. So half of them read without understanding or taking in an iota of what was in front of them and the rest of the class engaged in shouting and screaming and storming around the room in such a lunatic way that they wouldn't have noticed if thirty hippos suddenly fell through the ceiling. In a corner of the classroom, there was a clump of white paper bags. They were full of student caps.

All at once silence reigned. Senior House Master Grüne stood in the doorway and called up the first delinquent. Preben Mengel disappeared out the door with regal waves of his hand. Off with his head.

The huge commotion started again like Ragnarok itself as soon as Preben disappeared. Aksel jumps up onto a desk and roars:

'The class's first student. Long may he reign!' And a volley of protests erupted because Preben wasn't a student yet and wouldn't be one if we joked about it and shut the fuck up Aksel and trying to read here and get down off that desk dickhead.

I stuck a sweaty finger into one of my books and looked up Wordsworth. I stared at some of his verses but couldn't see the lines. 'In vacant and in pensive mood,' a voice said in my head. Tore was standing over in the corner talking to some of the lads. 'I wandered lonely as a cloud.' It was an airy and delightful sensation. I slapped the book shut. Stupid trying to read now. I could hear Tore discussing the chances of Shakespeare coming up. He wanted Shakespeare. Personally, I preferred poetry. We were both petrified of Civics.

Preben came back seconds later. It was as if he'd only just walked out the door. He was ambushed by a fusillade of questions. Most important of all. What subject had idiot features been asked about? 'Shakespeare of course.' What mark did he get? 'MG - Average of course.' They all smiled broadly. Then the real excitement started. The Principal himself comes gimping in and might he be allowed on behalf of the school and its staff to pass on his congratulations to the first student this year. And the old school and us the soon-to-be-not pupils any more stood there and were all actually moved beyond words. We looked over at Preben with his cap on and our eyes on stalks. Jesus do you know what? He looked cool. That goddamn fucking cap suited him.

Then the next one went up and the next and then it was me. I worked my way up the stairs. Trying to convince myself that the climb was what made my heart bang against my ribs. But once up there in the Gods, I forgot everything and believed as usual that I would pass out when I walked in front of that exam panel. Even though I knew this classroom so well, it looked like a different world with all the desks and chairs pushed to the sides and my school examiner and the external examiner planted in the middle of the floor.

Every time I'd done this, I'd tried to look at the familiar things around me to see whether they might calm me down. The tableau itself reminded me of a scene from the waxworks, where the two models, one known to you and the other totally strange, looked like figures in the house of horrors section. Deliberately put there to terrify the innocent children who'd been dragged in and forced to look at them. Before a second had passed, I'd sat down and pulled a number. The wax figures in front of me began slowly to come alive and bent over their table, opened books, moved their mouths, but no sound reached my ears yet. Eventually, finally finally finally, as if the words had floated over to me baked in dough, I picked up that Hr. Grüne wanted me to read aloud. 'Something from what, sir?' I didn't actually speak the sentence. Just mumbled it with closed lips. Then it dawned on me what he wanted. When I saw the slim volume with a selection of poetry down there in front of me. The mist slid from my eyes as, with precise care and a suppressed shake, I read the first lines of 'To Autumn'. I read and read and knew more and more in my heart that this was Keats and I was home and dry. No need for any more panic attacks. And I sat there and translated.

Inspired. Flowing, rhythmic and fluent. As if I'd composed it myself. My eyes were buried in the text but I still noticed that Master Grüne sent a look over to the external examiner. A look asking did he not also think I was wonderful. In fairness, Grüne himself must have been shocked, because he'd rarely seen me on such good form before. I translated and discussed the poem in English, as if this was my last chance ever in my life to talk about Keats and poetry, or anything at all for that matter. As if it was my last chance in the whole world ever to be happy like this. I didn't even hear when a thank-you was said from somewhere and just thundered on. Because I wanted to have it all said. Nothing could be left out. Eventually, and with a big vacuous smile on my face, I rose from my chair and bowed deeply to the two men in front of me. The men beamed their appreciation back at me and I nearly started bawling on the spot. I wasn't standing outside in the corridor two seconds when Master Grüne was standing in front of me taking hold of my hand and congratulating and saying I'd been given the UG Upper Grade as he was unable to give me anything higher and would I be a good lad and ask the next candidate to come up.

I swear my heart only struck a beat once every 60 seconds as I descended the staircase. Just one massive deliriously happy beat that made my chest bulge like a huge billowing sail.

Down on our corridor I blundered into the classroom where ranks of questioning eyes and mouths locked onto me.

'UG,' was all I said. 'Next one has to go up.'

'But what subject did you get?' they all roared. 'What subject for fuck's sake?'

'Keats,' I said. Then a load of them jumped on me and fished my cap out of one of the bags and planted it on my head. It felt so weird.

I spun round on my heels to look for Tore and he was standing right behind me holding his hand out. Just as on the other occasions, shaking hands with him was a rare and ceremonial moment.

'Mister Student Sir,' he said. 'That is just pure brilliant!'

'Mad. It's all just insane,' is all I said. My stomach was still gurgling.

'Soon be all over for you as well, mate,' I said, trying to gee him up.

'Phew,' he said. 'Now I'm starting to feel the pressure.'

Right that minute I couldn't have looked down on anyone in this world. Even Kurt, who was standing right next to me. I could have patted him on the shoulder and said 'you'll be fine, mate'. Not that I did any such thing.

There was nothing for it but to grab all my books. The whole fucking lot of them. And launch them right across the room. A feat which wiped the congratulations mask off the Principal's face as he walked through the door in that very same instant. He chose to ignore it though. Instead smiling sourly and saying something like I had done very well. As soon as he had disappeared, I went over to Tore again.

'I'm going downstairs to walk round in the street. Do a test run to see how it feels. I have to ring home as well.'

He nodded.

'Aye go on. Stop hanging around like a troghead.'

I scooted down the staircase, past other students who were going up and down. And we roared loads of things at each other and smiled at those poor creatures that were only doing the normal non-university exam. Down on the street. I didn't stop running till I got to a telephone box and had the coin in the slot.

The ready tone at the exchange exploded in my ear with a little bang and a second later I asked for our number. It was mum that answered the phone.

'It's over mum. I've passed,' I roared down the speaker.

'Did you pass, Janus my little man?' she asked with the start of a shake in her voice.

'I did mum and I got UG in English!'

There was no answer. But I could hear that my mother had started to cry. Which was only right.

'I got Keats, mum,' I said. Welling up in my breast. That same feeling of affection as when I was small and lay in bed. My mother tucking me up and caressing me.

'Ah Janus little love, congratulations,' she said. 'Well done, son.'

'Thanks a lot,' says I. 'Mum. I'm gonna run back to school now to see how Tore got on.' My legs were already doing bicycles.

'Well give Tore all our very best,' she said with a final sniffsob.

'Course I will,' says I. The phone was down and I was on the way back to school. It was just so wonderful to have someone to tell. Someone who also thought it was a wonderful thing. I didn't need to say anything to the people passing by. It shone out of me from a hundred miles away. I accelerated. Just to burn off some of that energy bursting in the pit of my guts and chest.

I swooped through the school gates like a jetfighter. It was like the whole school was imploding. All these people milling around, backwards and forwards. Talking, roaring, yelling. And radiant like they'd never been before. We went to see the caretaker and talked to him as equals and nothing wrong at all in inviting us in to his lodge for a beer.

Tore was sitting with a few of the last miserable remnants who still had to go up. They talked calmly. Subdued. But when they saw me, they all started shouting at once:

'Look a student! A genuine student!'

Tore got up. Making threatening gestures as he walked towards me.

'Get the fuck out of here,' he hissed. 'Go on. Piss off student wanker! Who do you think you are coming in here showing off with that pathetic cap?'

I took the cap off and tried to put it on Tore's head.

'Who's afraid of the big bad cap, the big bad cap, the big bad cap? Who's afraid of the big bad cap, tra lal lal la la!' I sang as he raised his arms to avoid the cap.

'Help!' He cried in a piercing voice. 'And it's me who's up next!'

The séance was interrupted when House Master Grüne came for Tore. We were quiet in an instant and then the procession disappeared through the door.

'All the best, mate,' I called to him as he disappeared.

Then I sat down to talk to the others. I nearly felt like going out to ring Ellen. But even having the idea sent an immediate rage through me. It was fuck all to do with her that I was only eighteen. She didn't give a shit whether I was a student or not. That was not what she was after. But what it was she was actually after, I didn't really have a clue.

'What's with the long face student?' one of the others asked. And I manned myself up and started thinking about something else entirely.

In the end it was too much to bear. I went out into the corridor to look for any signs of Tore. Quiet reigned everywhere. Not even the hint of a sound from the examination room. I walked across the corridor and looked out of the window.

It was like swimming. My mind. Just a mass of blissful elation revolving slowly round up there. My gaze moved from the windows opposite, to the slate roof shining in the sun. In between the chimneys and weather vanes, the sky was almost white. You could have almost believed the world had been emptied of humans but for the distant drone of traffic. I leaned against the window sill with an affectionate movement. As if this too was made of pure bliss.

Helle was standing down there in the street with her bike. I caught sight of her in the same instant that the sound of chairs being moved and scraped came from Tore's exam room. There was no time to wave to her because a door was opened and a second later Tore burst into the corridor.

'Oh Lordy Lordy,' was all he said. 'The House of Lords, what a question to get. Oh Lordy.'

I nudged his arm and pointed down to the street. Then he spotted Helle. He rushed over to the window, grabbed the hasps and flung the window open. Then he let out a roar so loud that Town Hall clock almost fell down:

'It's over, Helle. I've finished! It's all over!' He pulled me over to the open window. 'And look!' he roared again. 'Janus is a student! Janus has turned into a student.'

I took my cap off and swung it round in circles outside the

window. Then I started roaring as well.

'We'll be down in a bit!' Helle said something or other we couldn't hear. She wouldn't be finished until the following day, poor creature. We carried on shouting more nonsense down to her for a while longer and hardly paused for breath when Master Grüne appeared behind us and tapped Tore on the shoulder.

'Well, Tore. I'm sure you won't be too happy with that?' he asked with a little smile.

'Oh, I don't know,' said Tore. 'It could have been a lot worse.'

'Would you settle for just above average. An MG plus?' The House Master inquired.

Tore stuck out his hand but said nothing. Then he received Grüne's congratulations. He as near as slung Grüne's hand away from him, turned to the window and roared down to Helle: 'I got MG plus Helle! MG plus!' Then he turned round, grabbed House Master Grüne and heaved him to the window. 'House Master Grüne awarded me MG plus.'

Grüne smiled down towards the street and then pulled back, slightly embarrassed. Then he was gone from our thoughts and we dived down the staircase. Tell you. Never have I run so much as I did that day.

You'd never work out who kissed Helle the most, but we just kept going until we realised that half the school was hanging out of the windows, cat-calling and hollering.

'Get stuck in lads!' they cried. 'Think yez are holding back there a bit. Call yourselves men?'

In the end. Nothing for it but to turn, acknowledge the gallery and doff the cap with a flourish. Tore went to do the same. Then remembered he hadn't got his yet.

So the nutter hares off and returns some breathless moments later with his cap on and receiving the raucous acclaim of the swampies up above.

And so it went the whole day. And the day after was even worse because Helle was finished that day as well and Tore the Man created a great stir and scandal by beating out a celebratory fanfare on the bins in her schoolyard whilst an exam was still in progress. We did all the daft things that new fledged students are supposed to do. And I sang an old student song arm-in-arm with dad from the days of his youth and we both had big fat tears in our eyes and I had no thought of Ellen or anyone else for that matter.

The Three Musketeers went to Tivoli fun fair as well. In the same week, I held a party at my house. It was a brilliant party, where we didn't even manage to get out to the Little Mermaid and watch the dawn come up because Kurt spewed his ring so much that we daren't leave him.

I still felt wrecked when I woke the next day and remembered that Helle's party was that very evening. I hadn't seen Fru Junkersen in ten million years. She and all things about her were nothing more than just vague afterthoughts for me at this time.

The hour of my waking was not unusual – it was almost one o'clock. The early rays of afternoon sunshine beating through my window. Over on my table, three overturned beer bottles presented mute testimony to the night before. There was a rank odour of stale cigarette smoke. My student cap was there as well. Suitably stained. In truth, the last thing I wanted to do was get up.

Down down beneath the duvet I slunk. Then I heard mum's steps coming down the corridor. So I closed my eyes and let on I was asleep. She opened the door. Stood there looking at me for a while, before going over to the table and putting the beer bottles upright. She nudged at the ashtray. Then she came right over to the bed.

'Janus,' she said quietly. 'Janus, there's someone on the phone for you.' My ears pricked up at this.

'Hrrrm?' I said.

'It's a girl that wants to talk to you.' I opened my eyes. 'Who is it?' I asked.

'She didn't say what her name was.' She was fussing at one of the books on my shelf.

'Right. I'd better see who it is,' I said. I swung my legs out of the bed but held the duvet around my body still. Mum was removing the beer bottles.

'And how are you today?' she asked.

217

'Really good,' says I, going out the door, snagging my dressing gown from its peg as I did so.

It was Ellen at the other end. I'd told her a million times that I didn't want her ringing me at home. I blew my top straight away.

'What the fuck do YOU want?' I snarled down the phone. 'Haven't I told you not to ring me here.'

'I just wanted to hear how it all went,' she said. I gave no answer. 'Just to hear if you'd passed,' she continued. I emitted a low growl.

'It's just that there's so much in the paper about students and all that ... so I thought you were probably finished.'

'All finished,' I muttered tersely.

'Congratulations, Janus,' she said. I didn't reply.

'I've a day off from the office today,' she said. 'Or I mean. I just stayed off. Would you like to come over?'

I had forgotten her. I was finished with her. I never wanted to go over to her place ever again.

'Arr, I can't really. You know what it's like. Me just finishing my exams and then going out later tonight.' I spoke with rising irritation.

'Where are you going tonight?' she asked.

'Never you mind,' I said.

'But could you not just come over for the afternoon then?' I held the phone away from my ear. Ready to smash it down. Then my mum walked through the living room. I didn't dare get caught having a massive row with Ellen whilst mum was in the same room.

'All right, sounds good,' I said in a completely different tone of voice. 'I'll come over for a while this afternoon.'

'Janus,' she said at the other end of the line. 'Janus.'

I put the receiver down and turned towards my mum, saying quickly that it was one of Helle's friends. One of them going to the party that evening, and she wanted me to help her in putting something together for the party, and a whole load of other rubbish that made me feel like a total idiot. Then I bombed it back to my room.

I threw on my clothes in small explosions of annoyance.

She had no right whatever to intrude into our dream world. Unbelievable that a girl like that didn't have the basic nous to keep away. I'd even said it to her. Told her umpteen times that she was not to ring me at home. I was so annoyed at her that I literally quivered with rage over my whole body. Like a hysterical puppydog. But I would teach her.

As I launched myself, using the banisters as leverage, down the inner staircase leading to the street, a feeling of base meanness rose inside me. What kind of girl could make me behave in such an atrocious way? Why was I such a fucking awful person?

My heart knocked in my breastcage, fuelled by the poison of all the stale beer and mountain of cigarettes I'd consumed in the last week. I felt destroyed even before I got up on my bike. In a few seconds, I had reached top speed and was bombing my way towards town. I would teach that fucking cow. I wasn't wearing my student cap. This between me and Ellen was no student thing. Taking off on the bike like that actually made me feel better. I banged down onto the pedals so hard the muscles in my thighs screeched in pain.

Cars and traffic passing so close they nearly barged into me. I overtook a horse-drawn van and, as I passed it, the horse turned its head to me snorting and braying. It had a huge white eye, staring right at me as if it recognised something there. I slogged on.

Down at the bottom of Ellen's stair entrance, I threw my bike into the gutter and braced myself for the run up the stairs. But when I stood in the entrance to the building and the tension from the hinge and spring arm on top of the door began to close it behind me with a soft whoosh, I remained hovering where I was. If she started that blubbering now I was there, I would kill her. Tears were not what I wanted from her. Under no circumstances would I be made responsible for anything whatsoever where me and Ellen were concerned. Anyway. Why had she just sat there in that pub that time, taking dog's abuse without even a whimper? Just like she was allowing herself to be abused by me now. Without screaming or something? But if she stood there quietly weeping. Then

I would murder her. For a split second, I was two different people. From the street me looking in. Saw my own self standing there like a useless effigy in the open doorway. The watching part of me staring at the other half wanted to run, but this doppelgänger effect only lasted a single second. Then I began to walk up the stairs.

Outside her door, I stopped again. My overwrought tension had my knees nearly buckling. My heart bulged through my ribs and gave irregular beats that felt like a disgusting nausea. That old seasickness had a hold of me again and I just wanted to kneel down and throw up on her door mat. That would be my student exam gift to Ellen.

The door opened, and Ellen stood there looking at me. I hadn't even rung the bell. She pulled me in. Or rather, she took a step back and I walked into her tiny hall. The door closed behind me with a quiet double click. I led the way into her sitting room. It was by no means a sad room. Definitely not. She closed the door.

It was like being inserted into a Chinese puzzle. With layer after layer sliding in around you. The room had become far too small for the two of us. I began to flap and move my arms about. Like a bird on the brink of expiring. I flapped in her direction.

'Can you get me a glass of water?' I asked, like a wretch thirsting in the desert.

'I've a beer there,' she said.

'No, just a glass of water.' I made a meaningful gesture up to my forehead. She stared at me.

'Right. Water it is then,' she said. She went out to the kitchen for a glass of water.

I sat on the sofa and placed my palms on the insides of my thighs. They were tense and slightly bowed. Like oar blades. I hadn't killed her yet.

She came in from the kitchen with the glass and handed it to me. I shoved my tongue down into it, opened my mouth and drank like a beast. The water ran down through my insides like bursting waves. Maybe I should have drunk it more slowly. To give me some time. This thought only hit me when the last glug of it went down and twisted my throat so that I had to pull the glass away from my spluttering mouth. A hiccup that sounded like a strangled cry. Then the cough came.

It occurred to me that I might be able to cough all this raging insanity out of my body. Or maybe I could cough so violently that Ellen would just shatter into a thousand pieces from the destructive force of the sound waves.

The vibration of my heaving lungs and huge wheezing intakes of air filled the room with a demonic thunder. But this simply spurred me on to even greater feats of respiration. The offending block in my throat seemed to go on bulging outwards and take on the dimensions of a tumour. My barking cough turned to a scream and soon I noticed the taste of blood in my mouth. Ellen came towards me. Maybe to pat my back or lift my arms into the air. I fired my cough at her. Like some flame-spewing dragon. A terrible parching and stinging pains rose from my chest and lungs and the sounds emanating from my mouth were like the braying of a whipped animal.

'Stop it Janus,' Ellen said. 'Stop it. Just stop!' I could see from her face that she was terrified and I began to feel as if I was on top again. Across my gut came this feeling of something dying. The coughs still roaring out of me.

She came right up to me and took hold of my head. I barked straight into her mouth and felt that the soft fleshy part of my throat was now in shreds. Tears streamed out of my face. I gnashed my teeth and coughs exploded through my nose like snorts from a strangled horse. By this stage, my eyes were on stalks. She grabbed me around my neck with both her hands and pulled me into her. At the same time she kneeled in front of the sofa and dragged my face towards her neck. Slaver was falling from my mouth and ran down the front of her. My cough stopped.

I just let the whole thing slide. All my muscles relaxed at one and the same time and I rolled onto her with the weight of a dead man. We fell to the floor in a slow arc. She lay partly beneath me and my face brushed the carpet. Then we lay stock still. I lay with my mouth on the floor and my head at the side of her shoulder. One of my legs was in between hers. I felt like someone had twisted my innards with a wrench.

'What's wrong with you?' she just kept on saying. 'What is wrong with you?' She said this rhythmically. Like an incantation. Every time I drew breath, it felt like a surgical operation.

She made moves to get up, but I pulled her down again. Then I began to work at her. Bent the leg that was between hers so that my knee ran up to her crotch. She thrashed her upper body around like a captured fish wriggling in your hands. I grabbed the neck of her dress and began tearing at it. That was when she started to whimper. She managed to slide from under me, but I still had hold of her dress and breaking totally free from me would have meant ripping it to shreds. I went on ripping the material and she began to scream. In clumsy slow motion, she fell back to the floor again.

'Stop ripping my bloody dress up will you,' she screamed. She was in floods of tears now and I stopped ripping.

'There's no need to go ripping my dress to pieces Janus. No need at all!' I lay still by her side. The particular way she was crying left me with no urge to kill her on the spot. She began to pull up the skirt of her dress. When she had got it over her thighs, she rose onto her knees and began pulling her dress over her head. When she was still all caught up, I rolled myself over her and dragged her to me. She emitted a little cry and whimpered feebly for me to wait but, when she finally realised what I was after, her hands helped me with my trousers and the whole thing happened in a cut and dried way, ending with those white stains that quickly change to black patches of damp on the carpet between her legs.

I got up straight away and straightened my clothes. She just lay there on the floor like a headless woman. She was naked to beyond her navel and the rest of her body was still covered by her dress. Her hands lay flat and limp alongside her. The water glass had been knocked onto the floor but had not broken.

My state of exhaustion had changed now and was more like a paralysis of my whole body. Senseless. Like after a knockout punch.

'Hey. Ellen. Get up now,' I said to her. Like I was talking to a very young daughter of mine who was messing around on the floor.

She didn't look at me. A bit after, she did a half roll so she ended up lying on her side. This also fully revealed the stains on the carpet. Her dress fell down over her stomach when she sat up. She got hold of her knickers and started putting them on. She did a couple of jolts as she pulled them up over her backside and nearly ended up with her elbow in the stains on the floor as she supported her weight. I stamped in irritation. When was this pathetic bitch finally going to throw me out?

She got up and went out to the kitchen. Seconds later she returned with a cloth, kneeled down and began rubbing at the stains. She was just in front of my right foot. I couldn't even speak to her.

She was down there rubbing away. As if her innermost wishes would be fulfilled if she rubbed hard enough.

'Where are you going tonight?' she asked. I moved my foot nearer to her. She didn't retreat. Just kept on rubbing.

'Are you going out to see that girl Helle?' I pulled my foot back a bit.

'Are you?' Her hand still going backwards and forwards.

'You and Tore are going there, aren't you?'

The question unleashed my foot and the tip of my shoe rammed into her outer thigh. She fell back onto the floor with a scream that quickly turned into a continuous yammering bawl. She lay on the carpet, crying and crying and clutching the wet cloth into her. A morphine-like lethargy came over me. I bent down over her in some kind of reflex action, took hold of her and got her onto the sofa. She lay there with her legs tucked up under her and the hand holding the cloth resting on my knee. The damp from the cloth was soaking through my trousers.

She shook all over. But gradually she settled. I carried on stroking her hair. In the end, her body relaxed. I lifted her head up and lay down beside her. She stretched her body out and I felt how she clung into me as I began descending into a deep sleep. Nodding off like that felt like being drugged. Her movements felt like those of a surgeon and his team around the operating table, just before you slip into unconsciousness. The room disappeared from me. Zoomed out and exploded those hundreds of layers of Chinese puzzle. The liberation I felt was like a dark detonation as unconsciousness enveloped me.

I didn't know where I was when I first woke. But I had a bad feeling of how late it was. When I felt the pattern of the stitching in the afghan rug she had thrown over me, I knew the place I was in. Ellen was not lying beside me. I jumped up from the sofa and stood there. Dizzy for a moment. My watch was telling me it was half-past five.

The thought that I'd nearly overslept left me close to paralysis. I looked round the room, where the low afternoon was shoving its slants through the window. Then to the front door. Time to get the finger out.

Ellen appeared in the hallway from her kitchen just as I gripped the door handle to get away. She stood there with two tea cups and a little tray with cakes on it. Two of the cakes had a green-coloured buttercream topping. Jesus I was nearly sick on the spot. The sight of her attempts at being a housewife in the middle of this utter mayhem.

'We're going to have a cup of tea,' she said. Like it was a command not to be ignored.

'I have to go right now.' I had the door halfway open. 'I have to be there by 7 and I'm not even dressed yet.' She couldn't keep me back with her hands full of teacups, cakes and all, but she held her hands out anyway. As if trying to get a hold of me. I retreated a little.

'For fuck's sake, Ellen. You know I have to go. Can you not get hold of some girl friend to drink tea with?' This far down the road, I'd become so hardnosed I was capable of saying anything.

'Ring some friend or other. Anyone.' It was a straight taunt. The green cakes stared at me like poisonous snakes. If only this fucking miserable bitch would throw the whole fucking tray over me. But she just stood there. 'That's just so unfair of you!' she said.

It would have been brilliant to roar like fuck at her. I could have kicked this numbskull from one end of the room to the other. But still. She would have come crawling back and wrapped herself around me like a sick kitten. I could abuse her and mess her up. Wreck her flat. And yet there she stood brimming with tea and cakes.

I opened the door. Wide open. Went out onto the landing and the last I ever saw or heard of Ellen was a teacup being jammed into the doorway as a block and then the little smack when the door hit the china cup as I slammed it shut. Then I ran like mad. Same as I always did after being at hers.

I was still running when I went through my front door and through the living room. Mum's stare bored holes in my back and, as I rushed on, I heard Dad's 'ah the student has arrived!' like soft, quivering echoes in the air behind me.

My mother had put out all my clothes for me. My tux lay on the bed. Headless and observing me with a superior air. Made me even more nervous. Shaving was nearly impossible, my hand shook so much. I was wrecked. Contrived to slit open a good few parts of my chin with the blade and, when I leaned forward to repair the damage with cotton buds, the black bags under my eyes filled the mirror. It was getting on for half six.

Finally finally. I put on my famous student cap and went in to mum and dad to act the part. My mother gave me the once-over. Turned me round and brushed my shoulders. They spoke to me like I was an actor making his inaugural appearance. But at least I was well prepared. Mum had made sure everything was present and correct. White handkerchief. Cufflinks. Cigarette case. All my pristine and wonderful articles that lead you up the stairway to *Academe*. Within touching distance of higher minds and the truly wealthy. When the last pat on the shoulder had been performed, I tumbled down the stairs to a waiting taxi.

As we drove along, I noticed that my legs were still going ten to the dozen. I relaxed and fell back about half a yard into my seat. There was no traffic on the roads and, thankfully, I had a driver who was in no mood for small talk. We got out there in less than ten minutes. Junkersen Castle towered ahead. Toppling forward above glowing columns of light. There were three taxis at the front gate when I arrived.

With careful, deliberate movements, I opened my door and got out of the car as the driver came round to my side for his money. I handed over the money and a generous tip. The Castle. The area. My tux. All demanded nothing less. Slowly, I wound myself up to the requisite mood and, in truth, it wasn't that hard to begin smiling and passing the correct remarks, as I greeted Esben and Aksel who were unfolding themselves from the other cars accompanied by an assortment of girls. The girls obviously in thrall to the prestige of the occasion, but only showing it by displaying ridiculously false airs and graces. We moved as a group up the garden path to the house, whose whole battery of lights shone brightly. Not one but two maids, d'ye mind, were there to receive guests in the *Vestibule* as Fru Junkersen insisted on calling it. The other lads issued bursts of forced laughter, but couldn't really control their stunned faces, which revealed they were all star-struck astonishment at the whole show. I greeted the Junkersen maid, whom I'd seen on all the other visits, and suddenly felt like I was a close friend of the Household. At the very least, I was somewhere up above swamp level.

The plush carpets swept us into the ground floor rooms which were brilliantly illuminated. As if by floodlights. Everywhere was overflowing with guests. My eyes dogged Kurt who was gorging the whole ambience into him like a pig at a trough. Sweet Jesus if they didn't also have male waiters swanning round with cocktails on silver trays. Tore was in the room. Surrounded by small clumps of couples. There they were, showering him with their admiration and jealousy. Like flowers cascading over the Prince Regent. Helle was stood talking to some lads who had no female escorts. She spoke calmly to them. Stroking her hand across her face every now and again. As if attempting to draw a veil aside. A veil that irritated her and was preventing her seeing all about her with full clarity. I went over to her to say hello. She seemed as wrecked as I was. Looked that way anyway. A dull grey cast over her eyes. But she smiled when she saw me. I acknowledged those standing around with a finger salute to my locks.

The waiter was hovering near me with cocktails, and I took the cold glass and lifted it as a toast to Helle, who was drinking sherry. The trogs all about me were swilling cocktails into them at a ferocious rate. They obviously felt the need after so many days of debauchery. The gin seeped down into our guts and deadened the highly fraught nervous state and lack of sleep that affected all of us. In the twink of a drink, our noise levels screamed upwards ten thousand decibels.

Fru Junkersen had still not made her entrance. I was on the brink of forgetting her altogether. Standing there with drink number two in my hand, another olive in my mouth. Enjoying an inner glow of contentment when a door in one of the side rooms opened and she emerged into the function room like a slow-burning comet. A trail of spectacular dress flowing behind her. As if the waiters had gone round like lightning bolts administering a slap to each mouth in the clumps of chattering guests, all talk and noise died away. These dregs of Copenhagen's periphery had never seen anything like it. Helle's mother looked astoundingly good in all her brash sophistication. Imposingly tall and wearing a dress that made every other girl in the place look like a dejected street sparrow, even though most of them were 20 years younger than Fru Junkersen.

Immediately, she plunged over to Tore's group, which fell back to either side like the Red Sea. Kurt's face seemed to become hooded like a chameleon, as he watched Fru Junkersen thrust across the room. She offered her hand to him and he took it with a star-struck shake. As if it was Stanley meeting Sarah Bernhardt in the jungle, rather than Doctor Livingstone. They exchanged a pleasantry or two before she moved on to greet all the other guests. The murmurs and party hubbub began again and rose gradually to chatter levels. The second Fru Junkersen left one group, the girls were to be seen leaning up to the boys and whispering in their ears. Helle's mother manoeuvred between the groups like a long-tailed reptile. Then she gave me a terse greeting. The feeling of being a close friend of the household quickly evaporated. In his predictable way, Kurt managed to detain her ladyship with some remark or other that required a response. So she was forced to stand by his side for longer than she intended and listen to his tedious drone, whilst he grabbed the chance to gawp brazenly down her cleavage.

Helle was still stood next to me holding a tray from which I found relief via yet another cocktail.

'You're allowed one more,' she said.

'Thanks,' I said, scrutinizing her as I did so. Her usual smile seemed to have been wiped from her face. I suppose preparing for this whole bash had been a nightmare for her.

At some point, after all the guests had paid their respects to the hostess, the double doors to the dining room were opened. Once again a frisson ran like a sigh through the assembled guests. This time at the sight of a massive table – bedecked with a profusion of flowers that were surrounded by oceans of silver and porcelain.

The maids in the corridor had given each one of us a table card and I only noticed at this point, to my utter delight and surprise, that I was to accompany Helle to table. I went over to her and took her hand. I had never done it before. But I took her hand as if it was me that had just got engaged to her and was showing her to our positions at table. At the same time, I closed my eyes and bit my teeth into my bottom lip, because a vague odour of something hit me. Something that filled me with all the events of the afternoon. Back at me like a hard slap between the shoulder blades. But those three cocktails had already moved me to a place where I could shove Ellen and all our works to one side and concentrate on that hand in mine and that table before which we now stood.

Helle freed her hand from mine, but not without giving it a little squeeze first. So slight I wasn't sure it actually happened. She rose from her seat and tapped her glass. Then she sent a look down to her mother, who was sitting with her head bowed. Helle bade us welcome. Both she and her mother were delighted that we had come. Tore sat with his face fully turned to Helle. Embracing her with his eyes. He had Fru Junkersen to table. Following Helle's welcome speech, we sang the time-honoured Student Song.

The initial stunned shock at seeing the table also began to wear off and everybody was soon getting stuck into the meal. Two male and two female waiters made sure there was no shortage of anything. Slowly but surely the drink got a good grip of me and the same could be said of a lot of the trogs at the trough. We weren't that far into the steak and red wine when the din from the table began to reverberate around the room. I raised my glass to Helle time without number but she barely drank. Just sitting there nipping at the same glass, whilst mine was refilled continuously.

'Are you abstaining or what?' I asked, leaning into her.

'Remember I'm the mistress of ceremonies,' she said.

I nodded a bit mechanically. Like people do when they've had a drink.

'I thought your mother was,' I said.

'Yes, Janus. Mother's the real host. But it's my party.' She looked down the table at her mother with some annoyance. Mother and Tore were deep in conversation.

'Course it's your party, Helle,' I said, as I sought out her hand again under the table. But she pulled hers away.

'Any minute, I'm going to stand up and tell them what complete morons they all are,' says I to Helle. She smiled back at me. Then Børge got up and proposed that we sing some song or other, because if we didn't sing, we wouldn't build up enough thirst to drink all that lovely red wine, and what a shame that would be, blah blah blah. But we all laughed anyway and got drunker from all that standing up and toasting and roaring and I don't know what.

I made a vain attempt to get Tore and Fru Junkersen to return a toast. Her jaws were in full swing shovelling him into her. Tore was sat leaning over towards her. Engrossed in the movements of her mouth. As if he was scared of missing a single motion.

I panned down the table and through my own swimmy eyes saw a mass of similarly blank and shiny eyes and hands moving up and down with carafes and glasses, knives and forks and mouths opening and shutting, all uttering meaningless grunts and noises. One of the girls had such a piercing laugh she was nothing more than a fart balloon. Then I was back at myself and a plate in front of me with a bit of meat and sauce and a knife and fork placed next to each other. A bit down to my right was Helle's hand on the table, and some breadcrumbs from one of the small baguettes. I looked at this for ages. Then I agreed with myself that I would look up at Helle. Like a remote control crane, I turned my head towards her and saw that she was sat staring at her plate just as I had been. I stayed looking at her.

'You are the mistress of ceremonies,' I said. 'You said just before that you've arranged all this.' I stare at her. 'So it's you who decides what happens. Everything.'

She turned towards me.

'Will you pour me a bit more red wine?' she asked in a low voice.

I turned and lifted the carafe and poured into her glass, that was nearly full anyway. I also filled my own. Nobody noticed that we sat there so still and quiet. I was sat beside Earth's most pure and divine angel of God and couldn't even hold her hand over a mound of breadcrumbs. I mean. In all this madness, even if we had kissed each other full on the mouth right there and then, no one would have paid the slightest heed. Not even Tore. What a golden chance.

'Are you upset about something?' I asked.

She shook her head. Then she looked at me again: 'I'm just a bit nervous Janus. My mother's about to announce to the whole world that Tore and I are engaged.' She smiled. 'We're not going to wear rings.'

Inside me, a voice was saying that there was something not quite right about that. And then it hit me. I mean. It was me that was Helle's partner at table for Christ's sake. That was mad stuff. You couldn't do that at an engagement party. The engaged couple always sat together. I looked up wonderingly at her face. Then I lifted my glass and offered a toast to her.

'Am I allowed to offer my congratulations before the rest?'

We clinked glasses.

'And do I finally get a chance to kiss you properly, or will that only happen on your wedding day?' I pondered and pondered my brain to try and work out what was wrong with Helle. This lunatic party. The seating arrangements. But all I could come up with was the usual conclusion that everything always went to cock if I was involved in it.

'Are you not supposed to be sitting with Tore?' I asked her straight out. My nerves jangling all the way down to my fingers.

'Actually I am,' she says rapid fast. 'But my mother switched things at the last minute. She asked me who you had to table and, when I said you were coming alone, she told me to keep you company. And there was no time to start fighting about it.' Then in a miserable voice she goes – 'Ah Janus, I didn't mean it like that. It's not that I didn't want to sit next you. You know that. It's just that I thought. Well, today of all days ...' I laid my hand on hers and we sat like that for a while. Then I noticed that Kurt was watching us and I felt my cheeks going red hot and I let go of Helle's hand. From across the table, Aksel's girlfriend leaned forward and began talking to me. Cheers we cried to each other. This was picked up at the other end of the table and soon we were all cheersing each other and standing up and sitting down and standing up. And eating cheese with biscuits and even more red wine was drunk and then we sang again till I nearly couldn't see out of my eyes any more.

'Must be with the dessert,' says I to myself. 'That's when they'll announce it.' But that came and went and nothing. Fru Junkersen never rose from her chair. Never tapped her glass, crying she was thrilled to announce that Tore and Helle had chosen to celebrate their engagement on this wonderful night when all these happy young people were gathered under her roof with their white student caps and bright shining eyes and beating hearts just as it says in that beloved Swedish song *der klappar än med friska slag* – No. She just sat there huggermugging with Tore like he was some shady Underground Resistance Guy who had been forbidden to bring his documents so was obliged to spend the whole

231

evening reciting the Luftwaffe's battle code off the top of his head.

We got champagne with the dessert. And even though most of the trogs were already slaughtered, their eyes went on stalks again as the corks started to pop around the table.

It wasn't long before all I was seeing was foaming champagne in front of my eyes and I suffered some kind of partial whiteout. With buzzing in my ears and a dink dink dink tapping at my skull, I managed to get upstanding and could vaguely hear through the clouds that people were thanking Madame for the wonderful meal. Finds myself at some point standing in front of Fru Junkersen with my hand out and her voice a million miles away saying: 'You are more than welcome, Hr. Janus.'

The noise coming from the other rooms was deafening. One of the waiters was going round offering Havanas and most of the boys had lit up torpedo-size cigars. Puffing into the air and looking like their own dads at a confirmation do.

I collapsed down into a sofa and started a conversation out of the side of my flapping mouth with some idiot or other whose identity I never did discover. We drank cognac. Sitting there gassing about cognac. As if we knew the fuck about cognac and all that.

They had begun dancing in the next room and I made a couple of attempts to get up from the sofa. In the end I succeeded, driven by the fact that I was bursting for a piss, and I blundered out into the back garden. All around in the darkness beneath the trees and the wall of the house, the trogs were going at each other hammer and tongs. But I eventually managed to find a spot where I could open my flies in peace.

Even though I bumped into fifty trees on the way back to the house, I didn't feel a thing. The whole universe seemed to be one big swampy mass that had sucked me into its quagmire.

When I stumbled up over the terrace steps to the patio area, who was standing there smoking a cigarette only my Big Red Indian Chief. It was the first time we had been together that evening.

'All right, Tore? Out stargazing mate? Where's Helle?'

'Haven't a clue mate,' says he, as if he couldn't care less.

'It's all right for him,' – says I to myself. 'They aren't officially engaged yet. So he can afford to be a bit relaxed about everything!' I gave his shoulder a light punch: 'Tore the Man eh! ... you've done good, mate. Congratulations!' He raised his head a bit and I could see that he was, if anything, more pissed than I was.

'You are the world's last Totem Pole,' I said. 'The last Totem Pole in the whole world.' I lurched into him and we held each other up for a while. 'I don't give a fuck about anything else anyway,' says I to myself. 'I'm in some mad place so far gone anyway that nothing matters a shit any more. But I've got you haven't I, eh? So fuck the rest.' With massive concentration, I put my full weight on my front foot, pushed off from his shoulder and pointed my momentum in the direction of the French doors. Half falling as I crossed their threshold.

Sodom and Gomorrah was going full swing in every room. It was impossible to find even the tiniest space on a sofa where I could fall. Writhing, cavorting bodies everywhere. Spy a little triangular table with a gin bottle still on it and floor space beside it. So down on the floor it is. It was eleven o'clock. I managed to get my mouth round the neck of the gin bottle. Took two pulls on it and promptly fell asleep.

When I woke again, nearly all the house lights were off. Someone had turned them all off and it was pitch black. My head was pounding and nausea welled up to breaking in me. My gin glass had fallen out of my hand, but a waiter must have taken it away because there was nothing more than a little wet patch on the floor beside me. Somehow, I was belly down on the floor, crawling round as my gut heaved like the sea and a mass of saliva began to run out of my mouth. Using the back of an armchair, I dragged myself up and tottered towards the door, hoping to make it to the toilet.

The door to the downstairs toilet was half open but when I pushed it further back I saw Gregers spark out on the floor – fast asleep, legs near the door, head up near the wash bowl.

The stench was horrendous. I staggered backwards and found the staircase to try and get to the toilets on the first floor. My legs wouldn't lift over the steps properly, so it was a case of half dragging myself upwards by the banister.

I was halfway up when I saw Helle. She was walking by the banister that went along the first floor landing and for a second I thought it was her white ghost. She wasn't reeling or staggering. You couldn't say that. Rather she was staving her way forwards, then downwards, using the banister for help. Heading right towards me. I just stopped dead because I couldn't go a step further.

When she was right in front of me, she just stood there looking at me. Like I was some distant relative she was forced to acknowledge for a moment before continuing with doing the much more vital thing she had to do. I wanted to ask her why she had smeared her face with green powder, but she stepped to one side slightly and just continued her passage down the stairs, with her free arm straight by her side and the hand clenched in a fist. 'Don't tell me she's paralytic as well?' I thought. 'Is that the way Helle looks when she's pissed?' Waves of nausea rose in me again and I had to keep moving to avoid throwing up on the spot.

I had just pegged my way up onto the landing as Tore emerged from a door at the end of the corridor. He began stumbling towards me. I looked at him very intensely and had half raised my hand in a wave when I saw that he had no jacket on and no trousers either. His shirt looked like it was torn. I stopped again. Stopped now and unable to move and he was beside me. Making to go past me without looking at me and on down the stairs. I put my arms out and clasped them round him. So he had no choice but to stop. He made a slight move to free himself from me and turned his face away but I pulled him round again and saw that he was crying. He squirmed out of my grasp but I got hold of him again and squeezed him into me.

'I've got to talk to Helle,' he said. Once more he turned his face away. 'Just need to talk her,' he said.

'Tore,' I almost whispered. 'You can't go downstairs like

234

that. Tore listen. You can't go down there like that, mate.' I shook him. 'Where's the rest of your clothes?'

'I'm not going back in there,' he said nodding backwards.

'Ah Jesus no. Ah fuck,' I cried. Then half wrestled half tripped him so we both went crashing to the floor on the landing. His big body fell halfway across mine and his knee smashed right into my thigh. I pulled him into me again. Then I got up and ran down the corridor. There was no light on in Fru Junkersen's room, but I could make out her shape in the bed. For a second, I just stood there struck with terror in the doorway. But then I reached up and found a light switch and clicked. She didn't move. Just looked at me. And I should have killed her there and then.

Tore's clothes were on the floor, and I began picking them up. Out of the corner of my eye, I noticed one of her arms move. Then she spoke.

'Who gave you permission to come in here, little pup?' I was rooting around for his socks. 'You just can't keep away can you? You little lapdog.'

I was still on the floor and my hand grabbed part of his jacket. Me lying on the floor holding Tore's clothes. Him sat out in the corridor half-naked.

'But do cheer up, Janus,' she said. 'I must say he wasn't half bad ... takes a lot longer with these little innocents, but he got there in the end.'

I groaned. No ... This really was the end of the world. I got up and left the room. Half running back down the corridor, because I saw that Tore was on his way downstairs again. I could hear the trogs starting up a conversation down below and I dived after him on the stairs and dragged him back into Helle's room.

It was nearly impossible to get him dressed. It was like tangling with a demented child. In the end, I managed it. And when his shirt was finally tucked under his tux all the way round, we went downstairs.

When we got there, the waiters were vigorously engaged in removing every single disgusting trace of the night before. They had also chivvied the trogs up onto their feet. They were now standing or sitting around nursing their wounds. Helle was nowhere to be seen. So we ran out to the garden. Two hound dogs plummeting into undergrowth. Bumping and turning about each other, sniffing at things and whining slightly as we searched for her. Tore went right out into the road, running up and down the garden railings in the avenue. Not seeing or finding her and not really knowing what he was doing. His head was sunk down between his shoulders and in the rising light of morning he resembled an ailing vulture.

In the end, we gave up looking for her outside. We went back in and, as we passed through the French doors, were met by a chorus of hoarse voices. Crowing their homage to the coming day. A huge cold buffet had been set in the dining room. Some of the demons were already going hell for leather at the schnapps. I pulled Tore away and made for the kitchen but we were stopped in our tracks by Fru Junkersen.

Tore roared out some unintelligible words when he caught sight of her. She was wearing a sparkling new dress and looked fabulous. She took Tore's arm with consummate ease and ushered him back towards the buffet table. Then she spoke aloud: 'I'm sure there were some amongst us yesterday evening who felt perhaps a bit let down because they had expected a certain thing to happen that in the end didn't take place. But that was not due to it being overlooked. It's just that I felt now would be a more fitting moment – a lovely summer morning beginning to dawn outside our windows … Where's Helle?' She looked about the room. 'Helle has to be here for this …'

Tore flung her arm away from him and a quiet gasp soughed through the room. I was now by his side, holding onto his arm. He opened his mouth to say something but never got there because the screaming started that same moment. At first it felt like aeons away. But it came nearer and nearer, as if being played through a loudspeaker whose volume was being screwed upwards with every second that passed. The kind of scream you only know when you hear it. The unbearable anguish of someone screaming beyond their senses. The shrieking rose up from the bowels of the house and came closer and closer to the dining room as its power increased. The assembled company was now motionless. Frozen in place. Only Tore's face was in constant agitation, as we waited in a fathomless eternity till the door was flung open and the youngest of the maids walked in. Her fist was pressed hard against her mouth. As if now, standing in front of Madam's guests, she was trying to push her shrieks back down her throat out of sheer politeness.

'I went down to get an extra bucket,' she said. Then she began to cry. 'Frøken Helle is down in the garage.'

We ran through the corridors and down the cellar staircase, where the screams still sat in the walls like a long, ear-bursting cannonade.

Helle was sat in the backseat of the car. Even paler than the girl I'd seen on the stairs. The smell of leather and petrol vapour lay heavy as thunder in the enclosed room. It looked like she was sleeping. Her head was down to one side. Hanging right across her shoulder. The engine's neutral drone a soft lullaby.

Someone or other behind me let out a scream and in that same second I saw the blood trickling under the door and out over the car's running board. Her hands lay at either side of her and very little blood was flowing from her wrist by this point. God knows who thought to turn the engine off, but all was suddenly quiet. The garage door's shutters started rattling up into the ceiling. Cool air and the soft green light of morning flooded into the garage.

I watched Tore as he walked out and disappeared up the slope towards the garden gate. He wasn't walking like a normal awake person would walk. Nor did he look like a sleepwalker. More like someone walking with a weird, unthinking certainty. As if he was on the way to some great place. Somewhere he'd been looking forward to seeing for a long time.

I wanted to go after him but stayed rooted to the spot. Then one of the waiters appeared and drove us all up to the living room. The girls were weeping quietly. Everything looked grim and ancient in the sparse light of early day. I didn't see

Fru Junkersen again. Just walked all the way home. Hearing a million voices in my head with each step. Like I was walking in my own echo chamber. Repeating to myself that it was weird, so fucking weird that there was a man's cut-throat razor in a house where no man was. I mean. None of those women used a cut-throat razor. No chance did they use a cut-throat razor. It was all hair removal creams and them women things. What did anyone want with a cut-throat razor in that house?

Chapter 12

You enter the place through a large gateway off the street and pass a couple of security men sitting there reading newspapers, or keeping an eye on who's coming and going. Just after the gate, the concourse opens out and you're looking at buildings to all sides. There are several signs pointing the way to the different departments. Once you've done it a few times, you get a map in your head and it's easy.

By this stage, I've done the trip so many times I could do it sleepwalking and blindfolded. From the entrance to the complex, you turn down to the left and walk along a low, two-storey building with a rose bed in front. Then you come to a stairway, which in a weird way leads you through, and sort of under, a building that is at right angles to the one you've just passed. It's a kind of tunnel you have to walk through, and you feel much more intimate with the whole hospital once you've walked through it. When you're back up on ground level, you see new yellow buildings with tended lawns in front of them and more rose beds as well as a single bed with perennials. The sun warms your neck as soon as you emerge from the tunnel, and the patients sitting round about really look like they are enjoying the good weather. Leaning their heads back and letting the sun bathe their faces. Maybe they've not been let out in the sun for a good while. So it's a case of making hay while the sun shines.

If you go on past this section, you come to a point where things get a bit more complicated. The signs all but disappear and if you're not careful, you can end up like a tourist in a strange town. If you take the obvious road – the broad, quiet lane that takes you to the right, you actually go way off track and end up at a place you never want to be. Because this road brings you slap bang up against the kitchens and laundry building. There's something depressing about hospital kitchens. There they are boiling up food for so many human beings in monster cauldrons. The odours are a turn-off as well. Even when you've back-tracked to the fork in the lanes, the hang of sour mince is still in your nose. I swear.

No sir. You don't go that way. If you're a bit more on the ball, you'll see a smaller lane running off in an arc along a garden fence. This leads to the last department at the very rear of the hospital. Though it's just as well appointed. Just as visually pleasing as the other places with their roses, lawns and colourful perennials. At the very end of this path, you go past another building that has a row of outside coal bunkers, spaced well apart. Then you're finally at the home of the last department. Actually in a more modern building looking out over a large lawn and then a park. The patients in this ward who are up on their feet sit on the grass. It's funny, but if you look at them from one of the floors above, they themselves sometimes look more like exotic flowers with their blue hospital clothes against the verdant background. This department has both male and female patients who live in separate wings of the building.

Whenever I come on visits, Tore is usually to be found sitting on a white bench just outside the entrance to his ward. He actually looks good. Very tanned and, in a way, that weird belt the patients have to wear to keep their trousers up gives him the air of a Spanish Toreador. He's already swarthy enough to pass for a Spaniard. Mainly, he sits on his own, but sometimes he'll be chatting to one of the other patients. It's difficult to hear what they're saying if you're any distance away. Partly because everyone seems to lower their voice in hospitals. Even outdoors.

Tore always spots me straight away, no matter what time I turn up. He's so used to me coming that it's like he already instinctively knows when to put his head up and look in the direction of the building with the coal bunkers.

He always remains seated. Right till I get to his bench. Then he gets up and we start walking the paths round the park. Sometimes our conversation stalls and it gets difficult. But usually we just talk away, about everything under the sun. I tell him what's going on in town. Who I've seen. What's on at the flicks and that I was over seeing his mother. We stroll round the paths – weaving in and out of the bushes, sometimes meeting other patients as we go. I always give them a little nod. Because, of course, I know most of them by sight by now.

You wouldn't think that Tore was sick with something. But maybe I'm just saying that because I've got used to him the way he is. Sure, he can seem a bit detached sometimes. A bit wooden maybe. But it's more like a polite reserve. An almost imperceptible smile passes across his face when I tell him something. But for the most part, I'm certain he's not listening. That said, he can always answer the questions I sometimes throw at him to see whether he's actually there with me. It must be that he is actually split into two people somehow – the one that is listening to me, and another person who is listening to something else entirely.

We don't talk that much about the hospital itself and what they are doing to him. It's almost as if he's decided to take a break at a spa resort. Or decided to withdraw from the world because there was too much noise and distress in it. But I suppose after a year or so has passed by, you get used to only getting your impressions of the world via an outside intermediary. Maybe that's normal for him now.

I have managed to get him to tell me a little bit about the treatment they're giving him. He is anaesthetized. Numbed. And then given shock treatment. But first they make sure to inject him with some kind of venom so that his body spasms don't break his back or cause other internal injuries. After these sessions, he's bedridden for a while.

So when you arrive and he's not there on his white bench, you know it's that time again. Nothing for it but to go up to him. But you have to say his building is nice inside as well. You go through two glass doors and up a stairway that has potted plants on every landing. Sure, you do notice at first that the door handles look weird and are turned the wrong way, and that the mirrors are not made of glass but of polished sheet metal. But you soon get used to it all.

Tore sleeps on a ward that has eight beds. He's always on his back looking up at the ceiling when you come in and this makes you want to just sit by his side without saying anything. But in two seconds he turns his head, says hello, and then we start talking about all kinds of things until visiting time is over. On these particular days he soon gets tired. You can see that. Usually, with about a quarter of an hour before it's time to go, he starts looking a bit haggard, but he still keeps on chatting till it's time to leave.

Naturally, I haven't been to see him every day in this whole period. I usually do turns with Fru Riemer, but it's a fact that the hospital has become a big part of my life. I can see that more clearly now. Now that I've become more settled myself. Those who were in the know wouldn't have much trouble understanding how often I had to put a mental straitjacket on myself whenever I thought about what had happened. There was a kind of halfway stage when I didn't dare visit him, because I was terrified I might suddenly start screaming and they would detain me there on the spot.

But in the last six months, I've begun to understand the importance of these visits. Even though we switch at times between being weirdly polite to each other, then really good mates. Or whatever terms you use for this situation. It's the comradeship in the very air we breathe together that marks the last surviving thread back to our former existence. We hardly ever mention it, but I can still feel that it's alive in both of us in some remarkable way.

I don't know how best to describe it. Because it's not like we've finally accepted what's happened and got over it. Probably more like resigning ourselves to something we can't change. We never mention those bygone times, but regardless – the whole world we share revolves around them. When the palms of my hands get too hot, I swing them backwards and forwards to cool them off and then we carry on walking and talking non-stop.

At home, the days are a lot easier for me now. The whole

story has been registered now and the raging internal nightmare has faded into the background somewhat. I can even listen to my parents talking without throwing up. I'm also nearly at the stage where I could read a book.

I hardly need to say that Tore never got to deliver his valedictory student speech two years ago. He didn't turn up at our last day at school – for the certificates and prize-giving. In fact there was no farewell student speech at all that year. Any sense of ceremony was muted. The festive holiday mood that usually reigns on such occasions was completely absent. Even the younger trogs and swampies made much less of a commotion. The rumours had spread very quickly and a mixed feeling of heightened astonishment and wounding catastrophe filled the room with a sickening nausea. I had no idea why I was there.

Even what I did at Helle's burial service is mostly a mystery to me. Tore wasn't there. There were very few mourners and all I remember clearly is how the voices of two people coming from behind a curtain in the chapel shrilled in my ears.

Tore was sent to some people in the country in the summer holidays, and I talked to Fru Riemer a couple of times. I went over to her house and we sat there saying nothing till we couldn't bear it any more and I left. She cried sore when I was leaving. In the September, me and Tore started at university. Why we did, neither of us knew. We barely spoke to each other and, of course, Tore was a sensation because the rumours about him had spread like maggots in a corpse. Right through the university.

In the spring, Tore just stopped. He didn't come into lectures, nor anywhere near college. I never saw him there again after that. When I went over to him, to talk to him in his room, he didn't open his mouth for hours and would mainly just go and lie on his bed to sleep. He slept most of that spring away. In the end, he was admitted to hospital and he's been there ever since, but there's great hopes of a full recovery.

I was out seeing him today. It was as if yet another one of those deadening shrouds that had enveloped him for so long had fallen away. There were fleeting moments when I could see into the man himself again.

We were on a bench in the park, and Tore had his head back, basking in the sunshine. We'd been sitting looking at a blackbird that was zooming backwards and forwards, feeding a chick that must have just left the nest.

'You've always believed in me. Haven't you, Janus?' he goes. All of a sudden. I was shocked. He leaned his face even further back.

'I mean. You've always believed that – no matter what I did, it was all right. I could do no wrong.' He straightened himself on the bench and looked right at me. He held his hands down between his knees.

'But I'm not the only one here in this world, Janus. It's not me who's in charge of everything and says what's what.' He looked at me pleadingly. 'You wanted me to carry not just my own hopes, but yours and everybody else's. But that's just too much. It's just impossible. No human can be pure and strong the whole time. There has to be a chink in the armour somewhere, Janus. An Achilles heel. We're humans, not angels.' Tore leaned back again and the sun glowed on his face.

And I knew exactly what he meant. I'd actually been thinking along the same lines. That complete perfection cannot be realised without being somehow inhuman. I mean. No tree is allowed to grow so tall it can reach the heavens.

I smiled at him, but he didn't catch it. A few moments later we got up and this time Tore accompanied me all the way through the hospital. Right down to the main gate. He gave me the lightest of supporting hands as I stood still for a minute putting on my bike clips. He didn't seem so fraught and distracted as he had regularly been. And I could look at him longer than I'd got used to doing. Tore the Man had had his wings clipped. All his shining excellence had been flayed off him. But it appeared that he carried his ravaged shoulders with a sense of relief.

Talking of relief. The relief I felt on leaving him today was different from my usual feelings on leaving the hospital and Tore behind. As a rule, any relief I felt was only the kind of respite you get when you're in transit from one nightmare to the next. But for the last while, and especially today, I felt a real surge of liberation. I strolled out through the gateway and over to the bike stand. Maybe we were more like equals now. I don't know.

Before I jumped up on the bike, I turned and looked at him standing there under the arch of the gateway in his blue hospital jacket and I couldn't help calling out to him:

'See you Tore! ... Be seeing you real soon, mate!'

Translator's Afterword

'Porridge-head' doesn't work in English

The first editing note I made when I sat down to begin translating Klaus Rifbjerg's early masterpiece *Den kroniske uskyld* to English was this: 'Porridge-head doesn't work in English.' I had already read the novel as a young man whilst serving in the Danish merchant navy. Now, it was time to read the novel again. Translating a novel entails a much closer reading, and usually re-reading, of the work in question, and taking notes as you do so. Note-taking for each chapter is important, as a translator's choice of words and phrases must be consistent right across the translation for it to work; in other words, the translator does what the author has done, very often unconsciously. The problem, however, for a translator is that certain words or phrases can carry a host of different meanings or connotations in the source language, without always having a direct equivalent in the target language.

My porridge-head note related to a Danish compound noun with *grød* as its first element: *grødhoved*. As far as I can see, *grødhoved* was one of many words that Klaus Rifbjerg invented specifically for this novel. Indeed Rifbjerg's barrage of new words was one of a number of quite shocking things about *Den kroniske uskyld* when it was first published in 1958, and it presents a real challenge to the translator even today.

The word *grød* appears very frequently – with various appendages – in *Den kroniske uskyld*, especially in the early chapters. The dictionary might tell us that *grød* can be translated as 'porridge', 'stewed fruit' (as in compote) or simply as 'mush'. But this gets us nowhere near the real story of Danish *grød*. The word is a cultural marker for Danes, not just because they eat varieties of it in the morning and at Christmas, but also because of the way they pronounce it.

As students of Scandinavian languages or linguistics are only too aware, standard Danish pronounces the *r* in *grød* as an uvular *r*. This means that the *r* is vibrated at the back of the tongue using the uvula (the soft, fleshy part of the palate at the entrance to the throat), rather than the more typical Scandinavian *r* after hard or plosive consonants, which is rolled or trilled. Compare the sound of the *r* in Danish *grød* with Norwegian *grøt*, or Swedish *trappa* with Danish *trappe* and you'll very quickly get the idea.

Now why does this *r* in *grød* matter for our appreciation of *Den kroniske uskyld*? Well, because whilst the rest of Scandinavia tends to ridicule the Danish *r*, the Danes themselves are rather proud of it. In fact, one of the first things you will be asked to do by a Dane if you claim any mastery in the language at all is to be asked to say *rødgrød med fløde*. This is not only a rather delicious summer compote of red berries and cream but also a tongue-and-groove strangler for those whose uvular palate is not sufficiently practised.

So Danes enjoy their *grød* on many levels. It's therefore important, in my view, for the translator to get across (translate) the relish with which Danes, in this case, deploy their own particular sounds. For example, the first time I heard and properly digested the linguistic and social import of this uvular *r* was when a second mate on one of my ships called the crew on my watch *røvhuller* (literally, arseholes). Janus Tolne would have enjoyed this moment, as would his creator. Nothing more untoward had occurred than two paint pots being left on the afterdeck, but I marked very well the relish with which the mate said it. Now, as a more experienced linguist, I marvel at the way he could in fact roll that first *r* at the back of his throat.

The first *grød*-related word is on the very first page of *Den kroniske uskyld* – *grødædere*, literally porridge- or mush-eaters – and then on the second page Janus Tolne refers to all the scholastic *grød* that he and his classmates spent most of their time being force-fed. With this choice of metaphor,

Klaus Rifbjerg has captured this intelligent and likeable (but sometimes high-handed and self-satisfied) pubescent youth perfectly; ditto the sharp learning curve he undergoes as the book progresses. Janus likes the word *grød*, and all its works.

The term that provoked my first note (*grødhoveder*, porridge-heads) appears in the first chapter of *Den kroniske uskyld*. To understand the challenge facing the translator, it's worth comparing the text in Danish and English:

> Men de blev ved med hver dag at komme hen til vinduet og stå der og vende og dreje sig i timevis uden noget på andet end natkjole, som om de vidste, at der stod en hel flok grødhoveder ovre på den anden side og var lige ved at hoppe ud ad vinduet for at komme over til dem ...

> Because, for ages every day, they would move to and fro near their windows and stand there, or turn around and flaunt this way and that, and them not wearing anything other than a night shift, as if they could sense that a whole pack of grunts was gathered across the way and just on the brink of descending upon them ... (p. 22)

Most readers will recall this highly charged and evocative scene (again typical of pubescent boys). In this instance, I chose to translate *en hel flok grødhoveder* with 'a whole pack of grunts'. But in the same paragraph, when the same word crops up again in the source text, I translate it as 'numbskull heads', only to use 'trogheads' a bit further on in the text when it appears again. The problem here is that *grød* can carry a multiplicity of meanings, which Danes sense before they categorise them, but these meanings, in all their nuances, have to be carried across to the target text. One minute the context for *grødhoved* is raging schoolboy hormones, the next it's an image evoking beans on a raft, and then later the connotation is a squat, abusive figure.

Another example comes when Janus describes the moment a dyspeptic teacher must begin to engage with his class of miscreants by asking them questions about their homework. The pupils are described as a *grødfad*, literally a platter of porridge, in front of the teacher. As Janus Tolne puts it in my translation:

> ... then the Ancient up at the desk would clear his throat and start flicking through his book and was obviously getting sick at the thought that any moment he would have to begin conversing with one of the swamp creatures oozing below him ... (p.25)

In the translation, then, this morass (*grødfad*) of a class are swamp creatures, in Janus Tolne's imperious view. I felt that what Janus was talking about with his often scathing references to his school and fellow pupils was something like a morass or swamp, very often green of hue. My default word for all the different uses of *grød* became 'swamp', though I sometimes used 'swill' or 'morass' instead. The ones who inhabited that swamp, I decided, were going to be 'swampies', or 'trogs' (Janus's fellow pupils) and 'duffheads' (the teachers). For me, the word 'duff' carries the requisite resonances of chalk dust, wadding and blockhead, which Janus attributes to his teachers. 'Swampies' is already explained, but I found 'trogs' or 'trogheads' to be very useful words for Janus's often baleful view of his classmates, as it is redolent of hog, and thereby hog swill (taking us back to the swamp). 'Trog' is also an English word that was very popular in the 1960s, but is no longer in widespread use; not quite the right decade, but remote enough from us in time to be serviceable. 'Numbskulls' is another word I use for Janus's description of his fellow pupils, precisely because it harks back to mid-century cartoon images of creatures that are portrayed as inhabiting our brain. I also found the word 'grunts' useful to translate Janus's derogatory term for his classmates; it not only carries an aural hog quality but is redolent of the 'runt' of the litter.

Overall, my aim when researching and weighing up appropriate translations was not only to consider the language used in the relevant period, but also the atmosphere or *Zeitgeist* created in the novel. Atmosphere is sometimes all.

From Chronic to Terminal Innocence
My second note for the translation of *Den kroniske uskyld* into English told me that a literal translation of the novel's title to

English would not work. The Danish word *kronisk* can usually be translated as 'chronic' in English, but a literary translator is obliged to listen not only to meaning in the target language but also to cadence and flow. Like many other Germanic languages, Danish likes to keep definite articles where English often prefers to lose them, *Den kroniske uskyld* being a case in point. We can't have 'The (Den) Chronic Innocence' in English, but what about 'Chronic Innocence'? I took the view that 'chronic' in this instance, unlike the use of 'chronic' in a phrase like 'chronic tiredness', did not carry the requisite weight of the Danish title, so I came up with 'Terminal Innocence'. Fortunately, Klaus Rifbjerg agreed with this view when I met him two years ago.

My approach to translation is based on the view that I must reveal in the target language what I believe the author's essential intent is in the source language, rather than giving a literal translation of what the text says. This latter aspiration is impossible anyway, as the term *grødhoved* demonstrates, as discussed above. This inevitably leads me to the view that I am in a sense a co-author of the new text, because I am (if only to a limited extent) inventing new words, terms and phrases.

A good way of illustrating the need for co-authorship on the part of the translator (whether it is good authorship is another matter) might be to look at the figure of Fru Junkersen, mother of the tragic Helle, whom Klaus Rifbjerg portrays as an awe-inspiring and terrible Sphinx-like figure in *Den kroniske uskyld*. It is interesting that in star-crossed love dramas, it is very often the young lovers who must transgress social norms to be together, whereas Rifberg goes the Romeo-and-Juliet route by portraying adults as the real transgressors – from the 'masked-up' teachers and braindead parents whose whole lives are spent hiding their true selves and wearing bicycle clips, to the bully and wife abuser Poul, culminating in the dominatrix *par excellence* Fru Junkersen, who toys with Janus as a prelude (as Janus rightly intuits) to the trap she lays for Tore and Helle.

Crucial to the power relations between Fru Junkersen and Janus was an interesting translation dilemma, which cropped up in the fairly lengthy series of scenes at Fru Junkersen's coastal holiday home, culminating in the corruption of his innocence. The dilemma was the use of *De* and *du* – the formal and familiar forms of address in Danish, which in English are simply expressed by 'you' in both singular and plural. After the traumatic seduction event, Janus sits stunned on the sofa. Amongst many other speculations, he asks himself why he and his seducer cannot now *være dus* (say 'du' to each other), given the intimacy that has just occurred between them. Modern Danish society has largely done away with the formal *De*, except for some commercial contexts; the informal *'du'* is now the standard form of address, regardless of the social situation. While one option in translation is simply to use 'you' for both formal and informal forms of address, it was crucial in this context to communicate the distinction, especially in the kitchen scene. Here, according to the convention of the period, Janus must say *De* to Fru Junkersen and address her as *Fru*, whereas she can say *du* to him:

> Uden at se på mig spurgte hun pludselig: 'Hvor gammel er du?'
> Hun smed spørgsmålet som en tidsindstillet bombe foran mig på køkkenbordet. Hvor lang tid ville der gå, før den sprang? Lunten på spørgsmålet hvæsede i det stille køkken.
> 'Hvor gammel er du?' sagde kvinden. Det 'du' var sprængladningen. Det var som om hun allerede rørte ved mig.
>
> Without looking at me, she suddenly asked: 'How old are you, boy?'
> She lobbed the question across the draining board like a grenade. How long did I have before the blast? The fuse in the question hissed in the quiet of the kitchen.
> 'How old are you, boy?' the woman said. But it was the 'boy' that carried the dynamite. It was as if her hands were already upon me.
> (p. 175)

Here I use 'boy' to translate the sense of *du*, to ram home Fru Junkersen's immediate and terrible superiority in this situation. Simply saying 'how old are you' (the literal translation) doesn't cut it. In this example, we have not so much a Danish word like *grød*, with all the nuances it carries for Danes, but the need to recapture a persona that Klaus Rifbjerg has created.

In my view, whilst the denouement of *Den kroniske uskyld* is truly shocking and unforgettable, the scene where Fru Junkersen defiles young Janus at her holiday home is the most devastating. I don't agree with those who argue that the final chapter dealing with Janus and Tore looking to the future is the key to *Den kroniske uskyld*. For me, the key theme of this extraordinary, indeed visionary, novel is the cynicism of adults and their capitulation to existential despair – their failure to hope, or believe in goodness. For this reason, the turning point of the novel is, I would argue, Janus's extraordinary admission that he desperately wants to be corrupted by Fru Junkersen, and that in his head that corruption is already an accomplished fact. Here, innocence is revealed as a terminal condition, not merely chronic.

'As if I'd composed it myself'

The joy of academic rigour and excellence, of delving into the lives of poets and writers and coming to certain Eureka moments in the understanding of them, is a gift that my alma mater University College London gave to me. It is also, however, one of the key tenets that underpin *Den kroniske uskyld* and also the life of the author Klaus Rifbjerg himself. My meeting with Klaus in November 2013 is etched in my memory, not least because of his literary ardour combined with a forensic analysis. His knowledge and recall of Beckett astonished me. Let this translation stand as a homage to one of Denmark's greatest chroniclers.

I will finish with my translation of my favourite passage from *Den kroniske uskyld*, forever now conjoined in my mind with my meeting with Klaus Rifbjerg. The passage where Janus is sitting his English exam, and becomes truly alive, steps into his own character and calling, as Kierkegaard would have it, and is embraced by the Muse who watches over all writers and translators:

Before a second had passed, I'd sat down and pulled a number.

The wax figures in front of me began slowly to come alive and bent over their table, opened books, moved their mouths, but no sound reached my ears yet. Eventually, finally finally finally, as if the words had floated over to me baked in dough, I picked up that Hr. Grüne wanted me to read aloud. 'Something from what, sir?' I didn't actually speak the sentence. Just mumbled it with closed lips. Then it dawned on me what he wanted. When I saw the slim volume with a selection of poetry down there in front of me. The mist slid from my eyes as, with precise care and a suppressed shake, I read the first lines of 'To Autumn'. I read and read and knew more and more in my heart that this was Keats and I was home and dry. No need for any more panic attacks. And I sat there and translated. Inspired. Flowing, rhythmic and fluent. As if I'd composed it myself. (pp. 211-12)

Paul Larkin
An Charraig
Gaoth Dobhair
Tír Chonaill

December 2014

HANNE MARIE SVENDSEN

Under the Sun

(translated by Marina Allemano)

Written in 1991, *Under the Sun* is the story of Margrethe Thiede, the daughter of a lighthouse keeper in an unnamed small fishing community on the north-western coast of Denmark. We follow Margrethe through her childhood, her years as a student in the capital, her marriage to a mentally unstable man, her involvement in the peace movement, and her old age.

The novel is also about a changing community where fears of violence at sea and rampant commercialism on land are strong undercurrents. The building of a naval base and the ominous presence of foreign submarines intimidate the fishermen and their families, and an accident caused by one of these intruding vessels forms the catastrophic climax of the novel.

ISBN 9781870041621
UK £9.95
(Paperback, 256 pages)

KIRSTEN THORUP

The God of Chance

(translated by Janet Garton)

The God of Chance focuses on the relationship between Ana, a high-
flying Danish career woman from the international finance sector
whose work is her life, and the young teenager Mariama, two women
whose circumstances are completely different. Ana first meets
Mariama selling snacks on a beach in Gambia, and the girl gradually
becomes a substitute for the family she has never had. The novel
moves to Copenhagen and then to London as Ana brings Mariama
to Europe to be educated; the girl finds the cultural shock and living
with Ana intensely difficult, whilst Ana's obsession with her leads
to her own carefully controlled life descending into chaos. The
story depicts the gulf between European affluence and Third World
poverty; it explores our dependence on money, our need to be in
control in every situation, and the problematic relationship between
sponsor or donor and recipient. The scene moves from colourful
depictions of life in a luxury hotel in Africa, cheek by jowl with
desperate poverty, to elite designer flats in Copenhagen, and finally
the bustling multicultural community on the streets of London.

ISBN 9781909408036
UK £11.95
(Paperback, 302 pages)

SVAVA JAKOBSDÓTTIR

Gunnlöth's Tale

(translated by Oliver Watts)

This spirited and at times sinister novel ensnares the reader in a tangled encounter between modern-day Scandinavia and the ancient world of myth. In the 1980s, a hardworking Icelandic businesswoman and her teenage daughter Dís, who has been arrested for apparently committing a strange and senseless robbery, are unwittingly drawn into a ritual-bound world of goddesses, sacrificial priests, golden thrones, clashing crags and kings-in-waiting. It is said that Gunnlöth was seduced by Odin so he could win the 'mead' of poetry from her, but is that really true, and why was Dís summoned to their world?

The boundaries dissolve and the parallels between Gunnlöth's circle and the strange company into which Dís's mother is drawn as she fights to clear Dís's name grow ever closer. The earth-cherishing goddess seems set on a collision course with strategic thinker Odin who has discovered that iron can be extracted from the marshes where she resides, and environmental disaster also looms in the modern context, brought into sharp focus by a shocking world event.

ISBN 9781870041799
UK £9.95
(Paperback, 232 pages)

JØRGEN-FRANZ JACOBSEN

Barbara

(translated by George Johnston)

Originally written in Danish, *Barbara* was the only novel by the
Faroese author Jørgen-Frantz Jacobsen (1900-38), yet it quickly
achieved international best-seller status and is still one of the best-
loved classics of Danish and Faroese literature. On the face of it,
Barbara is a straightforward historical romance. It contains a story
of passion in an exotic setting with overtones of semi-piracy; there
is a powerful erotic element, an outsider who breaks up a marriage,
and a built-in inevitability resulting from Barbara's own psychological
make-up. She stands as one of the most complex female characters
in modern Scandinavian literature: beautiful, passionate, devoted,
amoral and uncomprehending of her own tragedy. Jørgen-Frantz
Jacobsen portrays her with fascinated devotion.

ISBN 9781909408074
UK £11.95
(Paperback, 304 pages)

C000065092

The CONNOISSEUR'S GUIDE TO
CIGARS

Discover the World's Finest Cigars

The
CONNOISSEUR'S GUIDE TO
CIGARS

Discover the World's Finest Cigars

ANWER BATI & SIMON CHASE

APPLE

A QUINTET BOOK

Published by Apple Press
7 Greenland Street
London
NW1 0ND

Copyright © 1997 Quintet Publishing Limited.
All rights reserved. No part of this publication
may be reproduced, stored in a retrieval system
or transmitted in any form or by any means,
electronic, mechanical, photocopying, recording
or otherwise, without the permission of the
copyright holder.

ISBN 978-1-84543-2003

Reprinted 1998, 1999, 2000, 2003, 2007

This book was designed and produced by
Quintet Publishing Limited
6 Blundell Street
London N7 9BH

Creative Director: Richard Dewing
Designer: Ian Hunt
Senior Editor: Laura Sandelson
Project Editor: Anna Briffa
Editor: Susan Martineau
Photographers: Ian Howes & Paul Forrester
Cover image: AGB Photo Library / Rex Features

Typeset in Great Britain by
Central Southern Typesetters, Eastbourne
Manufactured in China by
Regent Publishing Services Ltd
Printed in China by
Midas Printing International Limited

CONTENTS

ACKNOWLEDGMENTS

It wouldn't have been possible to update this book without the help and support of a number of people in the cigar trade, so the Publisher would like to thank the following for the help they have given:

Philip Thompson, C.A.O. International; Felipe Gregorio, Cigars of Honduras; Jean Clement; Janelle Rosenfeld, Consolidated Cigar Corporation; Christine Brandt and Raymond Scheurer, Davidoff; Oscar Rodriguez, Dominican Cigar Imports; Carlos Fuente Jr; Paul Garmirian; Eddie Panners, Gold Leaf Tobacco Co.; Alan Edwards, Hollco Rohr; Liz Facchiano, J.R. Cigars; Stanley Kolker; Brian G. Dewey, Lane Limited; Robert Newman, M & N Cigar Mfrs, Inc.; Oscar Boruchin, Mike's Cigars; Bill Sherman, Nat Sherman Incorporated; Jorge L. Padron, Padron Cigars; Chris Boon, Rothman's International; Patrick Clayeux, Seita; Mark Segal, Segal Worldwide; Dorette Meyer, Suerdieck; Ralph Montero, Tropical Tobacco; Sherwin Seltzer, Villazon & Co., Inc.

PUBLISHER'S
FOREWORD

$\mathscr{C}$igar culture has expanded on an unprecedented scale since this book was first published in 1993. In England and the United States in particular cigar-smoking has become a prestigious public pastime, and a hobby of the rich and famous. One rarely sees a movie or rock star without a cigar, and over the last 12 months alone the world has witnessed countless magazine covers sporting glamorous cigar-smoking women.

This boom in cigar culture has naturally had a tremendous effect on demand and while researching this edition, it was not uncommon to hear manufacturers admit to large back-orders in supplies—sometimes as high as six months worth. At the same time, there has been great scope for expansion, and several companies have taken advantage of this; new cigar brands have hit the market as fast as existing ones have been increasing their lines, and, with few exceptions, every brand has new sizes and many have a new look. There is a deliberate retrospective edge to current trends, and the *figuardo* shape, properly popular for the first time since the nineteenth century, has made a welcome comeback.

Despite the change of pace forced by the great boom in their industry, cigar manufacturers have contributed generously to this book for the third time. Their continued enthusiasm and praise for *The Cigar Companion* was evident at many levels within the trade; some brands use their entry as a basis for their own sales pitch, while others regard the book as their most reliable source. Whatever the reason, the book has played a major role in the cigar world over the last four years, and there is a definite indication that it will continue to do so for the foreseeable future.

MARCH 1997

INTRODUCTION

*T*he cigar has always had a very strong image in a way that the cigarette, despite its popularity, has never had. True, some cigarette brands evoke strong associations – the Marlboro cowboy, for instance – but only through advertising. Cigars, on the other hand, have acquired their image not only through the people who smoke them – one need only mention Winston Churchill, Edward VII, and any number of Hollywood film directors and producers such as Darryl F. Zanuck – but also through the occasions on which they are smoked. This applies to cigars in general, but handmade cigars, the subject of this book, in particular.

The aim of this book, whether you are a regular or occasional smoker of handmade cigars, is to tell you as much about them as possible and help you to understand the subject better. Above all, however, this book has been written to enhance your enjoyment of fine cigars and to encourage your interest in them.

ANWER BATI
AUTHOR
MARCH 1993

*M*y eighteen years in the cigar trade have been spent mainly in the company of Havana. You should know that they pay my salary, so watch out in these pages for self-serving bias. Having said that, we are all biased by our own taste in cigars. Mine is unlikely to match yours and, in the end, the choice is personal.

Cigars have seen heady days since the first appearance of this book. The "Cigar Boom," "The Renaissance of the Cigar," call it what you will, started for me at Cuba's El Corojo plantation in February 1992. Anwer Bati, Marvin Shanken, and I stood watching the massive wrapper leaves inching their way to maturity under the muslin cover. Not even Marvin could have foreseen quite what was to follow.

In revising and updating *The Cigar Companion*, I hope to do justice to Anwer's original work and, like him, to augment the pleasure you obtain from your cigars.

SIMON CHASE
AUTHOR, 2ND EDITION
MAY 1995

1

THE STORY

OF

CIGARS

The Cigar World

*N*obody knows for sure *when* the tobacco plant was first cultivated, but there is little doubt about *where*. The native peoples of the American continent were undoubtedly the first not only to grow, but to smoke the plant, which probably first came from the Yucatán peninsula, Mexico. It was certainly used by the Maya of Central America, and when the Maya civilization was broken up, the scattered tribes carried tobacco both southward into South America, and to North America, where it was probably first used in the rites of the Mississippi Indians. It didn't come to the attention of the rest of the world until Christopher Columbus's momentous voyage of 1492.

Columbus himself was not particularly impressed by the custom, but soon Spanish and other European sailors fell for the habit, followed by the conquistadores and colonists. In due course the

THE AMERICAN INDIANS WERE ALMOST CERTAINLY THE FIRST PEOPLE TO SMOKE CIGARS.

LEFT: CHRISTOPHER COLUMBUS. HIS MEN WERE THE FIRST FROM EUROPE TO ENCOUNTER THE NORTH AMERICAN HABIT OF SMOKING.

returning conquistadores introduced tobacco smoking to Spain and Portugal. The habit, a sign of wealth, then spread to France, through the French ambassador to Portugal, Jean Nicot (who eventually gave his name to nicotine, and *Nicotiana tabacum*, the Latin name for tobacco), and to Italy. In Britain, as every schoolchild knows, Sir Walter Raleigh was probably responsible for introducing tobacco and the new fashion for smoking.

The word tobacco, some say, was a corruption of Tobago, the name of the Caribbean island. Others claim it comes from the Tabasco province of Mexico. Cohiba, a word used by the Taino Indians of Cuba was thought to mean tobacco, but now is considered to have referred to cigars. The word cigar originated from *sikar*, the Mayan word for smoking.

Although the first tobacco plantations were set up in Virginia in 1612, and Maryland in 1631, tobacco was smoked only in pipes in the American colonies. The cigar itself is thought not to have arrived until after 1762, when Israel Putnam, later an American general in the Revolutionary War, returned from Cuba, where he had been an officer in the British army. He came back to his home in Connecticut—an area where tobacco had been grown by settlers since the 17th century (and before them by the Indians)—with a selection of Havana cigars, and large amounts of Cuban tobacco. Before long, cigar factories were set up in the Hartford area, and the attempt was made to grow tobacco from Cuban seed. Production of the leaves started in the 1820s, and Connecticut tobacco today provides among the best wrapper leaves to be found outside Cuba. By the early 19th century, not only were Cuban cigars being imported into the United States, but domestic production was also taking off.

The habit of smoking cigars (as opposed to using tobacco in other forms) spread out to the rest of Europe from Spain where cigars, using Cuban tobacco, were made in Seville from 1717 onward. By 1790, cigar manufacture had spread north of the Pyrenees, with small factories being set up in France and Germany. But cigar smoking didn't really take off in France and Britain until after the Peninsular War (1806–12) against Napoleon, when returning British and French veterans spread the habit they had learned while serving in Spain. By this time the pipe had been replaced by snuff as the main way of taking tobacco, and cigars now became the fashionable way of smoking it. Production of segars, as they were known, began in Britain in 1820, and in 1821 an Act of Parliament was needed to set out regulations governing production. Because

FERDINAND VII KING OF SPAIN. HE VIGOROUSLY PROMOTED
THE PRODUCTION OF CUBAN CIGARS.

of a new import tax, foreign cigars in Britain were already regarded
as a luxury item.

Soon there was a demand for higher-quality cigars in Europe,
and the Sevillas, as Spanish cigars were called, were superseded
by those from Cuba (then a Spanish colony), not least as the result
of a decree by King Ferdinand VII of Spain in 1821, encouraging
the production of Cuban cigars, a Spanish state monopoly. Cigar
smoking became such a widespread custom in Britain and France
that smoking cars became a feature of European trains, and the
smoking room was introduced in clubs and hotels. The habit even
influenced clothing—with the introduction of the smoking jacket.
In France, tuxedos are still referred to as *le smoking*. By the end of
the 19th century, the after-dinner cigar, with port or brandy, was a
firmly established tradition. It was given an added boost by the
fact that the Prince of Wales (the future Edward VII), a leader of
fashion, was a devotee, much to the chagrin of his mother, Queen
Victoria, who was not amused by the habit.

Cigar smoking didn't really take off in the United States until
the time of the Civil War (although John Quincy Adams, 6th
President of the United States, was a confirmed cigar smoker at
the beginning of the century; later, President Ulysses Grant was
also to become a devotee) with the most expensive domestic cigars,

ILLUSTRATION OF A MID-19TH-CENTURY CIGAR FACTORY IN
ENGLAND.

made with Cuban tobacco, called clear Havanas. The name Havana,
by now, had become a generic term. Some of the best-known
domestic cigars came from the factory at Conestoga, Pennsylvania,
where the long "stogie" cigar was made. By the late 19th century,
the cigar had become a status symbol in the United States, and
branding became important. Thus, there was Henry Clay, for
instance, named after the Senator. A tax reduction in the 1870s
made the cigar even more popular and widely available, and
encouraged domestic production. By 1919, Thomas Marshall,
Woodrow Wilson's Vice President was able to say in the Senate:
"What this country really needs is a good five-cent cigar," an
ambition not to be achieved until almost 40 years later when new
methods of cigar production allowed truly cheap cigars to be made
by machine. Cigar sales in the United States have, however,
declined over the last 20 years—from 9 billion cigars (of all types)
in 1970, to 2 billion today.

Machine production of cigars wasn't introduced until the 1920s
(in Cuba, the Por Larranaga firm was the first to attempt it, and
handmade production in the United States fell from 90 percent in
1924, to a mere 2 percent by the end of the 1950s.

It was a different story in Cuba, where the cigar became a
national symbol. Cuban peasants started becoming *vegueros*,
tobacco growers, from the 16th century onward, waging a constant

NOTE THE WOMEN SMOKING CIGARS AS THEY LEAVE A CIGAR
FACTORY IN MANILA.

battle against the big landowners as exports of the crop grew. Some of
them became tenant farmers or sharecroppers; others were forced
to find new land to farm, opening up areas such as Pinar del Rio
and Oriente.

By the mid-19th century, by which time there was free trade in
tobacco, there were 9,500 plantations, and factories in Havana and
other cities sprang up (at one stage, there were as many as 1,300,
though there were only around 120 by the beginning of the 20th
century), and cigar production became a fully fledged industry.
Export was mainly to the United States until tariff barriers were
put up in 1857. During the same period, brand and size differen-
tiation began, and the cigar box and band were introduced.

As the industry grew, the cigar makers became the core of the
Cuban industrial working class, and a unique institution was set
up in 1865, which lasts to this day: the reading of literary, political,
and other texts, including the works of Zola, Dumas, and Victor
Hugo, to the rollers by fellow workers. This was to alleviate the
boredom, and help the cause of worker education. During the last
quarter of the 19th century, faced with the growing political up-
heaval caused by the struggle for independence from Spain, many
cigar makers emigrated to the United States or nearby islands like
Jamaica, where they set up cigar industries in towns like Tampa,
Key West, and Kingston.

SUPERLATIVE CUBAN CIGARS ARE STILL MADE EXCLUSIVELY
FOR FIDEL CASTRO, THE CUBAN LEADER, TO PRESENT TO STATE
VISITORS AND DIPLOMATS.

These Cubans abroad were instrumental in funding the revolt against Spain, led in 1895 by José Martí, the Cuban national hero, and later the increasingly politicized cigar workers in Cuba were to take an important part in national life. Martí's order for the uprising was, symbolically, sent from Key West to Cuba inside a cigar. Cigar workers continued at the center of political consciousness after Fidel Castro's revolution against General Batista in 1959. After Castro started to nationalize Cuban and foreign assets, the United States embargo on Cuba, imposed in 1962, meant that Havana cigars could no longer be legally imported into the United States, except in small quantities for personal use. The cigar industry—much of which had been American-owned—was nationalized along with everything else and put under the control of the state monopoly, Cubatabaco.

Many of the dispossessed cigar factory owners such as the Palicio, Cifuentes, and Menendez families fled abroad, determined to start production up again, often using the same brand names they had owned in Cuba. As a result, cigars called Romeo Y Julieta, H. Upmann, and Partagas are made in the Dominican Republic; La Gloria Cubana in Miami; Punch and Hoyo de Monterrey in Honduras; and Sancho Panza in Mexico. In the case of Montecruz cigars, the name was slightly changed from the original Montecristo, and they were originally made in the Canary Islands, though they are now manufactured in the Dominican Republic. These brands using Cuban names usually bear no relation in terms of flavor to their Havana counterparts, however well made they may be. Entirely new brands, too, such as Don Miguel, Don Diego, and Montesino were also set up. After two decades of investment by both local and American companies, the Dominican Republic has seen rapid growth in its cigar industry during the 1990s. More than any other country, it has benefitted from the explosion of American consumer enthusiasm for handmade cigars touched off by the launch of *Cigar Aficionado* magazine in September 1992.

At the start of the decade, sales from the Dominican Republic to the United States had been expanding at a rate of around 5 percent per year. This leapt to 18 percent in 1993 when 55 million handmade cigars were shipped, accounting for just over half of all the handmade cigars imported into the United States. In 1994 growth continued, adding another 20 percent overall, with some factories claiming increases of nearly 40 percent. The greatest problem facing the Dominican Republican manufacturers today appears to be finding enough tobaccos of quality for handmade cigars.

The early 1990s have been less kind to Cuba. In the two years following the collapse of the Soviet Union, half of the island's gross domestic product evaporated. The cigar industry suffered less than most because its essential raw material—tobacco—is all grown on the island. Nonetheless, shortages of fertilizers, packaging materials, and even such mundane items as string, all of which had come from the former Eastern bloc, took their toll.

The weather played its part, too. Unseasonal rains in the Vuelta Abajo constrained the 1991 and 1992 harvests. Then the great storm of March 1993, which ended up depositing ten feet of snow on New York City, started life wreaking havoc in the Partido wrapper-growing region. Production of Havanas, which had topped 80 million in 1990, fell to around 50 million by 1994. If cigar enthusiasts around the world have been forced to search hard for their preferred Havana, their difficulties pale into insignificance alongside the trials of their Cuban counterparts. Domestic cigar production tumbled by well over half from a remarkable figure of 280 million in 1990, and stringent rationing was introduced as a result of this.

Such changes of fortune are nothing new to Cuba's hardy population. Just after the revolution, cigar exports dropped to 30 million.

THE ARCHETYPAL VIEW OF THE CIGAR SMOKER: GOOD WINE, GOOD TOBACCO.

Havanos SA, the company which recently took over most of the marketing responsibilities for Havanas from the state-owned Cubatabaco, arranged hard currency deals with its international partners to supply materials for the crops from 1995 onward.

There can be few symbols of capitalism and plutocracy more potent than the cigar. Tycoons rarely seem happier, or more prosperous, than when pictured puffing a large Havana. It says: power, privilege, prestige—and, above all, expense. But the irony, of course, is that Havana cigars are produced in one of the world's few remaining bastions of communism.

It would be quite wrong to give the impression that the growing of cigar tobacco and the production of cigars is limited to Cuba and the Dominican Republic. Nearby Jamaica has had its own industry for over a century, and several Central American countries like Mexico, Honduras, and Nicaragua enjoy traditions of cigar making that go back much further. Ecuador now produces a good-quality wrapper, oddly known as Ecuador/Connecticut, and Brazil brings its own unique flavor and style to the creation of cigars. Further afield, the Indonesian islands of Java and Sumatra have time-honored links with the cigar makers of the Netherlands, Germany, and Switzerland, as do the Philippines with Spain. Africa's contribution comes from Cameroon, in the form of some of the most sought-after, rich, dark wrappers in the world.

THE DOMINICAN REPUBLIC

The Dominican Republic, east of Cuba, has a similar climate and very good tobacco-growing conditions, particularly in the Cibao River valley. It has, over the last 15 years or so, become a major exporter of top quality handmade cigars, particularly to the United States, which imports over 60 million cigars a year from there. This accounts for half of the American handmade cigar market. It has attracted major cigar manufacturers such as General Cigar (with brands like Partagas) and Consolidated Cigar (brand names such as Don Diego and Primo del Rey). Consolidated moved its operations to the Dominican Republic from the Canary Islands. Most of the tobacco grown in the Dominican Republic is for fillers only. Virtually all the wrappers and many of the binders for cigars made there are imported from countries like the U.S. (Connecticut), Cameroon (for Partagas, for instance), Brazil, Honduras, Mexico, and Ecuador. Some fillers, too are brought in from abroad. Major efforts, led by the Fuente family, are now being made to extend the variety of tobaccos grown in the country. Wrappers, always the toughest challenge, are now to be seen on the Fuente's plantations … and, increasingly, on their cigars.

CONNECTICUT VALLEY

The sandy loam of the Connecticut valley (where conditions suitable for growing top-quality cigar tobacco are created under huge, 10-foot high tents), and the use of the Hazelwood strain of Cuban seed produces some of the world's best wrapper leaves, called Connecticut Shade. The leaves are very expensive to produce and sell for as much as $40 a pound, adding between 50 cents and a dollar to the price of a cigar. The growing cycle begins in March, with the harvest taking place in August. The drying process, though essentially the same as in Cuba, is helped, in Connecticut, by the use of careful heating from below using gas burners. Connecticut wrappers are used for cigars such as Macanudo, and the Dominican-made Davidoffs.

PINAR DEL RIO *an[e]*

There are those who disagree (the leaf producers of Connecticut, the Dominican Republic, and Honduras foremost among them), but it is still generally acknowledged that the finest cigar tobacco in the world comes from Cuba, and in particular from the Vuelta Abajo area of the Pinar del Rio province.

Pinar del Rio is the region at the western end of Cuba, situated between mountains and the coast, the island's third largest province. The area, which points toward the Mexican Yucatán peninsula, is undulating, green, and lush (it was under the sea in prehistoric times), rather resembling southeast Asia or parts of southern Louisiana and Florida. Life and living conditions there are primitive for the 600,000 inhabitants, with none of the sophistication or development to be found near Havana. But the agricultural conditions—climate, rainfall, and soil (a reddish sandy loam)—are perfect for tobacco production, by far the main industry. Tobacco is grown on smallholdings (many of them privately owned, but selling tobacco to the government at a fixed

price), totaling about 100,000 acres. They create a patchwork effect across the plains. Before the revolution, large tracts of land were owned by the main tobacco companies, but today, although vegueros *can own up to 150 acres, most cultivate from five to ten acres. Outside the tobacco season, maize is often grown on the same land. Vuelta Abajo takes up most of the 160 square miles of Pinar del Rio. Tobacco grows freely here, but the finest,*

VUELTA ABAJO, CUBA

*destined for cigars to be known as Havanas or Habanos, comes
from a surprisingly small area centered around the two towns of
San Juan y Martinez and San Luis. Not much more than 2,500
acres are devoted to wrappers and 5,000 acres to fillers and
binders. Amongst the best known plantations are El Corojo,
where the Corojo wrapper plant was developed, and Hoyo de
Monterrey, famous for its fillers.*

*The rainfall in Pinar del Rio is among the highest in Cuba,
with 65 inches a year, although significant for tobacco growth,
only 8 inches or so of rain—over an average of 26 days—falls
during the main growing months from November to February.
They come in the middle of La Seca, the dry season, by which time
the soil has had plenty of rain from storms in the period from May
to October. Temperatures during the growing season reach average
highs of 80°F, with around 8 hours a day of sunshine, and
average humidity of 64 percent. The Semivuelta area is the second
tobacco-growing area of Pinar del Rio, and produces thicker
leaves, with a stronger aroma than those of Vuelta Abajo. This
tobacco was once exported to the United States, but is now used
for the domestic cigar industry.*

*The Partido area, near Havana, also grows high-quality
wrappers for handmade Havanas. Remedios in the island's
center, and Oriente at its eastern end produce
tobacco, too, but not for top-quality
cigars.*

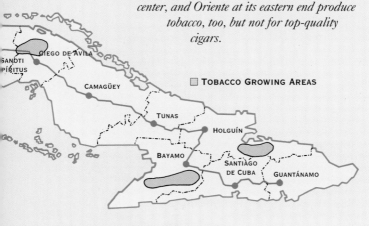

□ **TOBACCO GROWING AREAS**

GROWING CIGAR TOBACCO

The following passage is specifically for Havana cigars, but the process is, broadly speaking, similar elsewhere.

Cigars are a natural product, often compared to wine (though the comparison sometimes tends to get out of hand), and the quality of a cigar is directly related to the type and quality of leaves used in its construction, just as the quality of wine depends on the type and quality of grapes used.

Tobacco seedbeds have to be in flat fields, so that the seeds aren't washed away. After being planted, the seeds are covered with cloth or straw to shade them from the sun. This covering is gradually removed as they begin to germinate, and after around 35 days (during which the seed will be sprayed with pesticides), they are transplanted—usually in the second half of October—into the tobacco fields proper. The leaves are watered both by rain and the morning dew, and irrigated from below.

The tobacco plant is considered in three parts: the top, or corona, the middle, and the bottom. As the leaves develop, buds appear. These have to be removed by hand to prevent them from stunting leaf and plant growth. The quality of wrapper leaf is crucial in any

CUBAN TOBACCO PLANT

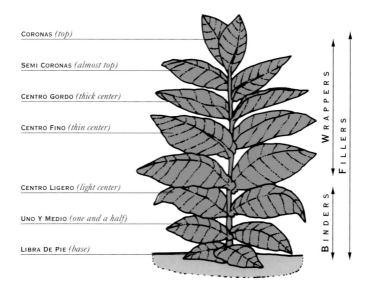

CORONAS *(top)*

SEMI CORONAS *(almost top)*

CENTRO GORDO *(thick center)*

CENTRO FINO *(thin center)*

CENTRO LIGERO *(light center)*

UNO Y MEDIO *(one and a half)*

LIBRA DE PIE *(base)*

WRAPPERS

FILLERS

BINDERS

cigar. Plants called Corojos, specifically designated to provide wrapper leaves for the very best cigars, are always grown under gauze sheets held up by tall wooden poles. They prevent the leaves from becoming too thick in a protective response to sunlight. The technique, called *tapado* (covering), also helps them to remain smooth.

When harvesting time arrives, leaves are removed by hand, using a single movement. Those selected as wrappers are put in bundles of five, a manojo, or hand. The leaves are picked in six phases: *libra de pie* (at the base), *uno y medio* (one-and-a-half), *centro ligero* (light center), *centro fino* (thin center), *centro gordo* (thick center), and *corona* (crown). The *libra de pie* section isn't used for wrappers. A week passes between each phase. The finest leaves found in the middle of the plant; the top leaves (*corona*) are usually too oily to be used for wrappers, except for domestic consumption, and are often used as binder leaves. The whole cycle, from transplanted seedlings to the end of harvesting takes some 120 days, with each plant being visited an average of 170 times—making it a very labor-intensive process.

Wrapper leaves grown under cover are classified by color as *ligero* (light), *seco* (dry), *viso* (glossy), *amarillo* (yellow), *medio tiempo* (half texture), and *quebrado* (broken), while those grown under the sun are divided into *volado*, *seco*, *ligero*, and *medio tiempo*. The ligero leaves from the top of the plant have a very strong flavor, the seco

EL COROJO WRAPPER PLANTATION IN SAN LUÌS ONE WEEK
AFTER PLANTING.

HARVESTED WRAPPER LEAVES ARRIVE AT CURING BARN,
LA GUIRA, CUBA.

from the middle are much lighter, and the volado leaves from the bottom are used to add bulk and for their burning qualities. The art of making a good cigar is to blend these, along with a suitable wrapper leaf, in such proportions as to give the eventual cigar a mild, medium, or full flavor, and to ensure that it burns well. The leaves are also classified by size (large, average, small) and by physical condition (unhealthy or broken leaves are used for cigarettes or machine-made cigars). If all the leaves are good, each wrapper plant can wrap 32 cigars. The condition and quality of the wrapper leaf is crucial to the attractive appearance of a cigar, as well as its aroma.

The bundles of leaves are then taken to a tobacco barn on the *vega*, or plantation, to be cured. The barns face west so that the sun heats one end in the morning, and the other in the late afternoon. The temperature and humidity in the barns is carefully controlled, if necessary by opening and closing the doors at both ends (usually kept shut) to take account of changes of temperature or rainfall.

Once the leaves reach the barn, they are strung up on poles, or *cujes*, using needle and thread. The poles, each holding around 100 leaves, are hoisted up horizontally (their position high in the barn allows air to circulate), and the leaves left to dry for between 45 and 60 days, depending on the weather. During this time, the green chlorophyll in the leaves turns to brown carotene, giving them their characteristic color. The poles are then taken down, the threads cut, and the leaves stacked into bundles according to type.

The bundles are then taken to the fermentation houses and placed in piles about three feet high, covered with jute. Enough moisture remains in the leaves to spark the first fermentation, a process like composting. Heat develops, but the temperature must be watched carefully so that it does not exceed 92°F during the 35 to 40 days that the piles are left intact. The leaves assume a uniform color.

The piles are then broken up and the leaves cooled. The next stop in their journey is at the *escogida*, or sorting house, where they will be graded according to color, size, and texture and where the fillers will have part of their stems stripped out. In preparation for handling, they are moistened either under a spray of pure water for wrappers or a mixture of water and the juices from tobacco stems for fillers.

THREADING THE WRAPPER LEAVES TOGETHER. THEY ARE HUNG
UP IN BATCHES OF 50.

CIGAR TOBACCO PRODUCTION

1 WRAPPER LEAF CURING BARN. THE LEAVES TURN BROWN AS CHLOROPHYLL TURNS TO CAROTENE.

2 SORTING HOUSE. UNPACKING "TERICOS" PRIOR TO MOISTENING AND GRADING.

3 INSPECTING WRAPPER LEAVES DURING PRIMARY FERMENTATION.

4 WRAPPER LEAVES BEING SORTED BY SIZE, COLOR, AND TEXTURE.

BACKGROUND PHOTOGRAPH: WRAPPER LEAVES GROWING UNDER CHEESE GAUZE "TAPADOS" TO SHADE THEM FROM THE SUN.

3

Traditionally, women perform the tasks of sorting and stripping. Each leaf is tenderly examined and graded. Broken leaves are set aside for use in cigarettes.

Flattened onto boards (*planchas*), the leaves return to the fermentation area. In dark rooms, they are built into stacks called *burros* up to 6 feet high. The second, more powerful fermentation begins within the damp leaves. A perforated wooden casing has been buried in the *burro*, into which a sword-like thermometer is thrust. The temperature inside must not exceed 110°F for around 60 days, longer for some leaf types, shorter for others. If it does, the bulk is broken down and the leaves cooled before it s rebuilt. Ammonia is released as the leaves shed their impurities.

Because of the fermentation process, cigar tobacco is much lower in acidity, tar, and nicotine than cigarette tobacco, making it much more palatable.

It is now time for the leaves to be sent to the factories or warehouses in *tercios*, square bales wrapped with palm bark, which helps to keep the tobacco at a constant humidity, and slowly mature until it is needed—sometimes for as long as two years.

These long and complicated processes of selection and fermentation have to be carefully supervised and are crucial to the final flavor of handmade cigars.

WRAPPER LEAVES FOR **C**OHIBA CIGARS MOISTENED
BEFORE GOING TO CIGAR ROLLER.

THE STRUCTURE OF A CIGAR

Handmade cigars have three constituent parts—the filler, the binder, and the wrapper. Each of the parts has a different function when the cigar is actually smoked.

The outside wrapper (or *capa*) dictates the cigar's appearance. As described, it is always grown under gauze and fermented separately from other leaves to ensure that is smooth, not too oily, and has a subtle bouquet. It also has to be soft and pliable so that it is easy for the roller to handle.

Wrapper leaves from different plantations have varying colors (and thus subtly different flavors, more sugary if they are darker, for instance) and are used for different brands. Good wrapper leaves have to be elastic and must have no protruding veins. They have to be matured for between one year and 18 months, the longer the better. Wrappers of handmade non-Cuban cigars might come from Connecticut, Cameroon, Sumatra, Ecuador, Honduras, Mexico, Costa Rica, or Nicaragua. The wrapper is the most expensive part of the cigar.

The binder leaf (capote) holds the cigar together and is usually two halves of coarse sun-grown leaf from the upper part of the plant, chosen because of its good tensile strength.

The filler is made of separate leaves folded by hand along their length, to allow a passage through which smoke can be drawn when the cigar is lit. The fold can only be properly achieved by hand and is the primary reason why machine-made cigars are less satisfactory. This style of arranging the filler is sometimes called the "book" style—which means that if you were to cut the cigar down its length with a razor, the filler leaves would resemble the pages of a book. In the past, the filler was sometimes arranged using the "entubar" method—with up to eight narrow tubes of tobacco leaf rolled into the binder—making the cigar very slow-burning.

Three different types of leaf are normally used for the filler (in fatter sizes, like Montecristo No. 2, a fourth type is also used).

Ligero leaves from the top of the plant are dark and full in flavor as a result of oils produced by exposure to sunlight. They have to be matured for at least two years before they can be used in cigar making. Ligero tobacco is always placed in the middle of the cigar, because it burns slowly.

Seco leaves, from the middle of the plant, are much lighter in color and flavor. They are usually used after maturing for around 18 months.

Volado leaves, from the bottom of the plant, have little or no flavor, but they have good burning qualities. They are matured for about nine months before use.

The precise blend of these different leaves in the filler dictates the flavor of each brand and size. A full-bodied cigar like Ramon Allones will, for instance, have a higher proportion of ligero in its filler, than a mild cigar such as H. Upmann, where seco and volado will predominate. Small, thin cigars will very often have no ligero leaf in them at all. The consistency of a blend is achieved by using tobacco from different harvest and farms, so a large stock of matured tobacco is essential to the process.

ROLLING A CIGAR

In making a handmade cigar, two to four filler leaves (depending on the size and strength of the cigar) are laid end to end and rolled into the two halves of the binder leaves—making up what is called the "bunch." Great skill is required to make sure that the filler is evenly distributed so that the cigar will draw properly. Wooden molds are used into which the filler blend (rolled into the binder) is pressed by the "bunchers," with a mechanical press than used to complete the process. In the Havana factory, the bunching is done by the same person who eventually adds the wrapper. The practice is slightly different in, for instance, the factories of the Dominican Republic, where specialist bunchers work in teams with specialist wrapper rollers. In both systems, the result is that each roller has a supply of ready molded fillers, prepared for what is being made on that day, at his or her work bench.

GATHERING THE BLEND OF FILLER LEAVES.

ROLLING A CIGAR

AFTER PRESSING, THE "BUNCHES" ARE READY TO HAVE WRAPPER LEAVES ROLLED AROUND THEM.

ROLLING COHIBA LANCERO CIGARS AT EL LAGUITO FACTORY, HAVANA.

THE "CHAVETA" IS USED TO TRIM SURPLUS TOBACCO.

THE FRAGILE WRAPPER IS GENTLY STRETCHED BEFORE ROLLING.

Surplus filler is trimmed from the end to form a round top. A wrapper leaf is then selected, the remaining stalk is stripped off the binder, and the wrapper is trimmed to the right size (using the central part of the leaf, placed upside-down, to avoid having any veins showing) with an oval steel blade called a chaveta. The cylinder of tobacco in its binder (the "bunch") is now laid at an angle across the wrapper, which is then stretched as necessary and wound carefully around the binder, overlapping at each turn, until it is stuck down using a tiny drop of colorless and flavorless tragacanth vegetable gum. The cigar is then rolled, applying gentle pressure, with the flat part of the steel blade to make sure its construction is even. Next, a small round piece of wrapper (about the size of a small coin) is cut out from the trimmings on hand to form the cap, which is stuck in place. In the case of cigars such as the Montecristo Especial, the closed end is sealed by twisting the end of the wrapper. This is a version of what is known as the "flag" method of capping a cigar—a highly skilled process in which the wrapper itself is smoothed down to form the cap. The flag method is only used on the best handmade cigars. Finally, the open end is guillotined to the correct length.

The construction of a cigar is a crucial factor in how well you enjoy it. If it is under-filled, it will draw easily, but burn fast, and get hot and harsh as a result. If it is over-filled, it will be difficult to draw on, or "plugged." Good cigars have to be consistent. That relies on skill, quality control, and the resources (reserves of suitable leaf, essentially) to guarantee that this year's cigars are the same as last year's, even if there is a bad harvest.

FITTING THE CAP

A SEPARATE PIECE OF WRAPPER IS USUALLY USED TO CAP THE CIGAR.

THE LEGENDARY PARTAGAS FACTORY, HAVANA.

THE HAVANA CIGAR FACTORY

The Havana cigar factory today is much as it was when the art of cigar making was standardized in the mid-19th century and the production of cigars became industrialized. There are only eight factories making handmade cigars in Cuba today (compared with 120 at the beginning of the century). The names of the factories were all officially changed after the revolution to what were considered more ideologically sound titles, but most of them are still commonly referred to by their pre-revolutionary names, and still display their old signs outside. The best known are H. Upmann (now called José Marti), Partagas (Francisco Perez German), Romeo Y Julieta (Briones Montoto), La Corona (Fernando Roig), and the elite El Laguito, which originally opened in the mid-1960s as a training school. Each factory specializes in a number of brands of a particular flavor. The Partagas factory, for instance, specializes in full-bodied cigars, producing six brands including Bolivar, Ramon Allones, Gloria Cubana and, of course, Partagas. Factories also often specialize in making a particular range of sizes.

The procedures in the various factories are essentially the same, though the size and atmosphere of each factory differs. The grand El Laguito, for instance, is an Italianate mansion (built in 1910) and former home of the Marquez de Pinar del Rio. It is located in three buildings in a swanky residential suburb. The rather gloomy three-story Partagas factory, on the other hand, which was built in downtown Havana in 1845, is rather more down to earth. Laguito was the first factory to use female rollers, and even today the majority of the 94 rollers there are women. The 200 rollers at the

THE MANUFACTURING PROCESS
OF HAVANA CIGARS

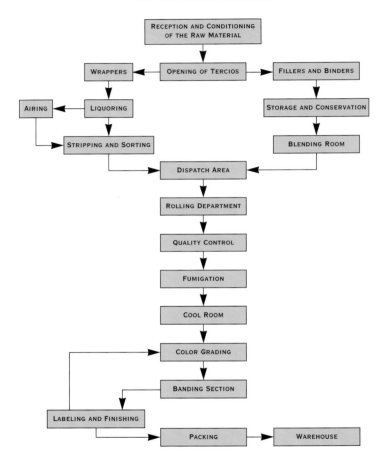

Partagas factory, the biggest for export production, turn out 5 million cigars a year. No matter which factory you go to, the walls of all of them display revolutionary slogans and portraits of Castro, Che Guevara, and others. Other slogans announced "La calidades el respeto al pueblo" (Quality is respect for people) or "Tu tambien haces calidad" (You have to care about quality).

It has been estimated that a handmade Havana cigar goes through no fewer than 222 different stages from seedling to the finished product, before being ready for distribution. And the care and expertise shown at the factory is not only crucial to the final

CIGAR ROLLER, HAVANA.

appearance of the cigar, but also affects how well it burns and what it actually tastes like. Not surprisingly, apprenticeship for the task of roller is a lengthy and competitive process, taking nine months. Even then, many fail, and those who succeed are confined to making small-sized cigars before being allowed to graduate to the larger, generally fuller-flavored, sizes.

The cigar rollers, or *torcedores*, work in large rooms where the old custom, dating from 1864, of reading aloud from books and newspapers continues to this day. The radio is also switched on, from time to time, to bring the news and important announcements. The worker who acts as reader (lector), selected by his peers for his expressive voice and literacy, is compensated by a small payment from each of the rollers, all of whom are paid piece work, according to the number of cigars they produce. Each roller is

TYPICAL WORKPLACE OF A CIGAR ROLLER.

responsible for seeing a cigar through from the bunching stage until it is finally trimmed to size. The ready-blended combination of filler leaves and binder are prepared in advance by each roller and pressed in wooden molds of the appropriate size. The use of molds started in around 1958, before the Cuban revolution. As a result, the cigar rollers—sitting at benches rather like old-fashioned school desks—each start with a quota of filler appropriate to the size and brand of cigar being made that day. All is concentration: errors are costly. But the atmosphere is cheerful, the torcedores taking great pride in their work. If a visitor enters the room, the rollers greet him by tapping their chavetas in unison on their tables.

There are as many as 42 handmade cigar sizes made today, and a good cigar maker can usually roll around 120 medium-sized cigars (though exceptionally skilled rollers can make as many as 150) a day—an average of four to five minutes for a cigar. But the average for the Montecristo A size is only 56 cigars a day. Some star rollers, such as Jesus Ortiz at the H. Upmann factory, can do much better: he can produce a staggering 200 Montecristo As a day.

The torcedores work an eight-hour day, usually six days a week, for around 350–400 pesos ($350–400 at the official exchange rate) a month. They are allowed to take home five cigars a day and can smoke as many as they wish while they work.

There are seven grades of worker in the Havana factory, the least experienced rollers (in grade 4) making only cigars up to and including the petit corona size; those in grade 5 making corona size and above, and those in grades 6 and 7 (the latter consists of a handful of star rollers) making the difficult specialist sizes such as

QUALITY CONTROL

QUALITY CONTROL. CHECKING THE GIRTH AND
LENGTH OF A COHIBA LANCERO.

MIRIAM LOPEZ, EL LAGUITO'S ONLY FEMALE
TASTER, ASSESSES A COHIBA LANCERO.

pyramides. The skill of the roller is reflected in the eventual cost per inch of the cigar. The smaller sizes are, in other words, cheaper than the larger ones.

Using colored ribbon, each roller ties his or her cigars into bundles (all of the same size and brand) of 50. Most of these bundles (*media ruedas*, or "half wheels") go into a vacuum fumigation chamber, where the cigars are treated against potential pests. A proportion of each roller's output is also taken to be checked for quality.

The man in charge of quality control at El Laguito, Fernando Valdez, tests a fifth of each roller's daily output (though only 10 percent of cigars are checked at the Partagas factory) according to no fewer than eight different criteria such as length, weight, firmness, smoothness of the wrappers, and whether or not the ends are well cut. Later, cigars from different batches are actually blind tasted by a team of six catadores, or professional smokers—themselves rigorously examined every six months—who must assess qualities such as a cigar's aroma, how well it burns, and how easily it draws. The important of each category varies according to the type of cigar. When testing a fat robusto, for instance, the flavor is paramount, but in the slim panatela size, draw is more important. There is a standard for each type of cigar. The catadores do their tasting in the morning only, smoking about an inch of each cigar, and refreshing their palates with sugarless tea. By the end of any given week, every roller's work will have been tasted.

After being removed from the vacuum chamber, cigars are held in special cool cabinets (*escaparates*) for three weeks, in order to shed any excess moisture acquired in the factory and settle down any fermentation that is taking place. A cabinet might hold up to 18,000 cigars, all kept under careful supervision.

When they are ready, batches of 1,000 cigars from a particular brand and size are sent in wooden boxes to be graded according to appearance. The cigars are classified into as many as 65 different shades—and each selector must be familiar with all of them. First the selector takes into account the basic color of the cigar (hues given names such as sangre de toro, encendido, colorado encendido, colorado, colorado pajizo, and clarisimo), and then the shade within that particular color category. The color grader then puts the cigars into transit boxes, making sure that all the cigars in a particular box are the same color. The darkest cigar is placed on the left of the box, and the cigars arranged according to nuances of shade so that the lightest is on the right.

FINISHING AND PACKAGING

CIGARS SORTED INTO DIFFERENT COLOR SHADES.

THE BAND IS ADDED.

CIGARS ARE BOXED ACCORDING TO COLOR.

Once the cigars are color-graded, they go to the packing department, where bands are put on. The cigars are then put in the familiar cedar boxes in which they will be sold. The packers also watch out for cigars which have escaped the quality control department. Once the final box is filled, the cigars are checked again, and then a thin leaf of cedar wood is laid on top of them.

The box is then sealed with the essential label guaranteeing that it is a genuine box of Havanas or Habanos. The word "Habanos" in red on a chevron has been added to boxes since 1994.

The practice of making handmade cigars is essentially the same wherever they're made, but in the Dominican Republic, for instance, the arrangement between bunchers and rollers is sometimes different (the jobs usually being separated). The large, modern American-owned factories of the Dominican Republic have state-of-the-art quality-control methods, using machines (at the bunch stage, as well as later) to check suction, and thus how well a cigar will draw. Despite this, other manufacturers still prefer to do everything by hand, particularly checking for gaps in the bunch, which will make a cigar overheat. In the Philippines, there is a method of rolling in which leaves are spiraled around two thin wooden sticks, which are removed when the cigar is wrapped.

HANDMADE VERSUS MACHINE-MADE CIGARS

The essential difference between handmade and machine-made cigars lies in the fact that, on the whole, most machine-made cigars aren't made with long fillers—fillers, that is, which run the whole length of the cigar—thus making the drawing and burning qualities (they burn faster and become hotter) of the machine-mades significantly inferior. Some machine-made brands, Bering for instance, use long fillers, making them better but still inferior to handmade cigars. The quality of wrappers on machine-made cigars is also usually inferior to those used on the best handmades.

For cheap, mass market, machine-made brands, blended filler is fed into rod-making machines—a process similar to cigarette making—and covered by a continuous sheet of binder. This creates a tube which is sealed at each end to the appropriate length. The wrapper is then added and the cigars trimmed.

In the case of more expensive machine-made, an operator sitting in front of a cigar-making machine feeds a mixture of filler tobacco (usually shredded leaves or scraps) into a hopper, and places two

THE DIFFERENCE
BETWEEN CIGAR TYPES

MACHINE-MADE: THE FILLER IS MADE OF SCRAPS OF LEAF.

HANDMADE: FILLER, BINDER, WRAPPER. NOTE THE
LONG FILLER WHICH RUNS THE LENGTH OF THE CIGAR.

binder leaves on a plate where they are cut. The two leaves are then positioned, overlapping, on a moving belt which feeds them into the rolling machine. This wraps the measured amount of filler and feeds out the cigar, which is then trimmed.

It is reasonably easy to tell the difference between handmade cigars and all but the best machine-mades: the caps on machine-mades are often very much more pointed; the cigars tend to be much less smooth to the touch; and the wrapper is likely to be much coarser, quite often with protruding veins. If a cigar doesn't have a cap, you can be certain that it is one of the cheaper machine-mades. Cellophane wrapping can also be a giveaway, particularly with Cuban cigars, but many very good non-Cuban handmade brands come wrapped in cellophane, so this is by no means an infallible way of telling whether the cigars are machine-made or not.

The Cubans recently introduced the concept of "hand-finished" machine-bunched cigars, with the Quintero brand for instance. These cigars have caps similar to handmades, long filler, and decent-quality wrappers. They can approach the experience of smoking a handmade cigar in flavor, though they wouldn't fool an experienced smoker.

Handmade cigars are so much more expensive than machine-mades quite simply because they take much longer to make, are labor-intensive, and use much more expensively produced and matured leaves. The handmaking process also leads to wastage.

THE CIGAR BOX

Cigars were originally sold in bundles covered with pigs' bladders (with a pod or two of vanilla to improve the smell); then came the use of the large cedar chests, holding up to 10,000 cigars.

But in 1830, the banking firm of H. Upmann started shipping back cigars, for the use of its directors in London, in sealed cedar boxes stamped with the bank's emblem. When the bank decided to go, full-scale, into the cigar business, the cedar box took off as a form of packaging for all the major Havana brands, and all hand-made cigars (though small quantities today are sometimes packaged in cardboard cartons, and single cigars of many brands come in aluminum tubes lined with cedar). Cedar helps to prevent cigars from drying out and furthers the maturing process.

The idea of using colorful lithographic labels, now used for all handmade brands, wherever they come from, started when Ramon Allones, a Galician immigrant to Cuba, initiated it for the brand he started in 1837. As the industry grew in the mid-19th century, so

H. UPMANN WAS AMONG THE FIRST USERS OF THE
CEDAR BOXES TO PACKAGE CIGARS.

did the need for clear brand identification. Labels or other illustra-
tions also appear on the inside of the lids of many Havana and
other brands. Boxes also usually have colorful decorative borders.
The cedar box is sometimes referred to as a "boîte nature." Paper,
usually colored, is normally glued to the interior of the box and is
used to cover the cigars it contains.

Finally, after being filled and checked, the box is nailed shut
and tightly sealed with a green and white label (a custom dating
from 1912) to guarantee that the cigars are genuine Havanas. The
practice of using a label, usually printed in similar colors and with
similar wording, to seal the box continues today for most handmade
brands, Cuban or not.

The Havana seal reads: "Cuban Government's warranty for
cigars exported from Havana. Republica de Cuba. Sello de garantia
nacional de procedencia."

Most sizes of the élite Cohiba brand come in varnished boxes, as
do one or two of the larger sizes of a handful of other Cuban
brands. The H. Upmann Sir Winston size, for instance, is available
in a polished dark green box. These polished boxes are usually
stamped with the brand symbol, rather than carrying any sort of
label other than the government seal.

The form of packaging called 8–9–8 is used for some cigars in
the Partagas and Ramon Allones brands. These boxes are polished,
have curved edges, and contain 25 cigars, arranged in three layers
with eight at the bottom, mine in the middle, and eight on top.
Cigars with this sort of packaging are relatively expensive.

CIGAR BOX STAMPS

THE HAVANA SEAL.

THE STAMP TELLING YOU THE CIGARS ARE HANDMADE.

A PREREVOLUTIONARY HAVANA BOX.

Hecho en Cuba has been stamped on the underside of Cuban boxes since 1961, when it replaced the English inscription "Made in Havana—Cuba." Since 1985, they have also carried a factory code and Cubatabaco's logo, the latter being replaced with Habanos SA from late 1994.

In 1989 the words "Totalmente a Mano" were added. Meaning "Totally by Hand," they provide the only cast-iron clue that the cigars are genuinely handmade in the traditional Cuban manner. "Hecho a Mano" or "Made by Hand" can cover a multitude of sins (European Union law permits cigars that are hand finished but machine bunched to be described as made by hand)—so the situation can be confusing.

Unless you have complete trust in your cigar merchant when buying older cigars, the only way to play safe is to buy post-1989 cigars with the "Totalmente a Mano" legend. If the box says: "Made in Havana, Cuba," it is almost certainly pre-revolutionary.

The factory code, on Havana cigars, is stamped in blue—using post-revolutionary factory designations. Thus, for instance:

JM stands for José Martí, formerly H. Upmann.
FPG stands for Francisco Perez German, formerly Partagas.
BM stands for Briones Montoto, formerly Romeo Y Julieta.
FR stands for Fernando Roig, formerly La Corona.
EL stands for El Laguito.
HM stands for Heroes del Moncada, formerly El Rey del Mundo.

Havana boxes also used to be stamped with the color of the cigars contained in them, but this practice has stopped, for the time being at least. Boxes, in the past, often read "claro," but this color classification was frequently inaccurate.

On non-Havana boxes, you might read "Envuelto a mano"— which only means hand-*packed*, but could deceive the unwary. "Hand rolled" means simply (as with Cuban "hand-finished" cigars) that the *wrapper* is put on by hand, the rest of the cigar is machine-made.

Underneath the boxes of American-produced cigars, there is normally a code: the letters TP, followed by a number identifying the manufacturer. Cigars imported into the United States don't show this code. Some cigars (Dominican Dunhills and the most expensive Macanudos, for instance) refer to a "vintage" on the box. This refers to the year of the tobacco crop, not the year of manufacture. Dunhills currently on sale, for example, are 1989 vintage—made from the Dominican 1989 harvest.

THE CIGAR BAND

The cigar band was introduced by the Dutchman, Gustave Bock, one of the first Europeans to get involved in the Havana cigar industry, somewhat after the introduction of the cigar box and labels, and for the same reason: to distinguish his brand from the many others on the market. His lead was soon followed by all the other brands, and cigar bands are still used by almost all handmade brands. When bands were originally introduced, other manufacturers followed Bock's example and had them made in Holland. Some cigars, sold in "Cabinet Selection" packaging—usually a deep cedar box containing a bundle of 50 loosely packed cigars tied together with silk ribbon—are sold without bands. This "half-wheel," as it is called, of 50 cigars is the way cigars were normally presented before the band was introduced. Some Honduran hand-mades are also often sold in Europe without bands (and usually singly), primarily for trademark reasons.

The band also has other minor functions, such as protecting the smoker's fingers from becoming stained (this was important when gentlemen wore white evening gloves) and, some claim, holding the wrapper together—though no decent wrapper should need help.

The cigar bands of older brands tend to be much fancier (with gold leaf in abundance) than those of modern brands. Those aimed at the very top of the market in particular—Cohiba, Dunhill, Montecristo, and Davidoff, for instance—are all simple and elegant.

The bands on non-Havana cigars with Cuban brand names tend to be similar to the Cuban originals, although they vary in small details (a typical one being that they bear the date of origin of the brand in the space where the Cuban version says "Habana").

Some Cuban brands use more than one band design, Hoyo de Monterrey, for instance, or Tomeo Y Julieta, where the Churchill sizes have a simple, slim gold band, but other sizes have red ones.

The question of whether to smoke a cigar with the band on or off is purely a matter of personal choice. In Britain, it has traditionally been considered a matter of "bad form" to advertise the brand you are smoking, an inhibition which doesn't apply elsewhere.

If you insist on removing the band, it is best to wait until you have smoked the cigar for a few minutes. The heat of the smoke will help to loosen the band from the wrapper and will make the gum on the band less adhesive and easier to remove. If you try to take the band off the cigar before starting to smoke it, you will risk damaging the wrapper.

CIGAR SIZES

There are countless cigar sizes. Cuba alone produces 69, 2 of which are for handmade Havanas. Each has a factory name, which usually bears no relationship to the name by which we know them, like Prominente (Double Corona), Julieta 2 (Churchill), Mareva (Petit Corona), Franciscano, Carolina, and so on. Some brands, Partagas for example, have 40 sizes, though several are machine-made. This is a throwback to the past when many selections were even larger. More modern brands such as Cohiba and Montecristo have just 11 sizes. Non-Havana brands tend to offer more manageable lines, although many, like Davidoff, which now boasts 19 sizes, have started to grow.

Sadly for the novice, there is no such thing as a standard size or a comprehensive list of sizes. Even the common Petit Corona can be found with different girths, and the name of Churchill covers a variety of alternative, albeit substantial, cigars. Listed below are the 25 most popular Havana sizes under their factory names. This may serve to indicate just how wide a selection is available, but it merely scratches the surface of the full panoply of choice offered by Cuba, let alone the Dominican Republic, Honduras, Mexico, and others.

The girth of a cigar is customarily expressed in terms of its ring gauge in ⅟₆₄ths of an inch. Thus, if a cigar has a ring gauge of 49, it is ⁴⁹⁄₆₄ths of an inch thick. Similarly, if a cigar had a ring gauge of 64, it would be an inch thick. Only a couple of cigars come into

CIGARS COME IN A BEWILDERING ARRAY OF SIZES AND SHAPES RANGING FROM THE 9¼-INCH GRAN CORONA TO THE 4-INCH ENTREACTO.

BASIC HAVANA SIZES

NAME	LENGTH: INCHES	RING GAUGE
HEAVY RING GAUGE		
Gran Coron	9¼ inches	47
Prominente	7⅝ inches	49
Julieta 2	7 inches	47
Piramide*	6⅛ inches	52
Corona Gorda	5⅝ inches	46
Campana*	5½ inches	52
Hermoso No. 4	5 inches	48
Robusto	47/8 inches	50
STANDARD RING GAUGE		
Dalia	6¾ inches	43
Cervante	6½ inches	42
Corona Grande	6⅛ inches	42
Corona	5½ inches	42
Mareva	5 inches	42
Londres	5 inches	40
Minuto	4⅜ inches	42
Perla	4 inches	40
SLENDER RING GAUGE		
Laguito No. 1	7½ inches	38
Ninfas	7 inches	33
Laguito No. 2	6 inches	38
Seoane	5 inches	36
Carolina	4¾ inches	26
Franciscano	4½ inches	40
Laguito No. 3	4½ inches	26
Cadete	4½ inches	36
Entreacto	3⅞ inches	30

**These sizes, having pointed heads, are often referred to as "torpedoes." This name suggests, incorrectly, that they should be pointed at both ends. Cigars which are pointed at both ends are termed "Figuerados."*

this size today, the 9-inch long Royal Jamaica Goliath, and the same length José Benito Magnum from the Dominican Republic. The Casa Blanca Jeroboam and Half Jeroboam come with a whopping 66 ring gauge.

The largest properly smokable cigar made was Koh-i-Noor, made before World War II by Henry Clay for a maharaja. The same size, called the Visible Inmenso (18 inches long, 47 ring gauge) was made for King Farouk of Egypt. There was also once a panatela measuring 19½ inches. At the Partagas factory in Havana, they keep a collector's item: a cigar measuring almost 50 inches. You can also see a cigar a yard long with a ring gauge of 96 kept at the Davidoff store in London.

The smallest regularly made cigar was the Bolivar Delgado—measuring under 1½ inches.

There are plenty of variations to be found within a particular brand, particularly if the choice is large. Different brands, on the whole, tend to be expert at making different sizes. So, while the large ring gauge cigars in a certain brand might be excellent, you shouldn't assume that the smaller ones will either taste similar or be as well made. It comes down to actually trying the cigars.

SELECTING A CIGAR

As a general rules, cigars with larger ring gauges tend to be fuller flavored (there is normally more *ligero* and less *volado* in the blend), smoke more smoothly and slowly, and heat up less fast than those with small ring gauges. They also tend to be better made than the smaller ones (which are the sizes recently qualified apprentices start on). Cigars with small ring gauges often have little or no *ligero* tobacco in the filler blend. Large ring gauge cigars are almost always the preferred choice—if there is no hurry—of connoisseurs or experienced cigar smokers.

The beginner, however, is advised to choose a relatively small cigar, say a minuto or carolina, and then move up to the bigger sizes of a mild brand (see The Cigar Directory). Jamaican cigars, such as Macanudo (also made in the Dominican Republic), tend to be mild, or try H. Upmann among Havanas. A cervante is probably the best cigar above the corona size to move up to when you feel you have gone beyond the beginner stage.

A number of cigar experts, including the legendary Zino Davidoff, have pontificated about a person's physical appearance related to cigar size, and the Cubans have a saying, "As you approach 30, you have a 30 ring gauge; as you approach 50, you have a 50 ring gauge." This is, on the whole, so much hogwash. What size of cigar you smoke is entirely up to you and your pocket. Having said that, smoking a fat cigar, if you are very small or thin, can sometimes look rather comic or pretentious. But there is a case to be made about what sort of cigar to smoke at what time of day. Most smokers prefer milder, smaller cigars in the morning, or after a light lunch. The seasoned smoker, however, might go for something like a robusto after a heavy lunch—a lot of flavor packed into a reasonably short smoke. Certainly, most experienced smokers prefer a big, full-bodied cigar after a heavy meal or late at night, partly because a thin cigar will not last very long, and a mild one isn't so satisfying on a full stomach. So they will select a belicoso, Churchill, or double corona. By the same token, smoking a heavy cigar before dinner is likely to spoil your appetite and play havoc with your taste buds. Much the same consideration applies when people have strong drinks like port or brandy after dinner, rather than something lighter, which they will take before or during dinner. If you want to compare cigars, it is best to smoke them at similar times of day, taking meals and location into account, too.

When you choose a cigar, you should first make sure that the wrapper is intact (if not, reject it) and has a healthy sheen. You should also make sure that it isn't too dry or brittle (otherwise it will taste harsh) and that there is a noticeable bouquet (if not, the cigar has probably been badly stored). A good cigar should be neither too firm nor too soft. If the wrapper is heavily veined, the cigar should be rejected: quality control went wrong somewhere.

The color of a cigar's wrapper (and that part of the filler that you can see) will give you some clues, though it is not infallible since the filler blend is the key, as to its flavor. As a rule of thumb, the darker a cigar, the more full-bodied and (since darker wrappers contain more sugar) sweeter it is likely to be. Cigars, if properly stored, continued to mature and ferment in their cedar boxes. This aging process, during which a cigar loses acidity, is not unlike the maturing of good wine. Fuller-bodied cigars, particularly those with big ring gauges, tend to age better than milder ones. But it should be said that some full-bodied brands, such as Cohiba and Montecristo (apart, perhaps from the very largest sizes) don't age particularly well because the tobacco is fermented for longer—a complete extra fermentation in the case of Cohiba—in the factory, thus leaving little room for further maturation. There are even those who argue that if tobacco has been properly fermented, it is very unlikely to mature further (and if it has been fermented too little, it can't mature at all).

Milder cigars, particularly those with pale wrappers, will merely lose their bouquet if kept too long. In general, you should smoke lighter cigars before darker ones. Wrappers which are destined to age well start off oily, and get slightly darker and oilier as they mature.

Most importers of fine handmade cigars take care to age them a little before releasing them to the public (about two years for Havana cigars taken into Britain). There is not hard and fast rule about how long cigars should be left to mature (it can often be a matter of luck), but some experts state that cigars aged for six to ten years will be in the peak of condition. Others warn, quite rightly, that even if they are stored under ideal conditions, most cigars will lose their bouquet. If storage conditions are less good, they will also become dry. Even if well stored, it's probably sensible not to keep cigars for more than 10 years—by that time, they're unlikely to get any better, and will almost certainly have lost some of their bouquet.

Cigars should be smoked either within three months of manufacture or, failing that, not for at least a year after they are made. The intervening "period of sickness" as it is known—when the maturing process starts—is the worst time to smoke a cigar.

WRAPPER COLORS

Cigar wrappers can be classified into seven basic colors, although there are dozens of possible shades:

THE BASIC COLORS OF WRAPPERS RANGE FROM CLARO (PALE BROWN) TO OSCURO (BLACK).

DOUBLE CLARO (also called AMS, American Market Selection, or candela)—greenish brown (for instance, as in Macanudo "jade.") The color is achieved by picking the leaf before it reaches maturity and then drying it rapidly. Very mild, almost bland, with very little oil. Cigars with this color have traditionally been popular in the United States, but are very much less so today.

CLARO—pale brown, like milky coffee. (For example, Havana brands like H. Upmann, or brands using Connecticut Shade wrappers.) The classic mild cigar color. The color is also called "natural," as is colorado claro.

COLORADO CLARO—mid-brown, tawny. (For example, brands, such as Dominican Partagas, using Cameroon wrappers.)

COLORADO—reddish dark brown, aromatic. This color is associated with well-matured cigars.

COLORADO MADURO—dark brown, medium strength, rather more aromatic than maduro. Usually gives a rich flavor, as found in many of the best Honduran cigars.

MADURO—very dark brown, like black coffee. (For example, full-bodied Havana brands such as Bolivar; cigars made with Mexican wrappers.) A color for seasoned smokers. Sometimes thought of as the traditional Cuban color.

OSCURO—more or less black. Very strong with little bouquet. Wrappers of this color, though once popular, are rarely produced today. If they are produced these wrappers tend to be from Nicaragua, Brazil, Mexico, or the Connecticut Broadleaf (as opposed to Shade) type.

The darker the color, the sweeter and stronger the flavor is likely to be, and the greater the oil and sugar content of the wrapper. Darker wrappers will normally have spent longer on the tobacco plant or will come from higher altitudes: the extra exposure to sunlight produces both oil (as protection) and sugar (through photosynthesis). They will also have been fermented for longer.

The term EMS or English Market Selection is a broad one, which refers to brown cigars—anything other than double claro (AMS) essentially.

All handmade cigars need to be cut at the closed end before they can be smoked. Just how you do this is up to you. There are a number of cutters on the market ranging from small, cheap, easily portable guillotines (which come in single or double blade versions, the latter being the best), to fancy cigar scissors—which need some skill to use properly. You can use a sharp (that's essential) knife. If you use your fingernails, just pinch off the very top of the cap. The important thing is that the cut should be clean and level; otherwise, you will have difficulties with draw and risk damaging the wrapper. You should cut the cigar so that you leave about ⅛ inch of the cap. Piercing the cap isn't recommended: it interferes with the passage of smoke by compressing the filler, and will make the cigar overheat, leading to an unpleasant flavor. Cutters which make a wedge shape in the cap aren't recommended for the same reason. You should never cut a cigar on or below cap level: it is a certain way of ruining the wrapper. The idea is to take off just enough of the cap to expose the filler leaves. Whatever you use, make sure it is sharp.

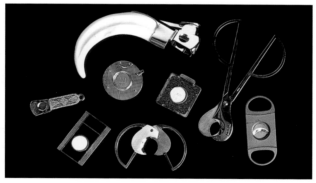

CUTTERS. THE GUILLOTINE TYPE IS THE SIMPLEST, CHEAPEST, AND BEST.

When you light a cigar you can use a butane lighter (though not a gasoline lighter, which will impair the flavor) or a match. There are special long slow-burning matches designed for cigar smokers available from high quality shops such as Dunhill or Davidoff, but a normal wooden match will do perfectly well. You should, however, avoid matches with a high sulfur or wax content. A properly lit cigar is always more enjoyable than one that isn't, so take it easy when you light one.

1 Hold the cigar horizontally, in direct contact with the flame, slowly revolving it until the end is charred evenly over its entire surface.

2 Only now do you put the cigar between your lips. Hold the flame about half an inch away from the end and draw slowly while turning it. The end of the cigar should now ignite. Make sure it is evenly lit; otherwise, one side will burn faster than the other.

3 Gently blow on the glowing end to make sure that it is burning evenly.

CUTTING A CIGAR. MAKE SURE IT'S NOT TOO NEAR THE BOTTOM OF THE CAP.

LIGHTING A CIGAR. DO IT CAREFULLY.

ALMOST READY TO SMOKE.

Older, well-matured cigars burn more easily than younger ones. If properly lit, the highest quality cigars have only a very narrow carbon rim at the lit end; mediocre cigars will have a thicker band.

To get the best out of them, cigars should be smoked slowly. They should not be dragged on or puffed too frequently. This will lead to overheating and spoil the flavor. Nor should the smoke—it hardly needs saying—be inhaled. The strong alkaline smoke and low nicotine content means that you will cough in reaction. A cigar like a corona will take about half an hour to smoke, with larger cigars taking an hour or more.

If your cigar goes out, don't worry: this is quite normal, particularly if you have already smoked half of it. Tap the cigar to remove any clinging ash. Then blow through the cigar to clear any stale smoke. Re-light as you would a new cigar. You should have a satisfactory smoke even if you leave the cigar for a couple of hours. Left much longer than that, it will taste stale, although a large ring gauge cigar smoked less than halfway down will still be smokeable, if not so enjoyable, the following day.

Cigars, unlike cigarettes, don't need to be tapped to remove the ash—it should fall off in due course. There is, on the other hand, no virtue in keeping a long cylinder of ash at the end of your cigar just because it is there: it impairs the passage of air and will make the cigar burn unevenly. The better the construction of the cigar, the longer and more "solid" will the ash cylinder be.

Once the cigar starts producing hot smoke and you get a strong aftertaste (usually when you are down to the last couple of inches), it is time to abandon it. As the French actor Sacha Guitry wrote: "If the birth of a genius resembles that of an idiot, the end of a Havana Corona resembles that of a five-cent cigar." It isn't necessary to stub out a cigar as you would a cigarette. Just leave it in the ashtray, and it will go out soon enough. Cigar stubs should be disposed of soon after they have gone out; otherwise, the room will acquire the lingering smell of stale smoke.

There are two things that really should not be done: first, don't roll a cigar near your ear. This is contemptuously known as "listening to the band" in the cigar trade. It tells you nothing at all about the cigar; second, you should never warm the length of the cigar before smoking it. This was originally done in order to burn off the rather unpleasant gum used to make some Seville cigars well over a hundred years ago. It is not necessary with today's high-quality handmade cigars, as they use a mere drop of flavorless, odorless vegetable gum.

2

THE
CIGAR
DIRECTORY

*T*he selected list of handmade cigars in this section doesn't claim to be totally comprehensive, but it should contain most of the brands you are likely to come across. Some of them are only available in the United States, others only in Europe: but these things change. The same applies to sizes within brands (always listed in descending order of length).

Notes on flavor and aroma are necessarily subjective, but construction, draw, and wrapper quality can be more objectively assessed. You might love the flavor of a cigar even though it is criticized in the directory. It is, after all, a matter of personal taste.

C The country of origin of the cigar is denoted as follows:
> Cuba, for example
> Honduras, for example

F The categories for flavor range through four strengths:
> Mild
> Mild to medium
> Medium to full-bodied
> Very full-bodied

As for quality, the assessment takes into account appearance, construction, and consistency—the latter being of particular importance in any brand. Even so, cigars being handmade, and cigar tobacco being subject to the vagaries of climate (not to mention politics in some countries), things have changed and will change from time to time even for the best-known brands. These entries, then, can only be a guide, good for the time being.

Q The four categories for quality are as follows:
> Could be better
> Good-quality leaf and construction
> Superior quality
> The very best quality available

AFTER BEING ROLLED, CIGARS REST FOR 15 DAYS TO LOSE
SOME OF THEIR MOISTURE.

*C*igar lore says that farmers raise tobacco and manufacturers make cigars. So, when the Fuente family, the largest producers of handmade cigars in the Dominican Republic, bought a plantation, eyebrows were raised on both sides of the divide. As word spread that the farm near el Caribe would grow wrappers, the same eyebrows arched. Virtually no one grew wrappers in the Dominican Republic and certainly not for premium cigars.

When a cigar wrapped with leaf from the El Caribe farm, now known as Chateau de la Fuente, topped *Cigar Aficionado's* fall 1994 tasting, beating several Havanas before it even went on sale, the eyebrows hit the roof.

1995 saw the creation of the Fuente Fuente OpusX® series which features the wrapper grown at the Chateau de la Fuente farm. Since then it has been a very popular line, but sadly limited in production. The Fuente family aim to remedy this, however, with 150 acres of newly purchased land adjacent to the Chateau de la Fuente farm. This land has not been worked previously so the top soil is very deep. The Fuentes believe it is as good, if not better than that of the Chateau de la Fuente for growing wrapper leaves, and eventually hope to double the production of this line.

There are plenty of other Fuente cigars to enjoy in both their standard range and their Hemingway series of big figurados. Rare Colorado Cameroon wrappers are Fuente's hallmark, although some sizes like Royal Salute come dressed in "natural" Connecticut shade. All these cigars are well-constructed and well-blended, giving a distinguished light to medium flavor which reflects the enthusiasm of their makers. The Double Corona and Rothschild enclosed in cedar-wood wraps are particular favorites.

FUENTE FUENTE OPUSX® SIZES

NAME	LENGTH: INCHES	RING GAUGE
Reserva A	9¼ inches	47
Double Corona	7⅝ inches	49
Reserva No. 1	6⅞ inches	44
Reserva No. 2	6¼ inches	52
Petit Lanceros	6¼ inches	38
Fuente Fuente	5⅝ inches	46
Robusto	5¼ inches	50

RESERVA A : LENGTH 9¼ INCHES, RING GAUGE 47

RESERVA NO. 2 : LENGTH 6¼ INCHES, RING GAUGE 52

ROBUSTO : LENGTH 5¼ INCHES, RING GAUGE 50

SIZES

NAME	LENGTH: INCHES	RING GAUGE
Canones	8½ inches	52
Royal Salute	7⅝ inches	52
Churchill	7½ inches	48
Panetela Fina	7 inches	38
Double Corona	6¾ inches	48
Privada No. 1	6¾ inches	46
Lonsdale	6½ inches	42
Flor Fina	6 inches	46
Cuban Corona	5¼ inches	44
Petit Corona	5 inches	38
Chateau Fuente	4½ inches	50

HEMINGWAY SERIES

Masterpiece	9 inches	52
Classic	6 inches	47
Signature	6 inches	47

"PETIT CORONA: LENGTH 5 INCHES, RING GAUGE 38

CHATEAU FUENTE : LENGTH 4½ INCHES, RING GAUGE 50

PRIVADA NO. 1 : LENGTH 6¾ INCHES, RING GAUGE 46

C Dominican Republic
F Light to medium
Q Superior quality

[59]

ASHTON

*O*wned by a Philadelphia enterprise but named after an English pipe-maker of high repute, these well-tailored cigars are made in the Dominican Republic. The come in three styles of flavor. One is known simply as Ashton. Then there is Ashton Cabinet Selection and Ashton Aged Maduro. All three are wrapped in Connecticut leaf, although the Aged Maduro is in broadleaf rather than shade, and is filled with a Dominican blend.

The mildest are the Cabinet Selection, owing to extra aging of the tobaccos (the Nos. 1, 2 & 3 are tapered at both ends). For a mild to medium smoke, go for the standard selection in a size like the Magnum, or if sweetness appeals, try a Maduro No. 10. The Ashton Crown series uses precious leaves from the Chateau de la Fuente farm.

SIZES

Name	Length: inches	Ring Gauge
Cabinet No. 1	9 inches	52
Churchill	7½ inches	52
Cabinet No. 10	7½ inches	52
No. 60 Maduro	7½ inches	52
Cabinet No. 8	7 inches	50
No. 50 Maduro	7 inches	48
Cabinet No. 2	7 inches	46
Prime Minister	6⅞ inches	48
No. 30 Maduro	6¾ inches	44
8–9–8	6½ inches	44
Elegante	6½ inches	35
Cabinet No. 7	6¼ inches	52
No. 40 Maduro	6 inches	50
Double "R"	6 inches	50
Cabinet No. 3	6 inches	46
Panetela	6 inches	36
Cabinet No. 6	5½ inches	50
Corona	5½ inches	44
No. 20 Maduro	5½ inches	44
No. 10 Maduro	5 inches	50
Magnum	5 inches	50
Cordial	5 inches	30

CABINET NO. 3 : LENGTH 6 INCHES, RING GAUGE 46

NO. 40 MADURO : LENGTH 6 INCHES, RING GAUGE 50

NO. 60 MADURO : LENGTH 7½ INCHES, RING GAUGE 52

CABINET No. 2 : LENGTH 7 INCHES, RING GAUGE 46

PRIME MINISTER : LENGTH 6⅞ INCHES, RING GAUGE 48

MAGNUM : LENGTH 5 INCHES, RING GAUGE 50

C Dominican Republic
F Mild to medium
Q Good-quality leaf and construction

AVO

vo Uvezian, accomplished musician and composer of *Strangers in the Night*, brings a clear understanding of harmony to the cigars which bear his name. Both in his standard selection and the more recent "XO" Series, the balance of flavor achieved between golden Connecticut wrappers and Dominican fillers and binders is well struck.

The "XO" Series, which can be identified by the two discreet letters on the side of the band, owes its premium price (no Avo is cheap) to a unique aging and fermenting process, although it is not clear quite what this entails.

The cigars are well constructed. The Pyramid and Belicosos sizes, however, should not be compared to the Cuban Piramides and Campana (often called Belicosos) sizes to which they bear little or no resemblance.

Flavors tend to intensify with the increase in girth of the cigars and can vary from a medium to a fuller, richer taste.

SIZES

Name	Length: inches	Ring Gauge
No. 3	7½ inches	52
Pyramid	7 inches	36/54
XO Maestoso	7 inches	48
No. 4	7 inches	38
No. 5	6¾ inches	46
No. 1	6¾ inches	42
No. 6	6½ inches	36
No. 2	6 inches	50
Belicoso	6 inches	50
No. 7	6 inches	44
XO Preludo	6 inches	40
XO Intermezzo	5½ inches	50
No. 8	5½ inches	40
Petit Belicoso	4¾ inches	50
No. 9	4¾ inches	48

XO MAESTOSO : LENGTH 7 INCHES, RING GAUGE 48

NO. 2 : LENGTH 6 INCHES, RING GAUGE 50

PYRAMID : LENGTH 7 INCHES, RING GAUGE 54

C Dominican Republic
F Medium to full
Q Superior quality

BANCES

A brand which comes in both hand- and machine-made sizes. The handmade sizes are all produced in Honduras from a blend of local tobaccos. The wrappers tend to be rather coarse, and tight rolling can give problems with the draw. Overall, these cigars offer a distinct, sweetish, slightly peppery taste at a keen price.

SIZES

NAME	LENGTH: INCHES	RING GAUGE
President	8½ inches	52
Corona Inmensas	6¾ inches	48
No. 1	6½ inches	43
Cazadores	6¼ inches	44
Breva	5¼ inches	43

C Honduras
F Mild to full-medium
Q Could be better

2¾

TOBACCO ✦ BANCES ✦ IMPORTED
1840 ESTABLISHED

CORONA IMMENSAS : LENGTH 6¾ INCHES, RING GAUGE 48

BAUZA

*E*choes of pre-revolution Havana are still to be found on Bauza boxes, although today the cigars are made in the Dominican Republic. The wrappers are rich Ecuador. The Mexican binder combines with a mixture of Nicaraguan and Dominican fillers to deliver a very pleasant, aromatic smoke with a mild to medium flavor. The cigars are well put together by hand, but watch out for the Presidente (not listed below) which is short filler and not to be compared to the rest. Prices are very reasonable.

SIZES

Name	Length: inches	Ring Gauge
Fabulosos	7½ inches	50
Medalla D'Oro		
No. 1	6⅞ inches	44
Florete	6⅞ inches	35
Casa Grande	6¾ inches	48
Jaguar	6½ inches	42
Robusto	5½ inches	50
Grecos	5½ inches	42
Petit Corona	5 inches	38

- **C** Dominican Republic
- **F** Mild to medium
- **Q** Superior quality

CASA GRANDE : LENGTH 6¾ INCHES, RING GAUGE 48

BOLIVAR

The famous Bolivar label and box featuring a portrait of the 19th-century Venezuelan revolutionary Simon Bolivar, liberator of much of South America from the Spanish empire, is one of the most instantly recognizable of all Havana cigar brands. At one time, the brand had the distinction of producing the smallest Havanas: the Delgado, measuring 1⅞ inches by 20 ring gauge, and even made a miniature box of cigars for a dollshouse in the royal nursery at Windsor Castle in England. It was founded in 1901 by the Rocha company.

There are some 20 cigars in the line, but many of the sizes come in machine-made versions, so be particularly careful if you think you've found a bargain. There are 19 handmade sizes, a selection of which is listed below. Bolivars are among the cheapest of handmade Cuban cigars and represent a good buy if—and this is a big if—their powerful flavor appeals to you, because as a brand, they are also among the strongest, fullest-bodied of Havanas. They are certainly not for the beginner, but appeal to many seasoned smokers. With their characteristic dark wrappers, they age well. Go for the larger sizes (Royal Corona upward)—which are well-constructed, draw and burn evenly, and have a strong aroma. The torpedo-shaped Belicosos Finos are a favorite with many, ideal after a heavy meal, whereas the mellow Royal Corona (robusto) is a very good post-lunch cigar. The Petit Corona is one of the fullest flavored available. The Palmas (panatela) which is produced in limited quantities should be avoided by those who expect a light smoke in this size. The distinctive Bolivar flavor comes not, as might be expected, because an unusually high proportion of ligero leaf is used, but because much more seco than volado is in the blend.

There are also Dominican versions of Bolivar on the market, not particularly noted, though good value, well made with Cameroon wrappers, and mild to medium in flavor. The Dominican line consists of only five sizes.

ROYAL CORONA : LENGTH 4⅞ INCHES, RING GAUGE 50

GOLD MEDAL : LENGTH 6⅜ INCHES, RING GAUGE 42

PETIT CORONA : LENGTH 5 INCHES, RING GAUGE 42

C Cuba
F Very full-
bodied
Q Superior
quality

C Dominican
Republic
F Mild to
medium
Q Good-quality
leaf and
construction

BELICOSOS FINOS : LENGTH 5½ INCHES, RING GAUGE 52

CUBAN SIZES

NAME	LENGTH: INCHES	RING GAUGE
Corona Gigantes	7 inches	47
Churchill	7 inches	47
Lonsdales	6⅝ inches	43
Gold Medal	6⅜ inches	42
Corona Extra	5⅝ inches	44
Belicosos Finos	5½ inches	52
Corona	5½ inches	42
Petit Corona	5 inches	42
Bonitas	5 inches	40
Royal Corona	4⅞ inches	50
Regentes	4⅞ inches	34
Corona Junior	4¼ inches	42

DOMINICAN SIZES

NAME	LENGTH: INCHES	RING GAUGE
Bolivares	7 inches	46
Corona Grand	6½ inches	42
Belicosos Finos	6½ inches	38
Panetelita	6 inches	31
Corona Extra	5½ inches	42

C.A.O.

*F*irst introduced in 1995, C.A.O.'s Honduran cigars are made at Nestor Plasencia's Fabrica de Tabacas Oriente factory and are made of Nicaraguan and Mexican filler tobacco, with binders from Honduras, and Connecticut shade wrappers. They tend to be very well constructed and offer a mild smoke. A new, superior line, C.A.O. Gold was introduced in 1996, and was an immediate success—so much so that, at the time of writing, C.A.O. International were five months behind orders. They are available in five sizes, all with Nicaraguan filler and binder, and Ecuadoran wrapper.

C Nicaragua
F Mild to Medium
Q Superior quality

SIZES

NAME	LENGTH: INCHES	RING GAUGE
Churchill	8 inches	50
Presidente	7½ inches	54
Triangulare	7 inches	36/54
Lonsdale	7 inches	44
Corona Gorda	6 inches	50
Corona	6 inches	42
Petit Corona	5 inches	40
Robusto	4½ inches	50

SIZES C.A.O. GOLD

NAME	LENGTH: INCHES	RING GAUGE
Double Corona	7½ inches	54
Churchill	7 inches	48
Corona Gorda	6½ inches	50
Corona	5½ inches	42
Robusto	5 inches	50

CHURCHILL : LENGTH 7 INCHES, RING GAUGE 48

CORONA MADURO : LENGTH 6 INCHES, RING GAUGE 42

PRESIDENTE : LENGTH 7½ INCHES, RING GAUGE 54

C Honduras
F Mild
Q Good-quality leaf
and construction

CASA BLANCA

*W*ell-made Dominican cigars with Claro Connecticut wrappers on all sizes and maduro on some. The filler is Dominican and the binder Mexican. Casa Blanca's specialty is gargantuan cigars. The 10-inch Jeroboam and 5-inch Half Jeroboam have ring gauges over 1-inch thick (66). In general, the cigars are well-built (they must have some rollers with big hands), mild, and smooth.

SIZES

Name	Length: inches	Ring Gauge
Jeroboam	10 inches	66
Presidente	7½ inches	50
Magnum	7 inches	60
Lonsdale	6½ inches	42
De Luxe	6 inches	50
Panetela	6 inches	35
Corona	5½ inches	42
Half Jeroboam	5 inches	66
Bonita	4 inches	36

MAGNUM XL : LENGTH 7 INCHES, RING GAUGE 60

HALF JEROBOAM : LENGTH 5 INCHES, RING GAUGE 66

LONSDALE : LENGTH 6½ INCHES, RING GAUGE 42

C Dominican
Republic
F Mild
Q Good-quality
leaf and
construction

V CENTENNIAL

*T*he Roman five in V Centennial signifies that the brand was introduced to mark the passing of the five centuries since Columbus discovered tobacco. It also serves as a reminder that the cigars are made of tobaccos from five different countries. The wrapper is American (Connecticut), the binder Mexican, and the filler a mixture of Honduran for spice, Nicaraguan for aroma, and Dominican to round it off. The cigars are made in Honduras.

Creating and maintaining a successful blend of such diverse tobaccos is far from easy. Few attempt it. Creating a compatible and palatable balance is the problem, but when it is achieved, the resultant flavor can make a refreshing change. Overall V Centennial succeeds both in its claro form and particularly in its maduro, which is available in some sizes.

These cigars are handmade and well-constructed, although the wrappers can be grainy. The line, which tends toward larger sizes, is well-priced. Its Torpedo resembles a blunderbuss rather than the classic Piramide shape, but nonetheless it offers an interesting variation and smokes well.

SIZES

NAME	LENGTH: INCHES	RING GAUGE
Presidente	8 inches	50
Numero Uno	7½ inches	38
Torpedo	7 inches	36/54
Churchill	7 inches	48
Cetro	6¼ inches	44
Numero Dos	6 inches	50
Coronas	5½ inches	42
Robusto	5 inches	50

C Honduras
F Medium to full-bodied
Q Superior quality

TORPEDO : LENGTH 7 INCHES, RING GAUGE 36/54

CETRO : LENGTH 6¼ INCHES, RING GAUGE 44

CHURCHILL : LENGTH 7 INCHES, RING GAUGE 48

COHIBA

$\mathscr{F}$or a brand so young (founded in 1968) in the annals of Havanas, it is remarkable how many myths surround Cohiba. One affects its very name, which was said to be the aboriginal Taino Indian word for "tobacco," but is now understood to have meant "cigar." Another centers on Che Guevara's role in its creation. His portrait may hang above the Director's desk at the El Laguito factory, but since he quit his post as Minister of Industry in 1965 and perished in October of the year before the brand was born, his association with it could at best be described as fleeting. A third is that all Cohibas are made at El Laguito, which, although it was the case for over twenty years, is no longer so.

La verdad—the truth—about Cohiba's origin is now offered by Emilia Tamayo, the Director at El Laguito since June 1994. This charming and highly capable woman confirms that it all began in the mid-1960s when one of President Fidel Castro's bodyguards enjoyed a private supply of cigars from a local artisan. They so pleased the president that their creator, Eduardo Ribera, was asked to make cigars of his blend exclusively for Castro, under strict security in an Italianate mansion in the Havana suburb of El Laguito.

At first, the brand had no name, then in 1968, under the name Cohiba, production began of three sizes, each a personal favorite of the President—the Lancero, the Corona Especiale, and the Panetela. All were originals, so they were given the new factory names of Laguito No. 1, No. 2, which had the unique feature of a tiny pigtail on their caps, and No. 3.

For 14 years these three Cohibas were reserved solely for government and diplomatic use. However, the same sizes, using different blends, were adopted first by Davidoff as the No. 1, the No. 2, and the Ambassadrice when he was granted his brand in 1969 and then by Montecristo in the early 1970s as the Especial, the Especial No. 2, and the Joyita.

The guiding hand over this period, and indeed for 26 years, belonged to Avelino Lara. (He took over from Ribera in 1968.) Affable and relaxed, Lara, the eldest of four top-grade cigar rolling brothers, laid down the three principles which have made Cohiba Havanas the premier brand and, arguably, the world's finest cigar.

The first he calls "the selection of the selection." The produce of the top ten vegas in the Vuelta Abajo is put at his disposal. In any year he picks the five best for his wrappers, binders, ligeros, secos, and volados. The next is a special third fermentation, unique among Havana brands, which is applied to just two of the leaf-types—the ligero and seco. Moisture is added to the leaves as they age in barrels to ferment out the last vestiges of harshness. And third, the making of Cohibas is confined to the ablest rollers in Cuba, all of whom at El Laguito are female.

By 1982 word of this fabled cigar was out, and the decision was made to offer it to lesser mortals than the King of Spain and other such heads of state. Seven years later, three more sizes were introduced: the Esplendido (a Churchill), the Robusto, and the Exquisito, another unique size measuring 5 inches by 36 ring gauge. Of these, only the Exquisito is produced at el Laguito. The other two are made at either H. Upmann or Partagas.

More recently, to celebrate the 500th Anniversary of Columbus's discovery of cigars in Cuba, five new sizes known as the Linea 1492 (the six former sizes are now called the Linea Clasica) were first revealed at a celebration in Havana in November 1992, then launched at a glittering dinner at Claridge's Hotel in London a year later. Named Siglo (meaning century) I, II, III, IV, and V, the five centuries since Columbus are commemorated in a selection which bears more than a passing resemblance to some of the Davidoffs no longer made in Cuba. Crafted at Partagas, they are said to offer a lighter flavor than the Linea Clasica, which notably in its heavier size boasts a rare richness.

Cohibas made in the Dominican Republic can be found in a few American cigar stores. These bear no resemblance to the cigars above, but reflect an adroit move by General Cigar to register the name in the United States early in the 1980s. When the day of the repeal of the U.S./Cuban trade embargo finally dawns, contrary to the belief of many, Cohibas and virtually all other Havana brands will not flood onto the shelves of American cigar merchants. Instead, lawyers will rub their hands with glee as the battle to untangle one of the world's most complex trademark issues begins.

SIZES

Name	Length: inches	Ring Gauge
Lancero	7½ inches	38
Esplendido	7 inches	47
Coronas Especial	6 inches	38
Exquisito	5 inches	36
Robusto	4⅞ inches	50
Panetela	4½ inches	26

PANETELA : LENGTH 4½ INCHES, RING GAUGE 26

EXQUISITO : LENGTH 5 INCHES, RING GAUGE 36

ESPENDIDO : LENGTH 7 INCHES, RING GAUGE 47

EDUARDO RIBERA,
CREATOR OF THE
ORIGINAL COHIBA BLEND.

ROBUSTO : LENGTH 4⅞ INCHES, RING GAUGE 50

CORONAS ESPECIAL : LENGTH 6 INCHES, RING GAUGE 38

LANCERO : LENGTH 7½ INCHES, RING GAUGE 38

- **C** Cuba
- **F** Medium to full-bodied
- **Q** The very best quality available

SIGLO I : LENGTH 4 INCHES, RING GAUGE 40

SIGLO II : LENGTH 5 INCHES, RING GAUGE 42

EMILIA TAMAYO, EL LAGUITO'S DIRECTOR SINCE 1994, WITH RAFAEL GUERRA, HEAD OF CIGAR PRODUCTION.

SIGLO SERIES

NAME	LENGTH: INCHES	RING GAUGE
Siglo V	6⅝ inches	43
Siglo III	6⅛ inches	42
Siglo IV	5⅝ inches	46
Siglo II	5 inches	42
Siglo I	4 inches	40

SIGLO III : LENGTH 6⅛ INCHES, RING GAUGE 42

SIGLO IV : LENGTH 5⅝ INCHES, RING GAUGE 46

SIGLO V : LENGTH 6⅝ INCHES, RING GAUGE 43

CUABA

*L*aunched in the fall of 1996, this is the latest Havana to hit the cigar market and is produced by the Romeo Y Julieta factory in Cuba. Its name derives from an old Taino Indian word for a type of bush, that still grows on the island today. It was used for lighting cigars at religious ceremonies—chosen because it burned easily. *Quemar como una Cuaba*—to burn like a Cuaba—is an expression still used by Cuban farmers today.

Available in four sizes, this line is reminiscent of vintage cigars. Each cigar in the line has a tapered end, known as "figuardo," a shape very popular during the nineteenth century, which then lost its popularity to the straight-sided or "parejos" cigars that have dominated the twentieth century.

This mild to medium cigar offers a smoke of outstanding quality.

SIZES

NAME	LENGTH: INCHES	RING GAUGE
Exclusivos	5⅝ inches	46
Generosos	5¼ inches	42
Tradicionales	4¾ inches	42
Divinos	4 inches	43

A TYPICAL TOBACCO FARM IN CUBA, WITH THE THATCHED CURING HOUSE AMID THE CROP.

GENEROSOS : LENGTH 5¼ INCHES, RING GAUGE 42

TRADICIONALES : LENGTH 4¾ INCHES, RING GAUGE 42

EXCLUSIVOS : LENGTH 5⅝ INCHES, RING GAUGE 46

C Cuba

F Medium to full

Q The very best quality money can buy

CUBA ALIADOS

*T*he band on every Aliados cigar bears the word Cuba. But it doesn't come from Cuba. It comes from Honduras. No doubt the hands that made it are those of a Cuban émigré. No doubt its production is supervised by ex-patriate Cubans, and no doubt the seeds for its tobacco are émigré Cuban seeds, but that doesn't make it Cuban.

In some ways, this is a pity because the cigars are good. They reflect the tireless devotion of that island's people to make fine cigars anywhere, and they possess the quality to stand on their own, no matter where they are from. The Piramides and Diademas shapes are masterpieces of the cigar-maker's art.

Most sizes come with a choice of Claro, Colorado Claro, and Colorado wrappers, which add interesting flavor alternatives to what is a medium to full-bodied taste. The Colorado has a particular richness.

SIZES

Name	Length: inches	Ring Gauge
General	18 inches	66
Figurin	10 inches	60
Diademas	7½ inches	60
Piramides	7½ inches	60
Churchill	7⅛ inches	54
Valentino	7 inches	48
Cazadore	7 inches	45
Palma	7 inches	36
Corona Deluxe	6½ inches	45
Fuma	6½ inches	45
Lonsdale	6½ inches	42
Toro	6 inches	54
No. 4	5½ inches	45
Remedios	5½ inches	42
Rothschild	5 inches	51
Petit Cetro	5 inches	36

ROTHSCHILD : LENGTH 5 INCHES, RING GAUGE 51

CORONA DELUXE : LENGTH 6½ INCHES, RING GAUGE 45

LONSDALE : LENGTH 6½ INCHES, RING GAUGE 42

C Honduras
F Medium to full-bodied
Q Good-quality leaf and construction

CUESTA-REY

*T*he name of Cuesta-Rey dates back to the time when Tampa, Florida, was the American capital of a flourishing cigar manufacturing industry. Founded in 1884 by Angel La Madrid Cuesta, who was soon joined by Peregrino Rey, "clear Havanas" (cigars made in the United States from Cuban tobaccos) were their trade.

These days, Cuesta-Rey is presided over by the Newman family, owners of the last of the great Tampa cigar houses. They, too, have a proud history dating back a century and recorded in a recent book by tobacco historian Glen Westfall.

There are two series: Cabinet Selection and Centennial Vintage Collection, celebrating the founding of the brand in 1884.

Cabinet and Centennial Vintage are all fully handmade in the Dominican Republic. Listed below is the Centennial Vintage Collection, a brand widely distributed throughout the world. These cigars are 100 percent handmade using Connecticut shade wrappers and Dominican binders. The filler is made from a blend of four types of long-filler tobacco.

SIZES

NAME	LENGTH: INCHES	RING GAUGE
Individual	8½ inches	52
Dominican #1	8½ inches	52
Dominican #2	7¼ inches	48
Aristocrat	7¼ inches	48
Dominican #3	7 inches	36
Riviera	7 inches	35
Dominican #4	6½ inches	42
Dominican No. 60	6 inches	50
Captiva	6⁹⁄₁₆ inches	42
Robusto	4½ inches	50
Dominican #5	5½ inches	43
Cameo	4¼ inches	32

DOMINICAN #1 : LENGTH 8½ INCHES, RING GAUGE 52

DOMINICAN #5 : LENGTH 5½ INCHES, RING GAUGE 43

CAPTIVA : LENGTH 6³⁄₁₆ INCHES, RING GAUGE 42

C Dominican
Republic
F Mild
Q Superior
quality

DAVIDOFF

$\mathscr{D}$avidoff is a byword for style and quality throughout the world. It encompasses men's fragrances, ties, glasses, cognac, humidors, and briefcases, but it is based upon cigars. To build such a multimillion dollar enterprise on a tobacco product in the late 20th century is a remarkable achievement, which owes its inspiration to Zino Davidoff and its present commercialisation to Ernst Schneider.

The life of Zino Davidoff, which ended in his 88th year on January 14, 1994, reads like a history of the 20th century. Born in Kiev, his family fled the pogroms to settle in Geneva and opened a tobacco shop where Lenin was a customer. Young Zino traveled the tobacco lands of Central and South America, ending up in Cuba, for which he formed a life-long affection. Amassing a hoard of Havanas from Vichy France, when World War II ended, he found himself with a rare stock of the finest cigars. His natural charm combined with a deep knowledge saw him first in 1947 create his Chateau selection based on Cuban Hoyo de Monterrey cabinets and then in 1969, aged 63, he was granted the accolade from the Cuban industry of a Havana brand.

His partnership with Ernst Schneider, one of several local Swiss importers at the time, dates from 1970. Schneider's Basel-based Oettinger Imex company saw the worldwide potential for the brand, and with Cubatabaco's expertise the cigar line was developed. There were three series of Davidoff Havanas, each with its own distinctive flavor. The fullest was the Chateau range, the lightest the Dom Perignon No. 1, No. 2, and Ambassadrice. In between there was the Thousand series.

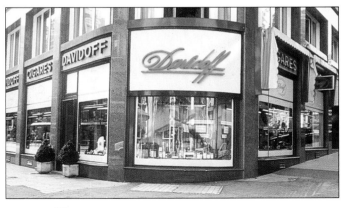

THE EXTERIOR OF THE **G**ENEVA BRANCH OF **D**AVIDOFF.

That these cigars should no longer be available is a tragedy born of a dispute between Oettinger and Cubatabaco, which resulted in the cessation of production of Davidoffs in Havana from March 1990 and the transfer of their manufacture to the Dominican Republic.

Much speculation has surrounded the reasons for the breakdown of what had been a highly successful marriage. It is perhaps best covered by Paul Garmirian in his book *The Gourmet Guide to Cigars*.

To their lasting credit, Davidoff and Schneider did not attempt to recreate the flavors of their former cigars. The sizes may be identical in many cases and the concept of different series with their own styles of taste is retained, but instead they have set out to create the very best of Dominican cigars. They accept that this will mean a lighter overall flavor, but believe that there are smokers who will be well pleased by it. Their success in several parts of the world suggests that they are right, but that is not to say that many previous devotees are not deeply disappointed.

DOMINICAN SIZES

NAME	LENGTH: INCHES	RING GAUGE
Aniversario No. 1	8⅔ inches	48
Double R	7½ inches	50
Tubo No. 1	7½ inches	38
Aniversatio No. 2	7 inches	48
3000	7 inches	33
Grand Cru No. 1	6³⁄₃₂ inches	42
4000	6³⁄₃₂ inches	42
Special T	6 inches	52
Tubo No. 2	6 inches	38
5000	5⅝ inches	46
Grand Cru No. 2	5⅝ inches	42
Tubo No. 3	5⅛ inches	30
Grand Cru No. 3	5 inches	42
2000	5 inches	42
Special R	4⅞ inches	50
Grand Cru No. 4	4⅝ inches	40
1000	4⅝ inches	34
Ambassadrice	4⅝ inches	26
Grand Cru No. 5	4 inches	40

Dominican Davidoffs, dressed in their claro Connecticut wrappers, are immaculately tailored. The "Grand Cru" range replaces the former Chateau range by offering the richest flavor. The No. 1, No. 2, No. 3, and Ambassadrice are as delicately mild as you can get, and the Thousand ("Mille") series are mild-flavored. There is a "Special" selection of heavier girth cigars, including the Special R (Robusto), the Special T (Piramides), the Double R (Double Corona) and the latest special "C" (Culebras).

Finally, there are two sizes of Aniversario (the name first used for a limited-edition Cuban cigar made to mark Zino's 80th birthday), which have a lightness remarkable in cigars of their size.

INSIDE THE DAVIDOFF SHOP, NEW YORK.

C Dominican Republic
F Mild to medium
Q Superior quality

DOUBLE R : LENGTH 7½ INCHES, RING GAUGE 50

SPECIAL T : LENGTH 6 INCHES, RING GAUGE 52

TUBO No 2 : LENGTH 6 INCHES, RING GAUGE 38

Made by Hand in th
Dominican Republ

DIPLOMATICOS

The Diplomaticos range was originally created for the French market in 1966. Although the brand's livery of a carriage and scrolls owes more to Walt Disney than to cigar tradition, it has been adopted recently by a Dominican Republic brand called Licenciados (also listed). The choice is limited, as is availability. They resemble Montecristos with a different label, and are cheaper.

Diplomaticos are very well-constructed, with a rich, but subtle flavor and excellent aroma. If you can find them, they are good value for the quality they represent. They are all good smokes, particularly No. 1, No. 2, and No. 3. The sizes, and numbering, are similiar to the Montecristo range—though the line itself is smaller.

DIPLOMATICOS NO. 1 : LENGTH 6½ INCHES, RING GAUGE 42

SIZES

NAME	LENGTH: INCHES	RING GAUGE
No. 6	7½ inches	38
No. 1	6½ inches	42
No. 2	6⅛ inches	52
No. 7	6 inches	38
No. 3	5½ inches	42
No. 4	5 inches	42
No. 5	4 inches	40

DIPLOMATICOS NO. 2 : LENGTH 6⅛ INCHES, RING GAUGE 52

DIPLOMATICOS NO. 3 : LENGTH 5½ INCHES, RING GAUGE 42

DIPLOMATICOS NO. 5 : LENGTH 4 INCHES, RING GAUGE 40

C Cuba
F Medium to
full-bodied
Q Superior
quality

DON DIEGO

*T*hese mellow mild to medium cigars (not too different from their rival Macanudo) are made in the Dominican Republic with claro and colorado claro wrappers. They are well made, and come in tubes as well as boxes. The brand was originally made in the Canary Islands—until the mid-1970s—and then had different characteristics. Connecticut wrappers are generally used, though some (mostly smaller) sizes come with fuller-flavored, sweeter-tasting, Cameroon wrappers. Some sizes are available in a choice of double claro (AMS) or colorado (EMS).

The Monarch tubes are very good for their type, as are the Lonsdales. The Royal Palms and Corona Major are also tubed sizes. Generally, with this brand, flavor, aroma, and burning qualities are all high class. Don Diego Privadas are more fully matured.

SIZES

NAME	LENGTH: INCHES	RING GAUGE
Monarch (EMS)	7¼ inches	46
Lonsdales (EMS/AMS)	6⅝ inches	42
Coronas Bravas	6½ inches	48
Grecos (EMS)	6½ inches	38
Royal Palms	6⅛ inches	36
Coronas (EMS/AMS)	5⅝ inches	42
Petit Corona (EMS/AMS)	5⅛ inches	42
Corona Major (EMS)	5¹⁄₁₆ inches	42
Babies	5⅛ inches	33
Preludes (EMS)	4 inches	28

LONSDALES : LENGTH 6⅝ INCHES, RING GAUGE 42

CORONA MAJOR : LENGTH 5¹⁄₁₆ INCHES, RING GAUGE 42

CORONAS : LENGTH 5⅝ INCHES, RING GAUGE 42

C Dominican Republic
F Mild to medium
Q Good-quality leaf and construction

DON LINO

*F*irst introduced in 1989, the Don Lino brand of handmade Honduran cigars has seen two new selections added in the last few years. The original blend covers fifteen very well-priced sizes wrapped in Connecticut shade and filled with a lightish mixture of Honduran tobaccos.

The seven sizes of the Habana Reserve line also come Connecticut wrapped and claim a special four-year aging before reaching the market. This mellows their flavor but adds to the price.

Darker Connecticut broadleaf wrappers are used for the four heavy gauge sizes in the Colorado series launched in 1994. These also show signs of aging and have a pleasing mild to medium taste. Each size is available in its own humidor, which can be refilled from standard cedar boxes.

If well-filled cigars appeal, any Don Lino is the cigar for you. However, they are sometimes too well-filled, which can impede the draw.

C	Honduras
F	Mild to medium
Q	Good-quality leaf and construction

COLORADO LONSDALE : LENGTH 6½ INCHES, RING GAUGE 44

SIZES

NAME	LENGTH: INCHES	RING GAUGE
Supremos	8½ inches	52
Churchill	7½ inches	50
Torpedo	7 inches	48
Panetelas	7 inches	36
No. 1	6½ inches	44
No. 5	6¼ inches	44
No. 3	6 inches	36
Corona	5½ inches	50
Robustos	5½ inches	50
Toros	5½ inches	46
Peticetro	5½ inches	42
No. 4	5 inches	42
Rothchild	4½ inches	50
Epicures	4½ inches	32

HABANA RESERVE SERIES

Churchills	7½ inches	50
Panetelas	7¹⁄₁₆ inches	36
Torpedo	7 inches	48
#1	6½ inches	44
Tubo	6½ inches	44
Toros	5½ inches	46
Robusto	5 inches	50
Rothschild	4½ inches	50

COLORADO SERIES

Presidente	7½ inches	50
Torpedos	7 inches	48
Lonsdale	6½ inches	44
Robustos	5½ inches	50

DON PEPE

his brand was launched in Brazil in November 1994, and is the latest addition to the lines produced by Suerdieck. It is already a popular choice in the United States. They are a blend of *mata norte* and *mata fina* tobacco, wrapped in Brazilian-grown Sumatra leaf. Available in seven sizes these cigars offer a medium to full smoke that is rich and earthy.

SIZES

Name	Length: inches	Ring Gauge
Double Corona	7½ inches	52
Churchill	7 inches	48
Petit Lonsdale	6 inches	43
Slim Panatela	5¼ inches	26
Robusto	5 inches	52
Half Corona	4¼ inches	34

A TOBACCO CROP IN BRAZIL. THE BOTTOM LEAVES
ARE READY TO HARVEST.

CHURCHILL : LENGTH 7 INCHES, RING GAUGE 48

ROBUSTO : LENGTH 5 INCHES, RING GAUGE 52

DOUBLE CORONA : LENGTH 7½ INCHES, RING GAUGE 52

C Brazil
F Mild to medium
Q Good-quality leaf and construction

[99]

DON RAMOS

*T*hese well-made, full-flavored, 100 percent Honduran cigars are made in San Pedro de Sula, mainly for the British market. There are a total of seven sizes, all available in bundles. Five come in tubes and four in boxes. The bundles are simply numbered; No. 11 is a Churchill, No. 14 a Corona, No. 19 a Rothschild, and so on, and offer good value for money. The heavy gauge sizes—6¾ inches, x 47 (Churchill/Gigantes/No. 11), 55/8 inches x 46 (No. 13) and 4½ inches x 50 (Epicures/No. 19) are substantial smokes. All sizes have a spicy richness. The list below gives the bundle numbers.

SIZES

NAME	LENGTH: INCHES	RING GAUGE
No. 11	6¾ inches	47
No. 13	5⅝ inches	46
No. 14	5½ inches	42
No. 16	5 inches	42
No. 19	4½ inches	50
No. 20	4½ inches	42
No. 17	4 inches	42

C Honduras
F Medium to full-bodied
Q Superior quality

NO. 16 : LENGTH 5 INCHES, RING GAUGE 42

NO. 14 : LENGTH 5½ INCHES, RING GAUGE 42

NO. 11 : LENGTH 6¾ INCHES, RING GAUGE 47

DON TOMAS

These are very well-made Honduran cigars which come in three lines at differing price levels. Special Edition incorporates five super-premium priced sizes using Honduran, Dominican, and Connecticut seed tobaccos grown near Talanga, Honduras. The International series offers just four sizes, identified by a distinctive slanting band, using an all Cuban-seed blend at a premium price. The standard series gives a choice of natural or maduro wrappers on a wide choice of sizes, including a so-called Corona with an unusually large ring gauge for this size, but a good smoke nonetheless.

S I Z E S

NAME	LENGTH: INCHES	RING GAUGE
Gigante	8½ inches	52
Imperial	8 inches	44
President	7½ inches	50
Panatela Larga	7 inches	38
Cetro No. 2	6½ inches	44
Corona Grande	6½ inches	44
Supremo	6¼ inches	42
Panetela	6 inches	36
Corona	5½ inches	50
Toro	5½ inches	46
Matador	5½ inches	42
Blunt	5 inches	42
Rothschild	4½ inches	50
Epicure	4½ inches	32

CORONA GRANDE : LENGTH 6½ INCHES, RING GAUGE 44

IMPERIAL : LENGTH 8 INCHES, RING GAUGE 44

BLUNT : LENGTH 5 INCHES, RING GAUGE 42

PRESIDENT : LENGTH 7½ INCHES, RING GAUGE 50

C Honduras
F Medium to full-bodied
Q Superior quality

DUNHILL

The old English company of Alfred Dunhill can claim a long association with fine cigars. It was to Dunhill that the Menendez y Garcia company first took their infant Montecristo brand in 1935. There were house brands like Don Candido and Don Alfredo. The 1980s saw the brief creation of Dunhill's own brand of Havanas, sporting a red band bearing the company's elongated "d" logo on sizes like the Cabinetta, and Malecon.

Today Dunhill's accolade is reserved for two lines: one from the Dominican Republic—the Aged Cigar—which can be found throughout the United States, Europe, and the Middle East; and the other from the Canary Islands.

There are thirteen sizes of Aged Cigars each made from Dominican fillers and wrapped in U.S. Connecticut leaf. Aged for a minimum of three months before they are distributed, these mid-priced

CENTENAS : LENGTH 6 INCHES, RING GAUGE 50

DOMINICAN SIZES

Name	Length: inches	Ring Gauge
Peravias	7 inches	50
Caberas	7 inches	48
Fantinos	7 inches	28
Diamantes	6⅝ inches	42
Samanas	6½ inches	38
Centenas	6 inches	50
Condados	6 inches	48
Tabaras	5⁹⁄₁₆ inches	42
Valverdes	5⁹⁄₁₆ inches	42
Altamiras	5 inches	48
Romanas	4½ inches	50
Bavaros	4½ inches	28
Caletas	4 inches	42

CORONA EXTRA : LENGTH 5 INCHES, RING GAUGE 50

PERAVAIS : LENGTH 7 INCHES, RING GAUGE 50

ROMANAS : LENGTH 4½ INCHES, RING GAUGE 50

C Dominican Republic
F Medium to full-bodied
Q Superior quality

cigars look good dressed with their blue
bands and are well made and blended.
They burn evenly and offer a distinctive,
medium to full, but in no way heavy
smoke, with a delicate aroma. Uniquely, a
vintage is declared for this brand, based on
the idea that its tobaccos are taken from a
single year's harvest.

The Canary Islands selection is smaller,
numbering just five sizes. Distinguished
by their red bands, these cigars offer a mild
to medium flavor with a touch of
sweetness. They, too, are well constructed, but offer a somewhat rougher, less
polished smoke.

CANARY ISLANDS SIZES

Name	Length: inches	Ring Gauge
Lonsdale Grandes	7½ inches	42
Corona Grandes	6½ inches	43
Panetelas	6 inches	30
Corona Extra	5½ inches	50
Coronas	5½ inches	43

C Canary
Islands
F Mild to
medium
Q Good-quality
leaf and
construction

EL REY DEL MUNDO

The name means "King of the World," a confident enough title for this brand, originally founded in 1882 by the Antonio Allones company. Many connoisseurs would rate it among their favorite brands. The selection is large, with some sizes available in machine-made versions. They are made in the Romeo Y Julieta factory along with other medium-flavored brands. There are also well-made (but much fuller-bodied) Honduran versions in 26 sizes (a selection is listed overleaf) from J.R. Tobacco with completely different names such as Flor de Llaneza, Imperiale, and Montecarlo, although they also list a Choix Supreme. Some contain a Dominican filler for a lighter flavor, aimed at the less-experienced smoker.

The El Rey del Mundo Corona was the favorite cigar of film producer Darryl F. Zanuck—former head of 20th Century-Fox—who once actually owned a plantation in Cuba. The British tycoon Sir Terence Conran is also a fan.

The Cuban are a well-constructed, high-quality line of cigars, with smooth, oily wrappers, particularly the larger sizes. Even the larger sizes are light and medium to mild (too mild for those for whom big cigars mean body), and the aroma is always subtle. These are good beginners' cigars, and very suitable for daytime smoking; even the larger sizes wouldn't be best appreciated after a heavy dinner.

CUBAN SIZES

Name	Length: inches	Ring Gauge
Elegantes	6⅞ inches	28
Lonsdale	6⅜ inches	42
Corona De Luxe	5½ inches	42
Choix Supreme	5 inches	48
Petit Corona	5 inches	42
Tres Petit Coronas	4½ inches	40
Demi-Tasse	3⅞ inches	30

HONDURAN SIZES

NAME	LENGTH: INCHES	RING GAUGE
Coronation	8½ inches	52
Principale	8 inches	47
Flor del Mundo	7¼ inches	54
Robusto Suprema	7¼ inches	54
Imperiale	7¼ inches	54
Corona Inmensa	7¼ inches	47
Double Corona	7 inches	49
Cedar	7 inches	43
Flor de Llaneza	6½ inches	54
Flor de LaVonda	6½ inches	52
Plantation	6½ inches	30
Choix Supreme	6⅛ inches	49
Montecarlo	6⅛ inches	48
Robusto Larga	6 inches	54
Originale	5⅝ inches	45
Classic Corona	5⅝ inches	45
Corona	5⅝ inches	45
Rectangulare	5⅝ inches	45
Habana Club	5½ inches	42
*Tino	5½ inches	38
*Elegante	5⅜ inches	29
*Reynita	5 inches	38
Robusto	5 inches	54
Robusto Zavalla	5 inches	54
Rothschild	5 inches	50
*Petit Lonsdale	4⅝ inches	43
Cafe au Lait	4½ inches	35

*Lighter Dominican filler

C Cuba
F Mild to medium
Q Superior quality

CORONA : LENGTH 5⅝ INCHES, RING GAUGE 45

CAFE AU LAIT : LENGTH 4½ INCHES, RING GAUGE 35

FLOR DEL MUNDO : LENGTH 7¼ INCHES, RING GAUGE 54

C Honduras
F Medium to full-bodied
Q Good-quality leaf and construction

EXCALIBUR

*E*xcaliburs are the very best of the Hoyo de Monterrey brand made by Villazon from Havana seed wrappers in Honduras (see also Hoyo de Monterrey entry). They are medium to full-bodied, rich, extremely well made, and among the best non-Cuban cigars on the market. They are sold with the Hoyo de Monterrey label in the United States (with the additional word Excalibur at the bottom of the band), but simply as Excalibur in Europe, for trademark reasons. Try the No. II.

SIZES

NAME	LENGTH: INCHES	RING GAUGE
No. I	7¼ inches	54
Banquet	6¾ inches	48
No. II	6¾ inches	47
No. III	6⅛ inches	48
No. V	6¼ inches	45
No. IV	5⅝ inches	46
No. VI	5½ inches	38
No. VII	5 inches	43
Miniatures	3 inches	22

C Honduras
F Medium to full-bodied
Q Superior quality

[110]

FELIPE GREGORIO

Felipe Gregorio is the flagship brand of Cigars of Honduras, founded in 1990. Named after the company's founder, it has enjoyed widespread success in the United States. The tobacco for filler, binder, and wrapper is all grown in the Jamastran valley of Honduras, and each cigar is made exclusively from tobacco grown in one *finca*, making each cigar a *puro*. Of particular interest is the fact that leaves of wrapper quality are used as binders. The cigars are available in six sizes and are very well constructed.

SIZES

NAME	LENGTH: INCHES	RING GAUGE
Glorioso	7¾ inches	50
Suntuoso	7 inches	48
Belicoso	6 inches	torpedo
Robusto	5 inches	52
Sereno	5¾ inches	42
Nino	4¼ inches	44

C Honduras
F Medium
Q Good-quality
leaf and
construction

*B*oxes of Cuban Fonsecas feature both New York's Statue of Liberty and Havana's Morro Castle, indicating that the brand was born at a time when relations between these two great cities were easier than they are today.

Since 1965, the brand has also been made in the Dominican Republic, originally using Cameroon wrappers, but now preferring light Connecticut shade. Mexican binders combine with Dominican fillers in very well-made cigars for a truly mild smoke.

The small range of Cuban Fonsecas come uniquely encased in white tissue. They are Barcelona's favorite cigar, where prodigious quantities are consumed by people who know their smokes. The flavor is light to medium with a slight saltiness.

DOMINICAN SIZES

Name	Length: inches	Ring Gauge
#10–10	7 inches	50
#7–9–9	6½ inches	46
#8–9–9	6 inches	43
Triangular	5½ inches	56
#5–50	5 inches	50
#2–2	4¼ inches	40

CUBAN SIZES

Name	Length: inches	Ring Gauge
No. 1	6⅜ inches	44
Cosacos	5¼ inches	40
Invictos	5¼ inches	45
Delicias	4⅞ inches	40
K.D.T. Cadetes	4½ inches	36

#10–10 : LENGTH 7 INCHES, RING GAUGE 50

K.D.T. CADETES : LENGTH 4½ INCHES, RING GAUGE 36

COSACOS : LENGTH 5¼ INCHES, RING GAUGE 40

NO. 1 : LENGTH 6⅜ INCHES, RING GAUGE 44

C Dominican
  Republic
F Mild
Q Superior
  quality

C Cuba
F Mild to
  medium
Q Good-quality
  leaf and
  construction

GRIFFIN'S

Griffin is the brainchild of Geneva-based Bernard H. Grobet, an early disciple of Zino Davidoff. He was among the first Europeans who over a decade ago saw the potential for cigars made in the Dominican Republic. More recently, both the manufacture and marketing of the brand have come under the influence of his old mentor's organization —Davidoff & Cie. The cigars look good in their light Connecticut wrappers and are well-constructed. The flavor is as to be expected from Dominican filler in this presentation, and they are quite costly.

SIZES

NAME	LENGTH: INCHES	RING GAUGE
Prestige	7½ inches	50
No. 200	7 inches	43
No. 100	7 inches	38
No. 300	6¼ inches	43
No. 400	6 inches	38
No. 500	5¹⁄₁₆ inches	43
Robusto	5 inches	50
Privilege	5 inches	32

C Dominican
Republic
F Mild to
medium
Q Superior
quality

HECHO A MANO

H. UPMANN

erman Upmann was a member of a European banking family and a lover of good cigars. It came as no surprise when, in around 1840, he volunteered to open a branch of the bank in Havana. The cigars he sent home proved so popular that, in 1844, he invested in a cigar factory. The company traded successfully as both bankers and cigar makers until 1922, when first the bank and then the cigar business failed. A British firm, J. Frankau & Co. saved the cigar brand and ran the factory until 1935 when it was sold to the newly founded Menendez y Garcia company.

In 1944 a new H. Upmann factory was opened in Old Havana's Calle Amistad to mark the centenary of Herman's enterprise. The brand is made there to this day, at present, under the direction of the talented Benito Molina.

Havana Upmanns are mild to medium-flavored, very smooth, subtle cigars. They are generally very satisfactory, although sometimes, particularly when they are machine-made, let down by construction and burning qualities, occasionally overheating and leaving a bitter aftertaste. They are, however, a good beginner's cigar, or one to be smoked after a light meal. Cuban Upmanns come in a bewildering choice of over 30 sizes, many of them similar to one another. A number of Upmann sizes (including machine-mades—so beware) are sold in tubes. Only handmade Upmanns are imported into Britain, however.

Handmade cigars bearing the Upmann name are also produced by the Consolidated Cigar Corporation in the Dominican Republic, with Cameroon wrappers and Latin American fillers. They are a very respectable, well-made, mild to medium smoke, usually in oily colorado wrappers. The 12 boxed sizes available include Corona Imperiales, Lonsdale, Corona, Petit Corona, and Churchill. There are also six tubed sizes. The label on non-Havana Upmanns reads: "H. Upmann 1844," whereas the Cuban version says: "H. Upmann Habana." The sizes given below are the standard Havana versions.

CUBAN SIZES

Name	Length: inches	Ring Gauge
Monarchs	7 inches	47
Monarcas (also called Sir Winston)	7 inches	47
Lonsdale (and No. 1)	6½ inches	42
Upmann No. 2	6⅛ inches	52
Grand Corona	5¾ inches	40
Magnum	5½ inches	46
Corona	5½ inches	42
Royal Corona	5½ inches	42
Corona Major	5 inches	42
Connoisseur No. 1	5 inches	48
Petit Corona (and No. 4)	5 inches	42
Corona Junior	4½ inches	36
Petit Upmann	4½ inches	36

UPMANN NO. 2 : LENGTH 6⅛ INCHES, RING GAUGE 52

CORONA MAJOR : LENGTH 5 INCHES, RING GAUGE 42

LONSDALE (AND NO. 1) : LENGTH 6½ INCHES, RING GAUGE 42

C Cuba
F Mild
Q Superior
quality

PEQUENOS NO. 100 : LENGTH 4½ INCHES, RING GAUGE 50

CORONA : LENGTH 5⅞ INCHES, RING GAUGE 42

LONSDALE : LENGTH 6⅝ INCHES, RING GAUGE 42

C Dominican
Republic
F Mild to
medium
Q Good-quality
leaf and
construction

HABANA GOLD

Available in eight sizes, these cigars come in three different bands, Black Label, White Label, and Sterling Vintage. Each type is different, with the Sterling Vintage coming highly recommended. All cigars are made in Honduras with Nicaraguan filler and binder, and it is the wrapper that gives each line its own distinctive flavor. The Black Label cigars have a natural Indonesian wrapper giving the cigars a smooth and spicy flavor. The White Label has a dark Nicaraguan wrapper, giving the cigars a rich chocolate flavor. Incidentally all of the tobacco for the White Label cigar is grown in one field making a "puro" cigar. The Sterling Vintage line has dark vintage wrappers from Ecuador, which give a mild to medium smoke of outstanding quality.

SIZES

Name	Length: inches	Ring Gauge
Presidente	8½ inches	52
Double Corona	7½ inches	46
Churchill	7 inches	52
No.2	6⅛ inches	52
Torpedo	6 inches	52
Corona	6 inches	44
Robusto	5 inches	50
Petite Corona	5 inches	42

HAND MADE
HECHO EN
HONDURAS

C	Honduras
F	Mild to medium
Q	(Sterling Vintage) Superior quality

CHURCHILL : LENGTH 7 INCHES, RING GAUGE 52

ROBUSTO : LENGTH 5 INCHES, RING GAUGE 50

CHURCHILL : LENGTH 7 INCHES, RING GAUGE 52

HABANICA

*F*elipe Gregorio launched this brand in Spring 1995, and it has yet to find the international acclaim enjoyed by fellow brand Petrus (also listed). Despite this it has been very well received and praised for its oily dark brown wrapper, and soft, slightly sweet flavors. All of the tobacco for these cigars is grown in the Jalapa valley of Nicaragua, and it offers an excellent mild to medium smoke.

SIZES

Name	Length: inches	Ring Gauge
Serie 747	7 inches	47
Serie 646	6 inches	46
Serie 638	6 inches	38
Serie 546	5¼ inches	46
Serie 550	5 inches	50

C Nicaragua
F Mild to medium
Q Good-quality leaf and construction

HENRY CLAY

*T*his was one of the most famous of the old Havana brands, dating back to the 19th century and named after an American senator with business interests in Cuba. In the 1930s, its manufacture was transferred from Havana to Trenton, New Jersey, to avoid the exuberance of the Cuban workforce. The brand is now made in the Dominican Republic. There are only three sizes, all medium to full-bodied with mid-brown wrappers.

SIZES

NAME	LENGTH: INCHES	RING GAUGE
Breva Fina	6½ inches	48
Breva Conserva	5⅝ inches	46
Breva	5½ inches	42

C Dominican Republic
F Medium to full-bodied
Q Good-quality leaf and construction

BREVA : LENGTH 5½ INCHES, RING GAUGE 42

BREVA CONSERVA : LENGTH 5⅝ INCHES, RING GAUGE 46

BREVA FINA : LENGTH 6½ INCHES, RING GAUGE 48

HOYO DE MONTERREY

There is an old wrought-iron gate overlooking a square in the Vuelta Abajo village of San Juan y Martinez which bears the inscription "Hoyo de Monterrey: José Gener 1860." It leads to one of Cuba's most renowned "vegas finas," a plantation specializing in sun-grown tobaccos for binders and fillers. Here, José Gener started his career as a leaf grower on prime land (a "hoyo" is a dip in a field much favored by farmers for reasons of drainage) before founding the Hoyo de Monterrey brand in 1865.

Hoyo's flagship, the Double Corona, has become a unit of exchange among cigar lovers with a value far exceeding precious metals and usually only transacted as a token of close friendship. It has a delicacy of flavor combined with a richness of taste which is a credit to the blenders and rollers at the La Corona factory where it is made. It is felt that other Hoyo sizes, some of which are machine-made, do not live up to their champion. There is some truth in this, but the Epicure Nos. 1 & 2, particularly in 50 bundles, are clear exceptions. It should also be remembered that Zino Davidoff first created his Chateau range using cabinet selection Hoyos in standard sizes. Davidoff's early success in Switzerland inspired the creation in 1970, by a rival merchant, of the Le Hoyo series, which has a spicier, somewhat fuller flavor.

This pales into insignificance however alongside the brand of cigars bearing the same name made in Honduras. What these

CUBAN SIZES

NAME	LENGTH: INCHES	RING GAUGE
Double Corona	7⅝ inches	49
Le Hoyo du Gourmet	6⅝ inches	33
Le Hoyo des Dieux	6 inches	42
Le Hoyo du Dauphin	6 inches	38
Epicure No. 1	5⅝ inches	46
Jeanne D'Arc	5⅝ inches	35
Le Hoyo du Roi	5½ inches	42
Corona	5½ inches	42
Le Hoyo du Prince	5 inches	40
Epicure No. 2	4⅞ inches	50
Margarita	4¾ inches	26
Le Hoyo du Depute	4¼ inches	38
Le Hoyo du Maire	3⅞ inches	30

cigars lack in fine tailoring, they make up for in sheer flavor. They are an "espresso" of a cigar, particularly in the larger girth sizes like the Rothschild and Governors. They are made by men who clearly appreciate the taste of tobacco.

It is important not to confuse the standard Honduran Hoyo line with the Excalibur series (also listed). These are sold as Hoyo de Monterrey Excalibur in the United States, but for trademark reasons, the Hoyo connection is dropped in Europe. They are among the finest of cigars and have a different style of flavor.

HONDURAN SIZES

NAME	LENGTH: INCHES	RING GAUGE
Presidents	8½ inches	52
Sultans	7¼ inches	54
Cuban Largos	7¼ inches	47
Largo Elegantes	7¼ inches	34
Cetros	7 inches	43
Double Corona	6¾ inches	48
No. 1	6½ inches	43
Churchills	6¼ inches	45
Ambassadors	6¼ inches	44
Delights	6¼ inches	37
Governors	6⅛ inches	50
Culebras	6 inches	35
Coronas	5⅝ inches	46
Cafe Royales	5⅝ inches	43
Dreams	5¾ inches	46
Petit	5¾ inches	31
Super Hoyos	5½ inches	44
No. 55	5¼ inches	43
Margaritas	5¼ inches	29
Sabrosos	5 inches	40
Rothschild	4½ inches	50
Demitasse	4 inches	39

HOYO DE MONTERREY

DOUBLE CORONA : LENGTH 7⅝ INCHES, RING GAUGE 49

CORONA : LENGTH 5½ INCHES, RING GAUGE 42

MARGARITA : LENGTH 4¾ INCHES, RING GAUGE 26

C Cuba
F Mild
Q Superior
quality

GOVERNOR : LENGTH 6⅛ INCHES, RING GAUGE 50

ROTHSCHILD : LENGTH 4½ INCHES, RING GAUGE 50

SULTAN : LENGTH 7¼ INCHES, RING GAUGE 54

C Honduras
F Medium to
full-bodied
Q Good-quality
leaf and
construction

[127]

J. R. CIGARS

Lew Rothman is a phenomenon. His J.R. Tobacco of America (J.R. stands for Jack Rothman, Lew's father) covers a mail-order, retail, and wholesale empire that handles 40 percent of all premium cigars sold in the United States.

He built it by playing Robin Hood to the manufacturers' Sheriff of Notthingham. He knows what a cigar costs and won't let his customers pay a cent more than they have to for it. The downside is that some manufacturers like to spend more time and money perfecting cigars to sell at prices Lew won't accept. His sales have

J. R. ULTIMATE

NAME	LENGTH: INCHES	RING GAUGE
Estelo	8½ inches	52
Presidente	8½ inches	52
No. 10	8¼ inches	47
Super Cetro	8¼ inches	43
No. 1	7¼ inches	54
Cetro	7 inches	42
Palma Extra	6⅞ inches	38
Slims	6⅞ inches	36
Double Corona	6¾ inches	48
No. 5	6⅛ inches	44
Padron	6 inches	54
Toro	6 inches	50
Corona	5⅝ inches	45
Petit Cetro	5½ inches	38
Habenella	5 inches	28
Petit Corona	4⅝ inches	43
Rothschild	4½ inches	50

C Honduras
F Medium to full-bodied
Q Superior quality

INSIDE J.R.'S CIGAR STORE, THE LARGEST OF ITS KIND IN THE WORLD.

No. 1 : Length 7¼ Inches, Ring Gauge 54

Petit Corona : Length 4⅞ Inches, Ring Gauge 43

Corona : Length 5⅝ Inches, Ring Gauge 45

rocketed in the cigar boom, so this doesn't seem to matter much. Anyway, no one has to sell to him, and several don't.

If it's the best price you are after, look no further than your nearest J.R. store or catalog where you'll find his own brands of J.R. Ultimate, Special Coronas, and Special Jamaicans.

SPECIAL CORONAS

Name	Length: inches	Ring Gauge
Pyramides	7 inches	54
No. 754	7 inches	54
No. 2	6½ inches	45
No. 54	6 inches	54
No. 4	5½ inches	45

No. 754 : Length 7 inches, Ring Gauge 54

J. R. Tobacco of America's Lew Rothman with his wife and partner LaVonda.

- **C** Dominican Republic
- **F** Mild to medium
- **Q** Superior quality

In ascending order of flavor, Special Jamaicans, now made in the Dominican Republic and wrapped in claro Connecticut leaf, are true to their Jamaican origins and as mild as their price. J.R. Special Coronas are also made in the Dominican Republic from a four-country blend of tobaccos— Ecuadoran wrapper and binder matched with a Brazilian, Honduran, and Dominican filler. They are richer in flavor, but are still mild to medium.

J.R. Ultimate is the flagship, and six new sizes have been introduced since the second edition of this book. Made in San Pedro Sula, Honduras, from a local blend wrapped in oily Nicaraguan Colorado leaf, they aim to come close to the taste of Havanas. They offer a rich, full-bodied smoke and rate highly among Hondurans.

All these J.R. cigars are very well put together by hand. Whether they are for you depends on how much you mind being seen with the same cigars as so many of the other chaps in Sherwood Forest.

SPECIAL JAMAICANS

Name	Length: inches	Ring Gauge
Rey del Rey	9 inches	60
Mayfair	7 inches	60
Pyramid	7 inches	52
Nobles	7 inches	50
Churchill	7 inches	50
A	6½ inches	44
Fancytale shape	6½ inches	43
Bonita Obsequio	6 inches	50
D	6 inches	50
B	6 inches	44
C	5½ inches	44
Pica	5 inches	32

SIZE D : LENGTH 6 IN / RING GAUGE 50

C Dominican Republic

F Mild

Q Superior quality

JOSE BENITO

*T*hese cigars, with their dark Cameroon wrappers, are made in the Dominican Republic. They are well constructed, and generally light to medium-bodied. They all come in attractive varnished cedar boxes (the huge Magnum, one of the biggest cigars on the market, is sold in a box by itself), and there are ten sizes.

SIZES

NAME	LENGTH: INCHES	RING GAUGE
Magnum	8¾ inches	60
Presidente	7¾ inches	50
Churchill	7 inches	50
Corona	6¾ inches	43
Panatela	6¾ inches	38
Palma	6 inches	43
Petite	5½ inches	38
Havanitos	5 inches	25
Rothschild	4¾ inches	50
Chico	4¼ inches	36

C Dominican Republic
F Mild to medium
Q Superior quality

CHURCHILL : LENGTH 7 INCHES, RING GAUGE 50

Joya De Nicaragua

*B*ack in the 1970s Nicaraguan cigars were rated by many as the next best to Havanas. The war put an end to that when plantations were laid waste and tobacco barns used to billet Sandinista soldiers.

Since 1990 things have been on the mend, but to re-establish quality in tobacco takes time. The local economy still faces formidable problems, but as every year passes, there is a noticeable improvement in Joya de Nicaragua's standards. Gone is the sweaty aroma of the early 1990s' cigars as maturer tobaccos come into use. The more rounded medium flavor with a touch of spice is returning, and the cigars are better constructed and more reliable than they were.

Surprisingly the choice of sizes available in Britain is larger than it is in the United States.

SIZES

Name	Length: inches	Ring Gauge
Viajante	8½ inches	52
Presidente	8 inches	54
Churchill	6⅞ inches	49
No. 5	6¼ inches	35
No. 1	6⅝ inches	44
No. 10	6½ inches	43
Elegante	6½ inches	38
No. 6	6 inches	52
Corona	5⅝ inches	48
National	5½ inches	44
Seleccion B	5½ inches	42
Petit Corona	5 inches	42
Consul	4½ inches	51
No. 2	4½ inches	41
Piccolino	4⅛ inches	30

PETIT CORONA : LENGTH 5 INCHES, RING GAUGE 42

ELEGANTE : LENGTH 6½ INCHES, RING GAUGE 38

CHURCHILL : LENGTH 7 INCHES, RING GAUGE 50

C Nicaragua
F Mild to
medium
Q Good-quality
leaf and
construction

JUAN CLEMENTE

*F*renchman Jean Clement hispanicized his name for the Dominican Republic cigar brand he founded in 1982. Wrapped in a claro U.S. Connecticut shade leaf and filled with a blend of Dominican tobacco, it offers a mild, straightforward smoke with a pleasant aroma, best suited to the morning. They have been criticized for their draw, but this seems to be improving. The Club Selection, bearing a white band, carries a darker wrapper and is well-blended. Over the last two years six new sizes have been added to this line, including the huge 13 inch Gargantua, and No. 5 in the Club Selection, an *obelisco*. Uniquely, the band is placed at the foot of the cigar, securing a piece of silver paper which serves to protect its most vulnerable point. Logical, if unconventional.

SIZES

NAME	LENGTH: INCHES	RING GAUGE
Gargantua	13 inches	50
Gigante	9 inches	50
Especiales	7½ inches	38
Club Selection No. 3	7 inches	44
Churchill	6⅞ inches	46
Panatela	6½ inches	34
Club Selection No. 5	6 inches	52
Club Selection No. 1	6 inches	50
Grand Corona	6 inches	42
Especiales No. 2	5⅞ inches	38
Club Selection No. 4	5¾ inches	42
Corona	5 inches	42
No. 530	5 inches	30
Rothschild	4⅞ inches	50
Club Selection No. 2	4½ inches	46
Mini-Cigar	4¹⁄₁₆ inches	22
Demi-Corona	4 inches	40
Demi-Tasse	3¹⁰⁄₁₆ inches	34

CLUB SELECTION NO. 2 : LENGTH 4½ INCHES, RING GAUGE 46

CLUB SELECTION No. 3 : LENGTH 7 INCHES, RING GAUGE 44

DEMI-CORONA : LENGTH 4 INCHES, RING GAUGE 40

ESPECIALES : LENGTH 7½ INCHES, RING GAUGE 38

C Dominican Republic
F Mild
Q Could be better

JUAN LOPEZ

(FLOR DE JUAN LOPEZ)

*T*his is an old Havana brand, no longer widely produced or distributed, but is a very light smoke, appealing to some European palates. There are only five sizes. They are fragrant, burn well, and good for daytime smoking. The cigars are only found in Spain, and the line will soon be reduced to only the Corona and Petit Corona sizes.

SIZES

Name	Length: inches	Ring Gauge
Corona	5⅝ inches	42
Petit Coronas	5 inches	42
Placeras	5 inches	34
Slimaranas	4¾ inches	32
Patricias	4½ inches	40

SLIMARANAS : LENGTH 4¾ INCHES, RING GAUGE 32

C Cuba
F Mild
Q Good-quality leaf and construction

LA CORONA

ormerly one of the great Havana brands, although its production was transferred to Trenton, New Jersey, in the 1930s. At present, a small selection of well-made, mild to medium cigars are made in the Dominican Republic by the Consolidated Cigar Corporation. There are also some cigars made in Cuba under this name, but they are either machine-made or hand-finished. The La Corona factory remains in Havana as one of the most important production centers making Punch and Hoyo de Monterrey among others.

SIZES

NAME	LENGTH: INCHES	RING GAUGE
Directors	6½ inches	46
Aristocrats	6⅛ inches	36
Long Corona	6 inches	43
Corona Chicas	5½ inches	42

C Dominican Republic
F Mild to medium
Q Good-quality leaf and construction

La Flor De Cano

*T*his is a relatively rare Cuban brand, not widely produced or easily available. Rumor has it that Habanos SA has decided to discontinue the handmade sizes like the much-vaunted Short Churchill (a Robusto). Should this prove correct, a group of British fans are considering a campaign to bring them back into production. They are cigars of undoubted quality and interest for those who look for something easy to handle. The Short Churchill, the Punch-Punch sized Gran Corona, and the Diademas are all worth trying, the latter particularly suitable for those who were once Davidoff Dom Perignon fans but don't want to move up to the fuller flavor of the Cohiba Esplendido. Watch out for the many machine-made cigars with names like Preferidos and Selectos that are also available.

C	Cuba
F	Mild
Q	Superior quality

SIZES

Name	Length: inches	Ring Gauge
Diademas	7 inches	47
Corona	5 inches	42
Gran Corona	5⅝ inches	46
Short Churchill	4⅞ inches	50

LA GLORIA CUBANA

*P*roduced by the Partagas factory, which specializes in full bodied cigars, this is an old brand which disappeared until it was revived a couple of decades ago to extend the factory's selection of different types of cigar. The Medaille D'Or brand comes in varnished 8–9–8 boxes and the others in labeled boxes.

These are very spicy, rather peppery, strongly aromatic cigars which sometimes fall down (the Lonsdale size, for instance) in construction. They are lighter (more refined, some would say) than the Partagas brand made in the same factory, though still a rich smoke. The line is small, almost all long sizes.

There is also the Gloria Cubana range made in the United States by Miami's Ernesto Carillo. Ernesto is a man of great integrity whose aim is simply to make the best cigars he can with the best tobaccos he can find. In the main his wrappers are darkish Ecuadoran leaves and his fillers and binders Dominican, Nicaraguan, or Ecuadoran. He blends with his Cuban ancestors in mind to produce full-bodied cigars. The Wavell is strongly recommended if you can find it.

CUBAN SIZES

Name	Length: inches	Ring Gauge
Medaille d'Or 1	7⁵⁄₁₆ inches	36
Tainos	7 inches	47
Medaille d'Or 3	6⅞ inches	28
Medaille d'Or 2	6¹¹⁄₁₆ inches	43
Cetros	6½ inches	42
Sabrosas	6⅛ inches	42
Medaille d'Or 4	6 inches	32
Tapados	5⁵⁄₁₆ inches	42
Minutos	4½ inches	40

C Cuba
F Medium to full
Q Superior quality

U.S. SIZES

NAME	LENGTH: INCHES	RING GAUGE
Soberano	8 inches	52
Charlemagne	7¼ inches	54
Churchill	7 inches	50
Torpedo	6½ inches	52
Wavell	5 inches	50

C United States

F Medium to full

Q The very best quality available

MEDAILLE D'OR 3 : LENGTH 6⅞ INCHES, RING GAUGE 28

MEDAILLE D'OR 4 : LENGTH 6 INCHES, RING GAUGE 32

MEDAILLE D'OR 1 : LENGTH 7⁵/₁₆ INCHES, RING GAUGE 36

MEDAILLE D'OR 2 : LENGTH 6¹¹/₁₆ INCHES, RING GAUGE 43

LICENCIADOS

*O*n the market since 1990, the makers of Licenciados chose to take the Disneyesque carriage and scrolls design found on Havana's Diplomaticos brand as their emblem. Blends of Dominican fillers are dressed in light Connecticut shade wrappers for the main range, while Connecticut broadleaf is used for a smaller maduro series, known as Supreme. The Robusto-sized Wavell comes in both wrapper colors. These are classic, mild, Connecticut Dominican Republic cigars, well-made and competitively priced.

SIZES

NAME	LENGTH: INCHES	RING GAUGE
Soberano	8½ inches	52
Presidente	8 inches	50
Churchill	7 inches	50
Panetela	7 inches	38
Excelente	6¾ inches	43
Toro	6 inches	50
Licenciados No. 4	5¾ inches	43
Wavell	5 inches	50
SUPREME RANGE		
500	8 inches	50
300	6¾ inches	43
400	6 inches	50
200	5¾ inches	43

C Dominican
Republic
F Mild
Q Superior
quality

PANETELA : LENGTH 7 INCHES, RING GAUGE 38

MACANUDO

his brand, founded in Jamaica in 1868, is now made by General Cigar in both Jamaica and the Dominican Republic, under the supervision of Benjamin Menendez. The blend is the same for both countries of origin: Connecticut Shade wrapper, binder from the San Andres area of Mexico, and a mixture of Jamaican, Mexican, and Dominican tobacco for the filler.

These are undoubtedly handsome, consistently very well-made cigars, which provide one of the very best smooth, mild smokes on the market. The word *macanudo* means fine, dandy, or a good thing in colloquial Spanish and, for once in a cigar name, is pretty near the truth.

There is a wide variety of sizes, some of which (mostly larger ring gauges) come in a choice of wrapper color: café (made with Connecticut Shade wrapper), the even milder jade (a greenish, double claro wrapper), and the fuller and nutty-sweet maduro (in which case, the deep brown wrapper comes from Mexico). The Hampton Court and Portofino sizes come in elegant white aluminum tubes. The Claybourne and Prince Philip sizes are made in the Dominican Republic, the others (normally) in Jamaica. Macanudos don't come cheap; the Connecticut wrapper sees to that. They normally come wrapped in cellophane. If there's one criticism, it's that they are somewhat short on aroma, but they are an excellent daytime smoke, or suitable after a light meal. The fuller-bodied Macanudo Vintage cigars are sold at much higher prices and designed for the connoisseur. They are all made in Jamaica, with Dominican filler.

SIZES

NAME	LENGTH: INCHES	RING GAUGE
Duke of Wellington	8½ inches	38
Prince Philip	7½ inches	49
Vintage No. I	7½ inches	49
Sovereign	7 inches	45
Somerset	7 inches	34
Portofino	7 inches	34
Earl of Lonsdale	6¾ inches	38
Vintage No. II	6⁹⁄₁₆ inches	43
Baron de Rothschild	6½ inches	42
Amatista	6¼ inches	42
Claybourne	6 inches	31
Hampton Court	5¾ inches	43
Vintage No. III	5⁹⁄₁₆ inches	43
Hyde Park	5½ inches	49
Duke of Devon	5½ inches	42
Lord Claridge	5½ inches	38
Quill	5¼ inches	28
Petit Corona	5 inches	38
Vintage No. IV	4½ inches	47
Ascot	4³⁄₁₆ inches	32
Caviar	4 inches	36

VINTAGE NO. I : LENGTH 7½ INCHES, RING GAUGE 49

DUKE OF DEVON : LENGTH 5½ INCHES, RING GAUGE 42

CLAYBOURNE : LENGTH 6 INCHES, RING GAUGE 31

C Jamaica
F Mild
Q Superior
quality

HYDE PARK : LENGTH 5½ INCHES, RING GAUGE 49

PORTOFINO : LENGTH 7 INCHES, RING GAUGE 34

PRINCE PHILIP : LENGTH 7½ INCHES, RING GAUGE 49

C Dominican Republic
F Mild
Q Superior quality

MATACAN

A minor brand from Mexico, made by the Consolidated Cigar Corporation, also responsible for the Te-Amo brand, in the San Andres Valley. They come in light brown and maduro wrappers. They are well made, less tightly rolled than Te-Amo (though they have similar coarse wrappers), draw well, and have a spicy, slightly sweet, if nonetheless rather bland, medium to full flavor. All things considered, they are somewhat superior to Te-Amo, even though they are cheaper. Try the No. 7.

SIZES

NAME	LENGTH: INCHES	RING GAUGE
No. 8	8 inches	52
No. 1	7½ inches	50
No. 10	6⅞ inches	54
No. 3	6⅝ inches	46
No. 4	6⅝ inches	42
No. 6	6⅝ inches	35
No. 2	6 inches	50
No. 5	6 inches	42
No. 9	5 inches	32
No. 7	4¾ inches	50

C Mexico
F Medium to full-bodied
Q Good-quality leaf and construction

MOCHA SUPREME

*T*hese are handmade cigars from Honduras, using Havana seed wrappers. They are well-constructed and, for a boxed cigar, well-priced. Generally they are medium to full-bodied in flavor, but noticeably milder than many Hondurans. There is a woody, nutty hint to their taste.

SIZES

NAME	LENGTH: INCHES	RING GAUGE
Rembrandt	8½ inches	52
Patroon	7½ inches	50
Lord	6½ inches	42
Allegro	6½ inches	36
Renaissance	6 inches	50
Sovereign	5½ inches	42
Baron Rothschild	4½ inches	52
Petite	4½ inches	42

ALLEGRO : LENGTH 6½ INCHES, RING GAUGE 36

LORD : LENGTH 6½ INCHES, RING GAUGE 42

PATROON : LENGTH 7½ INCHES, RING GAUGE 50

BARON ROTHSCHILD : LENGTH 4½ INCHES, RING GAUGE 52

C Honduras
F Medium to
   full-bodied
Q Good-quality
   leaf and
   construction

*M*ontecristo is the most popular Havana by far. Around half of the cigars exported from Cuba in any one year bear its simple brown and white band.

Ironically, perhaps, it started life in 1935 as a brand limited to just five sizes which its founders, Alonzo Menendez and Pepe Garcia, aimed to keep in restricted distribution. They had just bought the H. Upmann brand from the British firm J. Frankau, and their main task was to extend its volume. Montecristo, first known as H. Upmann Montecristo Selection and sold through Dunhill in New York, was a prestigious sideline to test Menendez's leaf skills and Garcia's knowledge of production.

The change of name simply to Montecristo was inspired by another British firm, John Hunter, which was appointed as the British agent. The rival company Frankau handled Upmann and wanted Montecristo to stand on its own. The outstanding red and yellow box design with its triangular crossed swords is attributed to the Hunter company.

World War II interrupted the flow of Havanas to Britain, so the brand's development was concentrated in the United States, mainly through Dunhill's stores. Film director Alfred Hitchcock was an early devotee and regularly sent supplies back to friends deprived by wartime restrictions in England.

After the war the Tubos size was added, but otherwise the line remained the same.

Shortly after Castro came to power, the Menendez and Garcia families moved to the Canary Islands. Some continuity was provided by a legendary figure who remained on the home island. He was Jose Manuel Gonzalez, known as "Masinguila." Considered in Havana to this day as the finest cigar maker ever and one of the hardest taskmasters for the rollers he supervised, "Masinguila" is generally credited with much of the consistency in quality and unique blending that is characteristic of the brand.

In the early 1970s, the Montecristo A and the Laguito (Cohiba) Nos. 1, 2, and 3 sizes were added as the Especial, Especial No. 2, and Joyita. Coincidentally, the brand took off. It became the firm showbiz favorite with the likes of singer Tom Jones and British movie mogul Lew (now Lord) Grade.

Some say success brought its own problems. Certainly to match the quality of the huge volume of Montecristos that go to Spain, for example, is a prodigious task, and many consider that higher standards are maintained only in smaller markets like Britain. However, this did not stop an outbreak of near civil unrest in Spain when the brand was withdrawn following a trademark dispute between Tabacalera (the Spanish monopoly) and Cubatabaco.

The signs are that the trademark issue has been resolved, at least in Spain if not in France. However, this has no bearing on the introduction of a line of Dominican Montecristos in the United States.

Montecristos, with their characteristic Colorado-claro, slightly oily wrappers and delicate aroma offer a medium to full flavor spiked with a unique, tangy taste. The No. 2 is the flagship for the Piramide size, while many devotees consider the No. 1 (a Cervantes) hard to beat.

MONTECRISTO

SIZES

NAME	LENGTH: INCHES	RING GAUGE
A	9¼ inches	47
Especial	7½ inches	38
No. 1	6½ inches	42
No. 2	6⅛ inches	52
Tubos	6 inches	42
Especial No. 2	6 inches	38
No. 3	5½ inches	42
Petit Tubos	5 inches	42
No. 4	5 inches	42
Joyitas	4½ inches	26
No. 5	4 inches	40

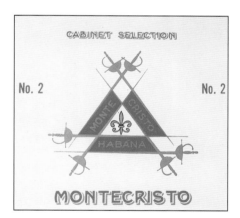

ESPECIAL No. 2 : LENGTH 6 INCHES, RING GAUGE 38

No. 2 : Length 6⅛ inches, Ring Gauge 52

Tubos : Length 6 inches, Ring Gauge 42

No. 5 : Length 4 inches, Ring Gauge 40

C Cuba
F Medium to
  full-bodied
Q Superior
  quality

MONTECRUZ

ontecruz was the brand name given to the cigars made by the Menendez family (former owners of the Montecristo brand) when they started a manufacturing operation in the Canary Islands after leaving Cuba. They were then made with Cameroon wrappers, with Dominican and Brazilian fillers. The cigars, with labels very similar to the Montecristo brand are now made (since the mid-1970s) at La Romana in the Dominican Republic, with mid- to dark-brown Cameroon wrappers, by the Consolidated Cigar Corporation. These very well-made, medium to full-flavored cigars (with a distinctive taste and bouquet) come in a very wide choice of sizes. They are described as "sun grown." The "boîte nature" selection is richer, and matured for longer. Montecruz cigars are also produced in a milder range (with different labels and lighter Connecticut wrappers) for Dunhill. The Dunhill cigars come in some of the same sizes as the Montecruz.

SIZES

NAME	LENGTH: INCHES	RING GAUGE
Indivuales	8 inches	46
No. 200	7¼ inches	46
No. 205	7 inches	42
No. 255	7 inches	36
No. 280	7 inches	28
Colossus	6½ inches	50
No. 210	6½ inches	42
No. 250	6½ inches	38
No. 201	6¼ inches	46
Tubulares	6⅛ inches	36
Tubos	6 inches	42
No. 276	6 inches	32
No. 281	6 inches	28
Seniors	5¾ inches	35
No. 220	5½ inches	42
No. 265	5½ inches	38
Juniors	5¼ inches	33
Cedar-aged	5 inches	42
No. 230	5 inches	42
No. 282	5 inches	28
No. 270	4¾ inches	36
Robusto	4½ inches	49
Chicos	4 inches	28

NO. 200 : LENGTH 7¼ INCHES, RING GAUGE 46

NO. 210 : LENGTH 6½ INCHES, RING GAUGE 42

NO. 220 : LENGTH 5½ INCHES, RING GAUGE 42

C Dominican Republic
F Medium to full-bodied
Q Superior quality

No. 255 : Length 7 inches, Ring Gauge 36

Tube Dunhill Sun Grown

Colossus : Length 6½ inches, Ring Gauge 50

MONTESINO

A medium-bodied brand made in Dominican Republic by Arturo Fuente with Havana Fuente seed wrappers, which are mid-brown to dark. These cigars are well made and reasonably priced for the quality.

SIZES

Name	Length: inches	Ring Gauge
Napoleon Grande	7 inches	46
No. 1	6⅞ inches	43
Gran Corona	6¾ inches	48
Fumas	6¾ inches	44
No. 3	6¾ inches	36
No. 2	6¼ inches	44
Diplomatico	5½ inches	42

C Dominican Republic
F Mild to medium
Q Good-quality leaf and construction

[159]

NAT SHERMAN

*T*he Nat Sherman store at 500 Fifth Avenue is a polished mahogany temple to tobacco, cigars, and smokers' requisites. Its business, which stretches far beyond its doors, was founded in New York's heyday of the 1930s and 40s with stylish cigarettes and strong connections in Havana.

Joel Sherman, its present custodian, anticipated the cigar boom back in 1990 and 1991, introducing four cigar selections, all made in the Dominican Republic but each with a different blend. An additional selection has been introduced since that time.

There is the Exchange Selection, named after New York's 1940s telephone exchanges, including the inevitable Butterfield 8 (a Lonsdale). Four different countries supply the blend of leaves for these cigars including the lightest of Connecticut wrappers. The flavor is mild.

Dressed in Cameroon wrappers, the Landmark Selection (Metropole, Algonquin, etc.) offers another four-country confection

THE FINE EXTERIOR OF THE NAT SHERMAN SHOP IN
NEW YORK.

with a bit more flavor and a chocolaty top taste.

Cigar-chomping editors of New York's former newspapers are commemorated by the four hefty, sweet-tasting Mexican maduro sizes in the City Desk Selection. Their mild to medium flavor belies their looks.

On the other hand, the Gotham Selection wrapped in a mid-tone Connecticut leaf delivers a surprisingly spicy, yet well balanced, taste. The latest line, the Metropolitan Selection, is named after some of the more famous gentlemen's clubs in New York. Available in five sizes the blend has a uniquely rich and balanced flavor.

Each series is identified by a different background color to the emblem of a clock on the band. go for gray; go for Gotham.

C Dominican Republic
F Varies according to selection
Q Superior quality

SIZES

NAME	LENGTH: INCHES	RING GAUGE
GOTHAM SELECTION		
500	7 inches	50
1400	6¼ inches	44
711	6 inches	50
65	6 inches	36
CITY DESK SELECTION		
Tribune	7½ inches	50
Dispatch	6½ inches	46
Telegraph	6 inches	50
Gazette	6 inches	42
LANDMARK SELECTION		
Dakota	7½ inches	49
Algonquin	6¾ inches	43
Metropole	6 inches	34
Hampshire	5½ inches	42
Vanderbilt	5 inches	47
EXCHANGE SELECTION		
Oxford 5	7 inches	49
Butterfield 8	6½ inches	42
Trafalgar 4	6 inches	47
Murray 7	6 inches	38
Academy 2	5 inches	31
MANHATTAN SELECTION		
Gramercy	6¾ inches	43
Chelsea	6½ inches	38
Tribeca	6 inches	31
Sutton	5½ inches	49
Beekman	5¼ inches	28

GOTHAM 500 : LENGTH 7 INCHES, RING GAUGE 50

CITY DESK TELEGRAPH : LENGTH 6 INCHES, RING GAUGE 50

LANDMARK VANDERBILT : LENGTH 5 INCHES, RING GAUGE 47

EXCHANGE MURRAY 7 : LENGTH 6 INCHES, RING GAUGE 38

OSCAR

These Dominican Republic cigars, named after the company's founder, are well-filled and elegantly presented in claro U.S. Connecticut wrappers. The fillers and binders form a mild to medium blend made from locally produced tobaccos. They have been on the market for nearly a decade and have benefitted from the general improvement in the quality of Dominican cigars. The line covers most needs, including a couple of useful smaller sizes alongside some giants.

SIZES

NAME	LENGTH: INCHES	RING GAUGE
Don Oscar	9 inches	46
Supreme	8 inches	48
#700	7 inches	54
#200	7 inches	44
#100	7 inches	38
#300	6¼ inches	44
#400	6 inches	38
#500	5½ inches	50
Prince	5 inches	30
#600	4½ inches	50
No. 800	4 inches	42
Oscarito	4 inches	20

C Dominican Republic
F Mild to medium
Q Good-quality leaf and construction

PADRON

ounded by Jose O. Padron in Miami, Florida, Padron Cigars has been producing long-filler premium cigars since 1964. Operating two companies in Central America, Tabacos Cubanica S.A. in Nicaragua, and Tabacos Centroamericanos S.A. in Honduras, Padron Cigars is one among a handful of companies that control every aspect of the manufacturing process.

- **C** Nicaragua/ Honduras
- **F** Mild to medium
- **Q** Good-quality leaf and construction

SIZES

Name	Length: inches	Ring Gauge
Magnum	9 inches	50
Grand Reserve	8 inches	41
Executive	7½ inches	50
Churchill	6⅞ inches	46
Ambassador	6⅞ inches	42
Panetela	6⅞ inches	36
Palmas	6⁵⁄₁₆ inches	42
3000	5½ inches	52
Londres	5½ inches	42
Chicos	5½ inches	36
2000	5 inches	50
Delicias	4⅞ inches	46

There is an emphasis on quality over quantity, and this is reflected in the two lines of cigars that are produced. The Padron—currently available in twelve sizes comes in both natural and maduro wrappers—is very well made, and offers a mild to medium smoke. The Padron 1964 Anniversary Series line has fewer sizes and the cigars are of limited production. All tobacco, from Nicaragua, is aged for at least four years, and wrapped in natural leaf. A medium smoke, this cigar gives very smooth, earthy flavors.

C Nicaragua/ Honduras
F Medium
Q Superior quality

1964 ANNIVERSARY SERIES SIZES

NAME	LENGTH: INCHES	RING GAUGE
Diplomatico	7 inches	50
Pyramid	6⅞ inches	42/52
Monarca	6½ inches	46
Superior	6½ inches	42
Corona	6 inches	42
Exclusivo	5½ inches	50

EXCLUSIVO : LENGTH 5½ INCHES, RING GAUGE 50

PARTAGAS

*P*artagas is one of the oldest of the Havana brands, started in 1845 by Don Jaime Partagas. The old factory still exists, in downtown Havana near the Capitol building (an architectural copy of the United States Congress). The name is still well known, not least because Partagas cigars are produced in large quantities: there are no fewer than 40 types available—many of them machine-made and cellophane-wrapped. There is also a Dominican version of the brand, made with Cameroon wrappers grown from Havana seed, and overseen by Benjamin Menendez and Ramon Cifuentes of the famous Cuban cigar families. The brand is manufactured by General Cigar. The differences between the labels are that Cuban versions carry the word Habana at the bottom of the label, whereas Dominican versions have the year 1845.

The brand was particularly famous between the two World Wars and has the distinction of being mentioned in cigar-lover Evelyn Waugh's novel, *Brideshead Revisited*.

The quality of Cuban Partagas can vary. The bigger sizes like the Lusitania, particularly in Cabinet 50s (a firm favorite with

SIZES

NAME	LENGTH: INCHES	RING GAUGE
Lusitanias	7⅝ inches	49
Churchill De Luxe	7 inches	47
Palmes Grandes	7 inches	33
Partagas de Partagas No. 1	6¾ inches	43
Seleccion Privada No. 1	6¾ inches	43
8–9–8	6¾ inches	43
Lonsdale	6½ inches	42
Corona Grande	6 inches	42
Culebras (twisted)	5¹¹⁄₁₆ inches	39
Corona	5½ inches	42
Charlotte	5½ inches	35
Petit Corona	5 inches	42
Series D No. 4	4⅞ inches	50
Très Petit Corona	4½ inches	40
Shorts	4⁵⁄₁₆ inches	42

ABC's Pierre Salinger) are very good indeed, but some of the smaller sizes, often when they are machine-made as opposed to hand-finished or handmade, can give draw problems. In general, the brand has a rich, earthy, and full flavor, which is particularly noticeable on the heavier ring gauge sizes like the Series D No. 4 (Robusto). There are two sizes in an 8–9–8 packing; one is a Corona Grande (6 inches x 42) and the other a Dalia (6⅝ inches x 43). The Dalia is seen by Ernesto Lopez, the factory's Director, as his flagship size. They have an altogether smoother finish, but retain the full flavor. There is a Connoisseur series of three cigars, available in some markets, which includes the No. 1, a cigar of the same dimensions as the Cohiba Lanceros but without the pigtail. In general, Partagas is a good choice after a heavy meal.

Handmade Dominican Partagas, although very well-constructed, occasionally have wrappers of variable quality, particularly the larger sizes. The best are very good. They are also relatively expensive. They normally come in colorado wrappers, but there is also a maduro—a 6¼-inch cigar with a 47 ring gauge. The fillers are a mixture of Jamaican, Dominican, and Mexican tobacco. There are 14 sizes, mostly numbered, of Dominican Partagas in all: smooth, medium to full-bodied, and slightly sweet. A selection of sizes is listed.

ERNESTO LOPEZ, DIRECTOR OF THE PARTAGAS FACTORY IN DOWNTOWN HAVANA.

SERIES D NO. 4 : LENGTH 4⅞ INCHES, RING GAUGE 50

CORONA : LENGTH 5½ INCHES, RING GAUGE 42

SHORTS : LENGTH 4⁵⁄₁₆ INCHES, RING GAUGE 42

C Cuba
F Very full-
bodied
Q Superior
quality

DOMINICAN SIZES

Name	Length: inches	Ring Gauge
No. 10	7½ inches	49
Tubos	7 inches	34
8–9–8	6⅞ inches	44
Limited Reserve Royale	6¾ inches	43
No. 1	6¾ inches	43
Humitube	6¾ inches	43
Limited Reserve Regale	6¼ inches	47
Maduro	6¼ inches	48
Almirantes	6¼ inches	47
No. 6	6 inches	34
Sabroso	5⅞ inches	44
No. 2	5¾ inches	43
Naturales	5½ inches	50
No. 3	5¼ inches	43
No. 5	5¼ inches	28
No. 4	5 inches	38
Purito	4⅞ inches	32

C Dominican Republic
F Medium to full-bodied
Q Superior quality

LIMITED RESERVE ROYALE : LENGTH 6¾ INCHES, RING GAUGE 43

PAUL GARMIRIAN

*P*aul Garmirian's P.G. cigars are among the best on the market certainly when it comes to non-Havanas. Garmirian himself, based outside Washington, DC, has a Ph.D. in international politics and is a real-estate broker. He is also a great connoisseur of handmade cigars, and author of *The Gourmet Guide to Cigars.* He decided to put his 30-year passion for fine cigars to work in 1991 with the launch of his own brand.

His cigars, available only in limited quantities, are made in the Dominican Republic with dark, slightly oily, reddish mid-brown colorado wrappers. They are very well made, have a subtle but noticeable bouquet, burn well and slowly, and are medium flavored. The cigars have a rich aroma, taste pleasantly sweet (the flavor gets richer as you smoke), and are very mellow and well blended. These are very superior cigars, as good as many Havanas, and better than quite a few. The Lonsdale will give you a pretty good impression of the line. Seven more sizes have been added since the first edition of this book, the most recent addition being the Especial.

C Dominican
Republic
F Medium to
full-bodied
Q Superior
quality

CORONA : LENGTH 5½ INCHES, RING GAUGE 42

SIZES

Name	Length: inches	Ring Gauge
Celebration	9 inches	50
Double Corona	7⅝ inches	50
No. 1	7½ inches	38
Churchill	7 inches	48
Belicoso	6½ inches	52
Corona Grande	6½ inches	46
Lonsdale	6½ inches	42
Connoisseur	6 inches	50
Especial	5¾ inches	38
Belicoso Fino	5½ inches	52
Epicure	5½ inches	50
Corona	5½ inches	42
Robusto	5 inches	50
Petit Corona	5 inches	43
No. 2	4¾ inches	48
Petit Bouquet	4½ inches	38
No. 5	4 inches	40
Bombones	3½ inches	43

CHURCHILL : LENGTH 7 INCHES, RING GAUGE 48

No. 2 : Length 4¾ inches, Ring Gauge 48

Belicoso : Length 6½ inches, Ring Gauge 52

Celebration : Length 9 inches, Ring Gauge 50

PETRUS

This brand has achieved inter-national acclaim since its debut in 1990, and has been praised by many, Arnold Schwarzenegger among them. Manufactured in Honduras by La Flor de Copan factory, Honduran filler and binder come wrapped in Connecticut-seed leaf grown in Ecuador. The cigar gives a mild smoke, with nutty flavors, and a dry finish. Currently available in 13 sizes, they offer a good choice of cigar at very reasonable prices. 1997 will see the introduction of a limited edition cigar, Etiquette Rouge, using a blend of Dominican, Honduran, and Nicaraguan tobaccos.

SIZES

Name	Length: inches	Ring Gauge
Lord Byron	8 inches	38
Double Corona	7¾ inches	50
Churchill	7 inches	50
No. 2	6¼ inches	44
No. 3	6 inches	50
Palma Fina	6 inches	38
No. 4	5⅝ inches	38
Corona Sublime	5½ inches	46
Antonius	5 inches	torpedo
Gregorius	5 inches	42
Rothschild	4¾ inches	50
Chantaco	4¾ inches	35
Duchess	4½ inches	30

... Tabaco Petrus Sublime ...

C Honduras
F Mild
Q Good-quality leaf and construction

PLEIADES

A very elegant range of Dominican cigars with Connecticut Shade wrappers. They are mild, well made, draw well, and are very pleasant cigars with a good aroma. The brand originates from France. Once made in the Caribbean, the cigars are shipped back to Strasbourg, where they are placed in boxes with an original built-in humidifying system, before being distributed in Europe and back across the ocean to the United States.

SIZES

Name	Length: inches	Ring Gauge
Aldebran	8½ inches	50
Saturne	8 inches	46
Neptune	7½ inches	42
Sirius	6⅞ inches	46
Uranus	6⅞ inches	34
Orion	5¾ inches	42
Antares	5½ inches	40
Venus	5⅛ inches	28
Pluton	5 inches	50
Perseus	5 inches	34
Mars	5 inches	28

C Dominican Republic
F Mild
Q Good-quality leaf and construction

URANUS : LENGTH 6⅞ INCHES, RING GAUGE 34

ORION : LENGTH 5¾ INCHES, RING GAUGE 42

SIRIUS : LENGTH 6⅞ INCHES, RING GAUGE 46

ALDEBRAN : LENGTH 8½ INCHES, RING GAUGE 50

POR LARRANAGA

*A*n old brand (the oldest still being produced), dating from 1834, but no longer among the best known. Production is limited, and the cigars aren't widely distributed, but these very full-bodied cigars are sought after by many connoisseurs of traditional Havana flavor. The selection is fairly limited, with about half a dozen machine-made sizes (the brand was the first to introduce machines), some the same (size, not quality) as handmade versions. "There's peace in Larranaga," claimed Rudyard Kipling in his 1890 ditty which includes the notorious line "A woman is only a woman, but a good cigar is a smoke."

These cigars, with their dark, reddish, oily wrappers, are a good choice for lovers of mid- to full-flavored cigars. With their golden bands, they have a distinguished appearance. They tend to be rich and aromatic, with a powerful (rather sweet) flavor, and an aroma less pronounced than some other brands of the same type (Partagas, for instance). The Lonsdale and Corona sizes are as good as most rivals, and the latter is a good after-dinner cigar.

There are also excellent Dominican cigars using the same brand name. They are extremely well made with Connecticut Shade wrappers, fillers blended from Dominican and Brazilian leaves, and Dominican binders. They are full of flavor, especially the Fabuloso (7 inches, ring gauge 50), which is essentially a Churchill.

CUBAN SIZES

Name	Length: inches	Ring Gauge
Lonsdale	6½ inches	42
Corona	5½ inches	42
Petit Corona	5 inches	42
Small Corona	4½ inches	40

FABULOSOS : LENGTH 7 INCHES, RING GAUGE 50

ROBUSTO : LENGTH 5 INCHES, RING GAUGE 50

CORONA : LENGTH 5½ INCHES, RING GAUGE 42

C Dominican Republic
F Mild to medium
Q Superior quality

C Cuba
F Medium to full-bodied
Q Superior quality

PRIMO DEL REY

$\mathscr{A}$ brand made by the Consolidated Cigar Corporation in the Dominican Republic. The main line consisting of 1–5 sizes dressed in a simple brown and white Montecristo-like band, offers a choice of Candela (double claro), Claro (natural), and Colorado (mid-brown wrappers). Just four sizes make up the Club Selection, which is identified by a red, gold, and white band featuring a coat of arms. They are all very well-made.

SIZES

NAME	LENGTH: INCHES	RING GAUGE
Barons	8½ inches	52
Aguilas	8 inches	52
Soberanos	7½ inches	50
Regal	7 inches	50
Aristocrats	6¾ inches	48
Presidentes	6¹³⁄₁₆ inches	44
Seleccion No. 1	6¹³⁄₁₆ inches	42
Seleccion No. 3	6¹³⁄₁₆ inches	36
Chavon	6½ inches	41
Churchill	6¼ inches	48
Nobles	6¼ inches	44
Seleccion No. 2	6¼ inches	42
Cazadores	6¹⁄₁₆ inches	42
Reales	6⅛ inches	36
Almirantes	6 inches	50
Panetela Extra	5¹⁵⁄₁₆ inches	34
Seleccion No. 4	5½ inches	42
Panetela	5⅝ inches	34
No. 100	4½ inches	50
Cortos	4 inches	28

REGAL : LENGTH 7 INCHES, RING GAUGE 50

SOBERANOS : LENGTH 7½ INCHES, RING GAUGE 50

NO. 100 : LENGTH 4½ INCHES, RING GAUGE 50

C Dominican
Republic
F Mild to
medium
Q Superior
quality

PUNCH

very well-known and widely distributed Havana brand (once very popular in Britain), with lower prices than many others, and as a result, familiar to beginners and occasional smokers. Cigar snobs thus tend to avoid it, mostly without good reason. There is a very wide selection of sizes, most from the La Corona factory, with many machine-made equivalents—as well as types such as Exquisitos and Palmas Reales, which are only machine-made.

The brand, the second oldest still in production, was founded in 1840 by Manuel Lopez with the British market in mind where an eponymous light-hearted magazine (similar to the New Yorker) was much in vogue. A contented Mr. Punch, cigar in hand, remains a feature of each box.

There is also a Honduran Punch brand which comes in three series; standard, Delux, and Gran Cru. These are exceptionally well-made cigars, particularly in the Delux and Gran Cru form. The standard line offers a straightforward, Honduran, fullish flavor, but there is a rare delicacy to the taste in the other two series, even

CUBAN SIZES

NAME	LENGTH: INCHES	RING GAUGE
Double Corona	7⅞ inches	49
Churchill	7 inches	47
Panetelas Grandes	7 inches	33
Punch Punch	5⅝ inches	46
Corona	5½ inches	42
Royal Coronations	5½ inches	42
Petit Corona	5 inches	42
Coronations	5 inches	42
Margarita	4¾ inches	26
Petit Coronations	4½ inches	40
Coronets	4½ inches	34
Punchinellos	4½ inches	34
Très Petit Coronas	4¼ inches	42
Petit Punch	4 inches	40

when maduro wrapped, which suggests substantial aging. The skilled hands and expert knowledge of Villazon's Frank Llaneza lie behind these cigars, which is always a good sign.

With such a large Havana line, it isn't possible for every cigar to be of the highest quality, but the larger sizes, with their fragrant bouquet, distinctive spicy aroma, and reasonably, but not very, full-bodied, slightly sweet flavor, are well-constructed and dependable—the Double Corona, for instance. One complication is that the same-sized cigars are sometimes known by different names in different countries. The famous Punch Punch (Corona Gorda), for example, can be found as a Royal Selection No. 11 or a Seleccion de Luxe No. 1, and even the Petit Corona del Punch is sometimes the Seleccion de Luxe No. 2 or Presidente. Find a trusty cigar merchant to guide you through this choice of first class mild to medium cigars.

There are tubed cigars in both the Cuban and Honduran lines, with names like Royal Coronation.

HONDURAN SIZES

Name	Length: inches	Ring Gauge
Presidente	8½ inches	42
Château Lafitte	7¼ inches	52
Grand Diademas	7⅛ inches	52
Diademas	7⅛ inches	52
Elegante	7⅛ inches	36
Casa Grande	7 inches	46
Monarcas	6¾ inches	48
Double Corona	6⅝ inches	48
Château Corona	6½ inches	44
No. 1	6½ inches	42
Bristol	6¼ inches	50
Britannia Delux	6¼ inches	50
Punch	6⅛ inches	43
Superiores Delux	5⅝ inches	46
Château Margaux	5½ inches	46
No. 75	5½ inches	43
Superior	5 inches	50
Rothschild	4½ inches	48

C Honduras
F Mild to medium
Q Superior quality

DOUBLE CORONA : LENGTH 7⅝ INCHES, RING GAUGE 49

PETIT CORONA : LENGTH 5 INCHES, RING GAUGE 42

PRESIDENTE : LENGTH 8½ INCHES, RING GAUGE 42

C Cuba
F Mild to
  medium
Q Superior
  quality

SUPERIORES DELUX : LENGTH 5⅝ INCHES, RING GAUGE 46

BRITANNIA DELUX : LENGTH 6¼ INCHES, RING GAUGE 50

MONARCAS : LENGTH 6¾ INCHES, RING GAUGE 48

QUINTERO

A Cuban brand notable for the fact that it was founded in the southern coastal city of Cienfuegos, and not Havana. Augustin Quintero and his four brothers, who worked in the nearby Remedios tobacco regime, started a small "chinchal" (cigar workshop) in the mid-1920s. By 1940, their reputation allowed them to open in Havana and introduce the brand bearing their family name using Vuelta Abajo tobaccos. Today several of the sizes are both handmade or machine-made, so check for the "Totalamente a mano" stamp on the box. The Churchill is a Lonsdale (Cervantes), but a good one if you like a light smoke. Overall the brand is mild.

SIZES

NAME	LENGTH: INCHES	RING GAUGE
Churchill	6½ inches	42
Corona	5½ inches	42
Nacionales	5½ inches	40
Panetelas	5 inches	37
Tubulares	5 inches	37
Londres Extra	5 inches	40
Puritos	4¼ inches	29

C Cuba
F Mild
Q Good-quality leaf and construction

RAFAEL GONZALEZ

*T*hese are among the best of medium-priced Havanas, long well-known and appreciated by serious smokers. The box of this brand, originally created for the English market, carries the unusual legend: "These cigars have been manufactured from a secret blend of pure Vuelta Abajo tobaccos selected by the Marquez Rafael Gonzalez, Grandee of Spain. For more than 20 years this brand has existed. In order that the Connoisseur may fully appreciate the perfect fragrance they should be smoked either within one month of the date of shipment from Havana or should be carefully matured for about one year." The box used to carry a portrait of the great smoker Lord Lonsdale on the reverse side of the lid. The brand is made in the Romeo Y Julieta factory.

These first-class cigars have a delicate, but rich and subtle flavor, and complex aroma (they are much lighter, but have a hint of Montecristo to them). The label is very similar to Montecristo in both color and design. They are very well made and have good burning qualities. The Corona Extra is particularly reputed, as is the Lonsdale. The Cigarrito is a very good example of a size which is often unsatisfactory. The selection of sizes is commendably small. These are, in general, very classy cigars, among the mildest of Havanas.

SIZES

Name	Length: inches	Ring Gauge
Slenderella	7 inches	28
Lonsdale	6½ inches	42
Corona Extra	5⅝ inches	46
Petit Corona	5 inches	42
Petit Lonsdale	5 inches	42
Panetela Extra	5 inches	37
Panetela	4⅞ inches	34
Très Petit Lonsdale	4½ inches	40
Cigarrito	4½ inches	26
Demi Tasse	4 inches	30

TRES PETIT LONSDALE : LENGTH 4½ INCHES, RING GAUGE 40

PETIT CORONA : LENGTH 5 INCHES, RING GAUGE 42

LONSDALE : LENGTH 6½ INCHES, RING GAUGE 42

C Cuba
F Mild
Q The very best quality available

RAMON ALLONES

*D*ating from 1837, Ramon Allones, although not one of the best known of Havana names, is a favorite with many connoisseurs, among the best of the full-bodied cigars available. They are near the top of the list of medium-priced Cuban cigars—i.e., below Cohiba and Montecristo, but up there with Upmann, Partagas, and Romeo Y Julieta. Most Ramon Allones are handmade, but there are a handful of machine-made sizes (Belvederes, Mille Fleurs, Delgados, and Toppers among them).

Ramon Allones are rolled in the Partagas factory (known for its full-bodied cigars) and have been since the factory was bought by the famous Cifuentes firm in the 1920s. The brand originated the 8–9–8 form of packaging.

The arms on the box are those of the Spanish royal house. Ramon Allones himself, emigrated from Galicia, in Spain, to Cuba, and was the first man to put colorful printed labels on his cigar boxes.

There is a good selection of Ramon Allones, all of them relatively full-bodied, and well made, with a strong aroma (similar to Partagas, but certainly less than Bolivar, also made in the same factory), good, dark wrappers, and excellent burning qualities. The smaller sizes tend to be lighter in color and somewhat milder. Rich in ligero leaf, these are not cigars for beginners. The 8–9–8 Corona is a good after-lunch choice, just as Gigantes (Prominente), 8–9–8 Churchill, or the Specially Selected (robusto) are all excellent choices after dinner. The very slim Ramonitas aren't recommended. These cigars age beautifully.

There are very good Dominican-produced Ramon Allones, with a similar band (but larger, and square, not round). They are very well made, mild to medium-bodied, and rather expensive. Most of the available sizes, unlike the Cuban brand, are named after letters of the alphabet. The Dominican brand, produced by General Cigar, have medium to dark Cameroon wrappers, Mexican binders, and fillers blended from Dominican, Jamaican, and Mexican tobacco. The Crystals are packed in individual glass tubes.

CUBAN SIZES

Name	Length: inches	Ring Gauge
Gigantes	7½ inches	49
8–9–8	6¹¹⁄₁₆ inches	43
Corona	5⅝ inches	42
Petit Corona	5 inches	42
Panetela	5 inches	35
Specially Selected	4¹³⁄₁₆ inches	50
Ramonitas	4¹³⁄₁₆ inches	26
Small Club Coronas	4⁵⁄₁₆ inches	42

DOMINICAN SIZES

Name	Length: inches	Ring Gauge
Redondos	7 inches	49
A	7 inches	45
Trumps	6¾ inches	43
Crystals	6¾ inches	43
B	6½ inches	42
D	5 inches	42

SMALL CLUB CORONAS : LENGTH 4⁵⁄₁₆ INCHES, RING GAUGE 42

GIGANTES : LENGTH 7½ INCHES, RING GAUGE 49

SPECIALLY SELECTED : LENGTH 4¹³⁄₁₆ INCHES, RING GAUGE 50

C Cuba
F Very full-
bodied
Q The very
best quality
available

C Dominican
Republic
F Mild to
medium
Q Good-quality
leaf and
construction

ROMEO Y JULIETA

*O*ne of the very best-known Havana brands, particularly popular in Britain, Romeo Y Julieta cigars come in a huge choice of over 40 shapes and sizes. Many of them come in aluminum tubes, and there are also a large number of machine-made sizes. Despite the vast range, which inevitably means that not all sizes can be trusted, there are some very good cigars produced under this brand, many of them among the best available in their size.

The brand's early success was directly due to the efforts of Rodriguez Fernandez. "Pepin," as he was known, was originally manager of the Cabanas factory in Havana, but unhappy at its imminent takeover by American Tobacco, he resigned in 1903 to branch out on his own. Using his savings, he bought a little-known factory which, since 1875, had made cigars called Romeo Y Julieta solely for the Cuban domestic market. But he had bigger ideas, and encouraging his employees by distributing 30 percent of profits to heads of department, he traveled the world promoting the brand. Within two years, with his 1,400 workers, he had to move to a larger factory.

For monarchs, heads of state, and others, he specialized in providing personalized cigar bands (at one stage the factory was producing 20,000 different bands). Pepin remained devoted, almost obsessed by his brand, naming his racehorse Julieta, and trying to buy the House of Capulet in Verona, where Shakespeare's play was set. He couldn't quite do that, but was allowed to have a stand under the famous balcony, so that until 1939, every visitor was offered a free cigar in honor of the ill-starred lovers who gave the brand its name. He died in 1954.

The famous Romeo Y Julieta Churchills also come in tubes. They are very well-made cigars, with an excellent aroma, but the tubed versions can sometimes be rather fresh and, as a result, are

MADE IN HABANA, CUBA

not as well matured as the boxed versions. The Churchill sizes, with their distinctive gold bands (the others, apart from the Cedros series, are all red) are, nonetheless, classic medium to full-bodied cigars. The Corona size, often with colorado maduro wrappers, is very well-constructed but inconsistent in flavor. The Cedros de Luxe No. 1 (Lonsdale), is a dark, smooth, medium-bodied cigar, though sometimes not enough for lovers of this size. The Exhibicion No. 4 (Hermoso 4), with its oily wrapper, provides a rich smoke after a heavy meal and is a favorite with many connoisseurs. The Cedros de Luxe No. 2 is a very good corona, with plenty of personality. The Petit Julietas are among the best made and fullest-flavored in their size.

There is no meaningful difference between the various Churchill sizes, but some claim that the Prince of Wales is milder

CUBAN SIZES

Name	Length: inches	Ring Gauge
Churchill	7 inches	47
Prince of Wales	7 inches	47
Shakespeare	6⅞ inches	28
Cedros De Luxe No. 1	6½ inches	42
Corona Grande	6 inches	42
Belicosos	5½ inches	52
Exhibicion No. 3	5½ inches	43
Cedros De Luxe No. 2	5½ inches	42
Corona	5½ inches	42
Exhibicion No. 4	5 inches	48
Cedros De Luxe No. 3	5 inches	42
Petit Corona	5 inches	42
Très Petit Corona	4½ inches	40
Petit Julietas	4 inches	30

than the tubed version. Be sure not to confuse the tubed No. 1, No. 2, and No. 3 *De Luxe* with the similarly numbered tubes without the words "De Luxe"—which are machine-made, and much inferior. In Britain all tubed sizes are handmade, so you can smoke them without hesitation. The Cazadores (6⅛ inches, ring gauge 44), although handmade, is one of the cheapest cigars in the range for the good reason that it is made from less well-selected leaves. They are thus cigars of a different quality.

Dominican Republic cigars called Romeo Y Julietas are also produced in a vintage line wrapped in Connecticut shade and standard selections using darker Cameroon wrappers. Both types are very good and well made, the former offering a particularly delicate smoke. As with the Cuban Romeo Y Julietas, only a selection of sizes is given below.

SIZES

NAME	LENGTH: INCHES	RING GAUGE
Monarcas	8 inches	52
Churchills	7 inches	50
Presidentes	7 inches	43
Delgados	7 inches	32
Cetros	6½ inches	44
Romeos	6 inches	46
Palmas	6 inches	43
Brevas	5⅝ inches	38
Coronas	5½ inches	44
Panatelas	5¼ inches	35
Rothschilds	5 inches	50
Chiquitas	4¼ inches	32

C Dominican Republic
F Mild to medium
Q Superior quality

C Honduras
F Medium to full-bodied
Q Superior quality

VINTAGE SIZES

NAME	LENGTH: INCHES	RING GAUGE
Vintage V	7½ inches	50
Vintage VI	7 inches	60
Vintage IV	7 inches	48
Vintage II	6 inches	46
Vintage I	6 inches	43
Vintage III	4½ inches	50

PRESIDENT : LENGTH 7 INCHES, RING GAUGE 43

MONARCAS : LENGTH 8 INCHES, RING GAUGE 52

CHURCHILL : LENGTH 7 INCHES, RING GAUGE 50

CHURCHILL : LENGTH 7 INCHES, RING GAUGE 47

BELICOSOS : LENGTH 5½ INCHES, RING GAUGE 52

EXHIBICION NO. 4 : LENGTH 5 INCHES, RING GAUGE 48

C Cuba
F Mild to medium
Q The very best quality available

ROYAL JAMAICA

*F*ormerly made in Jamaica, production moved to the Dominican Republic following a hurricane in 1988 which destroyed both factories and tobacco crops. They remain among the best of mild cigars. Most Royal Jamaicas have Cameroon wrappers, but the fuller-bodied Maduro range uses wrappers from Brazil.

SIZES

NAME	LENGTH: INCHES	RING GAUGE
Ten Downing Street	10 inches	51
Goliath	9 inches	64
Individuals	8½ inches	52
Churchill	8 inches	51
Giant Corona	7½ inches	49
Double Corona	7 inches	45
Doubloon	7 inches	30
Navarro	6¾ inches	34
Corona Grande	6½ inches	42
No. 2 Tube	6½ inches	34
Rapier	6½ inches	28
Park Lane	6 inches	47
Tube No. 1	6 inches	45
Director 1	6 inches	45
New York Plaza	6 inches	40
Royal Corona	6 inches	30
Corona	5½ inches	40
Buccaneer	5½ inches	30
Gaucho	5¼ inches	33
Petit Corona	5 inches	40
Robusto	4½ inches	49
Pirate	4½ inches	30

MADURO SIZES

NAME	LENGTH: INCHES	RING GAUGE
Churchill	8 inches	51
Corona Grande	6½ inches	42
Corona	5½ inches	40
Buccaneer	5½ inches	30

DOUBLE CORONA : LENGTH 7 INCHES, RING GAUGE 45

PIRATE : LENGTH 4½ INCHES, RING GAUGE 30

PARK LANE : LENGTH 6 INCHES, RING GAUGE 47

C Dominican
Republic
F Mild
Q Superior
quality

SAINT LUIS REY

This Havana brand was created some 50 years ago by British importers Michael de Keyser and Nathan Silverstone. The name originated after the success of the popular American film *The Bridge of San Luis Rey* (based on Thornton Wilder's play, and starring Akim Tamiroff and Alla Nazimova). By lucky chance, there was also a Cuban town called San Luis Obispo.

The characteristic cigars of the brand are heavyweight medium to strong cigars. They are made at the Romeo Y Julieta factory and are in many ways similar to Romeos. The brand has had many fans, among them Frank Sinatra and actor James Coburn. This is a very high-quality brand with a very limited production of only 60,000 cigars a year.

The cigars, which come in a predominantly white box and have a red label, are not to be confused with *San* Luis Rey, a brand made in Cuba for the German market. There is also a range of San Luis Reys machine-made in Germany for the mass market by Villiger using Havana leaf. San Luis Reys have a black label with a similar emblem.

These cigars are among the best Havanas available. The wrappers are dark to very dark, smooth and oily, and the flavor, although full-bodied, is very refined. The aroma of the best of these cigars is superb. The Regios (robusto) is a very fine smoke, as is the milder, and less full Churchill. Saint Luis Reys tend to be cheaper than most other Havanas (certainly others of comparable quality). The selection is small.

SIZES

Name	Length: inches	Ring Gauge
Churchill	7 inches	47
Lonsdale	6½ inches	42
Serie A	5⅝ inches	46
Corona	5⅝ inches	42
Regios	5 inches	48
Petit Corona	5 inches	42

CHURCHILL : LENGTH 7 INCHES, RING GAUGE 47

REGIOS : LENGTH 5 INCHES, RING GAUGE 48

CORONA : LENGTH 5⅝ INCHES, RING GAUGE 42

C Cuba
F Very full-
  bodied
Q Superior
  quality

SANCHO PANZA

Not a well-known brand, but good, reliable Havanas, if a little too light and short on flavor for the real connoisseur. But for some, they offer a subtle, delicate, even elegant smoke, particularly the Molino (Lonsdale), although this cigar sometimes has a slightly salty taste which appeals to some smokers, not to others. Their construction sometimes leaves something to be desired: they don't burn as easily as they should. But the Corona Gigante is very well made. Even the torpedo-shaped Belicosos are mild (perhaps the mildest) for their type. The same applies to the Montecristo A-sized Sanchos. The line is small. These are good beginners' cigars, or for daytime smoking. The brand appears intermittently in Britain, but is very popular in Spain. There are plans to distribute it more widely.

SIZES

NAME	LENGTH: INCHES	RING GAUGE
Sanchos	9¼ inches	47
Corona Gigante	7 inches	47
Molino	6½ inches	42
Panetela Largo	6½ inches	28
Corona	5⅝ inches	42
Belicosos	5½ inches	52
Non Plus	5⅟₁₆ inches	42
Bachilleres	4⅜ inches	40

C Cuba
F Mild
Q Superior quality

SANTA CLARA

*A*mong the best of Mexican cigars. Made in San Andres with wrappers from the same area. The brand was founded in 1830, is medium flavored, and well made. There is a choice, in most sizes, of pale brown and dark wrappers, with most recent additions including the Premier Tube, and Robusto sizes.

SIZES

NAME	LENGTH: INCHES	RING GAUGE
No. I	7½ inches	52
Premier Tubes	6¾ inches	38
No. III	6⅝ inches	43
No. II	6½ inches	48
No. VI	6 inches	51
No. V	6 inches	44
No. VII	5½ inches	25
No. IV	5 inches	44
Robusto	4½ inches	50
Quino	4¼ inches	30

C Mexico
F Medium
Q Good-quality leaf and construction

SANTA DAMIANA

*S*anta Damiana was once a famous Cuban plantation and brand name. Now it is the name given to a relatively new brand of high-quality cigars, handmade in La Romana on the southeastern coast of the Dominican Republic.

The La Romana factory, near the luxurious Casa de Campo resort, is one of the most advanced handmade cigar factories in the world, applying modern quality-control techniques to the age-old skill of cigar rolling. Different blends and size names are used for the line sold in the United States as opposed to those available in Europe. The American sizes, named Seleccion No. 100, No. 300, and so on, contain a lighter blend of filler unlike the European line which, using traditional names, is designed to appeal to a preference for something fuller-flavored. Both are very well-made, consistent cigars.

SIZES

NAME	LENGTH: INCHES	RING GAUGE
Seleccion No. 800	7 inches	50
Seleccion No. 100		
Churchill	6¾ inches	48
Seleccion No. 700	6½ inches	42
Seleccion No. 300	5½ inches	46
Corona	5½ inches	42
Seleccion No. 500	5 inches	50
Petit Corona	5 inches	42
Tubulares No. 400	5 inches	42
Panetela	4½ inches	36

C Dominican Republic
F Mild to medium
Q Superior quality

SOSA

*T*his is a three-country-blend cigar brand founded in Little Havana by Juan B. Sosa in the early 1960s, which then moved to the Dominican Republic in the early 1970s, and is currently starting production at its new plant at the Arturo Fuente factory. Ecuadoran wrappers in darkish, natural, and maduro tones combine with Honduran binders and Dominican fillers to offer pleasant and distinctive, medium to full flavor. There is a definite attempt here to go for the Cuban style of taste in a well-priced cigar.

SIZES

Name	Length: inches	Ring Gauge
Magnum	7½ inches	52
Piramides #2	7 inches	48
Churchill	7 inches	48
Lonsdale	6½ inches	43
Governor	6 inches	50
Brevas	5½ inches	43
Wavell	4¾ inches	50

- **C** Dominican Republic
- **F** Medium to full
- **Q** Could be better

SUERDIECK

One of the best-known Brazilian cigars, with a medium flavor. The line consists mostly of small ring gauge sizes, a number of which are very similar. These are by no means connoisseurs' cigars—they are not particularly well made, and the mid-brown Brazilian wrappers (the cigars also use Brazilian fillers and binders) leave quite a lot to be desired. But some people like the flavor.

BRASILIA : LENGTH 5¼ INCHES, RING GAUGE 30

SIZES

NAME	LENGTH: INCHES	RING GAUGE
Fiesta	6 inches	30
Valencia	6 inches	30
Caballero	6 inches	30
Brasilia	5¼ inches	30
Mandarim Pai	5 inches	38

C Brazil
F Mild to medium
Q Could be better

TEMPLE HALL

*T*his brand, founded in 1876, has been re-introduced by General Cigar. The Temple Hall estates are in Jamaica, and the cigars are a somewhat fuller-bodied version of Macanudo. Like Macanudo, the wrappers are Connecticut Shade and the filler blend a mixture of Jamaican, Dominican, and Mexican tobaccos. The binder is Mexican, from the San Andres area.

These are very well-made, subtle cigars, at or near the top of their line. Temple Hall make a special selection for Dunhill (slightly milder, with a different blend). The 450 is the only cigar which comes in a Mexican wrapper. The brand consists of seven sizes.

SIZES

NAME	LENGTH: INCHES	RING GAUGE
700	7 inches	49
685	6⅞ inches	34
675	6¼ inches	45
625	6¼ inches	42
550	5½ inches	50
500	5 inches	31
450	4½ inches	49

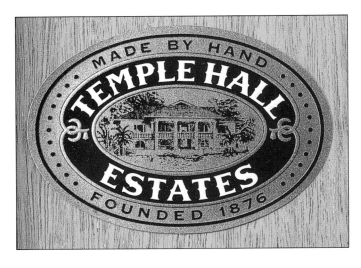

450 : LENGTH 4½ INCHES, RING GAUGE 49

550 : LENGTH 5½ INCHES, RING GAUGE 50

700 : LENGTH 7 INCHES, RING GAUGE 49

C Jamaica
F Mild to medium
Q Superior quality

2¾

TRESADO

*T*his is a relatively new Dominican brand, made and imported by the Consolidated Cigar Corporation. The cigars are well made and have a medium flavor.

SIZES

NAME	LENGTH: INCHES	RING GAUGE
No. 100	8 inches	52
No. 200	7 inches	48
No. 400	6⅝ inches	44
No. 300	6 inches	46
No. 500	5½ inches	42

C Dominican Republic
F Mild to medium
Q Good-quality leaf and construction

NO. 200 : LENGTH 7 INCHES, RING GAUGE 48

TRINIDAD

This cigar is still not to be found in any store, but a few—a select few—people have had a chance to smoke it recently. They were the 164 guests at Marvin Shanken's Paris "Dinner of the Century" in October 1994. The one and only Trinidad size, a Laguito No. 1 like the Cohiba Lancero, was served as the first cigar. With a darker wrapper than you would find on any Cohiba and a rich, earthy flavor, there were those present who felt it might have been better suited to the end of the meal.

Mystery now shrouds the origin of this cigar. Non-smoking President Fidel Castro had been credited with its creation as an exclusive gift for heads of state to replace Cohiba after it went public. However, in his interview with Cigar Aficionado (Summer 1994), Castro virtually denied any knowledge of its existence. He was happy to continue offering Cohibas to cigar enthusiasts of his acquaintance.

So, who's idea was it to ask the El Laguito factory to make Trinidad? As yet, outside official Cuban government circles, no one knows.

C Cuba
F Medium to full-bodied
Q The very best quality available

TRINIDAD : LENGTH 7½ INCHES, RING GAUGE 38

ZINO

reated by Zino Davidoff for the American market when his main brand was still made in Cuba, Zinos are well-tailored Honduran cigars which come in three brands. There is Mouton Cadet, appropriately clad in claret-colored bands and launched during a memorable mid-80s coast to coast tour by Zino himself accompanied by his partner, Dr. Ernst Schneider, and La Baronne Phillipine de Rothschild. These are medium-bodied cigars bearing interesting reddish-brown wrappers. There is the Connoisseur series of heavy-gauge cigars created for the opening of Davidoff's Madison Avenue store, and the standard line, with gold bands, including the 7-inch, 50 gauge Veritas, which gives rise to one of advertising's few classical Latin puns—In Zino Veritas.

SIZES

NAME	LENGTH: INCHES	RING GAUGE
Connoisseur 100	7¾ inches	50
Connoisseur 200	7½ inches	46
Veritas	7 inches	50
Zino Tubos No. 1	6¾ inches	34
Elegance	6¾ inches	34
Junior	6½ inches	30
Tradition	6¼ inches	44
Connoisseur 300	5¾ inches	46
Diamond	5½ inches	40
Princesse	4½ inches	20

MOUTON-CADET SERIES

NAME	LENGTH: INCHES	RING GAUGE
No. 1	6½ inches	44
No. 2	6 inches	35
No. 3	5¾ inches	36
No. 4	5⅛ inches	30
No. 5	5 inches	44
No. 6	5 inches	50

VERITAS : LENGTH 7 INCHES, RING GAUGE 50

CONNOISSEUR 100 : LENGTH 7¾ INCHES, RING GAUGE 50

MOUTON CADET NO. 6 : LENGTH 5 INCHES, RING GAUGE 50

C Honduras
F Mild to
  medium
Q Superior
  quality

THE STRENGTH OF CIGARS

Cuba is unique to the extent that all Havanas or Habanos are blended from tobaccos grown on the island. They tend to offer medium to full flavors but the enormous variety of leaves available can produce surprisingly mild smokes in certain brands.

Cigars from other places like the Dominican Republic and Honduras are usually made from tobaccos taken from several countries. Hard and fast rules on flavors are therefore impossible to lay down. As a rough guide: Connecticut shade wrapped cigars with Dominican fillers tend towards mildness; maduro wrappers bring a sweetness to the taste, and in general Honduran and Nicaraguan fillers add spiciness.

Below is a selection of cigars by strength of flavor:

COUNTY OF ORIGIN

C Cuba	**D** Dominican	**J** Jamaica
CI Canary Islands	Republic	**M** Mexico
	H Honduras	**N** Nicaragua

MILD

Ashton **D**	Macanudo **J**	Royal Jamaica **D**
Casa Blanca **D**	Pleiades **D**	H. Upmann **C**
Cuesta-Rey **D**	Rafael Gonzalez **C**	

MILD TO MEDIUM

Arturo Fuente **D**	Griffin's **D**	Rey del Mundo **C**
Avo **D**	La Invicta **H**	Romeo Y Julieta **C**
Bauza **D**	Joya de	Santa Damiana **D**
Canaria D'Oro **D**	Nicaragua **N**	Te-Amo **M**
Davidoff **D**	Primo del Rey **D**	Temple Hall **J**
Don Diego **D**	Punch **C**	

MEDIUM TO FULL

Aliados **H**	Dunhill **D**	Montecristo **C**
Cohiba **C**	Excalibur **H**	Montecruz **D**
V Centennial **H**	Henry Clay **D**	Por Larrangaga **C**
Don Ramos **H**	Mocha **H**	Paul Garmirian **D**

FULL

Bolivar **C**	Ramon Allones **C**
Partagas **C**	Saint Luis Rey **C**

3

BUYING AND
STORING
CIGARS

BUYING CIGARS

hen you buy a box of handmade cigars (certainly Havanas) you should ask to open the box to check the contents. No decent cigar merchant should refuse. If he does, he either doesn't know his business, or there is probably something wrong with the cigars. The first judgment to make is purely visual: they have to look good. Make sure that the cigars are all of the same color. They should be properly matched: darkest on the left, lightest on the right. If there is any significant variation in color, it would be sensible to reject the cigars, as as they are likely to be inconsistent in flavor, and the box might possibly have escaped final quality control in the factory. If the cigars differ significantly in color and the box is already open, it is more likely to mean that some of the cigars have come from another box (or somebody: customs, the cigar merchant, has been messing around with them)—another good reason for rejecting them. The spiral of the wrapper leaf should be in the same direction on all the cigars. Don't be afraid to smell the cigars to see if you find the bouquet agreeable—it is part of what you are paying for. If they smell good, they should taste good, too. Smell the cut ends, or take one cigar out, and smell the gap where it lay: that way you will experience the bouquet at its fullest.

And feel one or two of the cigars. They should give slightly when you press gently between finger and thumb, but spring back to shape. They should feel smooth. If they make a noise, they are too old or dry. If they don't regain their shape, they are not well

THE DAVIDOFF SHOP, JERMYN STREET, LONDON.

PREVIOUS PAGE: GEORGETOWN TOBACCO, WASHINGTON D.C.
OWNER DAVID BERKEBILE.

made. If the cigar shows no resilience when you press or is mushy, it has been badly stored and will smoke badly. A fresh cigar (less than three months old) will spring back to shape even if your finger and thumb make the two sides almost touch.

If possible, buy cigars in large quantities (boxes of 10 or 25, say) rather than cartons of five which are often less good and less consistent than larger quantities. Nor is it as easy to inspect a cellophaned carton as it is simply to open a cigar box. Some large cigar stores sell cigars in their own boxes or with their "own label." This is normally a marketing ploy: if you have an empty box or two at home, buy them loose; otherwise, you are simply paying for the fancy packaging. The same applies to cigars in polished boxes: if you have the option, buy them in regular cedar, unless you are very fond of boxes or want to present the cigars as a gift. Unless you have sophisticated storage facilities, buy only what you can smoke in the near future (a month or two, say).

Cigars in aluminum tubes lined with cedar (invented by H. Upmann), though very convenient to carry, can sometimes be rather dry as the tubes are not completely airtight. They occasionally lose their bouquet and tend not to be as well matured as cigars in boxes. This applies particularly to small sizes, whatever the manufacturer may claim on the tube. You can, on the other hand, find perfectly well-conditioned cigars in tubes. In the case of the famous Romeo Y Julieta Churchill, the tube states: "The rich aromatic flavor of this fine Havana cigar will be protected by the aluminum container until opened." But many would disagree.

Cigars wrapped in the cellophane can be just as good as those left loose in the box (except, that is, if they are machine-made). They keep well, but mature less. Sometimes cellophane turns brown by absorbing the oils from the cigar it contains. This shouldn't make a difference to the quality of the cigar, particularly if it is then properly humidified. Handmade Havanas rarely come in cellophane, although some sizes of Cohiba do, when sold in small packs.

Some cigars, the Havana H. Upmann Cristales (a corona size), for instance, come in hermetically sealed jars. These are meant to be "fresh" cigars, theoretically unmatured, and tasting like the cigar would shortly after it was actually made.

London (with shops like the 200-year-old Fox & Lewis, Davidoff, and Dunhill) is acknowledged to be the best place in Europe to buy handmade cigars, certainly Havanas. The London branch of Davidoff sells some 400,000 handmade cigars a year in 220 different sizes and brands. But British import and tobacco taxes

THE DAVIDOFF SHOP, NEW YORK.

THE HISTORIC DUNHILL SHOP, LONDON.

are high, and the cigars don't come cheap. Paris and Geneva (the headquarters of Davidoff) are also good places to buy. You are unlikely to find non-Cuban cigars using Cuban brand names in most of the leading European cigar shops, so there should be little confusion. Although Spain imports more cigars than anywhere else in Europe (the Spaniards smoke around 30 million Havanas a year, compared to 5 million in Britain), the quality of Havanas there, with many machine-mades on the market to boot, is often dubious, though prices are cheaper than in most of the rest of Europe. Smoking cigars is a particular custom at bullfights. There is a good selection of non-Cuban handmades to be found in London and, of course, in the major cigar stores in the United States.

Beware of apparent bargains—in sales, for instance. These are sometimes machine-made cigars bearing famous Havana labels. As always, check the box carefully. The same applies at airports, where duty-free prices can look very attractive. Storage conditions are often poor, but fast turnover can mean the cigars are smokable. Inspection is not permitted, so there's a risk. You should certainly steer clear of small tobacco stores, news stands, and the like: the cigars will almost certainly be old and badly stored.

Cigars, like any natural product, need to be carefully kept. They should be protected from extremes of temperature and kept in a humidified environment—ideally at 60°–70°F with 65–70 percent humidity. This may be difficult to achieve, particularly in air-conditioned or centrally heated homes. But at the very least, you should keep your cigars in an airtight cupboard or box, away from any heat source, in preferably the coolest place in the house. Keep the cigars in their cedar boxes—the cedar helps to preserve them. You could put a damp sponge in the cupboard. Put the cigar boxes in plastic bags if you like, to stop evaporation, spraying a little water into the bag before you put the box in. If you put a damp sponge or a glass of water in the bag, not too close to the cigars, it will help humidify them (as long as the bag isn't completely sealed—so that there is some air flow—and the box of cigars is partially open).

Some experts suggest that you store cigars in an airtight bag in the vegetable crisper compartment of your refrigerator, but in that case you should take a cigar out of the fridge at least half an hour before you want to smoke it, so that it can get back to room temperature. This is a method of storage which has many detractors, and one you have to be particularly careful with. If you put cigars in the refrigerator, the airtight bag (with excess air expelled before you close or seal it) is essential. You can also get small humidifiers from leading cigar merchants. These come in different shapes and sizes (ranging from pill box types to small strips of plastic), and you put them in the cigar box (having removed a cigar or two). The moistened sponge or chalk in these devices will help keep the cigars humidified (but be careful to check once a month that the sponge hasn't dried out). Metal tubes, which work in a similar way, are also available.

Many importers and merchants use Zip Lock or other sealable heavy plastic bags to send cigars to major clients, and they are very useful, particularly if you are traveling with cigars. Keep them in the box, and put a slightly damp sponge in the bag or spray the inside of the bag with a little water.

If cigars are stored in a warm climate, bugs can sometimes appear—the tobacco beetle, in particular. Heat allows the larvae to hatch. You should never store cigars anywhere near direct sunlight, or exposed to sea breezes. If you store cigars at a low temperature, you have to raise the humidity to compensate.

Humidors come normally made of wood such as walnut, mahogany, and rosewood (though there are also plexiglass models on the market), usually at fancy prices, and in many sizes. They are only really worth buying if you smoke cigars regularly. You should make sure that the lid, which should be heavy, closes tightly and that there is a hygrometer to monitor the humidity level. The humidor should be well made and unvarnished inside. Keep an eye on it, and remember, the humidor only looks after humidity, not the temperature, so you still have to find a suitable location for it. It's useful if the humidor comes with trays at various levels, so that you can store different sizes separately and rotate cigars within the box. Prices can range from $200 to over $2,000—but at the top end you are paying for the humidors as furniture as much as for its functional use. For example, Viscount Linley, cabinet-maker and nephew of Britain's Queen Elizabeth, now offers beautifully crafted humidors through Dunhill starting at $2,000. The plexi-glass models retail for under $200 and are serviceable enough. Choose your humidor carefully: many are ineffective or need care-ful monitoring.

Small humidors made of wood or leather are also available for travelers. Some first such as Davidoff even market briefcases with special cigar and accessory compartments, or built-in mini-humidors. There are a number of pocket cigar cases on the market. The best are made of leather, and the most convenient design is the expandable, rigid "telescope" type which can take large or small cigars. Some pocket cases come with mini-moisturizing units. For the cigar smoker who has everything, there are any number of items on the market such as brass, silver, and gold-plated cigar tubes, fancy lighters, and silver match holders.

HUMIDORS. THE SELECTION IS HUGE.

REVIVING DRIED OUT CIGARS

If cigars are very dry, they will be difficult to revive satisfactorily. But, essentially, if moisture can escape from a cigar, it can also be replaced. One of the simplest methods, which usually works, is to put the open box of cigars in a large plastic bag, which is partially, but not completely, closed (it is essential to have a little air flow). You should also put a glass of water or a moist sponge in the bag. Rotate the cigars every few days, remembering also to bring cigars from the bottom of the box to the top, and within three weeks or so the cigars should return to smokable condition. It is very much a matter of trial and error, and means that you have to keep a careful eye on things. They will, however, having been dry in the first place, have lost much of their bouquet and won't compare to a well-kept cigar. In any event, cigars lose moisture slowly and need to regain it equally slowly. You need patience: attempting drastic measures will only ruin the cigars for good.

Another simple way of reviving a box of cigars, after traveling for instance, is to turn it upside-down, and put it under a gently running faucet. Be careful: the bottom of the box should be moistened by the water, but no more. You could use a sponge as an alternative method of dampening the bottom of the box. Shake off excess water and put the box in an airtight bag. The cigars should be in good shape after a couple of days.

Some major cigar stores, particularly if you are a regular customer, will revive a box of cigars for you in their humidified room (it takes around a month) as a favor. The charming and knowledgeable Edward Sahakian of the Davidoff shop in London will even provide this service for people who aren't regular customers—at no cost. "The pleasure of doing it is sufficient for both him and myself," he says.

Top cigar stores will also store cigars for regular clients.

PLACING THE CIGARS IN A PARTIALLY CLOSED POLYTHENE BAG
IS ONE WAY OF REPLACING LOST MOISTURE.

The only serious collectors' market in cigars is in prerevolutionary Havanas. They demand premium prices, about 5 or 6 times higher than the current retail price. The best place to find them is in London, because of the old tradition of laying down large cigar reserves at the main cigar shops. These cigars usually come onto the market when someone realizes that he will never get through the reserve, or when he dies (sometimes there is no obvious beneficiary). They are particularly attractive to American smokers, who have been able to buy and import them with a clear conscience since the trade embargo was imposed on Cuba in 1962. Unopened boxes are the most sought-after, as are sizes and brands which have now disappeared.

You can tell a prerevolutionary box because, the underside will read: "Made in Havana, Cuba," as opposed to the use of Spanish after the revolution.

Whether such old cigars are actually worth buying is a different question. As with old wine vintages, it is a matter of luck. If they have been properly stored and date no earlier than the 1950s, they might well still provide very satisfactory and interesting smokes. But, however well stored, they could just as easily be mere shadows of their former selves, musty with little bouquet. Dark cigars (colorado, colorado maduro, or maduro) are the best bets. Cigars really shouldn't be kept, even in the best storage conditions, for more than 10 to 15 years: the longer you leave cigars, the more of their bouquet and aroma they will lose.

THE MARK ON ANY PREREVOLUTIONARY BOX OF CIGARS.

AUSTRALIA

MELBOURNE
Benjamins Fine Tobacco
Shop 16, Myer House
Arcade,
25 Elizabeth Street
Tel: 39 663 2879

Daniels Fine Tobaccos
Melbourne Central,
300 Lonsdale Street
Tel: 39 663 6842

SYDNEY
Alfred Dunhill
74 Castlereagh Street
Tel: 292 35 16 00

CANADA

CALGARY
Cavendish-Moore's
Tobacco Ltd
Penny Lane Market
Tel: 403 269 2716

TORONTO
Thomas Hinds
Tobacconist
8, Cumberland Street
Tel: 416 927 7703

Havana House
9 Davies Avenue
Tel: 416 406 6644

VICTORIA
Old Morris Tobacconist
1116, Government Street
Tel: 250 382 4811

VANCOUVER
R. J. Clarke Tobacconist
No 3, Alexander Street
Tel: 604 687 4136

Vancouver Cigar Co.
1938 West Broadway
Tel: 604 737 1313

FRANCE

PARIS
A Casa del Habano
69 Boulevard Saint-
Germain
Tel: 331 4549 2430

La Civette
157 rue Saint Honore
Tel: 331 4296 0499

GERMANY

BERLIN
Horst Kiwus
Kantstr. 56
Tel: 30 3124450

HAMBURG
Duske u. Duske
Großen Bleichen 36
Tel: 040-343385

Pfeifen Timm
Jungfernstieg 26
Tel: 040-345187

KÖLN
Pfeifenhaus Heinrichs
Hahnenstr. s
Tel: 0221-256483

MUNICH
Max Zechbauer
Residenzstrasse 10
Tel: 49 89 29 68 86

HONG KONG

The Cohiba Cigar Divan
The Mandarin Oriental
Hotel
Tel: 852 2522 0111

Pacific Cigar Company
Ltd
8/F China Hong Kong
Tower
Tel: 852 2528 3966

SPAIN

BARCELONA
Gimeno
101 Paseo de Gracia
Tel: 3302 0983

SWITZERLAND

GENEVA
Davidoff & Cie
2 Rue de Rive
Tel: 41 223 10 90 41

UNITED KINGDOM

BATH
Frederick Tranter
5, Church Street
Abbey Green
Tel: 01225 466197

CAMBRIDGE
Frederick Tranter
17, St. Johns Street
Tel: 01223 324515

EDINBURGH
Herbert Love
31, Queensferry Street
Tel: 0131 225 8082

GLASGOW
Herbert Love
9, St. Vincent's Place
Tel: 0141 226 4586

LONDON
Davidoff of London
35, St. James's Street,
SW1.
Tel: 020 7930 3079

Alfred Dunhill
48, Jermyn Street,
SW1Y 6LX.
Tel: 020 7838 8000

Fox/Lewis Cigar
Merchants
19, St. James's Street,
SW1.
Tel: 020 7930 3787

Harrods
Knightsbridge, SW1.
Tel: 020 7730 1234

Monte's Cigar Store
16, Halkin Arcade,
SW1X 8JT
Tel: 020 7245 0890

Desmond Sautter Ltd.
106, Mount Street, W1.
Tel: 020 7499 4866

Selfridges
Oxford Street, W1.
Tel: 020 7629 1234

Shervingtons
337, High Holborn, WC1.
Tel: 020 7405 2929

MANCHESTER
Astons
Unit 8, Royal Exchange
Arcade, M2 7EA
Tel: 0161 832 7895

STRATFORD-UPON-
AVON
Lands
29, Central Chambers,
Henley Street,
CV37 6QN
Tel: 01789 292508

UNITED STATES

CALIFORNIA
The Beverly Hills Pipe &
Tobacco Co.
218 North Beverly Drive
Beverly Hills
Tel: 310 276 3200

The Big Easy
12604 Ventura Boulevard
Studio City
Tel: 818 762 EASY (3279)

Century City Tobacco
Shoppe
10250 Santa Monica
Boulevard
(Century City Shopping
Center)
Los Angeles
Tel: 310 277 0760

Davidoff of Geneva
232 Via Rodeo/North
Rodeo Drive
Beverly Hills
Tel: 310 278 8884

Alfred Dunhill of London
201B North Rodeo Drive
Beverly Hills
Tel: 310 274 5351

Gus's Smoke Shop
13420 Ventura Boulevard
Sherman Oaks
Tel: 818 789 1401

CHICAGO
Jack Schwartz Importers
175 W. Jackson
Tel: 312-782 7898

Iwan Ries & Co.
19 South Wabash Ave.
Tel: 312 372 1306

Rubovits Cigars
320 South LaSalle St.
Tel: 312 939 3780

KANSAS CITY
Diebels Sportsmens
Gallery
426, Ward Parkway
Tel: 800 305 2988

LANCASTER
Demuth's Tobacco Shop
114 East King St.
Tel: 717 397 6613

MASSACHUSSETTS
David P. Ehrlich Co.
32 Tremont St.
Tel: 617 227 1720

L.J. Peretti Company,
Inc.
21/2 Park Square
Tel: 617 428 0218

Leavitt & Peirce
1316 Massachusetts Ave.
Tel: 617 547 0576

NEW HAVEN
The Owl Shop
268, College Street
CT 06510

NEW YORK, NY
Arnold's Cigar Store
323 Madison Avenue
Tel: 212-697 1477

Davidoff of Geneva
535 Madison Avenue
54th Street
Tel: 212 751 9060

De La Concha
Tobacconists
1390 Avenue of the
Americas
Tel: 212 757 3167

Nat Sherman Inc.
500 Fifth Avenue
Tel: 212 246 5500

OHIO
Straus Tobacconist
410–412 Walnut St.
Tel: 513 621 3388

OREGON
Rich's Cigar Store Inc.
801 SW Alder St.
Tel: 503 228 1700

PHILADELPHIA
Holt Cigar Co. Inc.
1522 Walnut Street
Tel: 800 523 1641

WASHINGTON
Georgetown Tobacco
3144 M North West
Washington DC
Tel: 202 338 5100

W. Curtis Draper
Tobacconist
640 14th St. N.W.
Tel: 202 638 2555

INDEX